WEIGHT OF INJUSTICE

A Corruption Universe Novel

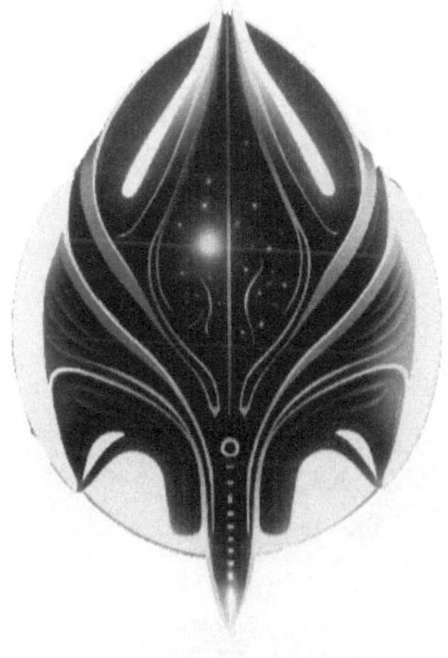

By J.F. Posthumus

Three Ravens Publishing
Chickamauga, GA USA

WEIGHT OF INJUSTICE By J.F. Posthumus
Published by Three Ravens Publishing

threeravenspublishing@gmail.com
P O Box 851, Chickamauga, GA 30707
https://www.threeravenspublishing.com

Credits:
WEIGHT OF INJUSTICE was written by J.F. Posthumus
WEIGHT OF INJUSTICE by: J.F. Posthumus / Three Ravens Publishing – 1st edition, 2025

Cover Design by: J.F. Posthumus
Edited by: Annamae Nedrow

Ebook ISBN: 978-1-966507-33-8
Trade Paperback ISBN: 978-1-966507-34-5

Table of Contents

Dedication

Dedicated to my eldest son, Chris Wagner.
Who answered all my questions and gave advice and
suggestions.

Ar scáth a chéile a mhaireann na daoine

'til Valhalla, son.

Special Thanks

This story, this series, the entire universe... It belongs to first responders and military vets.

This universe would not, could not, exist without them. The Injustice universe and K'lais in particular were built to show a place where lessons learned about what they deal with, the cracks they witness in the system, and even our society are actually appreciated and acted upon with the same dedication these people show in their callings of duty.

This is for them. These people see the worst humanity has to offer. And they still choose to help.

In duty, we prosper.

Chapter One

Violetta Cq'linns doubted she would ever grow accustomed to how many beings viewed Duels in the arenas. Lines poured through the doors of the main gates. Her steps faltered as they neared the smooth, swooping entrances that lined the edge of the street. The curved top reminded her of the underside of a soft, oblong mushroom and the doors and windows represented the mushroom's gills.

She was oddly delighted that Zane Morelli, the don of the Italian syndicate who owned the arenas, had chosen typical K'laisian architecture when the arenas were being designed. The blue-silver hue of the metals shone in the evening twilight.

Malik slid his hand around her waist. She glanced at him, tilting her head to the side.

"Are you well?"

"Yes," she replied, taking a step closer to him. "I guess I'm still trying to grow accustomed to how many people visit the arenas. How many enter and exit at a constant rate."

"I suppose you haven't had to deal with the crowds in homicide," Malik mused.

She shook her head.

"Not usually, no," she admitted. "When festivals are going full swing, especially for the winter solstice, it's usually too crowded for us to be on the streets. If there are deaths, we get called in by the beat officers."

"In other words, your 'slow time'," Malik commented.

"Exactly."

As a lieutenant detective of the 42nd District's police service's homicide department, her job was investigating the deaths of those who died outside of official Duels or the health care facilities of their world. Homicide's job was to determine if the being died from a Duel, official or otherwise, suicide, accident, or a more nefarious reason. Because Duels were a way of life, and killing in cold blood was punished by death, homicide stayed busy.

On a planet where Challenges could be issued between anyone for any reason, and Duels to the death were allowed and completely legal, cold blooded murder was seen as an incurable illness.

Why kill someone in 'cold blood' when you could Challenge them, then kill them during a Duel?

And yet, it did happen. Violetta had spent a short time only four months earlier as a wanted fugitive due to the murder of Ylvran Me'addn. Me'addn had been the chief of police prior to his death. Violetta had risked her life and everything she'd ever worked to achieve to clear her name with Malik Addelia's help. In the end, she'd discovered the corruption had gone as far as the district attorney of their city.

After five years of avoiding Malik, her childhood sweetheart, she'd quickly discovered nothing had changed between them. They'd picked up as though those five years hadn't separated them.

Against everything their society thought was proper, Malik had begun courting her. Taking her to concerts, out to eat, and even to the arenas where he was Master of Ceremonies.

She still didn't understand the entertainment value of the Duels, and she had a love-hate relationship with watching Malik Duel. Violetta now completely understood why she'd been told her mother had hated it when her Father Dueled, yet loved watching him.

She felt the same way towards Malik.

"I still prefer watching you from the other side of a weapon," she teased as they headed towards the main gates.

Malik laughed easily, his hand in hers.

The arena they were entering was where he spent most of his time as the Master of Ceremonies, compared to the other eleven in their city.

"So where are we going?" she asked once they passed through the entrance doors.

Malik smiled before answering, "Up to my box, after I check in with the shift manager."

His "box" referred to the moving platform that was solely used by the Master of Ceremonies in the arena. While similar in size and outward design to the private platforms reserved for high-paying patrons, the "Moc Box" was able to maneuver.

Private platforms were attached to pylons and sat above the duel fields at all six points of the K'laisian compass. The Moc Box had hover engines, so it undocked on ground level, and rose up. Usually, Malik's space was dead in the middle of the dozen duel fields that were allotted on the arena floor. If Malik so desired, or a patron paid for the privilege, he could hover between any or all of the private "boxes" and even dock next to one.

Or he could park away from all of them.

Further, his box was equipped with enough monitors to keep track of every person in every duel, even if all twelve fields were in play simultaneously. It gave him the ability to hype up any being or comment on any fight. Since the monitors were all below the line of sight of the crowds on the ground level pit or the common platforms which rose in stair-like design around the pit, he could appear to be omniscient about all activity within the arena.

Violetta had been in a couple of Malik's Moc Boxes in other arenas around the city. Those had been fun, so she anticipated a similar experience on this day. Her stomach grumbled slightly, which made her swear under her breath. Malik looked back at her and gave another smile.

"Shall I meet you in the food court? Oh, wait. No. Since we're at the main arena, go to the restaurant at the end of the court. It's the best eatery of all the arenas. And my favorite! Go select anything you like, and have them put it on my tab. Clearance is Z-6-2-T, and have them pour me an Earth bourbon. The lead server and bar attendants know my preference. Please?" he asked happily.

"Sounds perfect," Violetta allowed. She stepped to her right and began descending the nearby stairs. Malik continued his course along the walkway to the offices on the left side of the building.

While she walked down the steps and to the dark blue floor below, Violetta watched patrons of all measures moving about her. A small part of her mind gave each being she spotted a quick threat assessment.

Such was habit, and probably always would be.

Mostly, though, she enjoyed the sight of beings walking out of the pit area for the Dueling fields. Some excited and elated, others grumpy or at best, reserved. She only saw one being in a state of shock or loss, crying and being helped along by those near them.

Younglings and slightly older children rushed to the food court units, eager to get the edibles and beverages they craved. Adults tried to keep up or were resigned to having no chance of catching the younger beings or getting them to settle before their desires were purchased.

Following the flood of beings moving towards the different offerings, Violetta's eyes caught sight of the restaurant entrance. It was one of a very few enclosed eateries and, as Malik had said, at the back of the court. She took the space of a breath to determine the course of least resistance to the double door entrance, and then proceeded.

The journey took a scant two minutes. Once she was inside and the double doors closed, Violetta wondered at the sudden drop in sound. The cacophony in the food court was silenced by the closed doors. Activity still existed in the restaurant, but the hustle and bustle within was more controlled and pleasant in comparison.

The smooth, arching segments were clearly designated as the lounge area, the tabled area, and bar. There was a lead server at the entrance to both the lounge and tabled areas. The bar was open, but Violetta could see the silhouettes of muscled K'laisian women standing at either side of the entrance. Nodding in appreciation, she opted for the bar.

The bar itself wrapped around the attendants and liquor shelves in a long oval. The narrow end was closest to her, so she walked to an open chair on her right. There were tables in this section as well, but they were limited to the small, two patron variety. All of the chairs were tall-legged with conforming seats and backs. Violetta enjoyed sitting back in the available one while waiting for one of the attendants to come for her order. She had less than a minute to wait.

"Well met, dear patron." The unisex human attendant addressed Violetta with enough cheer to be genuine. Their hair was long, straight, and not in a particular style. Green eyes appeared neither tired nor resentful. "What may I provide for you today?"

"Well met," Violetta returned. "I am here to request a menu, along with an Earth bourbon for our esteemed Master of Ceremonies. Clearance is Z-6-2-T, if you please."

"Oh, at once!" the attendant eagerly said.

They pushed a section of the bar's surface. A menu projected in the air in front of Violetta. She had to blink a few times to verify that the prices next to the available items weren't misread numbers.

They weren't.

Her credit level hurt just looking at them.

More time was spent gawking at the menu and prices than Violetta realized, because the attendant seemed to appear a second later with a wide glass half filled with bourbon.

"Deciding what to order for yourself? Because I know what bures'o Malik prefers," the attendant offered.

The K'laisian word was a title which held great honor. The human equivalent was 'lord' for men and 'lady', or bures'a, for women.

"I'm sure you do," Violetta muttered aloud, and felt her mouth snap shut from embarrassment. She looked at the attendant and smiled. "Yes, he told me to get whatever I liked, on his tab."

The attendant nodded appreciatively, then gestured for Violetta to continue to consult the menu. Violetta tried to concentrate on the food options instead of the costs.

"You have sweet potato fries?" she suddenly blurted.

The attendant laughed merrily.

"Indeed we do! I shared my grandmother's recipe with the chefs, um, the preparers, here, and they acquisition the spuds to make them whenever they get a supply."

Violetta smiled at the human's slipup of using the Earther term for professional preparers of foods. She glanced at a few more items on the menu before making her decision. If Malik wanted to pay as much as a week's worth of food for her meal here, that was his choice.

"I will gladly try the sweet potato fries, along with grilled moratoes."

The attendant's face squished inward slightly. Their voice took on a concerned tone as they replied, "All those carbohydrates? You'll feel like you stepped into a gravity well. No offense, but may I suggest a serving of bruchi, perhaps topped with dried ro'shii petals?"

"What would I have to drink with that meal," Violetta asked curiously.

"I will go and get a second glass of bourbon, if you'd like," said the attendant.

"You know, that's a near-perfect suggestion. I will take that with my sweet potato fries!"

The attendant smiled and leaned forward. Long fingers tapped against the menu. A moment later, the menu disappeared.

"Your order shall be available shortly," they assured her. "Will this be for here or in the arena?"

"The arena," Violetta replied.

The attendant flashed a brilliant smile to go with the nod. They turned and strode away, leaving her alone with her thoughts. Hopefully Malik wouldn't complain about the tab. It took considerable effort to not shake her head at the prices. Eyeing the glass of bourbon, she lifted it to her lips and took a sip.

The bourbon burned across her tongue and as it slid down her throat. Admittedly, it was rather tasty. Considering Malik had been spending more nights with her than not, she doubted he would mind.

In fact, he had yet to object to anything she did with him, she thought in genuine amusement.

Within a very short amount of time, the attendant returned with a take-out box and the second glass of bourbon. A slight frown pulled at their lips for a brief moment before the smile returned. The smile did not meet their eyes, though. A fact Violetta found amusing.

She doubted many of the beings Malik entertained had ever stolen his food or drinks.

"Thank you," Violetta said brightly. "I'm certain Malik will appreciate the quickness of service. I certainly do."

"You are most welcome, bures'a," the attendant replied. With a short bow, they turned and departed, leaving Violetta to gather the food and make her way back to Malik.

The door slid open as she neared it, allowing entrance into the general food court and its noise.

Moving towards the wall, she surveyed the area. Her eyes traveled over the occupants, taking in every detail even as she searched for Malik. Amusement only grew as she noticed members of the military unit assigned to watch over her. A fact she'd learned while being hunted and trying to investigate the former Chief of Police's murder.

Violetta had always thought they were at her apartment to protect the data on her father's console, since she still lived in his apartment. Though he'd been murdered shortly after she graduated by a pure blood fanatic, she had been allowed to remain living in his apartment. Having been raised to trust the military, she hadn't questioned if there was more to it than that.

Yet there had been.

So much had changed over the past few months.

As she spotted Malik moving towards her, she couldn't help the smile that curved her lips. He moved through the crowd with ease, talking to those who recognized him and waving to others. An easy smile on his face.

Despite everything that had happened, she didn't regret any of it. Aside from, perhaps, the murder.

How could she have regrets when she had Malik? The rock she'd been missing for five long, lonely years.

Well, she thought, trying to not laugh aloud. She wasn't lonely now!

Moving away from the wall, she met him in the midst of people moving to and from the eateries and main area of the arenas.

"Hope you don't hate me for the tab you now have," she teased.

Laughter danced in his eyes. "Not even your bar tab can scare me off, Vi."

"I hope you remember that when you see it!"

"Perhaps your tab is small compared to others," he teased as he reached for the bourbon and takeout box. "Shall we continue to my private box?"

Irritation flashed through her briefly before she pushed it away. She'd lost the right to complain about past women who may have been part of his life when she'd ignored him. That was the past and she couldn't change it.

His brows furrowed. "Did I say something wrong?"

She shook her head. "No, just a reminder of what I missed by not keeping in touch with you."

"Ah," was her only reply.

Before she could say anything, her eyes caught sight of someone she recognized on the other side of the food court. "Is that Commander Fr'osst?"

Malik turned towards the direction she was looking. "Perhaps? It looks like it may be her."

A thought occurred to Violetta. "Are you wearing the comm?"

They had been given military comms while she'd been avoiding the local police service. The military had requested she and Malik keep their comms, as a method to contact them in any emergency. A part of their 'reward' for bringing to light the corruption in the District's police service, coupled with her being on their world's Watch List.

The Watch List was a very real list the military kept for beings of immense interest, who had done exemplary service to their world. She understood why her father would have been on the list, but didn't understand why she'd been placed on it. But she was and she didn't know how to learn why. Not yet, anyway.

Malik gave a slow nod.

"Oh, good. Hopefully this will work," she muttered. "Comm change. Military channel only." There was a soft chirp indicating the switch from the comm having both the police service channel and military channels. "Commander Jozelyn Fr'osst, Harbormaster of Crom's Drop Lake."

Understanding flashed across Malik's face a moment before he gave her a narrow-eyed look. "You know that command?"

Violetta tipped her head side-to-side in typical K'laisian fashion for a shrug.

"Violetta, this is a surprise," Commander Fr'osst's voice said in comm. "I'm afraid I'm not at the harbor, but how may I assist you? Congratulations on your promotion!"

Another result from bringing an end to the corruption was a field promotion from sergeant to lieutenant granted by the governor of the 42nd District.

"Thank you, Commander," Violetta replied. "Malik and I are at the arena. We were wondering if you would like to join us in his private box?"

"It would be a pleasure to have you," Malik added, the smile on his face evident in his words.

"Oh!" Commander Fr'osst exclaimed. "Ah, would it be acceptable for Atos to join us?"

"Absolutely! We would love to see you both," Malik replied brightly. "Shall we meet at my office?"

"That would be wonderful, thank you, bures'o Addelia," Commander Fr'osst replied brightly. There was no mistaking the delight in her voice. Violetta could see the grin on her face from where she stood. "We will join you there shortly!"

"We're looking forward to it," Violetta said warmly.

Together, she and Malik began towards his office. The box used by the Master of Ceremonies was accessible only through his office. He could invite anyone to it, but Violetta knew if you weren't invited, you couldn't get to it.

She nodded at the guards posted near his office to keep away unwanted visitors. They returned the nods, but otherwise kept their attention on their job.

"Commander Fr'osst, Harbormaster of Crom's Drop Lake and her mate will be here soon," Malik informed them. "Please allow her through."

The pair gave a nod.

Malik held the door open to his office and she stepped into the room.

Just like his other two offices, this one was filled with luxury and opulence. Thick carpet covered the floor, a large antique human-style desk filled a third of one wall. A high-end conforming chair sat behind it. This particular chair was shaped to mimic a high-backed office chair. It was almost throne-like in its design.

"I think I'm going to have a harder time growing accustomed to all the luxury you have at your fingertips," Violetta stated, afraid to even place her glass on the desk's top.

She watched as he placed his glass and takeout box on the desk, as though it were no different than her dining table. Her drink was taken from her hand and placed beside the box of food.

"It's all part of the position," Malik explained. "Both our people and the humans expect this with the position, and so…" He gestured towards the room. "It doesn't change who I am, Violetta."

"How long did it take you to become accustomed to it?"

Laughing, Malik shook his head. "I had, as the humans say, a 'crash course'. After my first day as Master of Ceremonies, I discovered how much I preferred my parents' lifestyle. But this helps those who wouldn't otherwise get it. So, I do it and accept everything that goes with it."

"In service, we prosper," Violetta said with a sigh. "People are going to question if I'm using you to get… this." She rubbed her arms at the chilling thought, her gaze on the floor.

Warm hands encircled her waist, pulling her close. She looked up, to find Malik's lips descending towards hers. She melted against him, giving into the kiss.

Loud humming, the K'laisian method of laughing for those who were pure blood, broke the moment. Startled, the pair looked up and towards the door. Commander Jozelyn Fr'osst and Atos stood in the threshold humming loudly at them.

"I see nothing has changed between you two," Commander Fr'osst teased, her eyes dancing with laughter. "Perhaps you should consider a lock on the door, bures'o Addelia."

"Please, just use my name," Malik implored. He didn't let go, instead leaning his head against hers. "The thought has crossed my mind a few times."

"I'd suggest a lounge chair, personally," Atos commented, glancing around the room. "A desk isn't very comfortable."

"Atos!" Commander Fr'osst practically shrieked, even as her skin darkened.

Violetta completely understood why the commander would be blushing. She could feel her own face burning. Though, unlike the commander, she knew the skin along her cheekbones would be turning slightly pink. The rest of her skin darkened, which was the norm for those who were pure blood K'laisian.

Being half K'laisian and half human, Violetta's blush was different from natives of their world. Her father had been a pure blood native. Her mother, who died in childbirth, had been human.

Atos hummed loudly, even as he kissed the tip of his mate's ear. One of the most sensitive parts of a K'laisian. It always caused a shiver of pleasure for Violetta.

"I may just do that," Malik mused.

Violetta could see a smirk forming from the corner of her eyes and she could feel her skin growing even warmer.

"Thank you for inviting us, Malik," Commander Fr'osst said, elbowing her husband in the side. "Please call me Jozelyn. Both of you."

"The pleasure is mine." His eyes shifted between them. "Did either of you desire refreshments?"

"We had dinner before coming," Jozelyn explained, a smile on her face. "We may acquire a beverage later. But for now, we're fine."

"Then shall we continue to the box?"

The harbormaster and her mate nodded. Kissing the top of her head, Malik finally released Violetta. She reached over and grabbed the glass of bourbon as Malik took the box and other glass.

Eyeing the amber beverage, Violetta suspected she was going to need another long before their evening was through.

"How have you been, Violetta?" Jozelyn asked as they followed Malik down the hallway to his box.

Smiling at the other woman, she said, "Trying to adjust to the promotion and having mostly military personnel as colleagues. Father never mentioned what it was like to work with those who were career military. Perhaps because I was so young."

Atos hummed loudly. "They are certainly a great deal different from civilians. Not just in behavior, but in language and their manner of speaking."

"Vrehn Cq'linns had one of the most unique crews in our service," Jozelyn admitted, referring to Violetta's father who had been commander of a battlecruiser. "Both he and Commander Mc'narrd, stars bless him, did. Which is probably why they worked so well together."

Commander, then Admiral, It'zarry Mc'narrd was considered to be dead by all but a very select few. Now a three-star admiral, he was most definitely not dead. A fact Violetta had discovered while trying to prove her innocence. When a weapon that could clone civilian, and potentially military weapons, became a known reality, Mc'narrd made his presence known to her and Malik. One of the highest ranking admirals, an overseer of their planet's black ops, had taken personal interest in the investigation and subsequently Violetta's life.

She still didn't know what promise he'd made to her father. Or how many both in and out of the military had made a promise to her father. Only that one had been made.

"Think he's listening?" Malik asked in a soft voice.

"Not likely," Jozelyn said brightly. "Lady Violetta is safe and unless some emergency occurs, that ghost isn't going to make his presence known."

"Let's hope that doesn't happen," Violetta grumbled. "I much prefer having a calm life dealing with homicides, to trying to outsmart and hide from my colleagues."

There was sporadic humming from Jozelyn and Atos, indicating chuckling, even as Malik chuckled like a human.

A moment later, the private box used by Malik as the Master of Ceremonies came into view.

There were worse things than spending time in a private box with someone you loved and two friends. Violetta was fully aware of many 'worse things' and had endured several of them. So she found herself treasuring the time spent with Malik, Jozelyn, and Atos.

Especially since she knew Malik was going to come home with her.

Chapter Two

Sitting on the edge of Issik Ha'kksworth's desk the next morning, she read over the day's incoming news. Issik had been her partner for the past five years. Neither of them cared about her new promotion. Their current captain, the former replaced due to the corruption in their department, hadn't seen a reason to alter their partnership.

Violetta and Issik had proven they worked well together and treated each other the same. So, the captain allowed them to continue as usual, despite Violetta being of a higher rank than Issik.

An open and half-empty box of two dozen pastries sat on Violetta's desk. Delivered with a note to share with her department. A gift from Malik's youngest sister, Syra, who ran the family bakery.

She'd been sending boxes and baskets of goodies ever since Violetta's name had been cleared. It had begun with a giant cake congratulating her. Issik and she had wondered if Syra was simply trying to fatten up the entire department.

Not that anyone was complaining. In fact, Syra had cheerfully reported business had only improved since she'd begun sending the treats. She'd even joked about how it made her wish she'd ignored Violetta and Malik's stubbornness and tried Matching them before now.

"Says here, a body was found near Malik's apartment," Violetta commented. "Know anything about it?"

Issik shook his head back and forth a single time. "Nothing on the blotter, aside from that report." Rolling his chair over to her desk, he grabbed a pastry from the box. "Does it say who got it?"

Scrolling through the report, Violetta searched for the names of the investigating team.

She paused when she noticed Issik had suddenly stilled, the pastry halfway to his open mouth. Following his gaze, her own jaw threatened to hit the floor.

Malik Addelia strode between two of the few police service homicide detectives who had managed to survive the military's investigation on corruption.

"What are you doing here, Malik?" Violetta called to him.

Detective Ra'keff Hy'szolis, a handsome K'laisian with dark tan skin, black hair, and gold eyes gestured towards the interrogation rooms. His partner, Osing Ad'miryz, another pure blood native with similar coloring, glanced towards Ra'keff before shaking his head. A smirk flashed across his face even as he continued escorting Malik towards the rooms.

"We brought him in for questioning," Ra'keff replied. His eyes slid to the box of pastries.

"Help yourself," Violetta offered. "Guess we know who got the case, now."

The words were directed towards Issik, but her eyes never left her fellow detective.

Ra'keff was also a lieutenant. Though he had more years behind him, they were now equal rank. He couldn't tell her to sit down and leave them alone and expect her to obey. Yes, he could do it to Issik, but not her.

"Mind if I listen in?" she asked, sliding from the desk. She slid the interface into its sleeve at her waist.

She'd been planning on meeting up with Malik for lunch, so she'd dressed for the occasion. The silvery blue tunic was snug and a wide belt wrapped around her waist. Her service weapon was at her waist, against her left hip, a stun baton beside it. Shackles were in the middle of her back. Long, loose black pants flowed around her ankles, hiding her military-style boots. The entire outfit hid the experimental biosuit the military had requested her to wear.

Another gift from the military and one that would ultimately help her fellow K'laisians, may they be human or of mixed heritage like her. Pure blood K'laisians already had biosuits that worked unquestionably with their physiologies and biologies.

Ra'keff's eyes swept over her once, then once again more slowly. A smile pulled at his lips.

"Have a date later, Violence?"

The room suddenly became very quiet. Most who called her Violence did so as an insult. Not that she could object: she'd earned the nickname as a child and it had continued to follow her throughout her entire life.

That did not alter the fact that those who had been from the military had quickly learned it was often used insultingly. Every one of them took exception to it. She suspected they'd been given an order to watch her back and protect her.

"You asking me out, Ra'keff?" she shot back.

The K'laisian's eyes widened and he blinked a few times. A clear indication from the pure blood K'laisian that she'd surprised, even shocked him.

She smirked. It was perhaps one of the few times she'd startled him into silence. Shifting her weight to one hip, she raised her brows. Humming and laughter quickly rose from around them.

"No." Without another word, he turned and stalked towards the interrogation rooms.

The laughter only grew as he walked away.

Violetta gave a very exaggerated shrug of her shoulders before following behind him.

Chuckles and teasing followed as she stepped into the small, adjoining viewing room, which was barely larger than a closet.

A one-way window separated the two rooms. A narrow counter held multiple interfaces. Each one was capable of anything required of a police officer. From replaying clips, to taking stillclips, to pulling up reports, and more. All while having a separate interface doing something different.

The biometrics for anyone in the interrogation room could also be viewed with ease, revealing if a being was lying, confused, or any number of other psychological and physical readings. The detectives doing the questioning could either use their own interfaces or have another one or two in the viewing rooms reading off what appeared on the displays.

Closing the door to the sound-proof room, Violetta touched an interface. Another tap allowed her to listen in to the questioning. She didn't bother with the biometrics. She knew exactly where Malik had been and what he'd been doing the previous night.

"What've you done to her?" Ra'keff demanded the moment the door shut behind him. "Before you assisted her in busting everyone's ass here, she wouldn't do anything remotely social. Now she's dressing up and going places with you."

Ra'keff moved until he stood opposite of Malik, his back to the viewing room.

"I don't know what you mean," Malik replied, meeting Ra'keff gaze without concern.

"You know ka'deshed well what I mean," Ra'keff snapped. "The only one she ever went to a bar with before that mess was her partner. Never did anything other than that or hitting the gym where she kicked everyone's ass. Only ever talked about work. Now she's out there all chummy with the replacements and being seen with the 'charming' Master of Ceremonies."

Oh, fark. Time to call for help, Violetta decided.

"Change comm frequency, military channel only. Emergency code Ya'aysha Mokuu."

The code 'violet violence', as the words translated to in Standard, had been chosen by Admiral Mc'narrd after a barroom brawl four months earlier. She suspected it was chosen to either annoy her or to tease her about her nickname of Violence. The nickname was well-earned, yes, but that didn't mean she wanted it used as a code when she needed to contact the admiral.

"Military command. Code Ya'aysha Mokuu acknowledged. What aid do you require, bures'a Cq'linns?" the feminine voice said in her ear. "Your biosuit shows you as being at the police station."

"Malik has been brought in for the questioning of a murder," Violetta said without preamble. "After leaving the arena, he was with me last night. According to the report, at least from what I've seen, the murder happened sometime yesterday evening."

"Malik Addelia?" the woman asked.

"Yes," Violetta replied.

"We'll inform the admiral."

"Thank you, bures'a," Violetta said, turning her attention to the trio in the interrogation room.

Malik was sitting seemingly comfortable in the conforming chair opposite of the window.

Standard procedure so far, she thought. But Ra'keff's questions had been anything but professional, let alone procedure.

She could tell Malik was on edge, though, from the tension in his body. Some things had not changed over the years, and her ability to read his body was one of them.

Was he wearing the earbud? she wondered.

"You aren't jealous are you? Hate the fact her old high school chum was able to bring her out of her self-imposed isolation?" Malik asked, his eyes still on Ra'keff.

"Malik Addelia, Master of Ceremonies," she said quizzically. "If you have your comm in, look at the window and not the two detectives in the room."

Malik's eyes shifted to the window and she saw him relax ever so slightly in the chair.

"Enjoying the reflection of your pretty face?" Ra'keff asked suddenly.

Violetta frowned. Malik's bronze eyes flashed with anger.

Only those of mixed heritage had bronze eyes, one of several traits she and Malik shared.

Both of them had dark hair, a skin tone humans called 'olive', and bronze eyes. The biggest difference between them was his father was human and his mother was K'laisian. Her hair was a dark auburn, almost black, and often wavy. His was black and straight. As a female, she had a Gift. He did not. Males of mixed heritage were never born with a Gift.

Both his parents were alive. Both of hers were dead.

"Wondering what you told Lady Violetta, actually." Malik smirked. "Detective Cq'linns, that is."

Oh, hox.

"I'm aware of her name," Ra'keff snapped back.

Touching a different interface, Violetta pulled up the camera in the opposite corner so she could view the two detectives.

Ra'keff's face was dark and his gold eyes were furious.

"What the hox is his problem?" she asked the empty room.

"Don't recognize a jealous male?" Mc'narrd's amused voice said in the comm. "You really were sheltered."

"Sir," Violetta said carefully. "I wouldn't have known from the way he treated me in the past."

"Bet he's unhappy your boyfriend's sister is sending you presents. Probably thinks it's Addelia doing it. Not to mention jealous of Malik taking you everywhere he probably wishes he could."

"Why was I brought in, detective," Malik said suddenly. His eyes fixed on Ra'keff.

"For questioning in the unexplained death of a colleague," Ra'keff replied.

"If he bites those words off any more, he's going to have indigestion," Mc'narrd commented.

Violetta barked a laugh. From the flash of amusement in Malik's eyes, she suspected Mc'narrd was speaking to them both.

"I've been meaning to ask, sir. Are you always this amusing with your people?" Violetta asked.

"Not always. Only when it amuses me," Mc'narrd retorted, stressing the word slightly.

"Lorenzo Tagliani was found deceased one block from your residence," Ra'keff stated. "He worked for Zane Morelli. Worked as a guard and did some protection."

Violetta blinked. Despite the window between them, Malik met her eyes. She had no clue how he knew where she stood, but he still managed to meet her eyes.

"Cq'linns? Your pulse just spiked and other readings have shifted suddenly. Since I know you aren't in the interrogation room, it's not because of Malik."

She remained silent.

"Are you concerned about saying anything there, detective?" Mc'narrd guessed.

"Yes, sir," she replied.

"Tagliani?" Malik was asking. He pursed his lips before giving a human shrug. "I knew of him. We crossed paths a few times. Can't say I knew him well, though. No clue why he would've been near my penthouse."

"Where were you last night between seven in the evening and midnight?"

A sly smile curved Malik's lips and he completely relaxed in the chair.

Oh, hox. Violetta knew that expression.

"I was with Lady Violetta at the Main Arena from twilight until around nine. Harbormaster Jozelyn Fr'osst and her husband can vouch for us, since they joined us in my private box." The smile grew and his eyes glinted as he continued to speak. "After we left the arena, we returned to Lady Violetta's apartment in the military district. I was there, with her, until late this morning." He paused before adding, "She left before I did."

"Malik." Violetta warned.

"Can anyone verify you were there?" Osing Ad'miryz asked, finally speaking.

"Aside from the lady?" Malik asked, his eyes shifting to Ad'miryz briefly. "It's a military apartment. I'm sure someone was there who witnessed us. Or you could view the cameras. If you have the clearance to do so."

"And what would Detective Cq'linns say if we asked her?" Ra'keff demanded.

"I'm certain she would verify we were together."

"Doing what?"

"Having a sleepover," Malik retorted. He leaned forward slightly. "The humans have a saying: a gentleman doesn't kiss and tell. Though, I suppose if you demand it…"

"Malik Addelia!" Violetta screeched in as low a voice as she could manage. Her eyes darted to the door, hoping no one heard her. She felt her face burn. "Don't you dare!"

"Uh oh, Addelia, she may actually Challenge you, this time." Mc'narrd drew the words out.

Ra'keff took a step forward. Malik was on his feet and closing the distance when Ad'miryz stepped between the pair.

Malik paused and glanced towards the mirror, fury showing in his entire face and body.

"I'm ending the meeting," Mc'narrd declared.

The comm became silent, even as Malik remained standing. His gaze hadn't shifted from the mirror. Ra'keff glanced towards the viewing room and understanding flashed across his face. The detective muttered something too low for even the cameras and comms to hear. Turning on his heel, he opened the door, and stalked out.

The captain stopped him on the outside of the door. Something was said and Ra'keff shook his head once before walking out of sight.

"If there are any further questions, I'll contact you personally, bures'o Addelia," the captain said smoothly. "My apologies for Detective Hy'szolis' behavior. I assure you, it will be addressed."

"I'm going to skin him," Violetta muttered under her breath.

Humming was the response from the admiral. Malik winced.

"Incoming," Mc'narrd said just as the door to the room opened, revealing Ra'keff.

"What?" she demanded, thankful there were two doors to the room. One on each side of the room.

"I wish to apologize," Ra'keff said. He stepped into the room, allowing the door to close behind him.

Violetta took a step closer to the opposite door. Ra'keff noticed and frowned. She swallowed hard, hating the flashback she was suddenly fighting off. Violetta wasn't certain which part of the flashback was worse: the feeling of helplessness or watching the former DA pointing a sidearm at her and waiting to die from it. Only to witness the DA's death instead, by a well-placed sniper's shot.

"I am not going to harm you, Violetta," Ra'keff said softly. He held his hands to the side, away from his body.

"Your vitals are all over the place," Mc'narrd stated, concern in his voice. His voice softened as he added, "If it's what I suspect, get out and come to the base. I'll contact Zh'oros."

Clenching her jaw, Violetta steeled herself, shoving away the past. "I'm not doing this right now. You want to apologize? Find me later when I'm not tempted to Challenge you both."

Opening the door, she slid out, refusing to turn her back on Ra'keff, who still wore a confused expression. Once outside the door, she swallowed hard as she closed her eyes.

"Take a walk, Violetta. I'll let the captain know you're going out to cool off," Mc'narrd said.

"Yes, sir," she said under her breath. "Thank you."

Turning, she strode through the short hallway to a side exit. From there, she strode towards the Fallen Memorial Fountain. It wasn't too terribly far from the police station, only a couple blocks. Even had it been further, the walk would've been welcomed.

Being in the room, angry and upset, had reminded her of being in the room with now-deceased Nyzril Lc'sonn, the former district attorney who had tried framing her and Monroe, her former homicide captain.

Her mind kept replaying the scene, no matter how much she tried to ignore it. Of Issik being shot by Lc'sonn. The weapon being turned on her. Then Victoria Delacruz sniping Lc'sonn, ultimately rescuing her with the perfectly-placed shot.

Violetta's mind put her back in that room with no weapon. At the mercy of an ill K'laisian willing to murder her simply because her father had been an accomplished soldier offplanet.

Shivering, she realized her feet had taken her to the plaque listing the names of fallen K'laisian soldiers. The water fell from the multi-tiered fountain into a three-foot deep basin.

"Are you well?" Malik's soft voice traveled easily to her.

He must have followed her. Or perhaps Mc'narrd told him where she was?

Rounding on him, anger flared again. "What the hox was that, Malik?"

"Uh oh," Mc'narrd muttered. "Looks like you're still in trouble, Addelia."

"Shut up, sir," she snapped under her breath. "Or I swear, by the seas and stars, I'm going to throw this comm into that basin. You can pluck it out, along with Malik!"

"Very well. Professional comments, only," Mc'narrd stated, the tone decidedly cooler. This time, Violetta didn't care. "You're to come to the base and see Sovereign Healer Zh'oros when you're finished with your argument."

"You're angry," Malik said simply.

"I'm seriously going to throw you in that basin," Violetta snarled. Her hands clenched into fists. "I'm furious! How *could* you? You said we had to go slow! That we couldn't let people know we were courting because of the trouble it might cause me! And you just told Ra'keff and Osing we're sleeping together!"

"I… I…" Malik closed his mouth and sighed. "I'm sorry. I should not have allowed him to goad me."

"Why? Why did you do that?" Violetta demanded.

"He wasn't the only one jealous," Malik admitted. He looked down and away from her briefly before lifting his eyes back to hers. "You never mentioned the fact that you had colleagues who wanted to court you. Pure bloods who probably were wondering how to convince Issik to Match you with them."

"Stars and Seas." Violetta groaned. "Save me from fools."

"You cannot tell me you don't find those pretty boys attractive."

"Actually, I can, you idiot. If I were attracted to just any pretty face, I wouldn't have Challenged those who even *mentioned* Matching me. Or kicked their asses in the gym before asking if they wanted to be officially Challenged," Violetta snarled. Malik's eyes widened and she wondered if Mc'narrd was talking only to him. "I wanted *you*. I've only ever desired *you*, and you…"

"Aww, how sweet! Your first lover's quarrel," a feminine voice said from near them.

Violetta and Malik turned to face the woman who spoke. Violetta's jaw dropped. She snapped it shut after two heartbeats.

The woman approaching them had long, beautiful honey gold hair, brilliant blue-gray eyes, and wore an elegant dark green gown and a long cape that covered only her shoulders, leaving slits for her arms.

"My husband thought you may need to be talked down," the woman said cheerfully. "I'm Alyssa Zelaya. Though I suspect you recognize me."

"Yes, sa'ii," Violetta managed to stutter, using the K'laisian word for 'ma'am'. A habit developed due to her own grandmother's preference of the K'laisian language over Standard, or even Earther words.

"Men have such a bad habit of shoving their feet into their mouths and making a meal of them," Alyssa stated, her piercing blue-gray eyes shifting to Malik. "Go to the base. Debrief and talk to Zh'oros while you're there. We'll be over shortly."

"And you two are going… where?" Malik asked, his eyes not moving from Violetta.

"I'm going to take her for a drink. Now, go," Alyssa said, her tone hardening as she spoke the last two words. "Maybe my mate will have some suggestions on how to apologize."

A bark of laughter erupted in Violetta's earbud, showing Mc'narrd hadn't actually turned it off.

"How much trouble am I in for what I said to him?" Violetta asked as Alyssa led her away.

"None," Mc'narrd's voice said in the comm. "You aren't under my direct command. Be thankful."

Alyssa snorted. "He's forgotten what he did on the *Laedschot*."

"I remember everything that happened," Mc'narrd countered.

"Then you remember what happened with the first policy master and what you did after that Duel," Alyssa countered.

Violetta glanced at the woman who was escorting her through the park and towards the little shops and cafes near it.

"Yes," was the grumbled reply.

"His jealousy caused so much trouble that day," Alyssa said with a chuckle. When she noticed Violetta's angry face, she laughed. "I'm not laughing at you, child. I'm laughing about how foolish men are and how much you remind me of those early days when I was rescued by the *Laedschot's* crew."

"I'm sorry-" Violetta began.

"Malik isn't as certain of himself as he appears," Alyssa continued. "He's probably afraid you'll suddenly decide that the pressure from your peers and those around you will win. That you'll decide it would be easier to accept someone of pure blood. Instead of the harder path of being courted by a fellow being of mixed heritage."

"How… why do you think that?"

"It's a fear we all have, child. Everyone in a relationship at one point or another fears someone else will be a better choice," Alyssa replied. "If you doubt me, ask Sovereign Healer Zh'oros."

"Did that ever happen to you?" Violetta asked after a few moments.

"A few times," Alyssa admitted with a small smile. "Being planetside when the man you love is lightyears away? With beings who all appear perfect?" She chuckled. "Oh, yes. I had that fear so often. But my love was never betrayed. Just as I never betrayed him."

"Malik's loyalty to you is unwavering. It was strong even while he was in the service," Zh'oros' voice came through the comms. Violetta recognized her from just a few months earlier. The Sovereign Healer had a very distinct voice. "He worries that he isn't worthy of you."

"And yet he admitted to my fellow detectives that we're sleeping together," Violetta bemoaned.

"Are you ashamed of it?" Alyssa and Zh'oros said the words together.

The answer came instantly.

"No. I wasn't ashamed five years ago. I'm not ashamed now."

"Then why are you angry?" Alyssa demanded.

"Because he said to not tell anyone. Yet, he did just that," Violetta retorted. "If he's going to tell my colleagues, then why can't the rest of the population know?"

"Okay, I'd be angry about that, too," Alyssa admitted. "Because now your department will know. Those who aren't military may choose to Challenge you because they don't approve and you can't always have Malik as your Champion."

"I'd prefer not having him as my Champion." Violetta glanced sharply at Alyssa. "Those were extenuating circumstances. As in: I was too injured to Duel."

"That's frighteningly familiar," Mc'narrd grumbled.

"Then train with Malik at the base," Alyssa said dismissively. "When he's not available, find me. I've had a few years of experience."

"You had 'a few years of experience' before you set foot on my ship," Mc'narrd grumbled. "A fact none of us were aware of."

"You didn't ask, either," Alyssa retorted. She winked at Violetta, a wide grin on her face. "Come on. Let's get that drink. Then we can go to the base and you can Challenge Malik to a Duel."

"That is very tempting," Violetta admitted.

"Then why not?" Alyssa asked, her brows furrowed. "Challenges don't have to be to the death. Or even require unconsciousness or a severe injury. They're a wonderful way of resolving arguments. Especially between spouses, lovers, or even friends. Because in those cases, neither wants to cause serious harm." She paused before adding with a smirk, "Usually."

"I really can't argue that," Violetta reluctantly agreed.

"Good. Then it's settled. We'll enjoy a drink and share contact information, then you can Challenge your lover. He can apologize later by buying you something pretty or maybe some chocolate." She paused, her eyes narrowing on Violetta. "You do like sweets, yes?"

"Who doesn't?" Violetta asked, brows raised. "I love sweet treats. I thought everyone did?"

Alyssa laughed and gestured towards a cafe. Violetta chuckled and entered the business, Alyssa following after her.

Having another woman to talk to helped. And Alyssa was as charming as her father had always claimed.

Chapter Three

The women were laughing and talking about life in general as Alyssa piloted her HAV through the gates of the military base before parking it in the hoverdeck. The guards on duty waved them through, calling a greeting to Policy Master Zelaya, who returned it easily. Taking the lift down to the ground level, they began towards the main building on the base.

Violetta's eyes swept over the multi-storied exterior of the building. The eight point spires reached for the clouds. The tall spires marked the six primary directions; North, Northeast, Northwest and the corresponding South points. A plenitude of sea glass allowed for strategic views out but a warped view looking into the interior.

"Beautiful, isn't it?" Alyssa said as she stood staring at the building made of blue-silver metal. "I didn't know what to expect when I learned about this world. Reading and viewing vidclips from an interface doesn't do anything on this planet justice."

"I love it, though my favorite has always been the interior," Violetta admitted, a smile on her face. "Dad would bring me to the base and I would just stare at it all."

Alyssa giggled. "I did, too. In total awe of it all. On the other hand, I think my staring at all of this allowed the K'laisians time to stare at me without appearing rude!"

Violetta chuckled. Alyssa had been the first human to interact, being-to-being with the K'laisians over three decades ago. Though one would never know she was over fifty by just looking at her.

The first ever human Master of Policies had been the first to also be injected with nanites. Her youthful appearance and health was attributed to the fact the nanites had never been programmed for a human before, so they treated her as a K'laisian more than a human. Those very same nanites removed the signs of age, illness, disease, and the like that were known to be part of a human's life.

Annoyance flashed across Alyssa's face briefly, causing Violetta to suspect Mc'narrd had said something to her.

"Don't forget, I am not under anyone's command, anymore," Alyssa muttered, confirming Violetta's suspicions. There was a brief pause. "I suppose that's better. You're still taking me out to Ossani's for that, though."

Ossani's Restaurant was an expensive, fancy Italian restaurant that was infamous for their classic, authentic dishes. It employed any being, but there were no robot attendants and the waiters took orders on notepads. There were no interfaces at the tables. It was old school to the extreme.

A common occurrence, she'd been told, on Earth and many other planets, but a rarity on their world.

"I'll see you in my office," Mc'narrd said over Violetta's comm.

"You know how to get there?" Alyssa asked as they stepped through the main doors.

Violetta nodded.

Understanding filled the other woman's eyes, even as Violetta turned her attention to the massive entry hall.

The walls and floors of the lowest level were made of dark blue dolomite. The handrails, stairs and doors were primarily made of manganese with other metals. The silver gray color of those objects shone against the dolomite. The ceilings and floors of all the other levels were a honeycomb of manganese and sea glass.

The visual was striking, while allowing anyone to look at the level above or below them. Violetta couldn't hide her fascination and appreciated the calm she experienced as she looked through the sea glass.

"Cq'linns," Mc'narrd's voice said in the comm. "Don't keep me waiting."

"Stop being militant," Alyssa snapped.

Violetta shot the woman an appreciated smile. "I'll go. I can always enjoy this later."

Giving her a nod, Alyssa turned and headed for the stairs. Taking a final look around the entry, Violetta traversed the corridors for the admiral's office.

It didn't take long for her to locate the door that opened to reveal Mc'narrd sitting at a desk. The office, void of anything declaring who used the room, was average in size and design. Two chairs sat in front of his desk.

Both were empty.

"Sit," Mc'narrd ordered when the door closed.

"May I speak freely, sir?" Violetta asked, not moving from where she stood just inside the door.

Mc'narrd's silver eyes met hers.

Anger burned in them, but it was the only emotion she could detect on his otherwise blank face. Unlike most K'laisians, he did not have any hair. His head was bald and he had no eyebrows. A long-lasting after effect of the human's using their first-gen nanites on him in an effort to keep him alive when an operation on Earth went deadly.

He wore a dark blue tunic and matching pants. Casual clothing to hide his true identity as Admiral It'zarry Mc'narrd. On the counter near the darkened window was a helmet. The tunic and pants were loose, allowing only the barest peek of the biosuit he wore beneath it.

After a few seconds, he gave a slight nod.

"I would like to apologize for my behavior, and especially my words earlier." Violetta met his gaze and held it. "I should not have spoken to you like that, or in that tone. I am sorry, sir."

Some of the anger faded from his eyes.

"Apology accepted," Mc'narrd said. He nodded towards the chair. "Please sit, Violetta."

"Thank you, sir," she said quietly, dropping her eyes from him briefly. "Thank you, also, for sending Alyssa."

The warmth that flashed through his eyes removed the last of his anger.

"She's a unique woman," Mc'narrd said. "I'm pleased she was able to help you."

"I, um… that is, can we return to how we were prior to my outburst?"

"In regards to how we communicate and speak with each other?" Violetta gave a nod. Mc'narrd smiled slightly. "Yes, we may. Since you asked nicely."

"Thank you, sir."

"Will you now explain how you knew Tagliani?"

"Yes, sir," Violetta said. When his eyes narrowed at her, she sighed. "I'm sorry. Habit with Dad when he would be angry at me. You remind me of him a lot." When Mc'narrd gave a nod, understanding filled his eyes. She smiled slightly as she continued, her tone more professional. "I only met him once. It was at Morelli's safehouse. He showed up to bring food and stuck around to, I think, annoy Malik. Said he was there to remind Malik of what not to do while protecting me."

"I'm certain there's more, but take your time," Mc'narrd said when she paused. There was no malice to his words.

"Why all of you thought Malik would do anything unprofessional is beyond me," Violetta grumbled.

Laughter was not what she expected from Mc'narrd, but it's what she received.

"The attraction between you two was so obvious to everyone except you, I think. Your father loved you very much, Violetta. I think he kept everyone else away simply because he saw it when you and Malik were too young to know what it was."

"Maybe. Probably," Violetta allowed. She tipped her head to the side in curiosity. "Is that what you would have done?"

"It's what I *have* done," Mc'narrd admitted gently. "Alyssa and I both have done it with our children."

It was common knowledge that Alyssa had given birth to a son. Then adopted a great many orphans. Human, K'laisian, and mixed heritage. The race didn't mean anything to them. They had a large family and each child was treated equally. They'd all succeeded in life. Many chose to be career military like their parents.

The only child they'd produced together had quickly risen through the ranks and now commanded his own battlecruiser. When he returned to the planet, he was known to be exceedingly protective of his family. Whether his siblings wanted it or not, was the rumor she'd heard.

Having met Mc'narrd, and now Alyssa, she didn't doubt their son's protectiveness.

"Malik made a comment about Tagliani having a poor record towards protecting those he was in charge of," Violetta said, changing the topic back to why she was there. "Malik called him an 'enforcer'. Instead of listening to the pair argue, and someone possibly issuing a Challenge, I punched Tagliani in the face. We left him unconscious behind the bar while we ate."

"So, you two beat up Tagliani together after you punched him first, left him unconscious, and went about your day," Mc'narrd repeated. Violetta nodded. Mc'narrd shook his head. "I am even more thankful you did not enter the military now. You are far too much like your parents."

"Thank you, sir," Violetta said sweetly.

"Your department has been informed of Malik's movements last night." Mc'narrd continued, ignoring her comment. His tone grew serious. "I would advise training harder with Malik and our own instructors. When your department learns of your relationship, I suspect there will be Challenges issued."

"Because I'm being courted by Malik?" Violetta surmised.

"You've done a decent job at keeping the opposite gender at bay, but that's changed drastically. Your behavior has shifted. You've changed. Some may think Malik will be able to influence you. And through Malik, Morelli."

"I hadn't considered that," Violetta admitted. She paused, her eyes dropping to her hands. "What did you mean by 'if it's what I think it is, leave'?"

"You were having a flashback to Lc'sonn's office."

Violetta glanced away from him.

"And you're trying to not think of it now," the admiral said. Something in his voice caused her to look up at him. "I've seen it before, Violetta. You'll need to talk to someone about it. You were cleared for duty after that event by Zh'oros. I assure you, she didn't do it just to get you back into the field."

"I would suspect the opposite to be true," Violetta admitted.

"Talk to her. Talk to Malik." He paused, then added quietly, "Or talk to Alyssa. She knows what it's like and she may have some suggestions on how to deal with it."

Violetta rubbed her face, her palms sliding over her eyes as though it would help remove the memory. "I hate it. I hate the feeling I get from that stupid memory. Having Ziph trying to kill me doesn't affect me the same way. So why should it?"

"Because you didn't feel helpless with him," Mc'narrd explained. She dropped her hands to stare at him. "Talking about it will help. I'm not a healer, but I am willing to listen. And I do understand."

"I'll… try." Violetta gave a heavy sigh. "I'm not always the most open being."

That received another round of loud, hearty human-style laughter. It was a musical sound most humans loved hearing. Violetta, though half K'laisian, had to admit she enjoyed hearing it, too.

"That is one of the biggest understatements I've heard yet," Mc'narrd said after he was able to talk. "Why did you contact us about Tagliani in the first place?"

"Actually, it was because of Malik," Violetta admitted, not looking at Mc'narrd. "He and Hy'szolis were close to Challenging each other. I was hoping someone could just send over confirmation of where he'd been. Camera vidclips or something, since I don't know what security clearance is needed to view the cameras at my father's apartment."

"Fair enough," Mc'narrd replied. A smirk flashed across his face. "Are you still planning on Challenging Malik?"

"Yes. He's earned it." She flicked her eyes up to his as she added, "Besides, Alyssa reminded me it's a good way of resolving conflicts."

"Very true. It's certainly been useful in my household over the years." He paused before chuckling. "As well as when we were together on the *Laedschot*. I suspect I was the only commander of a battlecruiser who's policy master frequently Challenged the battlecruiser's commander."

"I suspect that was because most commanders were not mates with said policy masters," Violetta countered. "Dad always said you two were a well suited pair."

"I often said the same about your parents," Mc'narrd admitted. His eyes twinkled with mischief. "I might be tempted to say the same for you and Malik, but he's got to survive your Duel, first."

"I don't think either of us are out for a death, sir."

"Only because you aren't as angry as you were in that booth."

Violetta opened her mouth to say something, then snapped it shut. "Do you have to sound like Dad all the time?"

"Only when you've earned it," was his cool reply.

"Whatever 'parenting school' you and Dad went to? Remind me not to go to it."

Mc'narrd laughed merrily as he stood. "I'll escort you to the gym. Malik's already there. I'll oversee it to ensure your temper doesn't get the best of you." He paused before adding, "Either of you."

"Thank you, Admiral," she said, standing.

She didn't know why Mc'narrd had taken such a personal interest in her, but she was thankful. He was still a force to be reckoned with, and certainly not a parent. But being able to talk with him so easily and openly was something she appreciated. Perhaps eventually they would be able to call each other friends.

Until then, she was going to enjoy what was being offered.

Chapter Four

The only difference in the gym this time was there were considerably more beings.

"Did you sell tickets?" Violetta teased.

The last time she and Malik had visited the gym, they'd sparred good-naturedly. She'd demanded a rematch and Mc'narrd had joked about selling tickets.

Mc'narrd laughed. "Not this time. Did you want this to be an official Duel?"

"I-" she broke off before considering the implications of what an official Duel would mean. She shook her head. "Were all the Duels with Alyssa official?"

"Onboard? Yes," Mc'narrd admitted. "But when we were planetside? No. Though many of those Duels were in this very gym."

"Unless Malik requests it, I don't think it needs to be official," Violetta said thoughtfully. "I'd rather we be able to use Duels as a way to resolve our personal problems. If they're always official, I don't think we'd be as apt to do them."

"There wouldn't be any publicity to worry about," Mc'narrd mused. "You'll have enough just by sparring with him."

"Exactly."

"I'll handle it," Mc'narrd reassured her. "Go pick out your weapon."

Violetta headed to the cabinet that held the weapons. Opening the door, she studied the options before her eyes landed on the swords. Taking one out, she gave it a few test swings. Holding it out straight, she studied the blade.

It hadn't been honed, so there were no sharp edges. A sparring weapon, though not padded. Glancing back at the others, she realized none in the cabinet had a deadly edge to them. It wouldn't stop an injury from happening, but it would take effort to cut through the clothes she wore.

Taking a few moments to remove her service weapon, baton, and shackles, she also removed the pouch that held her interface.

"Where should I place these?" she called out to Mc'narrd.

"I'll take them," a familiar voice said near her. She looked over and found Commander Ap'errson approaching her.

He'd been in charge of the squadron who had escorted her to the government center when she'd been prepared to exonerate herself. He was a pure blood native with straight black hair. Gold eyes shone brilliant against skin as dark as his hair.

"Good to see you again, Commander," Violetta said, offering the stack of items to him.

"Pleasure to see you, also, detective," he replied cheerfully. "Decided on a rematch, huh?"

"Oh, you were here for that?"

The commander hummed loudly. "I was, indeed. Though I suspect Malik won't go as easy on you this time."

"I'd be angry if he did," she admitted.

"*Angrier*, you mean," he said, humming. "You weren't too thrilled that day."

"Never liked being coddled, sir."

"No one ever does," Ap'errson agreed. He lifted the items slightly. "I won't be far."

"Thank you."

"A pleasure to be of assistance." He gave a slight bow before stepping back.

Turning, Violetta discovered Malik standing on the mats near Mc'narrd. His bronze eyes were on her and his black hair was pulled back into a braided ponytail. He wore loose clothes and study boots. His face was neutral, though his eyes shone with unhappiness.

"Are you ready, Violetta?" Mc'narrd asked.

She gave a nod and crossed to them. The moment her feet touched the mats, silence descended upon the gym. News of a Duel always traveled quickly. Today was no different.

There was no teasing from Malik this time, so she kept her thoughts to herself.

"Violetta Cq'linns, lieutenant detective of the 42nd Police Service has issued a Challenge to Malik Addelia. This is not an official Duel at the request of the issuer," Mc'narrd announced. His voice was loud and clear in the gym. "Do you agree, Malik Addelia?"

Malik started, his eyes darting between Mc'narrd and Violetta. They narrowed suspiciously on Mc'narrd. "Is this her choice or yours?"

"Mine," Violetta said loudly. "I would prefer we resolve our conflicts personally." She paused and looked blatantly around the gym. "Well, as personally as one can get with an audience watching the Duel. But it was, and is, at my request. Without urging from anyone."

"Do you agree?" Mc'narrd repeated. "If you desire, it can be made official."

"I agree with Violetta," Malik replied. His eyes met hers and held them. "If it is your wish, then may it be so. I would have accepted it as official, if you had desired it."

"I'd prefer our Duels not be official."

His lips rose slightly.

"An unofficial Duel has been requested between Violetta and Malik," Mc'narrd repeated.

He dropped the use of their titles and official designations. As it was now on record as being unofficial, they weren't required. It also wouldn't need to be recorded and submitted to the proper places.

"Do you accept the Challenge, Malik?"

"I do."

Two words and they had so much meaning. Violetta stared at Malik with wide eyes.

He'd seen the wedding videos of her parents. They'd had a human wedding with K'laisian traditions incorporated into it. Those two words were spoken to each other during the ceremony.

Humming and laughter filled the gym briefly. Even Mc'narrd chuckled at Malik's choice of words.

Official language used by Challengers was 'I accept'.

Malik's words sounded like a promise for something else entirely.

"I don't need to ask her," Mc'narrd stated as he smiled.

He held a hand up between them. Violetta raised her sword in salute to Malik, who did the same towards her.

Taking a slight step to the side, she held her sword out at shoulder height. Uncertainly, Malik tapped his sword against hers. When she flipped it down, some of the sadness left his eyes. He did the same, tapping her blade easily. They both slid back into their former positions, determination shining in their eyes.

It was a promise and declaration to each other. Something they'd done since they'd begun sparring, then Dueling together. A tradition of their own. Violetta refused to forgo it for anything.

Even her irritation at him.

"Begin!" Mc'narrd called out, once they'd resumed their former stances. His hand slashed downward. With the agility that only a native K'laisian could possess, he slid backwards away from the pair.

There was no cautious tapping against each other's blades, or a formal crossing. Violetta charged forward and thrust her sword at Malik's chest in an unmistakable kill move. Malik brought his own blade down in a vicious arc while pivoting to his left.

The momentum of the two brought them around in a full circle. Malik positioned his sword in a line across his chest and neck. The perfect move to block the expected downward swing from Violetta.

He did not anticipate her right foot. Immediately after the swords clashed, she launched a strong front kick right into Malik's exposed thigh.

The muscle seized and Malik had no choice but to go to one knee. Violetta had to move back after the kick to regain both feet on the floor. She gave no quarter and began a series of thrusts that aimed for the vital areas of Malik's neck, chest, and back.

Malik managed to block and pivot while on one knee, keeping the thrusts from landing even as harmless sparring hits. The strain cost him, as both Violetta and Mc'narrd could see he was already showing signs of fatigue and exertion.

A mild opening came, giving Malik a chance to take a hard swing at Violetta's legs. He gave a milder swing, with the flat of the blade. It was enough to make her jump back and give him some breathing room. He used the opportunity to roll further away and come back into a standing position. He favored the leg not kicked, but only just.

When she came again, the flat of her sword dipped towards Malik's uninjured leg. Malik easily slapped away the attack with his blade, and then moved his torso against hers. His free hand caressed her cheek.

"Too obvious," he cooed into her ear. "Do better."

With surprising grace and speed, he spun around her and playfully slapped her rear. With his hand, although she realized he could have just as well used the flat of his sword. Which would have been a strong point against her in this Duel.

In response, her sword swung up towards his crotch. Malik sidestepped the maneuver before striking her blade away from him.

"Violetta," Mc'narrd said in a warning tone.

She ignored him and pressed the attack. Her swings and thrusts favored against Malik's injured leg, forcing him to rely on it more and more. He started to become slower.

Thinking she sensed an advantage, Violetta moved around Malik. He began hopping on his good leg to keep her within his sight. She rushed in, prepared to deliver a series of swings to finish him.

And ran right into Malik's extended, injured leg. His foot compressed her diaphragm and stomach, making her stumble back as the air rushed from her lungs.

"I'm disappointed she ignored that possibility," Mc'narrd confessed aloud.

"I did not become Master of Ceremonies by talking a good duel," Malik declared.

Violetta shook her body and inhaled deeply. Her lungs accepted the air gratefully.

The Duel continued.

Malik took the offensive. He was starting to hobble slightly, making his strategy of attacks that required

Violetta to extend her body over and over difficult for both of them. Finally, her mind cleared enough to see the pattern.

At his next deep arc aimed for her sword arm, she moved in close. He tensed at the change in dynamic, his sword arm faltering for the moment.

She threw a punch at his face with her sword hand. He ducked, but instead of popping back into a full stand, his body tucked in and began to slip to her side.

Pivoting awkwardly, Violetta brought her sword around and down. She smiled in satisfaction as the flat of her blade slapped against Malik's exposed neck just below the ear.

Her smile ended when she realized that the dull point of Malik's sword was poking against the two middle vertebrae of her back.

"A draw. However, I do concede that the advantage goes to Violetta. Her spine and lung might be healed enough to continue living. Malik certainly would not continue without his head," Mc'narrd commented with a chuckle in his voice.

"Master Malik," a younger, excited voice interrupted.

All three turned to see a K'laisian male barely into adulthood, wearing the staff outfit of the gym. He smiled uncertainly at Malik.

"My apologies, but the overseer at the city's primary arena has been quite insistent about contacting you. Since this is obviously a spar, I presumed it would be appropriate to intercede. The Overseer claims there is an overbooking and needs you to decide on- Oh!"

The young male's head snapped towards Mc'narrd.

His voice became faster and half an octave higher. "Judge Ta'ba! A pleasure to see you, your Honor! This is unexpected."

"As unexpected as you interrupting?" Violetta demanded.

The staff member flinched as if struck by a shock rod.

"Laying judgment over crimes gets tedious. Master Malik asked that I give an impartial view on this unofficial Duel. Your eagerness to pacify the overseer has led you to interruption, not an intercession," explained Mc'narrd in a pleasant tone. The same one he used for his alias as "Judge Io'siph Ta'ba".

The staffer immediately dropped to his knees, head hung low.

"Mercy, please, Judge! Master and Lady!"

"Detective," Violetta growled. The young male prostrated himself further.

With his face almost touching the floor, the male said, "I have brought dishonor to myself and the gym by my actions. Pray, tell me what punishment will settle this debt!"

"Get up and face it with respect and honor," ordered Malik. "Mewling and cowering on the floor is not the way of K'lais."

Typically Violetta would giggle or smile at 'mewling', an ancient Earther word. Today she found herself irritated at the intrusion.

The male got to his feet, forcing himself to look at the wall behind the three beings.

"Give me a minute to grab a proper blade," Violetta began.

A brief whimper came from the male.

"Violetta, take your anger out on me, not the help," Malik suggested calmly. He then addressed the staff member. "You will tell Overseer T'ac that he will await my response at my disposal. Not his. And you will not speak of this incident other than to convey to T'ac that you nearly lost all in bringing his request to me. Go."

The male staffer ran out. Violetta and Malik finally moved from how the Duel had ended. As they both stood and stretched, Mc'narrd collected the swords.

As he was placing the practice weapons on their racks, Mc'narrd spoke in a casual, conversational tone.

"That was really quite a show. Do find me when the inevitable re-Challenge happens, will you?"

"You will be one of the first to be informed," Violetta said, bowing low to Mc'narrd. "Thank you for overseeing this one."

Malik bowed, also. "It has been an honor and pleasure, sir."

Mc'narrd chuckled. "Are you satisfied, Violetta?"

A mischievous grin flashed across her face. "For now, anyway."

That brought a round of laughter from everyone in the gym, including Malik and Mc'narrd.

"Good luck with her." Mc'narrd gave Malik a small bow. "I suspect she is going to leave you fatigued more often than not."

"In more ways than one," Malik agreed.

"I give up!" Violetta exclaimed, throwing her hands in the air.

"Your items, Lady," Ap'errson said, suddenly appearing beside them.

Accepting them, Violetta began reattaching the items to her belt.

"At least medics aren't being required," another familiar voice said from behind Violetta. "Unlike certain times on a certain battlecruiser."

She turned to find Sovereign Healer Zh'oros stepping forward. The silver biosuit was a stark contrast against the woman's hair that was so dark it had blue and purple highlights. Her skintone wasn't nearly as dark, instead it was a beautiful olive shade, similar to what Malik and Violetta possessed.

A gray tentacled mollusk with its wings spread wide on her shoulder revealed her to be a healer. Three brands wrapped around her cuffs with three starbursts above them signaled her rank. Violetta knew it meant she was a Sovereign Healer on level with a three-star admiral.

Mc'narrd laughed. "I suspect that will come later."

Violetta glanced at him sharply, but there was nothing but amusement on Mc'narrd's face and in his eyes.

"I saw the readouts from your biosuit," Zh'oros said without preamble. "Let's go to medical and you can explain to me what happened." She paused before glancing at Malik with her gold eyes. "Would you like him to join you? Or would you prefer it to be private?"

"I think I'd like Malik to be there," Violetta admitted. "I'd end up telling him, anyway."

The look in Malik's eyes had her mind going in all the wrong places. Places that included a comfortable bed and complete privacy.

"As you wish. Shall we, then?" Zh'oros hummed loudly. "As procedure dictates, I'll need to examine you both after the Duel, anyway. We can do it all concurrently."

Violetta nodded, even as Malik stepped beside her. His hand slid into hers and he squeezed her fingers.

"I think this was certainly a better method of resolving our problems," Malik admitted, his eyes shining as he looked into hers. "I suspect we will be coming here more often."

"Of that, I have no doubt," Mc'narrd said dryly. "Go and discuss things with Zh'oros. You know how to contact me."

Violetta and Malik gave a nod. Then, in perfect synchronization with each other, they followed Zh'oros from the gym.

"I wonder if anyone won any bets?" Violetta muttered as she walked through the crowd.

There was even more laughter.

"I'm certain someone did," Zh'oros said, amusement in her voice.

Chapter Five

Tired and pleasantly exhausted, Violetta trudged back to the police station.

She'd spent several hours talking with Zh'oros. The woman had then cleared Violetta for duty once again. Malik had remained to continue discussing PTSD and coping techniques with Zh'oros and a few other healers.

He may have ended his instruction for becoming a healer, but he hadn't ended his interest in the subject.

"Comm frequency change: police frequency normal," Violetta said when the front steps came into view. The comm chirped once signally the change. The soft hum of dimmed voices filled her ear. "Comm code D-4-2-V-C."

The noise went silent. She was eternally thankful for the ability to silence the idle chatter of the comms. If someone spoke her name, or if Issik spoke, she'd hear it. Otherwise, she had silence in her ear.

A welcome change, in her opinion.

"Violetta."

Ra'keff Hy'szolis brought her to a full stop near the bottom steps that led into the station. She turned to find him approaching her slowly. She offered a smile and he relaxed, though he didn't appear any less cautious.

"I wanted to apologize, again," he said, stopping a few feet from her. He kept his hands slightly away from his body. As though hoping to reassure her that he meant no harm. "I thought perhaps it would be better to do it out here. Where there's more space." He tipped his head side-to-side in a K'laisian version of a shrug. "I should not have said what I did. I was out of line. I apologize for all of it."

"Did the captain tell you to apologize?" she asked with a sigh.

He grinned slightly. "He actually suggested I give you time to cool off. But no, he didn't tell me I had to do so."

"Apology accepted, then." When he remained in place, she raised a brow. "Was there something else?"

"May I ask a question?"

Ra'keff was watching her closely and Violetta wondered what she'd done this time.

"Sure. Go ahead. Seems to be a day for interrogations."

He shook his head slightly. "Did I do something wrong earlier? In the booth? If I… troubled you, I wish to apologize for that, also."

Violetta leaned against the railing of the steps, trying to find the proper words that wouldn't insult her fellow detective.

"Please, do not think it was anything you did. I meant no insult then, and I mean none now. My reaction was… from an event I experienced. PTSD, if you will." Her lips curved up in a smile, but she knew it didn't meet her eyes. "I've been cleared by a sovereign healer for duty. Again. But I'll still need to work through the vestiges of that event. It will be a struggle, but nothing that should hinder my job."

Ra'keff tipped his head to the side. A universal sign of curiosity, even thoughtfulness, from a native K'laisian.

"A recent event, then. Something to do with Lc'sonn, probably." When she remained silent he hummed a little. "I've heard the words 'required security clearance' thrown around more in the past four months than my entire time in the police service and military combined. Doesn't take a good detective long to figure out something bad happened with the former D.A."

"He's very astute," Mc'narrd's voice said in her ear.

Guess he'd been listening, Violetta grumbled silently.

"I'm sorry, I can't say," Violetta admitted, true regret in her voice.

"It's fine, Lady," Ra'keff said with an easy smile. "If there's anything I can do to assist, please let me know. Even if it's to let others know to be easy around you in the booths."

"Thank you," she replied, the smile finally meeting her eyes. "I appreciate that, Ra'keff."

"See you around, detective," he said, lifting his chin and dropping it in a K'laisian nod.

She returned the gesture and began up the stairs.

"Lady Violetta."

Pausing at the top step, she looked down at him, wondering what he wanted now.

"Calling you 'Violence' has never been meant as an insult. At least not from me." With that declaration, he bowed to her before spinning on his heel and striding away.

Turning, she began up the stairs, staring at the main doors in complete confusion.

Laughter filled her ear.

"Not helping, sir," she muttered under her breath.

Traversing the main foyer, she continued down the hallways and corridors in silence as she made her way to homicide. The interface to the main area flashed green, then slid open as she reached it.

When the door opened, the scent hit her first. The sight of her desk was second.

Flowers of various types sat in vases. They covered the entire top of her desk with just enough room for a small envelope.

"Nope," she said aloud and turned to walk away.

"Cq'linns." The captain's voice filled her ear, stopping her. "Take the rest of the day off. Issik, take her to lunch. She can deal with her desk later."

"Yes, sir," Issik replied. She could see him standing and walking towards her, a wide grin on his face. He snatched the envelope from her desk, never breaking his stride as he did so.

He met her outside the door to homicide.

"Did you see Hy'szolis?" he asked as they headed towards the nearest exit. "He's been wanting to apologize."

"Yeah, he caught me outside." She glanced at him warily. "Who sent the flowers?"

"They started arriving about ten minutes after Malik left. Every one of them has the words 'I'm sorry' on them."

Issik hummed. He held the envelope up. She plucked it from his fingers but didn't look at it.

"Not a single one is from Ra'keff. He was actually pretty impressed when they kept arriving."

"Malik," she said with a groan. "As though that declaration in the booth wasn't enough."

"He couldn't get them into your apartment," Mc'narrd's voice said in her ear. "I believe they're your favorite flowers, too."

"Excuse me a moment, Issik," she said to her friend. "And how would you know that, sir?"

"A voice in your ear?" Issik asked. She nodded. His response was humming. "Must make work interesting."

"You have no idea," she muttered.

Mc'narrd laughed. "We have a dossier. It's a rather thick file, actually." He paused for a moment, allowing the words to sink in. "There's also the fact Malik was in my office when he began placing the orders. It might have slipped out."

"Any other information on Tagliani's death?" Violetta asked, turning her attention to Issik. It was definitely a safer topic, in her opinion. "I didn't get to finish going over the file."

Issik's face brightened. "Was wondering when you were going to come back to that. Nothing new has been learned. An autopsy has been scheduled."

Fishing her service-issued interface from its holder, Violetta touched the screen. A few taps later and she had the file up.

As they walked, she scrolled through the file.

"Where are we heading?" she asked, not looking up.

"Ku'rtiiz," Issik replied.

It was a favorite bar of theirs. Good food, good drinks, and semi-private booths. It also wasn't a favorite for most of the police service. Which meant they didn't have to worry about running into fellow officers.

Violetta nodded, even as she frowned at the screen.

"What's wrong?"

"His place of employment puts him as a guard across the river. Yet he was found near Malik's penthouse." Violetta continued scrolling. "Why? Why would he be close to where Malik lives? They aren't friends or even close associates. They didn't like each other at all."

"We didn't hate each other," Malik's voice said in her ear. "But it was close. Adversaries would be a good description."

"You're comm off?" Issik asked.

"Usual code for silence."

Issik nodded. "At least I don't have to ask how you know they didn't like each other. Though I wouldn't say anything to anyone else at the department."

Violetta gave him a disgusted look, causing him to humm.

"It's rather obvious that I spend a great deal of time with Malik. I don't think anyone can miss the flowers. Or the notes on them. And, oh yeah, there's the fact anyone on comms heard what was said in the interrogation room." She paused, trying to curb her irritation. "It's not like our comms aren't linked or anything."

Which, everyone knew, the comms they used *were* linked. Everyone in their department could easily hear each other, if they so chose. Violetta often found the constant background noise of talking annoying, so she generally muted her comm. Allowing it to be silent unless someone spoke to her or it was Issik talking.

A benefit of knowing how to program a comm.

Issik hummed louder. "That was rather amusing. Never thought I'd see Ra'keff being anything but professional."

"So delighted to be the subject of such amusement," Violetta said dryly.

"I am sorry for that, Vi," Malik said over the comm. "Do you want me to stop sending the flowers?"

Violetta paused, feeling her heart squeeze at his words.

"No," she muttered. At Issik's questioning look, she tapped her ear. Her partner's humm only grew. "They are lovely. Even if I don't have the energy to deal with them right now."

"Right," Issik teased. "Back to our corpse. Do you think he was trying to cause problems?"

"I don't know," Violetta replied. Her fingers flew across the interface.

"What are you doing?"

Mc'narrd's voice and Issik's overlapped each other.

"Playing a hunch," Violetta said thoughtfully.

"You aren't supposed to be accessing COD," Issik said blandly, using the favorite abbreviation for the police service's criminal organization division. "That's the department for the organized syndicates and gang affiliations."

"Really? Would never have guessed," Violetta said dryly. "There's nothing here, anyway."

"You sound disappointed," Issik said thoughtfully.

"I was wondering if the Moyii Tsaa might have something going on around there," Violetta admitted.

"I'll check with Commander Al'erryn," Mc'narrd said thoughtfully. "Despite taking out the one cell, there are others in the city. She's in charge of investigations and eliminations."

"What investigations do we have?" Violetta asked, copying the file on Tagliani over to another folder on her interface for easy access later.

"You're supposed to be taking the day off," Issik teased as they neared the bar.

"I didn't say I was going to begin the investigation with you," Violetta argued. "But I'd like to know what we've got."

"An investigation at the corner of Rt'aasn Street and Issunde Street. A male of mixed heritage was found deceased there," Issik replied.

He held his hand out for the interface as he paused near the entrance to the bar. Violetta handed it to him as she stepped past him.

Myia met them in the small foyer. A cute K'laisian with silver hair cut in a bob with bright silver eyes, she'd been a constant at the eatery for the five years she and Issik had been going there. She wore the bar's uniform of a black short-sleeved tunic and matching, snug pants.

"Oh! Good afternoon, detectives. Would you like your usual booth?" Myia said cheerfully.

Issik and Violetta both smiled and nodded.

"Would you like your usual drinks and meal? Or something different?" the woman asked brightly, leading the pair to a booth along the far wall.

The booths along that side were empty, aside from them.

"An ual cider would be lovely," Violetta said, knowing the hard liquor was on the menu. She slid onto the conforming bench seat, even as Issik settled opposite her.

If she was off-duty, she was going to enjoy a strong beverage.

Myia blinked a few times. She quickly recovered from her surprise, though. "Absolutely! What about you, Issik? Same or the usual?"

"The usual. I'm still on duty," Issik replied.

"Ah, that explains it, then!" Myia exclaimed, humming. "I'll get your drinks and be right back. Then you can let me know what you'd like to eat."

As she sauntered off, still humming, Issik finished tapping on the interface. He handed it back to Violetta.

"Theories?" she asked, as she scrolled through the data.

It was their usual method of discussing cases.

"None yet," Issik admitted. "Report shows it was a beating. It's possible the responsible party didn't mean to cause death."

"Perhaps," Violetta allowed. Pulling up the initial scan of the body, she enlarged it and began going over the image slowly. "Are these from us or the coroner?"

"Coroner."

Both paused in speaking as Myia returned, a tall tankard of cider in one hand, a tall glass of kaerik root for Issik.

"How about the usual," Issik suggested.

Violetta thought for a moment then nodded.

"Two tsak burgers with full trimmings and salted potato fries coming up," Myia replied. "It'll be out shortly!"

Without another word, the woman turned and headed towards the actual bar.

"And that is why I love this place," Issik said with a grin.

"Because of the view or the fact they give us privacy?" Violetta teased.

"Both," Issik replied, tipping his head to the left before lifting it again in a K'laisian style wink.

Laughing, Violetta turned back to the interface. Something about the image still bothered her.

"Do you have your interface?" she asked, looking up at Issik. He gave a slow lift of his head in a nod. "Can I borrow it?"

"What did you notice?" he asked, pulling out his interface and opening it for her.

"I'm not sure," she said honestly. "Something about this is bothering me. But I can't pinpoint it."

"The only other one you've seen today is the one for Tagliani," Issik stated. His fingers moved across the screen with a nimbleness Violetta envied. "Come to think of it, he was beaten, also."

"I'm surprised no one thought I did it," she quipped. Issik hummed loudly as he handed her the interface, the initial scan already on the screen. "Probably because no one realized I'd met him."

"If anyone had met him, they'd want to do the same to him," Issik muttered. Violetta raised a brow. "He worked for Morelli and has been brought in a few times. So, yes. I've met him multiple times."

Nodding thoughtfully, she set the interfaces on the table between them. She shifted the scans until they both showed the sides of both bodies. Then enlarged the injuries.

"*Ka'desh,*" Issik breathed. He leaned forward. "That can't be a coincidence."

"Doubtful. Those are done by someone who has been taught," Violetta said softly. "Dad taught me when I was little. I'm sure it's standard in the military."

"Do you think Ad'miryz and Hy'szolis know?"

"That depends on if they've checked out ours," Violetta mused.

"Probably not, then. *Most* of us don't look at everything in the database."

"I like to be thorough."

Lifting the glass of cider to her lips, she took a long pull. The cider was as delicious as she expected it to be. The alcohol was dark and smooth with a sweet, yet woodsy undertone. It left a light, spicy aftertaste in her mouth. It took considerable effort to not smack her lips like an uncouth human.

She took another, shorter pull, before settling the glass on the table.

At Issik's raised brows, she asked, "What?"

"What happened in the booth with Ra'keff? He said you hightailed it out as though you thought he was going to punch you. Left him baffled and worried."

"Did he actually say that?"

"Not exactly, but I could read between what he did say. So what happened?" He took a sip of his own drink. "We were both in Lc'sonn's office. I don't know everything that happened, but I can guess."

"I had a flashback," Violetta admitted. "When… I was told to take a walk, the military called me in to talk to their healer. The same healer who cleared me originally. It's why it took me so long getting back to the station."

"Going to be well?" Issik asked, his eyes sympathetic. "You aren't planning on drowning it out with drinks, are you?"

"No, the drinks are because I got in trouble when yelling at Malik," Violetta replied laughing. "Then there was the unofficial Duel with Malik. And talking to the healer and requiring clearance before being returned to duty. Again."

"Busy day," Issik commented, leaning back in the booth. "You'll get through it. But if I think you're hitting the bottle, as the humans say, I'll call your scrawny ass out on it."

"It's not scrawny," she retorted, though there was laughter in her voice.

"Really? Have you looked at it lately?"

It was a standard joke between them. One Violetta appreciated.

Issik paused, before reflecting. "Though you have been eating more recently. Maybe it isn't as scrawny as it was."

"I may have to Challenge you for that," Violetta said indignantly.

Issik's humming joined with the laughter in her earbud. It sounded distinctly like Mc'narrd's laughter, too.

"So, what's the plan, Cq'linns?" Issik asked, gesturing towards the interfaces. "You've been told to take the day off. If Captain Os'shye finds out you're investigating, he'll have your head.

"Doubtful. *Commander* Os'shye isn't that bad," Violetta retorted.

Their captain had been military prior to taking the position of their captain. His military title was higher than that of any of their captains, but he accepted the title without argument.

"I'm still uncertain if he isn't actually still active military and there to keep an eye on everything from inside."

"That's a good guess," Mc'narrd commented in a neutral tone.

"It's certainly possible. Most of the military who have moved over are certainly willing to have your back without question," Issik stated. "It's like you've suddenly gained a few dozen protective older siblings."

Mc'narrd burst out laughing. Violetta wanted to warn the admiral Issik might hear him.

"I am not saying that to any of them. You can do it," Violetta joked.

"Think I'll pass," Issik said flatly. "I'd rather not have to contend with that many Duels. And that doesn't answer my question."

"We need to view the bodies. If we can confirm they're linked, it may allow us to put together a more complete profile," Violetta replied, her eyes on the interfaces. Taking another pull of her cider, she tapped the table with a finger. "Do we know if the deaths occurred there or if the bodies were moved or dumped?"

"Nothing in the reports. Since they didn't lose a lot of blood, it may be difficult to determine. I'll go by after we leave. I can use my Gift. Maybe it'll shed some light on the subject."

"How many new cases have there been?"

"These two and another were discovered near Sl'enthwar Street. Though general consensus is that one was from a Duel."

"It's near the poorest area, so that makes sense," Violetta admitted. "Any cameras pick it up?"

"There were a few in the area. Cassias and By'rricks are investigating that one. I can check to see if it's been confirmed to be from a Duel."

"What's your plan when you leave here?"

"I'm supposed to go home," Violetta commented. "Though I may drop by Syra's bakery."

"Isn't that near…" Issik trailed off, shaking his head. "You're going to get into so much trouble."

"Don't know what you're talking about Ha'kksworth. I'm going to visit Malik's sister and thank her for all the pastries she's been sending to the department. Maybe grab something to take home."

"Right. And since I'm supposed to ensure you get home in one piece, I'm going to be accompanying you."

"You don't have to."

"I like my job, thank you. The captain may like you, but that doesn't mean it extends to me."

Violetta was still chuckling when Myia arrived with their food. "Need a refill, Violetta?"

"Actually, how about a glass of drekka berry lemonade?" Violetta asked, smiling at Myia.

"Coming right up!" she exclaimed. "Had me worried there for a minute, Lady."

"Can't have that," Violetta teased.

Myia hummed, bowed slightly to them, and hurried off to get the other drink.

"Better?" Violetta asked Issik.

"For now," he relented. "Think you can get some reassurance my ass won't be in the fire for you not obeying our superior?"

"If the captain doesn't know what he was getting into with you, that was his mistake," Mc'narrd commented. "I'll make sure nothing happens to either of you. And have a talk with Commander Os'shye if he causes problems for you or your partner."

"I'm sure we won't end up in the proverbial fire." Violetta checked her burger to ensure everything she enjoyed was on it before picking it up. "You'd think someone would have warned Os'shye before he took the job."

Mc'narrd chuckled. "Wasn't my job to warn him about you."

Issik hummed, even as he dove into his meal.

The conversation shifted to more mundane things as they enjoyed their lunch. The screens of the interfaces dimmed, then shut off as time passed.

At least some things were still the same, Violetta thought.

Chapter Six

Malik's youngest sister, Syra, had taken over Sweet Uáts, after their parents retired. Or 'Sweet Treats' as the humans called it. Her Gift was in baking, which fit well with her chosen profession. The bakery had originally been a front for the Morelli syndicate.

Their father, Carmine, had been a member of the Morelli syndicate who moved to K'lais and ended up meeting his mate, a native K'laisian. Isima and Carmine had always welcomed Violetta into their home. Now, Malik's sister ran the bakery and had taken it upon herself to pull Violetta back into the Addelia fold.

The fact Sweet Treats was near the Master of the Dead's building meant Violetta could use the store as a sort of cover.

Or that was the plan, anyway.

The building used by the Master of the Dead was one of the very few buildings in the city made of stone, girders, and mortar. Centuries old, it was a piece of their ancestry. As much of a beautiful work of art as the modern buildings on the block. Carvings wrapped around the narrow stone ledges with what appeared to be sharp points following the curve of the roof's ledge. Humans often commented the building appeared to be wearing a crown, an Earth symbol of royalty.

The colors of the stones varied, shifting from a dark blue to white, giving the building a beautiful gradient appearance. It reminded Violetta of a tall waterfall, with the water crashing into rapids. Soothing. Peaceful. Everything the dead were promised in their eternal sleep.

Since Issik drove, she was able to enjoy the view of the building as they approached it.

On the other side, considerably shorter than the towering, seven-floor building, was the pastry shop Malik's sister, Syra owned and operated.

Her partner parked between the two buildings. Violetta stepped out of the HAV, her eyes sweeping over the beings moving along the sidewalk. Not seeing a threat, she turned to Issik. He met her at the front of the HAV. Together they walked towards the building where the Master of the Dead worked.

Most called the K'laisian a coroner. A word from the humans for someone who processed the dead, performed autopsies, and similar activities.

The Master of the Dead did all that and more. They handled the bodies of all those who died, regardless of the reason. Giving them the utmost respect while ensuring answers were given to families, the police service, and military. They performed funerals for all with great gravity.

Issik entered ahead of Violetta.

The first time she'd visited the building had been when her father had been murdered. Malik had been beside her that first time, as well as her grandparents. Since then, she'd visited the building many times over, in a professional capacity.

A human with long red hair wearing loose clothes of a pastel green and a simple style met them in the foyer. The brilliant lights gave a cheer to everything. Bright flowers filled vases, giving the air a pleasantly floral scent.

K'laisians believed in celebrating a person's life, not their death. Even in the midst of grief, they believed in remembering a being's triumphs, accomplishments, and service. Not the loss of a life.

Humans, Violetta knew, found it strange and unusual. It was a culture shock to many.

"How many I be of service?" the woman asked. "Detective Cq'linns, I presume?"

Violetta gave a slight bow.

"You must be here to see the Master of the Dead Eineit Ki'monl."

Issik raised a brow. She gave a subtle shake of the head.

"We are, but how did you know?" Issik asked. "We haven't seen you before now."

The woman smiled brilliantly, showing perfect white teeth as she did so. "I recognized the detective. She's the 'talk of the town' since being seen multiple times with Master of Ceremonies Malik Addelia." At their confused expression, the woman chuckled. "It's a human phrase. It means a great many women are envious of your position with Master Addelia."

"Ah," Violetta said, suddenly uncertain of what to say.

"Few women have ever managed to join him in his private box. Rarer still is seeing that being there so often. Normally his female companions have their own boxes, which he joins. Not actually in his box as he works." The woman turned away from them and began down the hallway, leaving them to follow. "Yet you've been there frequently since that horrible mess earlier this year."

"It's that much of a conversational topic?" Issik asked, nudging Violetta.

"Oh, yes!" the woman replied brightly. She glanced over her shoulder at Violetta. "I personally think it's lovely to see him with someone who is service-centric."

"You don't think anyone else was service-centric?" Issik asked when Violetta remained silent.

"They may have been lovely women, but none had a job that truly helped the people," the woman replied. "I've been on K'lais for a decade. Though I didn't begin this job until after Commander Cq'linns' death. My duties are with the human sector, but Edtari is at lunch, which is why I am the greeter at the moment. As for the women the Master of Ceremonies has previously been seen with? They wouldn't dream of getting their pretty fingers dirty. All had office jobs. Lady Cq'linns is a much better choice, in my opinion."

"Despite being of mixed heritage?" Violetta finally found her tongue.

"A being's lineage is not as important as the being," the woman replied as she paused before a door.

Sharp blue eyes met Violetta's bronze as the woman turned to face her.

"My ancestors were Irish. Centuries ago, back on Earth, they would have been treated like dirt simply because of where they were from. Worse than dirt in many places. Women on that planet had to fight their way to a position of respect. I remember *my* ancestors' history. K'laisians are a far better race compared to my own. If any of those purist idiots bothered with reading the history of Earth's people, they'd realize what sort of trap they're falling into."

Violetta bowed deeply to the woman.

"Thank you, Lady."

Startled, the woman smiled at her. "Bridget Doyle. A pleasure to meet you, Lady Cq'linns. I'll leave you with Master Ki'monl. You may go on in."

With a bow, Bridget turned and swept away, her long red hair bouncing with each step.

Shrugging her shoulders, Violetta touched the door's interface. It slid open, allowing them entrance.

Issik gestured and Violetta entered before him.

The room reminded Violetta of a mix between a library and museum dedicated to the dead. Shelves filled the walls on two sides. The third was what at first appeared to be large windows, until you looked closer. As with the military base, sea glass was strategically placed to give a calming feeling to those in the room. Books and items associated with death and the dying filled the shelves.

Small tables had conforming chairs nestled around them. The tables held small glowing globes.

Moving towards them was a K'laisian with long flowing silver hair, brilliant silver eyes, and snow white skin. He bore a solemnity and gravity that few other K'laisians could claim. He wore a snug tunic that criss-crossed over his chest. Loose pants billowed as he walked. A long jacket swirled around his ankles, the bell sleeves hiding his hands.

The entire ensemble was shades of silver and the palest blue possible.

"Lady Cq'linns and Detective Ha'kksworth. How may I be of service to you today?"

"A pleasure to see you again, Master Ki'monl," Violetta said, moving towards the K'laisian. "Though perhaps one day it won't be for business."

A brilliant smile formed on Master Ki'monl's face.

"It is always a pleasure to see you well, Lady Cq'linns," Master Ki'monl said easily. He gripped her left shoulder firmly in the K'laisian version of a handshake. Violetta did the same. They released each other's shoulders at the same time. "Who have you come to speak about today?"

"There are two beings, this time," Issik said, moving forward. He and Ki'monl gripped shoulders briefly, also. "Both men. Found at similar times. Similar cause of death."

"Would either of you care for a refreshment?" Master Ki'monl asked.

They both gave a single shake of their head causing Master Ki'monl to humm.

"Little ever changes with either of you," Master Ki'monl stated. His brilliant silver eyes twinkled. "Let us go to the morgue and we can discuss the bodies there."

Violetta and Issik gave nods.

Master Ki'monl smiled, turned, and crossed to a wall on the right side of the room. Touching a well-concealed interface, a door slid open. Violetta and Issik followed him into another room, then into a lift. Moments later, they were in the lower level where the dead were kept in tubes tucked into the walls.

Humans, K'laisian, those of mixed heritage, and other races could be seen in the tubes. Even in this room the lights were bright and a floral scent could be detected.

"Who are the beings in question?"

"Nicholas En'ingo and Lorenzo Tagliani." Issik spoke up before Violetta could say anything.

"What do you wish to know about them?" Master Ki'monl asked, folding his hands together before him. The bell sleeves overlapped, hiding his hands completely.

"While examining the initial scans, I noticed the bruising appeared similar," Violetta stated. "They reminded me of injuries that could be sustained by someone who was trained."

"Perhaps military training?" Master Ki'monl suggested, a sly gleam in his eyes. "That is certainly possible." He stepped to the center of the room. "Full size holcrom images of Nicholas En'ingo and Lorenzo Tagliani. Overlay and overlap injuries. Detect and highlight similarities and identical injuries."

"Acknowledged," a feminine computerized voice said. "Processing."

As with most tech on K'lais, the voices were feminine. Healers had long past discovered a feminine voice was accepted and listened to far faster than a masculine one, regardless of the gender of the living being.

Holograms of the two deceased beings appeared above the floor in front of Master Ki'monl. Their bodies and injuries copied down to the shade of bruised skin and imperfections on their nude bodies.

Unlike humans, K'laisians had no shame when it came to a body. Whether it was their own or someone else's. Nudity was accepted, as were the emotions of a being. If two people were engaged in romantic behavior, they were ignored. Though most K'laisians preferred partaking of such actions behind closed doors. There was no shame seen in exhibiting a romantic or sexual attraction towards another being.

The bodies slid over each other, and the injuries were highlighted, revealing the patterns were, indeed, identical. The depth of the bruises and the locations.

"That does, indeed, answer that question," Issik stated. "Good catch."

Violetta merely nodded.

"Violetta? Are you well?" Mc'narrd's voice said in her earbud.

"Were the deaths deliberate? Or could they have been accidental?" Violetta asked, ignoring Mc'narrd.

"Though the tests have not been concluded just yet, my initial response would be that they were deliberate. Especially after viewing this data."

"Thank you." Violetta turned to look at Master Ki'monl. "Could you send copies of this to myself and Issik? We'll handle informing the detectives handling the other case."

"Of course, Lady," Master Ki'monl replied, bowing slightly. "I'll have them sent to you and Issik directly, locked only to you both."

"Thank you." Turning to Issik, she added, "We should be going."

"Agreed. Our thanks, again, Master Ki'monl."

Master of the Dead Ki'monl bowed to the pair. "It is a pleasure to be of service to you both. Be well, be safe."

Issik and Violetta both returned the bow before taking the lift up. Silence engulfed the pair as they exited the building. Once outside, Issik touched Violetta's arm.

"What did you realize?" he asked quietly.

"Comm off, privacy code P'awsks Linaa." The comm chimed in her ear. Issik took a moment to turn his bodycam and comm off completely, even as she pulled him towards the building. Once they were out of the path of other beings moving past them, she turned to him completely. "En'ingo was found at the corner of Rt'aasn and Issunde."

"And?"

"Malik lives on Mc'ktass."

"Oh, fark."

There was some rather impressive swearing in her comm from Mc'narrd, also.

The corner of Rt'aasn and Issunde was only a block and half away from Malik's penthouse.

Violetta nodded. "Two corpses with identical patterns. Two murders. One murderer. And all we know is it wasn't Malik."

"Did he know the other being?" Issik asked, his voice quiet. "Or are the bodies being left as a threat? Or a warning?"

"Or promise?"

"You still want to visit Sweet Treats?" Issik asked, touching her arm again. "Are you well?"

"Yes, and I'll be fine. Just need to locate Malik," Violetta said wearily. "Remember what you said about not 'hitting the bottles'?" Issik gave a nod. "I think I might hit them tonight."

"Nah, you won't," Issik stated, his eyes narrowing on her. "Come on, Violence. You didn't fall apart before when your life was on the line. You won't do it now."

"True," she said in a tired voice. "If I was able to handle that, I can handle another murderer. All I have to do is stop thinking of Malik as my suitor. If I could put my feelings to the side four months ago, I can handle this." She grinned brightly. "Come on. I'll treat you to something from the bakery. We can hit the streets tomorrow."

"That's my girl," Issik said, patting her on the head. "I'll see what I can dig up while you take the rest of the day off."

"Set up an alert on your interface, also. If any more deaths by beatings come in, we need to know about it. I'll do the same on mine."

"Good plan," Issik said thoughtfully as they headed towards the bakery. "I'll see what I can find out from Ra'keff, too. If there's someone committing multiple murders, we need to know. We'll have to work together to locate the being and bring them to justice."

"Agreed." Violetta nodded. "So, what do you want from the shop?"

The conversation quickly changed to the options and which treats were superior.

As they entered the shop, Malik's sister immediately noticed them. There were two other beings in the eatery. Both were sitting at one of the few tables in a small alcove to the side of the main entrance.

Most people, Violetta knew, preferred to purchase their treats and eat them elsewhere. In front of the store was a long display case filled with pastries and desserts. Syra provided a wide variety of human and K'laisian treats. Many of the pastries and treats were unique combinations of both cultures.

"Hey, Vi!" Syra called out cheerfully.

Malik's sister stepped from behind the case to pull Violetta into an embrace, which Violetta returned with a broad grin.

"Good to see you, too, Syra," Violetta said brightly.

"Issik," Syra said in greeting, crossing her arms at the wrists before holding her hands out to him.

Issik crossed his own at the wrists, before grasping Syra's hands. It was a traditional K'laisian greeting between close friends or beloved family. Far more intimate and warm than grasping shoulders.

"Are you keeping Vi out of trouble? Or helping her to get into it?"

"Trying for the former, managing the latter," Issik said while humming.

They dropped hands as Syra laughed in delight, her bronze eyes twinkling. Like Malik, Syra was also of mixed heritage, just like the rest of his siblings.

"What would you two enjoy today?" she asked brightly.

"Anything new?" Issik asked, glancing towards the case. "You always seem to have something new and interesting to try!"

"I have a few new combinations," Syra replied. She gestured towards the far end of the case. As Issik turned to examine the treats, Syra turned her attention back to Violetta. "Will you be seeing Malik today?"

"You have to ask?" Violetta teased. "But, yes. I thought I'd have Issik drop me off at the arena before he returns to the station. I've been granted a reprieve thanks to your brother's mischief."

"Oh, my," Syra said, leaning against the case. "What did my darling brother do now?"

"We'll start with him turning my desk into a miniature florist's business."

"That's not nearly as interesting as what he said earlier," Issik commented.

"Shut up, Issik," Violetta snapped.

Syra raised a brow and she felt her face warming.

"I don't think I've ever seen your face darken that much," Syra teased. "Though you still have that little tiny bit of pink along your cheeks. So cute!"

"He told my colleagues we were sleeping together," Violetta muttered.

"And?" Syra asked bluntly. "Not like either of you are ashamed. I'd think you'd be more smug."

"He's the one who was saying we should keep it quiet," Violetta countered.

"Ah, you're cranky that it's taken him this long to finally admit his feelings publically. That's fair. But, you have to admit, there may be consequences from certain groups," Syra said, her voice solemn. "Be certain of what you want. Otherwise you both are going to be in a lot of pain."

"I made my choice that night five years ago, Syra," Violetta said quietly. "I was an idiot for ignoring him after that night. He's not getting rid of me that easily. Even if I have to Challenge him daily just to knock some sense into him."

Syra snorted, then burst out laughing. "Good. Hopefully you won't need to do that, though."

"If anyone can do it, it's her," Issik commented. "I'd love to have one of each of your new combinations."

"Of course!" Syra said cheerfully. To Violetta, she added, "I'll give you some treats to take to Malik. He said he'll be at the main arena today. I'm certain he'd love to see you there."

"Thanks, Syra," Violetta said warmly. "I'll tell him you send your greetings and love."

"Anytime," Syra replied cheerfully, stepping back behind the counter. "Give me a few to get your orders together!"

Issik nodded to Syra. His eyes flicked to the pair in the alcove. Violetta turned to find the pair watching them.

"It'll be known eventually," Violetta said with a shrug. "I'll never be ashamed of my relationship with Malik."

"Just be prepared for the attention," Issik warned.

"For him? I'd do anything," Violetta said, too quiet for anyone else to hear.

"Just remember that when Ta'natha hears," Issik muttered.

Violetta shrugged. She was confident her work would speak for itself.

Within twenty minutes, the pair had departed Syra's eatery and Issik had dropped Violetta off in front of the main arena.

Staring up at the entrance for a few moments, Violetta headed for the main doors. The carryout container from Syra's business held tightly in her left hand. Her steps were brisk as she followed the beings into the arena. Instead of following the general traffic down the stairs or to the right, she continued along the walkway towards the offices.

"Military frequency only," she said as she walked.

Her comm chirped and her smile brightened. Having only the military channel meant she had more privacy and quiet. No one in her department could eavesdrop. Even if they wanted to. It was the same as if she'd turned it off and left it somewhere.

The number of beings dwindled as she moved further to the left of the main part of the building, and subsequently, the arena's 'pit'. Though she hadn't been to this side before, she could easily read the labels on the doors. She was amused to see they were written in the native language of their world.

Locating the shift manager's office, she touched the interface.

Instead of it chiming, followed by the typical request for her name, the door slid open.

Blinking in surprise for a couple heartbeats, she stepped through the threshold and into the office.

The furniture was standard. A desk, a console, even the conforming office chair. The interfaces covering practically every surface and lining each wall were not standard supply for any office she'd ever entered. The interfaces showed every part of the arena. The crowds in the pit, the beings in the private boxes, the restaurants and eateries, the main floor. The Duels filled the interfaces directly opposite of where the shift manager was sitting.

A K'laisian male, he wore his long silver hair in a loose ponytail that draped down his back. His silver eyes shifted from the displays to her, a polite smile taking the place of an initial frown.

"Lady Cq'linns, this is a pleasant surprise," he said in greeting. "Well met and greetings!"

"Greetings and well met," Violetta replied, trying to remember the K'laisian's name. It finally came to her. "I was wishing to know if anyone was using the private box often kept on hold, bures'o Ku'stkel. Malik mentioned-"

"That you could use it whenever you desire," Ku'stkel interrupted cheerfully. "Of course! None have requested the use of it today, Lady. Are you aware of its location?"

"Not exactly," Violetta admitted.

"Very well! When you return to the main foyer, go straight. It's in the Southwest section," the shift manager replied. "The interface has already been programmed to give you allowance."

"Thank you, bures'o," Violetta replied, bowing slightly.

As she turned to leave, Ku'stkel spoke again. "Lady Cq'linns." She shifted so she could face him. "Malik will be Dueling shortly. Someone has Challenged him over his position as Master of Ceremonies."

Violetta blinked at him in surprise. She gave him a slight bow. "Thank you for the warning. Please don't inform him I am here. I would prefer he be centered upon his Duel, not me." She couldn't stop the smirk from forming on her face. "Hopefully I can be a pleasant surprise after he wins the Duel."

A smile flashed across Ku'stkel's face. "I will not inform him. I'm certain it will be a pleasant surprise." He tilted his head to the side. "You're very confident in Malik's skills."

"Of course," Violetta replied, puzzled. "I've Dueled him. Unofficially, that is. He is… impressive. I suspect my father would be very proud of him."

"Vrehn would have been," Mc'narrd said easily on the comm. "He isn't the only one."

Bowing a final time, Violetta departed the office.

"I think that's the first time I've heard you compliment him, sir," Violetta said quietly as she strode towards the private boxes in the Southwest section.

"Just don't tell him I said so," Mc'narrd retorted.

"Wouldn't dream of it, sir." There was no stopping her soft snickering. "One day, you will have to explain why there is so much animosity between you two."

"One day," Mc'narrd teased.

She took just enough time to acquire a couple of carbonated beverages from one of the eateries near the private boxes. Pausing in front of the appropriate lifts to the private boxes, Violetta's eyes swept over them. It took less than two minutes to locate the one kept on hold for dignitaries, celebrities, and high ranking military service members.

Touching the interface, she input the required code. It flashed green, then the lift door slid open. Stepping inside, the door closed briefly. When it opened, she stepped from it and into the private box.

Unlike Malik's Moc Box, the private boxes were stationary. There were a couple conforming chairs for those who wished to relax or sit. Though native K'laisians' biologies were built for standing or walking for extended periods, not all races were designed for such. Humans and other races enjoyed the private boxes as much as the K'laisian natives. As such, they were designed for comfort for all.

Interfaces were spaced everywhere in the boxes, allowing for those within the boxes the ability to view any Duel below them in the arena with ease. If there were multiple beings in a box, multiple Duels could be viewed. A being could even enlarge it to be viewed on the windows of the boxes. The floor of the boxes were clear, designed to magnify the Duels directly below them. They could even change the camera angle to focus directly on the Master of Ceremonies and his box.

"Talk about strange," Violetta muttered to herself. She placed the container of treats and drinks on the table between the chairs.

Or so she thought, until Mc'narrd spoke. "What is strange?"

"Being in a box without Malik," she admitted. "I now understand why beings bring friends or family with them."

"It does make viewing the Duels more enjoyable," Mc'narrd allowed.

"I wonder how long it will be until Malik Duels?" she mused, touching the interfaces on the console at the front of the box. "Oh. Not long, at all."

"Concerned?" Mc'narrd teased.

"Only for his opponent," Violetta replied truthfully. "There would be very few beings I'd be concerned about him Dueling. You being one."

"I have no interest in Dueling either of you," Mc'narrd said sincerely. "You have a very high opinion of Addelia."

"Are you saying it isn't earned? Or deserved?"

"No, Violetta. He has earned his position as Master of Ceremonies. And as a Champion at the arenas."

"Good, because he's walking out now," she said quietly.

Touching the screens, she altered everything so it appeared she was watching him from the edge of the arena.

Neither Malik nor his opponent appeared strangely distorted or unusually large.

She found herself adopting a calm pose as though she were watching a Duel at a gym. Her eyes shifted between Malik and his Challenger. The pure blood native was confident in her stride as she walked the perimeter of the arena. Likely she was marking the space in her mind to minimize the possibility of misstep or misjudging how much room she would have to maneuver.

"Iadra Ja'rafeyn," a new male voice spoke up, "You have Challenged the Master of Ceremonies for the right to bear the position he currently holds. Are you cognizant that doing so forgoes any right to Challenge him again for at least one year's time, for any reason? And that your life may be forfeit in the event of defeat in this Duel?"

Iadra shook her long dark hair out. Her gold eyes locked onto Malik as she declared, "I understand both conditions and accept them."

Malik seemed disinterested in the entire affair. He lazily swung his sword back and forth, as a student might when first handed a new weapon. His eyes stayed in line with his opponent's while he gave a single, dismissive shrug.

"Why isn't the overseer on the arena floor?" Violetta asked Mc'narrd.

"In a Challenge for a Ceremony seat, no overseer wants to be on the floor. Too easy to be wounded or killed," Mc'narrd explained, as though the answer was self-evident.

"It's that severe?" she asked.

"It's that… vicious. And violent. I believe you can respect that."

Before she could decide on a reply the overseer's voice boomed out again.

"Commence!"

Iadra charged toward Malik. He continued to stand as though bored and waiting for something interesting to do. As the tip of her sword flashed out Malik brought his sword up to parry the attack towards his abdomen. Rather than carry through the jab, Iadra used the momentum she'd built to go into a flying kick aimed at Malik's head.

With fluid ease, Malik batted the foot away before it could make contact. Iadra recovered with a controlled landing, facing her opponent with both feet firmly on the mats.

"You're not the only one who researches their opponents before a Duel, Iadra," Malik warned. "This will not go well for you."

"I will not miss your banter, Malik," Iadra said. "It bores me, as it does so many others."

She swung at his sword arm. When he stepped away from the swing, Iadra kicked out at his exposed ankle.

Violetta winced in anticipation. She had never seen anyone attempt such a move, and did not know how she would avoid being struck.

She was surprised again as Malik leaned into Iadra's kick. His weight was mostly against the ankle that Iadra's foot struck. His sword lashed out as she made contact, puncturing Iadra's abdomen to the left of her navel. Iadra yelped, jumping away from the sword.

In response, Malik shrugged and casually twirled his sword. He strode a few paces away from her, with no apparent damage to his ankle or leg.

"Oh, fark, he's toying with her," Violetta groaned.

Mc'narrd's amused response came in over the comm.

"No, he's just being Malik."

"Just being Malik" apparently incited his opponent. She gritted her teeth, wiped silver blood from the hand she'd pressed to the wound before gripping her sword. Using the strength in both arms, Iadra swung with the intent to split Malik in two.

With a vicious backhanded swing, Malik swatted Iadra's wrists with the flat of his blade as he stepped to the side. Once her weapon was clear, his free hand crashed into Iadra's jaw and lower lip.

Iadra nearly dropped her weapon as she staggered back to recover from the blow.

To the tune and beat of the theme music played when he was officiating as Master of Ceremonies, Malik sing-songed a single sentence.

"Not going well for you at all."

After spitting blood to the mat, Iadra declared, "Fark you, Malik. This isn't going to go easy for you."

Malik gave a shocked expression, and said, "You think this is easy? Hardly so!"

In what could be seen as direct opposition to what he'd said, Malik then held his sword to one side and began to do a little dance.

"I hate you," Iadra growled.

Malik kept dancing as he spoke. "That is becoming obvious. And you let it affect your technique. Which, until you Challenged me, I have adamantly admired. Cry off, Iadra. Come for my title when you can keep your mind and emotions focused. There is no shame in that."

"I'm not here for your title. I am here for *your head*!" she screamed.

As she came at Malik, she contradicted her own words. Instead of aiming attacks at his head or neck, Iadra jabbed at his shoulders, arms, and legs. The complexity of her series of moves was difficult for Violetta to keep track of. Iadra did not seem to move as a single body subject to momentum, but as several independent parts that occasionally agreed to move in tandem.

Malik had to continually move or give ground to avoid serious injury. But even with his impressive footwork, Violetta saw several shallow cuts on his limbs. When she looked at Malik's opponent, she recognized the expression on Iadra's face. The malicious grin of someone who felt they had the advantage.

Iadra went for Malik's neck. That was her mistake.

Malik moved faster than he had in this Challenge. He moved into Iadra's swing.

The cross hilt of her weapon struck Malik's neck, but the blade did not. Although he was forced off his balance by the blow, he carried through with his plan. The strike against his neck seemed to be a minute interruption. He drove his forehead into Iadra's left eye and brow. His chest struck against hers and she was pushed back. Malik pivoted, both hands grabbing Iadra's sword arm.

Even as he used opposing leverage and force to separate the cartilage in Iadra's elbow, Violetta realized he did not have his sword. She looked around while Iadra screamed, her sword dropping from a barely usable hand.

When her eyes found his sword, she had to blink, and give her mind a moment to catch up with what must have happened.

He had jammed it point down into the mat when Iadra had swung her sword at his neck. Malik had gone at his opponent with only his body. His sword was standing erect not three feet from him. Once he released Iadra, he walked over and plucked his weapon out of the mat.

His opponent was still shrieking in rage, pain, or both as she gathered up her sword in the remaining usable hand.

"I am being kind, Iadra," he said loudly, so the screaming opponent could hear him, "Every bit of damage you have, can heal. But I will not let you take my head. Yield or you will not be able to-"

Iadra ran and leapt at Malik.

She jumped and kicked straight up, aiming for his jaw. Malik moved away. She landed more gracefully than Violetta expected, able to deliver another fierce kick from one side so quickly that Malik could only keep moving, rather than try to attack or block.

Without slowing, Iadra shifted her weight as the one foot came back to the mat so she could kick out again. Malik had no time to move fully out of the way. His sword was in the wrong position to block or cut.

He pivoted to avoid the full force of the kick catching him in the abdomen or chest. He took most of it on his left side. The grunt of pain, the way his body arched, and the all too familiar sound of the impact made it clear that Iadra had cracked, perhaps broken, at least two of Malik's ribs.

Pressing the momentary advantage, Iadra lunged with her sword, and stabbed Malik right where her foot had been. The sword tip sank three inches into his body before Malik could move away.

With his left arm cradled against the wounded side, Malik began spinning his sword in a wide, almost figure-eight pattern ahead of his body. He advanced on Iadra. She tried to jab her sword between the spins, only to have her blade smacked away by his moving blade. A second attempt while trying to retreat yielded the same result.

When she tried to throw her body against Malik, the edge of his sword sliced against her scalp, cheek, collarbone, and the forearm above her sword. She kept retreating. Malik continued to advance, his sword spinning faster.

"Such a waste. You had real potential, Iadra," Malik spoke softly while he kept coming.

"Shut up! Shut up! *Shut up!*" Iadra shrieked, and tried to thrust her sword under his relentless maneuvers.

With a quick twist of his body, Malik brought his downward swing to meet her attack. This time the blade met the wrist instead of the flat part of the blade. Iadra's hand separated from her arm so easily it might have been waiting to do so. The sword and hand began their descent to the mat.

Before either did, Malik spun in a tight circle. The momentum of his sword took Iadra's head as easily as it had her hand.

Malik stood still, facing away from his opponent's body and parts as they all came to a final rest on the bloody mat.

"I hate this part of my job," he confessed quietly.

The audio on the Duel vidfeed did not mute out the statement. Which meant that Violetta, and anyone else watching, heard him.

Watching Malik walk out of the arena, Violetta doubted he cared.

After a minute, she began to gather up the goodies she'd brought. Not sure where Malik would go to be seen by a healer, she was determined to find out.

"Oh! Syra gave you goodies? What did you bring?" Malik asked as he parked his personal box against the private box she was in. Violetta turned at the sound of his voice. She watched as the interlock between the boxes engaged and the entryway slid open. He walked in, with his left arm still cradled against the wound on his left side. Which was still bleeding.

"You should be with a Healer! Why aren't you being tended to?" Violetta blurted.

Malik cocked his head at her, before looking down to the bloody spot on his torso.

"Oh," he said casually. "Yes, I've got a scratch. It'll get looked after. So, what did Syra send?"

"Um, most of my favorites, but she also sent a few stuffed scones? They're still warm," Violetta heard herself say. She couldn't take her eyes off his left hand, and the large patch of blood beneath it.

"Ah, may the seas bless my sister. She knows my weaknesses well," Malik exclaimed as he sat beside Violetta with some difficulty. He continued in a strained voice. "Ever since my human aunt introduced us to scones, I could never get enough of them."

Violetta stared at Malik for a moment. Resigned to his willful ignorance of his injuries, she shook her head and fished out a pair of scones. She handed the first one to Malik. He took it with a grateful smile. "Thank you."

"Does she use Earth ingredients for the scones?" Violetta asked.

"Except for the berries or other filling. As it turns out, scones pair wonderfully with K'laisian fruits and vegetables. Ooooooo, these have cho'ba berries," he replied before taking a large bite out of the scone. He groaned.

"Sovereign Healer Zh'oros?" Violetta asked over the comm.

There was a moment of silence, then the healer's voice filled her ear. "I'm here, Violetta."

"Just how seriously injured is Malik?" she asked. There was more silence and she muttered a few words under her breath. Words her father had used. None were polite. "You tell him all the time. It's only fair."

There was a snort. Violetta suspected it was from Mc'narrd. Then skittered humming from the healer.

"I highly doubt Vrehn was aware you knew those words," Mc'narrd commented.

"But you are right," Zh'oros interjected. There was no amusement in her voice as she continued speaking. "Malik has two broken ribs, a cracked rib, and internal bleeding. As well as a punctured lung."

"You are such a stubborn male," Violetta grumbled. "How is he reacting to his 'suit?"

"The nanites are currently working on healing his lungs and internal bleeding," Zh'oros replied. "He should have gone directly to the medical rooms there for assessment, then treatment. Including being brought to the base."

"Here's where you're hiding," grumbled a new voice. A male native in a military biosuit came into view as the lift brought him to the box. His 'suit had the insignia for healers.

"Let me finish my scone before you ruin the rest of my day," Malik complained.

"Eat it on the way. Now that I've found you, I'm keeping you in my sights until you're healed," the healer rejoined.

Before Malik could object, Violetta stood and held a hand out to help him to his feet. Malik sighed in resignation and took her offered hand.

"So, I'm going to be unable to talk for a little while once he gets me on a slab," Malik began once they stepped onto the lift. "Can you tell me why you aren't at the station or working on a case?"

"You can answer with monosyllabic responses," Violetta stated firmly. She glanced at him from the corner of her eyes. "Unless you remember the signs we used in school."

Military signs? he asked as the lift doors opened. The fingers of his free hand moved with a frightening speed and efficiency.

"Yes, that one," she replied dryly. Mc'narrd's laughter in her comm did not help improve her mood. "Issik and I were assigned a case. They're connected. Ours was found at the corner of Rt'aasn and Issunde."

Malik turned to their left, down a narrow corridor. His steps were sedate and she slid an arm around his waist. When he leaned against her, she gave him a smile.

"Remember the grousing you did when I was injured four months ago?" she asked. He gave a slight nod of his head. "My turn."

There was considerable humming from the healer escorting them, as well as from Zh'oros. Even Mc'narrd was humming, instead of laughing as a human. Which Violetta was considering his normal response.

"Not far from my place," Malik said, his voice pained.

"Indeed," Violetta replied, concerned. "I'm hoping we're nearing the medical rooms here."

"To the right, Lady," the healer said pleasantly. He turned towards a set of double doors, which slid open as he approached them. "We'll use the first room."

The room was small, but the bed was standard for medical offices everywhere. She helped Malik onto it. As he leaned back, the bed rose automatically and conformed around him.

Malik glowered at the healer, even as Violetta slid his hand into hers.

"And I thought I made for a very poor patient," she teased. When the glare turned to her, she laughed. "My turn to worry over *you*."

It's just a scratch, he signed, refusing to meet her eyes.

"We both know that's a lie," Violetta replied calmly. "And I have Zh'oros in my ear. So you can't try to claim otherwise."

"That's just mean," he muttered.

"That's just fair," she retorted.

The healer paused beside the bed, studying her and Malik. He gave a K'laisian style-shrug, his silver eyes amused.

"Normally, I would advise you to leave. But I suspect he might actually behave better with you in the room." The healer turned his attention on Malik. "You know the routine, Master Addelia. Stabilized here, then transported to a hospital. In your case, the military base."

"Fine," Malik grumbled. His eyes shifted to Violetta. "Tell me what you know?"

Violetta nodded. Though she didn't know a lot, it might just keep him on the bed and behaving.

Chapter Seven

Stretched out on her sofa, Violetta tried to lose herself in the book she was reading. But her mind refused to read the words on the pages, let alone comprehend them.

She was, she realized, bored and growing restless. Somewhere in the past several months, she'd allowed herself to find entertainment with Malik. Typically not in her home or his penthouse.

It was her scheduled day off. Typically she'd be content being home alone. Or she would have had plans with Malik. But, she was unable to be drawn into any of her books. She didn't know where Malik was currently and she had no interest in vidhopping on her interface.

"Are you there, sir?" she asked, hoping the admiral could give some suggestions.

"For now," Mc'narrd allowed.

"May I ask your opinion on something?"

Amusement mingled with curiosity in the admiral's voice as he replied. "You may."

"Do you have suggestions on how to cure boredom?"

"I believe that's the first time I've actually been requested to help with someone's boredom," he admitted with a laugh. "I must really remind you of Vrehn."

"You really do, sir." She paused, then in a quiet voice added, "I miss him. Every day."

"I know," he said gently. "I'm honored you think of me in a similar way."

She didn't know what to say, so she remained silent.

"As for your 'boredom', I often spend my downtime in the gym, swimming, or going fishing on Crom's Drop

Lake." He chuckled. "Often annoying our esteemed harbormaster in the process."

"Fishing?" she asked doubtfully. "Swimming I can understand. Even going to the gym. But fishing? No."

"There's several books I could suggest," he added. "Both on the fish and types of fishing methods favored by both humans and K'laisians."

"No, thank you," she said, shaking her head. The idea was anything but appealing. "I think I'll pass."

"It's a very enjoyable pastime, though," he insisted. There was definitely laughter in his voice. "It allows one time to commune with the fish. Though they never seem to want to be tossed back. A fact I keep telling Jozelyn, though she insists I'm wrong."

"No." Violetta stated firmly. "I am never asking for your help with boredom again."

There was a snort. Then loud laughter.

"I'm honestly surprised you're bored. Isn't Malik there?"

"No," she grumbled. "I'm not sure where he is. I know he was released from the base's medical wing and sent home late yesterday evening. I also know he was completely healed."

"What did you do during your high school days?" Mc'narrd asked. "Give me a few and I can tell you where he is, if you'd like to know."

Ducking her head, she glanced down at her hands. "You would do that?"

"I just asked, didn't I?"

"Yes, sir, you did." She couldn't help the smile on her face. "I'd appreciate knowing."

"Answer my question, and I'll tell you where the boyfriend is."

"I'd visit the museums, the parks, spend a lot of time at the local libraries." She tilted her head to the side. "Do they still have the skates for rent at the nature preserve?"

"They do," Mc'narrd replied. "You think you remember how?"

Violetta laughed. "Maybe. It's been a while since I went there." She paused before adding thoughtfully, "I may actually purchase a personal interface. Something I can listen to music on."

"That should prove amusing, since you'll end up having something in each ear, if you do that." Mc'narrd chuckled. "Malik is currently at his penthouse."

"Did you put a unit on him, also?" Violetta asked, genuinely curious.

"We've added an extra," Mc'narrd admitted. "With the information you've discovered, we felt it best for his safety and yours."

"Thank you, sir. For everything," Violetta said as she stood. "It's appreciated."

"Are you planning on dropping in on him?"

"I think I'm going to go shopping first. I should be able to purchase a personal interface capable of what I want without too much trouble."

"Considering you've barely spent anything on anyone aside from solstice gifts for Captain Ae'staa and her unit over the past few years? You'll be fine." He paused before adding, "I'll have Malik meet you, at least long enough for that. He'll help you get what you want."

"Thank you, admiral," Violetta said warmly.

"In service, we prosper, Violetta," Mc'narrd replied. "You make it easy." Then he had to ruin it by adding, "When you aren't giving into your temper, anyway."

***

Thirty minutes later, Violetta was browsing the storefronts in the business district. Pausing in front of one of the many jewelry businesses, she gazed in the storefront window at the displays. Sparkling jewelry was lit from beneath with tiny lights. The lights reminded her of stars illuminating the rings, necklaces, and entire sets.

Her eyes were drawn to a particular set of deep blue ibja gems set in a delicate silver design. The ibja gems were surrounded by sparkling white sinspars. It was an entire collection: a necklace, bracelet, and several rings.

The rings were typical of what humans favored as wedding bands. Complete with a silver band with tiny ibja and sinspar inlaid into the metal for one of the spouses, typically a male human.

"You always did have good taste," Malik murmured in her ear.

Lips kissed the tip of her left ear. A shiver ran down her spine, sending her thoughts in all the wrong places. Leaning back against his chest, she smiled up at him. Every K'laisian was aware that ear tips were sensitive places. And Malik knew it applied to her. Of course, she also knew it affected him, too.

"Want to go look at it?" he asked, his arms wrapping around her waist. At her widened eyes, he brushed his lips against hers. "Come on. You may see something else you like better, and I need ideas for the winter solstice!"

Not giving her the chance to argue, he began walking her forward towards the doors of the business. She gave a slight sound of denial.

"You might as well give up," Mc'narrd suggested. "He'll just drag you in."

"I would, indeed," Malik said quietly. "It isn't as though I can't afford it, Vi. Please?"

"Fine," she said with a sigh. "But only because you both teamed up against me."

Mc'narrd laughed even as Malik kissed her ear again before stepping around beside her. His arm did not leave her waist. She leaned against him, knowing her body's reaction to Malik was being sent back to the military base.

"I do not want to know how many have access to my readouts," she muttered as she turned her head against Malik's chest.

"Only the highest ranking healers," Mc'narrd reassured her. "And myself."

"That's something, at least."

A pair of K'laisians stood behind the counter talking quietly to themselves, until they noticed Malik and Violetta approaching them. The pair paused their conversation and turned towards them, all smiles and bright eyes. One had dark hair, gold eyes, and tanned skin while the other had silver hair and eyes with pale skin.

Both wore jewelry that sparkled in the unique lighting of the store, designed to make everything sparkle more than it would in their natural sunlight. Or any other light, for that matter.

Irritation flashed through their eyes briefly, but the smiles remained.

"How may we be of service? I am Asharii and would enjoy assisting you both today."

Malik kissed Violetta on the temple, even as she wanted to just turn and walk right back out the door.

"We would like to see the ibja set in the window," Malik said, ignoring the irritation his behavior was causing.

Asharii's eyes narrowed slightly, but she gave a stiff nod and went towards the window.

"You have a good eye," the other woman said pleasantly. "I'm Kimina. It's a wedding set. We have many and they can be customized as you desire. Not all K'laisians wear the ring meant for a human spouse."

"We are certainly interested in discovering what size ring Lady Cq'linns wears," Malik stated calmly. "As for the set, that depends on how well your associate treats us."

The woman's eyes flashed to Asharii. "Of course, Master Addelia."

"Surprised, detective, that she recognizes Malik?" Mc'narrd teased. "He's one of the few POPIs that are rather infamous in this city. You'll end up just as popular once he places that ring on your finger." He paused, then his tone grew sly. "Have you told your grandparents yet? I'm certain they'll be delighted to know he's viewing jewelry with you."

POPIs, Violetta knew, stood for 'people of public interest'. It wasn't the most polite term used when spoken by a being in the military. But she couldn't detect any sarcasm or disgust in the admiral's voice.

She kept a polite smile on her face, refusing to give into Mc'narrd's goading. She would've been able to succeed, if Malik hadn't kissed the tip of her ear just as Asharii was walking back to them. Melting against him was not what she had intended to do, but it's what she did.

Asharii stopped in midstep, anger flaring in her eyes.

"Give me the jewelry," Kimina ordered. "Go to lunch. Now." The other woman opened her mouth to say something, but Kimina interrupted her. "You are dismissed for lunch. Go before it becomes longer."

The dark-haired woman bowed stiffly before stalking past Kimina and to the curtained opening. Asharii passed through it, vanishing from sight.

"My apologies, Master Addelia, Lady Cq'linns. Please, may I see your ring finger?" she said, picking up the gem-laden ring Violetta had been admiring.

Deciding it was better to just give in, Violetta did as requested by holding her hand out. Kimina slid the ring onto her middle finger. Humans, Violetta knew, wore their wedding bands on their third finger, but K'laisians always wore them on their middle fingers.

The ring slid on as though it was meant for her.

"A marvelous fit! Oh, and it looks perfect on you, too," Kimina said in amazement. "We've had several women try that ring on. But none have matched the ring as well as it does you."

"It does look lovely," Violetta admitted reluctantly.

"You don't have to decide today, Lady," Kimina reassured her. The silver eyes met Malik's easily. "I can hold it for you, if you wish."

"May I purchase the necklace today? The rest can be decided at a later time."

"Of course! It's an honor, Master Addelia," Kimina said smoothly. Her gaze drifted to Violetta briefly. "It really does look lovely on you. And it can be altered to fit whichever finger you desire."

"I… um… he would need to speak to my grandparents first," Violetta finally managed to say.

"Ah, that explains much," Kimina said thoughtfully. "Allow me to replace the pieces, and then I'll take care of the purchase." She glanced at Violetta, as she removed the ring. "I hope you enjoy the necklace. I am certain it will be just as lovely as the ring."

"Thank you, bures'a," Violetta said before turning her gaze to Malik. "If you don't mind, I think I'll wait for you outside."

Something flashed through Malik's eyes. "Of course. Then we'll go get that new interface for you."

"You're spoiling me."

"It's a delight," he said, kissing her eartip.

Smiling at him, she gave the saleslady a bow, then made her exit as fast as she felt was reasonable without insulting anyone.

"Did he just spend a small fortune on a single necklace?" Violetta asked under her breath once she was outside.

"Yes," Mc'narrd said simply. "I suspect it won't be long before he contacts your grandparents and the Fangs."

Crossing to a bench, she sank onto the conforming seat. Propping her elbows on her thighs, she dropped her head into her hands. "I've never even thought about a wedding. Or celebration. Or anything."

"You may want to start," Mc'narrd suggested. "Though you could always locate a planner or even allow Laraeda to plan it. She enjoyed helping your parents. I'm certain she'd love the opportunity to help you."

"Not helping," Violetta muttered. "I just wanted to shop for a personal interface."

"You could always Challenge him again."

"I'm definitely going skating after this. I should make you go, too."

"I'll take you fishing."

"I'll stick with finding a murderer," she grumbled.

"Did I do something wrong?" Malik asked. Violetta looked up to find him standing in front of her. A small bag hung around his wrist. "Should I have not bought you the necklace?"

"Are you going to approach my grandparents?"

"Eventually," he admitted. That gleam flashed through his eyes again. "But first, we're going to make sure you have a personal interface that isn't going to fail after a year." He held his hands out to her. She took them in hers and he pulled her up with ease. "I won't be able to stay after, not if we still want to meet up as we'd planned."

"That's fine. After we get the interface, I plan on loading the music I like and going skating at the preserve."

"I'm actually jealous," Malik admitted. "I haven't done that for a long time. Most of my clients wanted to go to the arenas, concerts, and the like. They weren't interested in the preserve."

"We can always go later," Violetta offered.

"I'd like that."

Chapter Eight

To reach the nature preserve, one had a few options. The main park, though, was directly off Preserve Highway. It was located near the housing for retired military personnel. Most of the personnel took pride in having the preserve close to them. Her father's apartment was part of that section.

Parts of the nature preserve were only accessible to military personnel. All of it was protected and guarded by the military. Violetta parked her HAV at her complex and headed for the park. It was only a few blocks over and she walked further while investigating unknown deaths.

Malik had spent a good amount of time going through the interfaces at the store before helping her decide between three. Since she'd only ever had a service-issued interface, she was thankful for his assistance.

Once again, he'd purchased the gift, but this time she hadn't complained after seeing the price. Their departing kiss had been long and heartfelt. She still felt giddy. Even Mc'narrd's ribbing couldn't cut through her happiness.

Locating the rental booth for skates, she paid for a pair. Carrying them to a bench, she settled onto it and slid her feet into the boots. The tiny wheels were in a narrow line. After lacing them up, she stood cautiously. It'd been at least eight years since she'd gone skating.

She wobbled a few times, but quickly found her center of balance on the skates. Glancing around, she noticed Faulkner paying for a pair with another of the unit. Smiling, she moved slowly on the skates.

Deciding she'd be fine on them, she moved slowly away from the bench, giving her guards time to get their skates on. As she skated around the main area, acclimating herself to the skates, she noticed people pausing and watching her.

Years ago, when she and Malik had skated together, they'd often danced and twirled while wearing them. As she became more comfortable with the skates, she began skating backwards, adding in twirls and spins. Old skills returned and she grew more comfortable. Both with herself and those watching her.

"Momma! Momma! It's *her*!" a young voice cried out.

Violetta slowed and smiled at a young girl, around six or seven, who was bouncing up and down, tugging her mother's hand. When she glanced up at the mother's face, she found recognition in the woman's features.

"Detective Cq'linns?" the mother said.

Skating closer, Violetta gave a K'laisian nod, since the pair were natives. Both had dark hair, gold eyes, and dark caramel skin.

"I am," Violetta said in a pleasant voice. "Well met and greetings to you both."

"My daughter loves watching the Master of Ceremonies," the mother explained apologetically. She laughed. "I think she has a crush on him."

At the words, the woman's eyes widened and she blinked several times.

Turning her eyes to the young girl, Violetta winked at the girl in typical K'laisian fashion. She tilted her head to the right then back up. "Master Malik *is* very charming, isn't he?"

The little girl nodded in a human fashion, her little head bobbing made her dark hair swirl around her. "He's amazing! I want to Duel like him when I get bigger!"

"You'll have to practice a lot," Violetta said in a firm, but warm tone. She knelt and leaned towards her conspiratorially. "If you want to be like Master Malik, you'll have to learn to use both hands equally." Violetta glanced around as though to make certain no one was watching. "Would you like to know something?"

The girl bounced up and down. "Yes!"

"We grew up together. Went to school together. I was once able to win against him easily. I can only hold my own against him, now."

"Really?" the girl asked in awe.

"Really. He practices a lot," Violetta said.

"Are you trying to make my reputation greater?" Malik teased in her ear. "Or is this some sort of reverse psychology? Hoping I won't think you're as good as you truly are?"

Smiling at the little girl, Violetta stood again. Meeting the mother's bemused expression, she said, "Your daughter is darling."

"Thank you, bures'a," the mother said. "It was a pleasure meeting you."

"In service, we prosper," Violetta replied, bowing to them slightly. "It was a pleasure, Lady."

The pair strolled away, leaving Violetta to skate in the opposite direction. Several other beings waved or stood talking in groups while watching her.

"Why do I feel as though I may need an extraction?" Violetta murmured as she pulled out her interface and began to scroll through it.

"I did warn you people would recognize you," Malik said via the comm.

"The mother recognized me, also," Violetta stated, her voice low. "As a detective. Probably from all the vidclips from when I was wanted earlier this year."

"Good point," Malik said thoughtfully. "She called you 'detective', not lady or bures'a."

"You handled it well," Mc'narrd said when Malik remained silent. "You still are. Even your biosuit is showing normal levels."

Tucking the interface back into its sheath, Violetta turned down a path away from the open area. The path headed away from the more crowded popular general area of the nature preserve. Taking a route with fewer people, she found herself choosing paths that were empty.

The entire preserve had paths open to the public. Though, somewhere deep in the forest, there were paths that veered off into military-only areas. Her father had often taken her skating through those areas. A way to have some time together without worrying about crowds or worrying about anyone approaching them.

"Do I have permission to go on your side of the preserve?"

"As long as there are no other civilians around when you veer off, yes," Mc'narrd replied. "A benefit of being on the Watch List. Have fun, Violetta. Mc'narrd out."

The comm went quiet and she decided he must be taking some time off.

Pushing off with her left foot, she pulled out her new interface. The case was meant to help protect it from the elements and dropping it. As she began skating down the wide path, she tucked the earbud into her opposite ear. Tapping the screen, she pulled up the music she had added. It had old favorites and new suggestions from Malik and Mc'narrd.

A song with a hard rhythm and beats began playing and she picked up speed. Tucking the interface into the holder at her waist, she twined along the path.

Delighted and thankful for the newly discovered outlet, she followed one path after another, moving deeper into the preserve. The stone path was smooth beneath her skates, the trees and other flora pleasant on each side. Wildlife moved among the branches, even as birds sang. With the brilliant sun shining down from above, Violetta found herself relaxing completely.

Finding herself as the only being on the paths, she took a single, narrow path to the side. Concealed among the bushes, she ducked down it and allowed the slight downhill slope to guide her speed. The branches crossing above her head dappled the sunlight. She could see the fauna more easily. Turning the interface off, she enjoyed the pleasant sounds of the forest, even as she took another, wider path that led in the direction of the base.

Within minutes, Faulkner was skating beside her. She shot him a grin and he returned it.

"I'm guessing we've 'crossed over' to your side?" she asked.

"Yup," he replied cheerfully. "Having fun?"

"Absolutely. I'd forgotten how enjoyable this was," she admitted.

"How long are you planning on being out here?"

She shrugged. "I was planning to meet up with Malik later. I didn't exactly give him a set time, though."

"Why didn't he join you?" Faulkner asked. He paused, then snickered. "Or would that be 'us'?"

"You know, I don't even know what he's doing," Violetta admitted, though the grin didn't fade.

"Paperwork," Malik grumbled. "I'm stuck doing farking paperwork instead of enjoying time with you and Faulkner."

Violetta tapped her ear. "He's doing paperwork. Rather jealous of us." She batted her eyes at her friend. "Said he wouldn't even mind it being a threesome."

Faulkner burst out laughing, as did Mc'narrd.

"Not funny, Violence," Malik stated. Then he chuckled. "Good thing I love you."

Wearing a smug smile, she said, "I regret nothing."

"You realize it will take an hour to get back?" Faulkner's eyes twinkled as he added, "Hope you're going back to his place tonight. You're going to want to use that hot tub of his."

"Do I want to know how you know he has one?"

"Probably not," he admitted.

Shaking her head, she began to slow down. "Have you forgotten I prefer to walk everywhere?"

"Yeah, but skating uses different muscles," Faulkner countered. "Just ask your suitor or any of the healers."

"I'm certain Malik knows some massage techniques to aid in sore muscles," Violetta said innocently.

Mc'narrd groaned even as Faulkner burst out laughing.

"Indeed I do," Malik cooed over the comms.

"You two never stop," Mc'narrd grumbled.

Faulkner and Violetta exchanged grins, even as Malik laughed.

"Shall we head back?" Violetta asked, sliding to a stop on the skates.

All amusement slid away as she noticed the two dark-clothed figures standing on the path in the direction they'd been heading. The pair began to distinctly move towards them.

Violetta whispered to Faulkner as they turned on the skates. "Those aren't your people."

"No," Faulkner said, all humor gone from his voice. They began retreating down the path in the direction they'd originated from.

"Thought we were off the reservation."

"We are. Not sure where the rest of the crew are, though," he replied. "Captain, you there?"

"We're two minutes out. You two got pretty far ahead on those skates," was Ae'staa's curt reply.

"Looks like we get to play alone for a bit," Faulkner observed.

"Are you carrying any weapons?" Violetta asked.

"Ballistic retractable knife, collapsible shock rod. You?"

"My work sidearm," she replied, feeling like a rookie.

"You need to ask your 'uncle' for some toys," Faulkner said, his voice a little strained.

The two of them had been keeping their rapid pace, but the strangers were gaining, somehow. Neither of them wanted to take long looks back, and Violetta hadn't spotted the pursuers wearing any kind of skates.

"Fark me flying, they're fast!" exclaimed Faulkner. "Captain, we have imminent contact in less than thirty seconds."

"Acknowledged," responded Ae'staa. "We are still one minute until interception. Wait, two dots active just to your northwest and northeast!"

The warning rang in Violetta and Faulkner's ears almost too late. From either side of the skate path, a single figure leapt out directly in front of them. Violetta hunkered down and rammed into the being in front of her. As she cleared the sprawling body, she saw Faulkner deliver a vicious right cross punch to the being in his path.

The presumed attacker's face snapped hard to the side, accompanied by a much louder crunch than expected.

Light gleamed across something in Faulkner's clenched fist.

The unextended shock rod, she realized.

He had used it to enhance his punch.

The other attacker had recovered from being knocked aside by Violetta, and clipped Faulkner's right leg with something. Faulkner went down with a pained grunt, the shock rod snapping open as he went to one knee.

Using the skates to do a fast ninety degree turn, Violetta then sped back. The successful attacker was going over to Faulkner, who was trying to regain his feet. Faulkner swung the rod low, hitting the attacker in the ribs. A moment later, Violetta kicked out, smashing the attacker's face with her left skate. The being made a strange sound while falling to the ground.

"Kick them again!" Faulkner barked.

For a moment, Violetta was confused. The attacker she had just kicked was prone on the ground and not moving. No longer a perceived threat. She looked at Faulkner, knowing she appeared puzzled.

"Oh, for fark's sake!" Faulkner growled, finally getting to his feet.

He made one uneasy step on his right foot, before the second attacker sprang from the ground and tackled him. The two rolled, and Violetta heard Faulkner curse, cry out, and then curse again. She started to move towards the two, when the first attackers were upon them.

"Lethal force, detective!" Mc'narrd ordered through the comm. "Free use is authorized!"

Part of Violetta's brain was startled at the admiral's voice giving the official kill order used by the police service.

Her training did its part. The sidearm was in her hands, changed to a lethal setting, and pointing towards the standing pair of beings that were rapidly coming towards her.

But she'd only heard that order given once in her police career so far.

The circumstances had been a Va'nu'ian that had taken offense at a conceived insult. He had quickly strangled a fellow service member, then begun using that officer's sidearm to shoot anyone near him. When the weapon had been disabled, he'd began using the bladed weapons of those who had died or were critically injured to cleave through even more innocents.

It had been early in Violetta's career, and her senior partner had shot first. She had fired as well, but Issik's first shot had terminated the perpetrator. Her shot had struck the being's chest, but it was an unnecessary wound. Her mind was holding up the training now, uncertain she should end lives.

Her ears and eyes changed that problem. Faulkner gave out a painful yelp. Mc'narrd was demanding she take action. The two arrivals were almost upon her, and in their hands were knives. A long serrated blade and a small carving blade.

Along with a pair of heavy cleavers.

The firearm discharged in Violetta's hands. One, two, three times. Each energy burst removed their target effectively with deadly precision.

Her body pivoted, led by the barrel of the weapon she held, until the sights had centered on the back of the attacker that was on Faulkner. The gun went up and fired when the back of the attacker's skull was centered along the barrel.

Due to the design and advancement of their weapons, there was no question of over-penetration. It simply did not happen.

The weapon was moving again, her body taking it around to point at the attacker that Faulkner had told her to kick a second time. Her mind was still trying to catch up with what was happening.

Ae'staa came into Violetta's sight, accompanied by another soldier. Violetta pointed the firearm down and away from them. As she was starting to gain her full senses, she witnessed the two soldiers pummel the kicked attacker with their shock rods. They were quick, efficient, and brutal in their actions. Violetta's ears were ringing, and her vision had narrowed at the edges.

"Are you well?" Mc'narrd's voice pushed through the ringing. "Acknowledge individually! Is everyone well?"

Violetta heard Ae'staa say her name and that she was unharmed. The other soldiers did the same. Faulkner wheezed his name and requested healers.

Ae'staa shook Violetta, her eyes looking up and down.

"Detective? Violetta! Are you wounded?" the captain demanded.

"Acknowledged." Violetta breathed. "I'm intact. How is Faulkner?"

The other soldier responded, from a position kneeling next to Faulkner. "He has deep lacerations across his right hamstring, left pectoral, and a puncture wound through the right forearm. Biosuit is doing its job, but he'll be out for two days without a healer. And I think there's nerve damage in the leg."

"Good job, detective," Ae'staa said to Violetta, but she could barely comprehend what was being said.

"Bring them in," Mc'narrd ordered over the comm. "Cleanup crew will be there in forty-five seconds."

"Acknowledged. C'mon, Violetta, let's go."

For some inexplicable reason, Violetta simply stood there, staring at Captain Ae'staa.

"Get her out of there."

Anger did not come close to describing Mc'narrd's voice. The words were snapped out, curt, and frigid. Compared to his usual jesting, it was easy to understand why he was career military. Why he was at the top and ran their covert ops division from the shadows.

She was very thankful he wasn't angry at her. She just wasn't certain who he was angry with or why.

"Are you well, Violetta?" the admiral asked.

His tone was slightly warmer, still furious, but she knew the fury wasn't aimed at her. Knowing he wasn't angry at her, she allowed herself to be turned and guided down the path towards the entrance.

"I will be. Eventually," she admitted.

"Shock." The voice was in her comm. She recognized it as Zh'oros. "Her pulse is too high and her blood pressure is climbing."

"Bring her to me." Malik's voice was the rock in the storm and she found herself clinging to it like a drowning sailor. She inhaled sharply. He must have heard because he added, "I'm here, Vi."

"She should be treated," Zh'oros replied, though there was no change in her tone.

"Please, Commander?" Violetta said. For whatever reason, she had immediately thought of him as Commander Mc'narrd. Or had she been thinking of her father? It was all a blur to her at the moment. "Admiral. Sorry. Admiral. Sir."

Violetta swallowed hard as she noticed the dark shadows of what she knew were bodies to her left. Wrapping her arms around herself, she kept moving forward. One foot in front of another. It took a moment to realize she still wore the skates.

"I'll protect her," Malik's voice remained gentle and warm, but there was a firmness to it. "Add more guards and send a healer here, if you need to."

Mc'narrd's voice filled her ear. "Pick, Violetta. Malik or the base?"

Suspecting he was talking only to her, she closed her eyes, trusting her feet to not stumble or falter. "Malik. Please. Let me go to Malik."

"Take her to bures'o Malik Addelia's penthouse. Escort her to his building, then to his penthouse. Hand her over personally into his care." Mc'narrd's tone allowed for no argument. "There will be a squadron outside the building, Addelia. Is it worth it?"

"You even have to ask?" Malik said incredulously. "I'll take care of her. Do you want us to come to the base tomorrow?"

"First thing in the morning."

"If her condition worsens, let us know immediately," Zh'oros stated, though there was intrigue in her voice. "Perhaps you are a better option, Malik. Her vitals are returning to their norms. It's slow, but they're dropping."

"Malik?" Violetta asked.

They were nearing the entrance to the park.

"I'm here. Not leaving you," Malik replied, a promise and vow to the words.

"Keep talking?"

"I can do that. I can talk to you all night. Though, eventually, you'll need to sleep."

"So will you," she replied.

"I suspect you'll sleep before I will," he teased.

She couldn't stop the smile from flashing across her face. "Maybe."

"I'll make sure of it." There was promise in the words and Violetta felt herself relax a little more.

"You know they can hear us," she said as the group escorted her to a marked military HAV.

It was parked in the opening where no vehicles were typically allowed. In fact, the entire entrance was filled with military HAVs.

"I switched it to a private channel. Only the commander of your escort, my command here, myself, and Zh'oros are on it. It's the best I can do for now." Mc'narrd sounded apologetic, but firm.

"Thank you, sir," Violetta said quietly as she climbed into the backseat of the HAV.

There was a soldier on each side of her, a driver and passenger, as well as three in the seat behind her. Mc'narrd was not taking chances with her. She didn't recognize any of the soldiers.

"Syra called me. She said you and Issik went by the shop," Malik continued, changing topics. "She claims you tried to actually purchase the treats from her. Threatened to put it on my tab."

"She lied. I've never had to pay for them. Tried the first time. Never again. You have to pay for your treats?" Violetta asked, her mind latching onto that bit of information. "Your parents never made me pay, either. Did they make you?"

"We had to work for our treats," Malik informed her. "Syra now makes us all pay for them. My parents, as I've said before, adore you. Always have. As do my siblings. Syra is merely keeping up the tradition."

"Oh."

"She also begged to be allowed to make whatever type of celebration or wedding cake you decide on. Though, I suspect she wants to make something large and elaborate." Malik chuckled. "And of course, there will be all your favorite pastries."

"We haven't… I'm confused again," Violetta admitted. "Why did she say that?"

"She was informed we visited the jewelry business."

"How?"

"You poor thing." Mc'narrd actually sounded sympathetic. "You haven't realized the popularity of your suitor, have you? Cameras are everywhere, Violetta. You're aware of that. What you may not realize, is there are very, very few who do not recognize Malik as the Master of Ceremonies. People watch the cameras. They see you with him everywhere. And they've now seen you go into a jewelry business."

"Where we looked at the set," Violetta said. She tilted her head back on the seat and slid down it slightly. "And you bought me the necklace."

Her feet suddenly felt very heavy. Looking down, she realized why. She quickly untied the laces and slid her feet out of the skates.

"Which you have yet to try on." Malik's voice could have melted a polar ice cap.

"Well, that's certainly one way to help with the shock," Zh'oros said in genuine amusement.

"It works, too," Mc'narrd murmured.

"You two are horrible," Violetta muttered, though there was no malice in her voice.

"Are you objecting?" Malik asked. The tone hadn't changed, either.

"Not even close, my love."

And suddenly there was a HAV full of humming and laughing soldiers.

"I believe that's the first time you've said that around people," Malik teased. "How far out are they, admiral?"

"We're pulling up now," the commander said. "Ah. I see you're already awaiting us."

"I've been standing out here since I learned about what happened," Malik admitted.

The door of the HAV opened and it was all Violetta could do to not climb over the soldier to rush into Malik's arms. But she waited for the man to slide out before she exited the vehicle.

One moment she was stepping out of the HAV, the next she was wrapped in Malik's arms, her face pressed against his chest. They stood there for a few moments. Then Malik turned and they began walking into his building with her huddled against him.

A memory of him holding her throughout her father's funeral ceremony and the trial flashed through her mind. He'd held her the same way then. Comfort and protection. Sanctuary and safety in the middle of a dark storm.

The unit fell into formation around them.

Violetta knew they had an audience. A military escort was not a common occurrence. And there was seemingly no reason for it. Yet, here she was being escorted to the Master of Ceremonies as though someone had died.

And Malik had taken her into his arms in front of everyone who may have been watching.

There would be no going back to hiding their relationship.

The fallout, she was certain, would come. But for now, she needed him. She needed his strength and the protection he and his penthouse afforded her.

***

Malik's penthouse was just as luxurious as everything else in his life. The outside was just as beautiful and elegant as the interior. A newer building, it was an architectural work of art. Dark blue curving beams swept up the sides of the building, making it appear as though the entire building swirled to the side. An optical illusion, but one that fooled even a native K'laisian's eyes. Windows filled each section between the sweeping, curving beams.

He had the very top floor, the entire floor not just part of it, for his residence. To add to it, the top floor had two levels. Windows filled entire walls, giving spectacular views of the city, including the main arena. The bottom level held the main living room, which featured a large entertainment interface and luxurious conforming chairs and sofas. Pillows lined the backs of the conforming sofa.

Between the conforming seats, were cushioned chairs and a long cushioned sofa. Human-styled furniture that many beings enjoyed. Blankets were draped over all the furniture, in easy reach for anyone who grew chilled, or simply wanted something to snuggle under.

Tables dotted the area, many filled with potted, flowering plants. The kitchen, a small library, an office, four guest bedrooms, and a full lavatory or bathroom as the humans called them, were also located on the lower level.

The upper level held the master bedroom, a full lavatory connected to the master, and two more guest rooms. Each of the guest rooms on the upper level shared a full lavatory.

Everything gleamed.

Holograms of Malik's family filled a bookcase against one wall, while art of popular artists dotted the walls.

What had caught her attention and gave her pause the first time she'd entered was all the stillcaptures of them. From their childhood throughout their high school years, including images of them at her father's funeral. They had only added to the collection with newer ones taken during the past few months. All candid with both of them smiling at the interface.

If she'd ever questioned his love for her, it had been answered the moment she stepped into the penthouse.

She registered all of it as she had done every time she'd visited. Except this time, she didn't feel overwhelmed.

"Do you want us stationed outside the penthouse, sir?" the commander asked. Violetta suspected he was asking Mc'narrd. "Or outside the building?"

"Outside the building," Mc'narrd replied. "They're in?"

"We're in my penthouse," Malik stated.

"Keep in contact. I won't require the suits to remain on."

Violetta closed her eyes and just leaned against Malik. She just didn't have it in her to respond.

"If anything changes, contact us immediately," Mc'narrd said, concern evident in his tone. "Take care of her, Addelia."

"I'll let you know if we need to come in sooner," Malik replied, holding her close. "Thank you, Commander."

There was no reply, aside from the door sliding shut.

"Lockdown engaged," Malik said aloud.

The immediate sound of locks clicking and the room suddenly becoming considerably darker for a brief moment had Violetta looking up and around. The windows were now black. The interior lights had grown brighter to adjust for the lack of light from the moon and stars.

"One of the benefits of this place," Malik explained. "The security is phenomenal. There's a five-point redundancy to the power, also."

"Can I fall apart now?" she whispered, her voice breaking with the words.

Malik studied her closely and she understood why.

Her body was shaking and she couldn't make it stop.

Sweeping her up into his arms, he carried her to the sofa where he settled onto the cushions with her in his lap. She leaned against him. Wrapping her arms around his neck, she wept.

Arms tightened around her, holding her close and secure. Lips brushed against the top of her head. She reached up, took out the comm, and handed it to him. He took it from her and there was a soft 'clink' when he put it on a nearby table. Hands unbuckled her belt, and she shifted so it could be removed. It was tossed to the side.

"I'm sorry," she whispered.

"For what? For 'falling apart', as you put it?" Malik asked. He kissed the tip of her ear. "You've never had to kill before, Violetta. Mc'narrd and Zh'oros told me. None have suffered a death from anything you've done before now. You've been protected and sheltered. Through luck or others, I don't know which. You just watched someone you care greatly for be seriously injured. Then killed three beings." He lifted her chin until her eyes met his. "You're allowed. You're in shock. And I love you. Never apologize for being alive. For having feelings. And especially for showing them to me."

"I know you have," she whispered, her face against his chest.

"In Duels, yes," Malik replied, his arms tightening around her. "It's not the exact same as what you had to do, though. But it still doesn't change the fact that I have taken lives in the arena. You've now witnessed two such deaths that have happened during Duels." He paused, before sighing. "I have never enjoyed having to kill in a Duel, though. Ziph being the exception. I would prefer accepting a yield, or even incapacitating a being, but there are always those who refuse to yield. Those who leave no choice if I wish to survive the encounter."

"Did Mc'narrd tell you who attacked us?"

Malik nodded. "He said it was the Moyii Tsaa. Do you know why they attacked, admiral?" There was a pause. "Mc'narrd believes it was to do with you insulting them when they had you earlier this year. They tend to hold grudges, apparently." When he snorted, Violetta gave him a questioning look. "He also said we should be discussing anything except the attack."

"Understanding why the attack happened helps with… the rest." Violetta retorted. "And I don't think they could have known about me insulting them the last time. No one from that group acted as though they wore comms. Plus, the military would've found them."

"Good point," Malik conceded.

She shook her head slightly. "No. This attack happened after we went shopping together. They're purists to an extreme."

Malik blinked at her. "You think maybe they're unhappy about two 'halfers' being a couple?"

"To say they're 'unhappy' would put it mildly." Violetta snuggled against him, thankful for his warmth. She felt Malik shift, then a blanket was pulled around her. "Still love me?"

She could hear Mc'narrd's laughter through the comm Malik still wore.

"I will always love you." He paused before turning the question back to her. "Do you still love me?"

"Forever and always." She kissed his collar bone. She repeated it in their native language. "Forever and always, my love."

"You aren't going to get angry when I speak to your grandparents, declaring my desire to take you as my mate?"

"No," she replied, her eyes drifting shut. "Not if you keep talking until I'm asleep."

"As you wish," he murmured.

The last thing she remembered before sleep claimed her, was him singing softly to her. A song from their teen years they'd sung together so often she heard it even in her dreams.

Chapter Nine

The following morning, Violetta awoke to the smell of fresh jakka and proteins being cooked on a stovetop. She did not remember undressing, let alone being tucked into Malik's bed. Shoving her dark auburn hair from her face, she sat up in the bed, trying to orient herself. She still wore the biosuit, though.

Probably too difficult to remove, she thought in amusement.

Malik wasn't a fan of the 'suits when they were alone. Normally, neither was she, but considering the previous evening, she understood why he'd left it on her.

Shaking her head, she tossed the covers back and climbed from the bed.

Padding from the bedroom, she paused long enough to admire the honeycomb-lattice work of the railing that wrapped around the upper level. The off-white color was bright, but not sharp to the eyes. Just soft enough to be easy to look at. The walkway curved around the main living area, giving a pleasant view of the lower level and was divided by the short, wide steps that led down to the main level.

Descending the stairs, she found Malik in the kitchen, adeptly fixing breakfast. Two cups of steaming jakka sat on the bar opposite of the utilities.

She made her way towards him. He paused in what he was doing, slid the skillet to the side, and met her at the edge of the kitchen.

His eyes searched hers, before sweeping over the rest of her. "How did you sleep?"

"It was restful," she replied. "Thank you."

"It's just shy of noon."

Blinking at him, she opened her mouth to say something, then snapped it shut. "Why did you let me sleep so late?"

"You needed it." He gave a very human shrug of his shoulders. "Zh'oros told Mc'narrd to shut up when he grumbled. Agreeing with me that allowing you to wake on your own was better than insisting you come in for her to check you out. You'll have to be cleared for duty, but rest is the best thing for your body and mind."

"Are you sure you haven't been taking instruction on the side?" she teased. "You sound like a healer."

Malik tipped his head to the side briefly in a wink. "I'll let her know you said that when we go by the base later."

Violetta laughed and kissed his cheek. "Thank you for last night."

His fingers brushed her cheek. "I'm pleased I could be there for you."

Her stomach took that moment to grumble. Causing them both to laugh.

"Sit, enjoy your jakka, and tell me what you'd like to eat."

"Whatever I'm smelling? I'd love to have some," she replied, crossing to the bar and settling onto a stool. "I'm not sure I've ever been this hungry before."

"Your body went through shock," Malik explained. "Your pulse went through the roof. Blood pressure, also. Your entire body reacted harshly to what you went through yesterday. Your mind was trying to comprehend something you've been trained against doing your entire life. Something every K'laisian is taught from birth. Hence, experiencing shock."

"It… it was different than with…"

"Lc'sonn?" He glanced over his shoulder at her. She nodded. He turned back to the cooking food, even as he put some on a plate. "A completely different event. You were shellshocked, as some people refer to it, but that was from seeing your would-be murderer being killed." He chuckled. "I assure you, the Fangs have all killed in cold blood before and they aren't troubled by the lives they take in those instances."

"How do you know that?"

"They're mercs." He shrugged. "Victoria took that shot with expert precision with a very short amount of time to plan for it. You don't just wake up one day and do that. They deal with worlds where murder isn't treated the same as our planet. Where it's sometimes rather common."

"That… makes sense."

He turned and slid the plate in front of her. Pulling silverware from a drawer, he handed her the eating utensils.

"It still bothers you, doesn't it?"

"I think I'm adjusting?" Malik raised his brows and she sighed. "I can't feel guilt or shame for killing someone who was going to kill me and Faulkner. That was the second time I've ever been told to take a shot and make it lethal. The first time, though, Issik fired first."

"But?" Malik prompted.

"But I do feel guilt for not acting more swiftly."

"That's understandable. You've always felt guilty when you couldn't protect someone." Malik looked pointedly at the food. "You are going to eat, yes?"

"After it cools some, yes," she retorted. "I am not going to let your food go to waste."

"So, what do you plan on doing? Mc'narrd, I might add, is unhappy you aren't wearing the comm so he can talk directly to you." Malik smirked. "He's lucky I'm wearing mine."

"I'll put it in after I finish my breakfast." Violetta giggled and began spearing the fried meat and scrambled eggs with her fork. "As for what I plan on doing? I'm going to start wearing my sword, as well as my other service-issued weapons."

"Think your colleagues will take it as a Challenge?" Malik asked as he turned back to the stove. Piling his plate with the rest of the food, he turned the stovetop off before returning to the bar. "Not many detectives wear bladed weapons suited for Dueling."

"Don't know," Violetta said between bites. "Don't really care, either. Doubt it'll take long for news to spread about what happened. Unless the military plans on keeping it underwraps."

Malik frowned, slid off the barstool, and stalked to the living area. Violetta watched as he grabbed something from a small table before turning to her. He had her comm in his hand, which he offered to her. Brows furrowed, she tucked it into her ear.

"Morning, sir," she said without preamble.

"Should be more like 'noon'," he grumbled. "But I cannot overrule a healer's orders. Not that I expect Malik to listen to anything if he thought you should sleep, anyway."

"Doubtful," Violetta said, even as Malik smirked as he began preparing the perfect bite of food. "I find it difficult to believe you were interested in hearing me eat. What do you need from me?"

"Actually, it's regarding what we are doing, as the military," Mc'narrd replied. "Your captain, and subsequently the entire department, has been informed that an unprovoked attack was made against you by the Moyii Tsaa. It's been disclosed it occurred at the nature preserve while the military was actively patrolling the area. A member of the guard was seriously injured while protecting you."

Oh, fark.

"I hear an 'and' coming. What's the 'and', sir?"

"And due to a member of the police service being openly attacked, and not in a Challenge, the military will be issuing a guard detail for the officer who was attacked until our investigation is complete."

Violetta looked at Malik, her fork halfway to her mouth.

"Did he mention that to you?"

Malik shook his head slowly.

"How are you able to do that without it appearing that I'm receiving preferential treatment?" she asked.

"Technically, you are," Malik muttered.

"What was that, Addelia?" Mc'narrd drew the words out, his tone cooler.

When Malik began chewing his food, the admiral made a disgusted sound.

"The police service is an extension of the military, which you're aware of. We prefer to allow the local services to handle local problems. Complete with their own internal structure. It allows the military to handle national and international problems with greater ease. When a cartel, such as the Moyii Tsaa, decides to attack someone for an unprovoked reason? That makes the military unhappy. Especially when it occurs on military property and involves military personnel."

"That's the official story?" Violetta asked. "How's Faulkner?"

"It is," Mc'narrd stated. "He'll be up and in physical therapy in three days. We have nanites working on him and he's responding as well as you did. Because of the nerve damage, it's taking longer to ensure a complete recovery."

"He'll be back on Captain Ae'staa's unit, then?"

"He will. He did suggest we offer you a few new 'toys' as an early solstice gift. Just in case your playmates decide to schedule another date." Mc'narrd chuckled. "We'll discuss it when you arrive."

"How close will the unit be to Violetta?" Malik asked suddenly.

"One unit will be within eyesight. Another will be escorting her when she hits the streets. None will interfere with any investigation. They may assist, though, should it be required. Or if they decide to take an interest in the case."

"Syra's gonna need to send at least two baskets until the Moyii Tsaa problem is resolved."

Malik snickered. "I'll let her know."

"Before anyone else asks, the case we're working involves a being of mixed heritage. Did you know Nicholas En'ingo, Malik?"

The sudden stillness from Malik had her reaching over to touch the hand that was on the counter. Softly, she asked, "Are you well?"

"Nick? Nick En'ingo?" Malik asked, lowering the fork to his plate. He looked at the food and slid the plate to the side. He twined his fingers through hers. "We worked together a few times. Remember I said I protected clients?" Violetta gave a nod. "He was a guard a few times. He taught me the ropes when I first started working for Morelli. He was a good man, though I haven't seen him in the past few months. Last time was before I helped you."

"I'm so sorry, Malik," Violetta said gently. "He was the being I told you about."

"Why didn't you tell me then?"

Violetta raised a brow. "As injured as you were? Wasn't about to do so."

Malik opened his mouth, then closed it. "I can't argue that. And yesterday was your day off. You never discuss work on those days." He paused, tilting his head to the side. "You weren't supposed to tell me then. I suspect you're not supposed to be telling me any of this now."

"You've got the clearance to know anything I do." She smiled softly. "Wasn't that the reason for you renewing your security clearance?"

"Part of it," Mc'narrd muttered. "Sorry, Addelia. Looks like you're going to have to listen to her discussing murder cases for the rest of her career."

"It's a fair trade. She has to deal with the popularity of being the Master of Ceremonies' mate." His grin widened at the dismay on her face. "Well, once we get everything smoothed out with her grandparents and have the ceremony."

"That's going to occur long before you two have the ceremony," Mc'narrd teased. "Have you managed to convince her to wear the necklace yet?"

"It's a bit shiny for work, sir," Violetta retorted dryly, taking a drink of the jakka.

"Wear it next time we go to the arena," Malik suggested. Mischief shone in his eyes.

"And why do you suggest that?"

"Because people will be staring at it more than they'll be staring at you."

There was the distinct sound of coughing, as though someone had choked on something they drank.

"Not likely," Mc'narrd managed to gasp.

"Please, sir, I'm trying to convince her to wear it. You're not assisting that in the least."

Malik actually sounded somewhat respectful. Violetta narrowed her gaze at him, not trusting his reason at all.

"No, no, you are correct. A great many eyes would most definitely be on that necklace." There was a long pause before he spoke again. "We'll be certain to add more guards when you decide to do that."

"I'm obviously missing something important here," Violetta grumbled. She speared the last of her food. "Will I regret wearing it?"

"No more than you'll ever regret wearing a wedding ring," Mc'narrd commented.

"I really cannot argue that."

"There's something you won't argue?" Malik teased. Violetta glowered at him. "You're cute when you're angry."

"Not what you were thinking the other morning."

"Very true."

"If you two have finished, we need you at the base. You need to be cleared before you can return to work. I'm afraid it will take a few hours, at the least, for a complete eval."

"I'll go get dressed." Violetta drained the last of her jakka and stood. She'd moved a portion of her wardrobe to Malik's penthouse shortly after they'd begun their courtship. "I'd like to stop by my apartment before going to the police station, if that's possible, sir."

"Absolutely. Faulkner is in our medical wing. Drop by on your way to Zh'oros. I'm certain he'd enjoy seeing you both."

"Malik can come?" Violetta asked as she headed for the stairs.

Malik fell into step beside her.

"He won't be there for the evaluation. But I don't believe we'd be able to stop him from accompanying you."

"He probably wouldn't be able to be there even if he were a healer," Violetta said thoughtfully. "He's too close to me."

"Indeed. Let me know when you're prepared to leave."

"We will," Violetta reassured him.

As they ascended the stairs, Violetta suddenly realized she felt comfortable in Malik's home. For the first time in her entire life, she wondered if she'd be moving out of her father's apartment. If she would be willing to lose another connection to her father for a new one with Malik.

Chapter Ten

Full psychological evaluations were long, extensive, and exhausting. The questions were meant to evoke reactions. The answers, may they be physical, emotional, or verbal were used to determine the true psychological state of the being in question.

Violetta had spent many hours over the years having them done. They were required for the security clearance that allowed her to retain possession of her father's console. She'd received one after being accused of murder and subsequently being witness to Nyzril Lc'sonn's death. Now she was going through yet another after being authorized to kill in what surmounted to cold blood in their society.

Her morals had not changed: she would always believe in Challenges and Duels. The honorable way to resolve problems. That those who kill in cold blood for no just reason were ill.

She believed extreme situations require extreme solutions. She was prepared to survive at any cost. To kill if it was a last resort. Or if it was ordered. But do it willingly for an unjust and unwarranted reason? No. Never.

When she was finished, she felt as though the evaluation had dug deeper within her psyche than ever before. The questions had been varied and encompassed far more than any other previous evaluation. When she checked the chronometer for the time, she was shocked to see she'd been in the eval for nearly six hours.

No wonder she felt as though she'd been run over by a HAV. All the previous ones had only been three hours, tops.

Sunset was just shy of three hours away. Which gave her a few hours to catch up with Issik and find out the latest on their case.

"You're free to return to work, detective," Mc'narrd said, meeting her as she exited the medical wing. They fell into synchronized steps. He offered her a bottle of kaerik root. She accepted it with a thankful look. "You did well in there."

"That was the longest evaluation I think I've ever had. Even the one for Dad's console wasn't that long."

"We're aware." Mc'narrd glanced at her from the corner of his eyes. "Zh'oros wanted to be thorough. Especially since you went to Malik instead of here last night."

"Right. And if there *was* any other reason, you wouldn't tell me, anyway."

The smirk that flashed across his face was answer enough for her.

"Next stop is my apartment, then the station."

"Have you decided if you're going to move in with Malik?" Mc'narrd suddenly asked. "Eventually you'll have to decide."

"Will I lose my father's console?"

She took a long pull of the beverage, savoring the coolness as it traveled down her throat and to her stomach.

"No, Violetta. If you chose Malik's penthouse, the console will need to be moved into a secure location at his apartment. Said room will be evaluated by the military and given approval prior to the console being moved." He patted her left shoulder. "It will be required that you keep it off all subnets. The rules that apply to it and the room it is in, will apply at Malik's penthouse."

"Oh."

"You have some time to discuss it with Malik."

"I suspect he already has a room in mind."

Mc'narrd chuckled. "Considering who we're discussing? I'm certain of it."

"Just how much of a file do you have on us?"

"Do you really want to know? After what you've just gone through?"

"I-" she broke off and bit her lower lip. Shaking her head, she admitted, "No, no, I don't think I want to know. The next eval will probably be two days long, instead of just six hours."

Laughing, the admiral squeezed her left shoulder. "You certainly understand how the military works far more than one would expect. Your parents would be proud."

The rest of the walk to his office was done in comfortable silence. Oddly, she didn't even feel apprehensive about the imminent meeting with the admiral. She supposed a six hour psych eval would do that to a being.

Admiral Mc'narrd opened the door, and gestured for her to enter before him. Drawing a breath, she let it out slowly before stepping into the almost-empty office.

There was nothing to indicate it was an active office used by a single being. No decorations or personal articles rested on shelves, desk, or counters. The furniture was standard-issue. Even the interfaces and console were standard. The sole unique item was the helmet currently sitting on the desk beside the main console in the office.

He gestured to one of the chairs before settling into his own behind the desk. Violetta found herself choosing the far left chair. A habit of old.

"Your adherence to the guidelines of your chosen service is considerable. Even commendable. But it no longer serves you or a greater purpose," Mc'narrd began.

Violetta immediately felt as though she was being sat down and lectured to by her father. Unconsciously, she sat up straighter.

"I apologize if you see some flaw in my approach to the work I do," she said with complete sincerity.

"Oh, no, no, this isn't a review of your work or an admonishment of any kind. I am endeavoring to help you realize that the scope and rules of your life have changed. Since life is a matter of adapt or perish, I prefer that you adapt, and quickly."

"Sir?"

Mc'narrd gave her a tired smile. "From the moment you were first attacked by agents of the Moyii Tsaa, you have been authorized for use of lethal force. 'Free use' is now your permanent method of operating."

Violetta felt struck. "I… what? But as a member of our police service-"

"As a person with your level of security clearance with the military," Mc'narrd rejoined. "And someone who is an active target of an identified crime syndicates, the use of lethal force is on your service profile. It does not and *will not* go away."

"Sir, I mean, admiral." Violetta struggled to compose her thoughts. "The police service is obligated to use non-lethal methods until all other options have failed."

"Or a direct threat to all beings is identified. I am fully aware of the service's guidelines, Violetta. I helped create them. It is also part of my current position to continue to update and create new ones as needed."

Violetta's mouth snapped shut.

"Since you chose police service over military service, there is little reason for you to be aware that the operating parameters work differently. As you know, since it's part of general education, the police service is very much a lesser branch of the military. Which means that in addition to holding service personnel accountable, the military branch supersedes the police."

She nodded.

"Within the military, members who serve for longer than one to two years, are placed into positions where their service will be of best use. Those who are placed into specific programs are given completely different guidelines than those who only serve the required year."

Violetta gave another nod. It was all information she already knew, though the reminder didn't hurt.

"Those in the command, and especially, security programs are taught when to use lethal force. It is a notation placed in their records and it remains there. Those who are sent offplanet on battlecruisers receive those same instructions, as well as the same notations." He leaned forward slightly in the chair. "Every being on our battlecruisers are authorized to use lethal force when it's required. Every commander and military unit on our planet receives the same. They have all been trained extensively to know how and when to do so." He paused, allowing the words to settle in the air around them. "Do you understand?"

"Yes, sir," she said, giving another nod.

"While you are an active member of the police service, Violetta, you are also a person of vested interest to the military. Your father insured that from your conception, and it has only grown during your time in the service."

Violetta leaned forward. "You're informing me that I function as someone above my station? A member of the military who would have received those same instructions?"

"Correct. Because you *did not* enter the military, you are not accustomed to using lethal force, which is a cornerstone of our society. Just as Challenges and Duels are another cornerstone. You must become accustomed to when such must happen. And in using it. There is no resistance from any military branch for you to have this. And no, this is not due to myself nor your father. This has been earned."

"To clarify, my service record now states I have been granted use of lethal force when it is required. Including, and especially, outside of Duels when dealing with the Moyii Tsaa." Mc'narrd gave a nod even as she continued. "And I will not be charged for murder in cold blood, due to the excessive force that would be required in such situations."

There was another nod from Mc'narrd.

"How many people, outside the military, are allowed such… permission? Is that even the right word?"

What she'd just been told went against all her training from the academy. It did not go against the training her father had taught her, though.

Survive at all costs. No matter the price.

"It is," Mc'narrd allowed. "To answer, it is very, very few. Those few had to also earn it."

"I'm quickly learning there are vast differences between the military and the police service," she admitted.

"Just remember what you've been told." Mc'narrd intoned. His eyes met hers. "I suspect you will need it."

***

Compared to the discussion with Mc'narrd, the trip to the police service was uneventful and oddly quiet. As was her arrival at the station. Even entering the station with a dozen soldiers fanning out around her was relatively uneventful. If one didn't include the stares from fellow officers and civilians alike.

Issik was still at his desk when she entered.

The flowers were still on hers. Someone had even been adding water to them.

"Someone certainly likes you," Toriz Da'kaw, the commander of the unit, stated.

A pure blood native, he had a gorgeous mane of black hair, which he wore braided back away from his face. His skin was only a few shades darker than Violetta's olive tone.

"Her suitor," Issik quipped as he approached them. "You well, Vi? The captain informed homicide what happened. Said you'd be eval'ed before coming in."

"Really? Would've thought it was the Moyii Tsaa from the attention they're giving her," Commander Da'kaw drawled. His gold eyes twinkled with laughter. "Who would think Addelia would send her flowers?"

Issik hummed loudly. "Good to know your guards have a sense of humor."

"We try." Da'kaw gestured towards his men, who fanned out against the walls of the room. "I'll get out of your hair. Pleasure meeting you, detective."

"An honor, commander," Issik replied with a slight bow.

"So, what do we have? Aside from a flower-filled desk?" Violetta asked, moving towards the vases. "Where am I supposed to sit? Let alone work?"

"Hox if I know. Want to use one of the meeting rooms? We can put the interfaces up on a larger screen."

"Sounds good. Did you talk to Ra'keff? Or Osing?"

"Did you get to ask Malik about our corpse?" Issik countered as he led the way towards one of the meeting rooms.

The meeting rooms for homicide were along both sides of the 'pit' where all the detectives had their desks. It was easier to discuss cases in the open area. The captain had his own office, for privacy. It was in a corner on the left side of the room, between the meeting rooms and the interrogation rooms. The interrogation rooms and booths were along the farthest wall, opposite the main doors.

"He knew Nick," Violetta said quietly. Issik looked at her sharply. "En'ingo worked for Morelli, also. Malik seemed upset to hear of En'ingo's death."

"Fark."

"That about sums it up, yes." Violetta shook her head. "Have there been more deaths with the same or similar cause of death?"

"None yet. But I spent most of the day investigating where En'ingo's body was found. Tried using my Gift, but the only thing I can tell is he was killed there. Yet somehow no one heard or saw anything."

"Fark."

"That does sum it up," Issik quipped as he opened the door to the meeting room. "I did talk to Ra'keff, since he asked how you were doing." He paused. "What did you say to him? First time he's ever been friendly and concerned about your welfare."

"Nothing! I told him the problem was I've got PTSD and I accepted his apology."

She stepped through the door and into the meeting room. A bare room with a long table with a dozen conforming chairs around it. A large interface with a stylus pen attached to it filled the wall opposite the door. Smaller interfaces rested flat against the table's surface, all of them turned off.

"He apologized, offered to be of assistance, and said he's never meant my nickname as an insult. You aren't the only one baffled." She moved to an interface and touched the screen. It rose into the air above the table. As her fingers moved over the screen, she asked, "So what did he have to say?"

"He agrees the cases are linked. Suggested we work together, especially since it may not be safe for you on the streets right now." Issik moved to an interface of his own. The wall interface turned on and he shifted his screen so it also showed on the wall. "He's wondering if we should go to the captain now or wait."

"What did you tell him?" Violetta glanced at him as she pulled up the day's list of deaths. She sent her screen to the wall, also. Enlarging the words, she settled onto the chair.

"Told him we need to be certain of what's going on before we go to Os'shye. Need to know if there's going to be only these or if there's going to be more rolling in."

There was a knock on the door. Issik glanced at her. She shrugged. Together, they turned towards the door. The windows showed only the people in the room, not what was on the wall or any interface.

Captain Os'shye was speaking with Commander Da'kaw outside the door. The door opened and the pair stepped into the room. Commander Da'kaw moved to the side, though he didn't move far. Os'shye wore a bemused expression.

"He has orders and they're equal to my own," the captain explained dismissively. He gestured for Violetta to remain sitting. "Can't fault him for doing his job."

"What can we do for you, Captain?" Violetta asked, shifting in the seat so she could face him easier.

"Are you doing well, detective?" Captain Os'shye asked, instead. "I'm surprised to see you in today, all things considered."

"I think the eval was what I needed," Violetta admitted. "It was rather intense, but I think it helped clear up a few things I was questioning."

"Good to hear. It's what our healers are for," the captain replied. "You have a visitor. Zane Morelli wants to speak with you. Preferably in private. But he's aware that won't be permissible due to current circumstances."

"Do you know why he's here?" Issik asked.

Violetta glanced at him, aware that Issik also worked for Morelli. In fact, Issik had been the one who told Violetta to go to Morelli for help four months earlier. Morelli had allowed Malik to be who helped her. She owed Morelli for more than just the use of a safe house and HAVs.

Morelli hadn't Matched her with Malik, perhaps not intentionally, but it had ended with the same result.

"No. Said he wanted to speak to Detective Cq'linns about an investigation."

"You won't be able to dismiss Da'kaw, but Morelli won't say or do anything to jeopardize you," Mc'narrd said in her ear. "It's your choice: speak to him there, or elsewhere."

"I'm fine with talking to him. It'll make asking him about the case a lot easier if he's here." Violetta smiled impishly. "Will you ask if he'd be willing to speak with Issik, also?"

"He'll be here in five minutes," the captain replied, giving them a nod.

When he left, so did Da'kaw. Though the commander took a position beside the door. He stood far enough away he could use either the sword at his side or his military-issue sidearm. Every being in the unit sent to guard her wore their preferred Dueling weapon. None were service-issued, for every K'laisian had the right to choose their own preferred weapon for a Duel.

Though most in the police service did not wear their preferred weapons, some did. Violetta had simply become one of those few beings.

"Any theories?" Violetta asked Issik.

"None. First time he's been to the station for anything other than to bail out a being."

Shrugging, Violetta turned back to the screens. "Have we found anything helpful? Any sort of clue pointing to a possible perp?"

"Did you get the reports from Ki'monl?"

"I haven't read them yet. Were they sent straight over to my inbox?"

"Yup."

Violetta's fingers flew over the interface. She found the files and pulled them up, sending them to the wall to read easier.

"Nothing new on the cause of death," she murmured. Glancing towards the window, she noticed the captain walking towards the room with Zane Morelli. "Any particulates that might be helpful?"

Issik glanced at her sharply. "None were searched for because it was a beating."

"Look at the face." Violetta gestured to the enlarged image on the wall.

The cheek and part of the nose, lips, and chin were visible. There was a tiny pattern left on the face. As though the force of the impact of the fist had left a pattern. But it was easily missed until she'd enlarged the image to the size of the wall's screen.

"I'll send a message to Ki'monl," Issik said. "Incoming."

Violetta cleared the wall interface and stood in one fluid movement.

The door opened two seconds after she stood.

"Detective Violetta Cq'linns," Captain Os'shye stepped into the room with Commander Da'kaw beside him. The commander moved to the side once more, allowing Morelli to enter. A second soldier entered behind Morelli. "This is Zane Morelli. Do you feel comfortable being in here with him?"

"Sorry, but if you don't have two, one for each, it will seem strange." Mc'narrd's voice was not the least bit apologetic. "Lieutenant Drabek will leave with the captain."

"As long as he doesn't mind speaking in front of Detective Ha'kksworth and the commander."

"A pleasure to meet you, Lady Cq'linns," Morelli said, giving her a slight bow. "I do not mind speaking in front of either being."

Morelli was a large human male with a pleasant demeanor. The first time she met him, he'd been putting together a little sailing ship. Today, he wore a dark blue button-up shirt and black dress pants. His black hair was slicked back. He still had the day-old stubble on his wide jaw and around his thin lips. Brilliant, intelligent dark gray eyes met hers with ease.

Those dark eyes watched as the captain and the one soldier, Drabek, departed the room.

Drabek took a position to the side of the door.

"Well met and greetings," Violetta said, choosing a more common K'laisian phrase. There was no need to lie for anyone's benefit, though she knew humans frequently did it with ease. "How may I be of service?"

"It has come to my notice that someone is killing my employees," Morelli said without preamble. "I would like you to investigate."

Startled, Violetta's eyes widened as she blinked at him several times.

"You may or may not be aware, but three of my employees have died within the past two days. The third was found near one of my housing centers."

Morelli's eyes did not move away from hers as he spoke. She could tell he was upset, possibly angry, from the tenseness of his body. His shoulders were tight, as were the muscles around his neck.

"Would you like to sit?" Violetta offered, gesturing to the table.

Issik had moved to the opposite side of her, allowing the end of the table to be free.

"Thank you, lady," Morelli said, settling into the chair at the end. Violetta and Issik followed his lead. "I'm pleased to see you came out on top with your earlier problem. Complete with a promotion, I believe."

"Yes, sir. To lieutenant. Thank you," Violetta said, smiling at the don.

"How's the Master of Ceremonies treating you?" There was definite mischief in the don's blue eyes when he asked the question.

"Malik and I are doing well together," Violetta informed him. She noticed the commander smirk at her comment. "What does he have to do with your 'people' being killed?"

"Those who have all died have been human or of mixed heritage. Two were found near where he lives. The third was located near a housing center he has used in the past." Morelli didn't even glance towards Issik. "I do not know the methods used by K'lais' homicide department. But on

Earth, those facts alone would make the police consider Malik a suspect."

"Malik Addelia is not a suspect," Issik stated as he leaned back in the chair. "His location has been verified by our military. The proof is indisputable."

"That is good to hear." Morelli finally turned his attention to Issik. "The third being located was Xela Devries."

Violetta put the name into her interface. She scrolled through, finding a brief basic report. The report showed a woman of mixed heritage identified as Xela Devries had been discovered dead on Lithlaur Street. Her body had been delivered to the Master of the Dead for an autopsy. There were scans showing the body, location, and preliminary reports.

"This says suspicion of death caused by possible unofficial Duel," Violetta commented, her voice neutral.

"Xela uses a mace, not a blade. She also wouldn't be involved in anything unofficial."

"Do you know why she might have been in that area?" Issik asked before Violetta could speak up.

"That's the other thing," Morelli stated, his gray eyes darting between them. "She lives… lived near the business district. Hates that part of the city. Is… *was* terrified of it, to be honest. My people there? They say they saw a dark, older HAV in the area just before her body was found."

"You think someone dropped her body there," she commented, not looking up as she typed on her interface.

When he didn't answer, she raised her gaze to meet his eyes. The anger burning in their depths was understandable.

"I can give you every camera video in and around that housing center for the past six months."

"We only would need the past month," Issik said, amused. "I doubt the military would allow us to view anything during the time Violetta may or may not have been in that area before then."

"Very astute, your partner," Mc'narrd mused. "Wonder why he hasn't been promoted yet?"

Did he have to ask those questions when she couldn't reply? He was such an ass, she thought crossly.

Aloud, she said, "Any assistance you can give us in locating the being doing this, would be greatly appreciated."

"I would consider it a… favor, if you investigated all of these murders and located the being killing those in my employ." Morelli locked his eyes with hers. "Bring this bastard to justice. I don't care how you do it, either. Duel. Arrest. Whatever it takes to end this sick being's murderous behavior."

"I would advise 'arrest', if at all possible," Mc'narrd drawled. "Though I'd be thinking the same if it were my people."

Commander Da'kaw cleared his throat, seeming to remind Morelli that he was in the room and listening. Morelli didn't even react. Mc'narrd merely chuckled.

"I will do everything within my power and capabilities to locate the being behind these murders," Violetta vowed. "Would you be willing to send the information you have to me? Those vidclips will help."

"They'll be in your inbox within the hour," Morelli promised. He hesitated. "I don't know what part Malik has to do with any of this, but you might want to let him know."

"I will." Violetta glanced at Issik, then Commander Da'kaw, before turning back to Morelli. "Do you have any theories?"

Morelli leaned back in his chair, a thoughtful expression on his face.

"If Malik isn't a suspect, then someone is leaving the bodies near him for a reason," Morelli mused. "In the old days of Earth, the syndicates did it as a warning. Something along the lines of 'get off my turf or I'll kill every one of your people'. Another was as a warning. 'I'll kill everyone you know and then I'm coming after you'."

"If we figure out the reason, we may be able to figure out who it is," Issik suggested. He glanced at Violetta. "Think Malik would be willing to talk to us again about this?"

"Maybe. Provided no one pulls another stunt like earlier."

Morelli's eyes shifted from Violetta to Issik before returning to her. "I suspect I'm missing something."

"You're missing a lot," Mc'narrd muttered. "Thank your lucky stars for it, too."

"Only some jealousy," Violetta said dismissively. "We'll need to inform the captain about what is going on." Morelli raised a brow even as he frowned. "If there is someone committing grotesque murders of multiple beings, he needs to know. I'll request taking point on the case. That should keep me in the office and in the middle of everything."

"Do you think your captain will allow it?" Morelli asked, doubt in his voice. "No offense, detective, but you are rather young compared to many. Including your partner, here."

"She didn't do too shabby four months ago," Commander Da'kaw commented. "Even with the entire city *and* the entire police service searching for her."

Morelli chuckled. "Very true, commander."

Pushing himself up, he offered Violetta his hand. She stood and accepted it. Just as he did the first time they met, he gripped her hand firmly. She returned the gesture with equal force.

"I'll be in contact, detective. Thank you for meeting with me."

"It has been a pleasure," Violetta said, a smile on her face. "Thank you."

Understanding flashed through Morelli's eyes. He flashed her a pleasant smile before leaving the room. Commander Da'kaw gave them a nod before following Morelli out the door.

"Curious how they don't consider you a threat," Violetta said to Issik. "Did you suddenly get some security clearance?"

Issik hummed loudly, even as Mc'narrd laughed in her ear.

"Nah. They've probably realized I'm the only one who you've never Challenged or beat up in the gym."

"Close enough," Mc'narrd said between chuckles. "Close enough."

Violetta smiled, though she wasn't feeling a lot of amusement.

"Captain Os'shye, could you please join us in the meeting room?" Violetta asked over the comms. "We have some disturbing news."

"In relation to?" the captain responded.

"The murders and why Morelli was here," Violetta replied, her voice grim. She met Issik's eyes. "This isn't small, sir."

"I'll be right there."

An hour later, Violetta was sitting at the table with Issik, having gone over everything they knew about the cases. They had also included the possibilities Morelli had given them.

Captain Os'shye sat at the end of the table, his face indecipherable. Commander Da'kaw stood on the side of the door opposite the captain and near Violetta.

"You suspect there will be more bodies before this is over," the captain said after several long minutes.

"That's our concern," Violetta admitted. "I'll ask Malik to come in. Perhaps he will have some insight we don't." She gestured towards the enlarged photos of the faces belonging to the beings that had been beaten to death. "As you can see, there is a pattern of some sort on the faces. We've contacted Master Ki'monl, who is investigating what could have caused it. He's also taking a closer look at the bodies in the hopes of finding particulates of some sort."

"His initial belief is that it's a fabric of some type. Perhaps from gloves," Issik added.

"I'd like to be the one to take point, Captain." Violetta tipped her head towards the commander. "As I've become the target, at least briefly, of the Moyii Tsaa, this would allow me to be of service. I'm also capable of convincing Malik to come in again." She chuckled. "Without anyone being Challenged to a Duel."

"You would also be in the midst of all the information," the captain stated blandly. "I know you're capable of being impartial. You're able to catch details others would miss. Perhaps you are the best suited for this particular case." He paused before leaning forward against the table. "Are you prepared for any Challenge it may incite?"

"Because of my age? Or the sudden promotion?"

"Both and more." There was a grimness in Captain Os'shye's entire body as he continued. "Morelli sought you out. You're being courted, openly, by Malik Addelia. Addelia works for Morelli. And now I'm placing you in a position that will give you all the information on murders where the bodies are being located near Addelia and places he's been."

"If I'm Challenged, I can handle them." Oddly, she didn't even feel angry about anything the captain said, only cool determination. "I was able to remain professional four months ago. This doesn't change anything. My relationship with Malik has no bearing on my job."

"I'm aware of that, as is Commander Da'kaw and his entire unit. So is the one sending in the orders from the military base." He paused, a smile curving his lips. "I suspect of everyone here in the police service, your security clearance is the highest."

"He isn't wrong, detective." Mc'narrd's voice filled her ear. "Wrap it up for the day. I don't want you and Malik out late."

Chapter Eleven

Malik and she enjoyed a chauffeured ride home in the same marked military HAV that had taken them to their workplaces. A fact that neither minded, since it allowed them extra time together.

No longer wearing the biosuit, Violetta changed into a soft, silk, emerald floor-length sleeping gown. Wrapping a matching robe around her, over the gown, she belted it loosely at her waist. Neither were planning on leaving and Malik had enabled the lockdown features once again.

Malik had cooked dinner again and they'd enjoyed the meal with tall glasses of an Earth-made red wine from his stash.

He was waiting for her in the living room, wearing a matching robe and lounge wear that hid his toned physique beneath the loose garments. A smile formed as he noticed the interface in her hand.

"Can we use your entertainment interface to watch some vids?" Violetta asked, crossing to him. She handed him her police-issued interface. The files had already been pulled up and ready to be played. "I thought maybe you'd be willing to help me out… like you did before?"

"Let's gather some snacks and drinks before we delve into this list," Malik suggested, scrolling through them briefly. "We might as well enjoy ourselves this time around."

Violetta chuckled. "Deal."

"What are these, Vi?" Malik asked as he headed towards the kitchen

"Morelli sent them to us. He came for a visit. Asked to see me, specifically. He's wanting me to investigate the murders of his people. Said he'd consider it a favor."

Malik's movements slowed and he turned to look at her.

"A third person was found dead. Xela Devries. She was discovered at the safe house we used."

"Xela Devries?" Malik repeated. His eyes closed and she watched as his face fell, sorrow washing over it. "Fark."

"I'm sorry, Malik. I didn't realize you knew her," she said, crossing to him.

She brushed her fingers over his cheek. He caught her hand and kissed the pulse point of her wrist before turning her hand back over and kissing her knuckles.

"I didn't know her well, but she was a good person." His eyes met hers. His fingers squeezed her briefly before he released them. "Let's get that food and some drinks. I'll do what I can to help you."

"Let's find this person and put an end to the deaths," she said softly, then brushed her lips across his.

He gave a nod, a small smile on his face. It wasn't a lot, but she'd take it.

***

Ten minutes later, Violetta was reclined on the sofa beside Malik. She hadn't realized the bottom most portion of the sofa could be extended and lifted like a tall footrest. It certainly made it easier to be comfortable.

As they played one video after the next, she couldn't help but laugh.

At Malik's quizzical expression, she explained. "I wonder if I could put in a request for an upgrade at the station? Gotta admit, this is much more comfortable. And having the large-screen interface makes looking for clues a lot easier."

"Probably an entire year's budget." He grabbed a fruit slice and offered it to her. Mischief brightened his eyes as he added, "We could always have viewing parties here. Have Syra cater them."

Laughing, Violetta accepted the fruit and munched it happily. "Could be fun. Think the captain would go for it?"

"I suspect you're going to have to settle for your own two-person viewing parties," Mc'narrd's voice said in her ear. "I doubt the captain would be thrilled with such an event."

"What a shame. We'd keep it all on the up-and-up. Limit the alcohol. Make sure nothing naughty happens in the bedrooms," Violetta teased. As she spoke, her eyes caught the slightest movement in the vidclip. "Pause that, please?"

Malik, in control of her interface, did as requested.

Mc'narrd's chuckle didn't even distract her as she took the interface from Malik. She backed it up a few seconds. "At the corner of the building? Does it look like a person is there?"

Malik took the interface and touched the screen a few times. The image enlarged. He grabbed his own interface and touched a few controls. The screen brightened slightly and became sharper. It wasn't perfect, but it was certainly clearer.

What appeared to be a long-haired being wearing a HAVcycle helmet, with a reflective shield was looking around from the shadows of a building. The front of the helmet was pointed towards the camera facing Morelli's safe house.

"Can you take a stillclip?" Violetta asked, handing Malik the interface.

"Done." His fingers flew over the interface before he handed it back.

She ignored the fact he did the same on his own. Playing the video, they watched as the being moved down the alley.

"Human or mixed?" Violetta suggested. "I don't know a single K'laisian who has a heavy step like that being."

"Some of the actors used to be able to mimic any race with ease," Malik pointed out. "It's not impossible. Just something most K'laisians don't try to do. In fact, it's not even required anymore due to having enough of the other races to fill the parts."

"Really?" Violetta asked, her eyes glued to the entertainment screen. "I remember when we were little almost all the actors were K'laisian natives. They were fantastic at the parts."

"Truly." Malik tossed a drekka berry into his mouth, chewed and swallowed. "I need to take you to more plays."

"You need to take her to more everything," Mc'narrd teased.

"Is there any time you aren't listening in? Or are we your favorite entertainment?" Violetta asked good naturedly. "Maybe I should start calling you 'Pops'."

"That was not nice," Mc'narrd said dryly. "How about 'Uncle'?"

"Uncle… what?" Violetta retorted.

"I can think of a few options," Malik interjected. "Though I suspect I may be Challenged if I utter any of them."

Violetta snickered as the admiral grumbled under his breath.

"How about 'Uncle Me'ngki'," Mc'narrd suggested. "If you're good, I'll send some gifts to you tomorrow under that name."

Stunned, Violetta looked at Malik, who was staring right back at her. It was an ancient title from the days when the clans of K'lais were constantly at war with each other. Long before they began working together and advancing their technology and lifestyles for the betterment of the world. It was given to the men who promised to care for another's child, should the parents ever die before the child reached adulthood.

It had turned into a clan name, then a surname, several centuries after the warring ways of their people came to an end. Those with the name were renowned for being caretakers and healers, continuing the meaning and honor of that ancient word.

Most people weren't aware of the history it was steeped in, but Violetta hadn't been a typical child with a normal parent. She'd loved the history of her parents, of both Earth and K'lais. Subsequently, she'd dragged Malik down the path because it had always fascinated her. Her father's stories about their world's violent history might have aided in that fascination and interest.

"Do I get to call you that, too?" Malik asked, a smirk forming on his face.

"After you wed her, yes." Mc'narrd paused, before adding slyly. "Whenever you manage that feat, that is."

The smirk slid from Malik's face faster than it had formed.

"I'm going back to the vids," Violetta announced. "I am not asking. I do not want to know. I do not need another six hours or more in an eval to gain the clearance needed for those answers."

"Six hours?" Malik asked suddenly. "Your evaluation was six hours?"

"On top of the three from yesterday," Violetta confirmed. "Does yesterday's count?"

"It does," Mc'narrd confirmed. "Nine hours total."

"Nine hours." Malik turned his eyes back to the video. "Nine hours in psych evals."

"Say what you're thinking, bures'o," Mc'narrd encouraged.

"Your clearance just rose," Malik stated, not meeting Violetta's eyes. "If they call you in again, you may actually end up with a higher clearance than mine."

"Is he right?"

"Affirmative."

"Mine's now equal to his, isn't it?" Violetta asked, leaning against Malik.

"Affirmative." There was a pause. "Congratulations on the rise in clearance, Lady."

"Thank you… Uncle Me'ngki." She leaned forward and paused the vidclip. "That's the HAV Morelli mentioned, but there's no plate or number on it anywhere. Do we know where it went?"

"Which vidclip and what is the timestamp?" Mc'narrd asked. Violetta rattled off the information. "We'll try to track it. But as you're aware, the cameras are often not very good in that area. If the HAV was dumped in an area with similar makes and models, it may cause problems."

"Or if this being had an accomplice," Violetta suggested, not hiding the dread in her voice. She glanced at Malik, who's eyes were hard and cold. "Morelli thought this may be a warning or some sort of macabre promise towards you."

"He mentioned it earlier today," Malik admitted. He turned to look her in the eyes. "I swear to you, Violetta, I will not search for this being. On my heart and by my love. I will not do so. But I will help in any way needed to find this being."

"I'm supposed to ask you if you'll come to the station for more questions. But I want some answers before you do that."

"Anything."

"You say that now, but I know the questions at the station aren't going to be easy. Or the ones I may ask," she warned. He shrugged, but didn't look away from her. "Is there anything the three beings had in common? Aside from knowing you and working for Morelli? Were all of you involved in anything? Do something together? Go somewhere together? Anything?"

Malik leaned back on the couch, his eyes looking up at the ceiling. The honeycomb pattern glittered in the lights, reminding Violetta of stars in the night sky.

After several minutes of silence, he shook his head.

"Together? Nothing. I can list off a dozen or so events or protection jobs each one of us were at or worked separately, but none that we were at together as a group."

"If you think of anything that might link you, aside from working for Morelli, let me know?"

"Absolutely." Malik nodded towards the interface. "Shall we continue through the vidclips? Do you have the footage for the others?"

"I have access to anything that goes through a camera that's not on military property," Violetta replied. "That permission came with the promotion, apparently."

"Or someone decided to give it to you so you could do your job better," Mc'narrd mused aloud. "Rather difficult to solve crimes when you can't view the needed footage."

"He does have a point, though." Malik touched her interface to start the vidclip before pulling her closer. "We'll go through these, then start up clips for the others. Hopefully one of us will notice something."

"I have to admit, I prefer this to hard chairs and a room filled with haphazardly stacked ancient interfaces," Violetta commented, snuggling against Malik.

Four months ago, they'd spent hours going over vidclip footage from bodycams as she put her case together against her fellow officers. It had been at the famous munitions expert's lab and she'd been afraid a sneeze would knock everything over.

"I don't think anything would dislodge that setup," Mc'narrd said. "The design isn't by accident, I assure you."

"Good to know," Violetta replied, reaching for a fruit slice. "I suspect we've got the best we're going to get on our suspect. But I want to be certain before we call it a night."

"Agreed."

Settling in for a long night of perhaps one of the most boring parts of her job, Violetta smiled as she munched the fruit. At least this time, it was somewhere comfortable.

Chapter Twelve

The next morning, her mind was still churning over the information that hadn't been found the previous night.

The only possible lead they had was the figure in the still capture she'd sent to Issik and the captain. Mc'narrd hadn't been able to track the HAV that dumped the bodies or follow the driver after the HAV left the area near Morelli's safe house.

Malik had no clue how anyone outside the syndicate could know about the safe house without having actually been there. The mole had been ferreted out and dealt with just over three months ago, according to him. Though he didn't explain what that meant. She wasn't asking, either.

Plausible deniability was something any being could try to claim. For all she knew, the person leaking information to the police service had been Challenged to a Duel and died as a subsequent result.

"You'll be at the arena again?" Violetta asked as the HAV stopped in front of the police station.

"With an escort if I go out for anything," Malik replied. He did not sound pleased.

"You won't have them forever," Violetta reassured him. "At least, I don't think so. You'd have to ask Uncle Me'ngki."

There was stunned silence in the HAV. Someone snickered. Then there was skittered humming. Then the HAV filled with loud humming and laughing.

"I'm so delighted you all find that amusing. Perhaps I should reassign everyone to the task of scrubbing the latrines in the public parks."

Violetta ducked her head even as Malik burst out laughing. She could feel her face warming. She knew her skin was darkening. Months earlier, she'd asked a drunk female soldier if she'd scrubbed the latrines to an extra shine. It had been the incendiary comment that pushed the woman to try throwing a punch. Simply because Violetta and Malik had gone to the bar for drinks, food, and conversation.

"I feel as though I should apologize, sir," Violetta quipped, though a smile was forming on her face.

"Don't you dare," Malik gasped, as he tried to curb his laughter. "I know you don't feel guilty for that comment or what happened after. Don't even try to apologize. For it or using the name."

"And you wonder why I've taken such a keen interest in listening to your conversations," Mc'narrd said in her ear. Humming followed the words. "I'm thankful for the opportunity that was given earlier this year. Without that inciting event, I wouldn't have been able to enter your life. Something your father always lamented the times we spoke."

She knew he was talking only to her, because no one else reacted. The smile on her face grew as the door to the HAV opened.

"I'm thankful for all you've done, sir," Violetta replied. She leaned over and kissed Malik's cheek. "Until this evening, my love. Stay out of trouble."

Still chuckling, Malik brushed his lips across hers in a fleeting kiss. "Or as much as they'll allow."

Giggling, she climbed out of the HAV. Not waiting for her guardians, she headed into the station. They would catch up and she was safer at the station than anywhere else. At least for now.

It was only a matter of minutes before she was abandoning her flower-filled desk for Issik's pastry-laden desk.

"Can we request a new counter?" she asked. "Maybe that will help with all the baskets Syra is sending."

"It would certainly help my desk." Issik glanced at hers. "What are you going to do about those?"

"Once I can use my HAV again, I'll take them home."

"Who's home? Seems like you've got two now," he teased.

She made a face and snatched up an ahvara cake with drekka berries and drizzled with ro'shii nectar. Biting into the delicate cake, she made a sound of utmost pleasure as she chewed.

"Why did I avoid Malik, again?" Violetta asked when she finished her mouthful. "His sister is part of the 'family package', as the humans say."

"Because you were an idiot," Issik teased. "Too stuck on traditions to realize what was best for you."

"I'm not sure these pastries are that good for my waistline, though," she retorted.

"Knowing you?" Issik asked, a brow raised. "You'll work it off in the gym this week or next. Or while hitting the streets to investigate. You're the only one I know who would rather walk the entire length of this city instead of taking a HAV."

Before she could respond, Captain Os'shye stepped out of his office. Moving to the front of the 'pit', he waited for everyone to quiet. It didn't take long.

"It's been brought to my notice that multiple deaths, now identified as murders, have occurred within two days. We have three deaths, two by the same cause of death. All linked." He paused as he allowed the division time to consider his words. "Detectives Ha'kksworth and Detective Cq'linns, would you please take over?"

Eyes shifted towards them.

"The first of the two deaths was a human by the name of Lorenzo Tagliani, an employee of Zane Morelli. The second was another male of mixed heritage by the name of Nicholas En'ingo." As Violetta spoke, Issik was tapping his interface, sending the report they'd compiled to the other detectives. She noticed several detectives were looking at their screens. "A third, a female of mixed heritage, was identified as Xela Devries."

"The first two were located near Master of Ceremonies Malik Addelia's residence." Issik continued, when Violetta gave a subtle gesture to him.

"Lady Cq'linns' suitor," Osing said loud enough for everyone to hear.

"The military has established his location at the time as being in an entirely different sector of the city," Ra'keff added, his eyes meeting hers. "The reports for his location are indisputable, complete with witnesses not related to Detective Cq'linns. Seems her neighbors are rather talkative beings when not questioned about military operations or their personnel."

"So he's not a suspect?" a female's voice asked.

Violetta recognized it as belonging to Valerie Carllio.

"Not unless he can evade an entire military squadron," Osing retorted dryly. "The third body appeared across the city near the lower-income residences. Time of death for Devries was during the time Addelia was in his penthouse with Cq'linns after the attack on her by the Moyii Tsaa."

"I believe we can all accept the fact that Master Addelia would not have left the detective alone in his penthouse. Nor did he evade the military positioned outside his house," the captain said loudly.

"He is, however, someone the murderer appears fixated on," Violetta stated above the chatter.

That brought about a dimming of the voices.

"It's been established that all three beings worked for Zane Morelli. According to our records, though Morelli is suspected of a great many things, he has been found guilty of nothing." She paused for a few heartbeats before continuing. "Thus far. Someone is taking extreme measures to leave the bodies in the vicinity of Malik's residence or a place he was known to visit: such as the housing in the poorer area of our city."

"The only beings who have died have been a human and two of mixed heritage?"

"Correct. Theories, Detective Ty'rett? Or do you have something to add?" Violetta called out.

Aleos Ty'rett, a full blood native with silver hair and eyes, had originally spent several years in the military before turning to the police service. He'd been at the department longer than Issik. They'd only ever talked business.

"Have you checked with our criminal organization division? It's possible the Moyii Tsaa are involved," Ty'rett stated. "They've already attacked you once. It might have been an attempt to continue this string of murders."

"It's not the Moyii Tsaa," Mc'narrd stated in her ear. "A report will be put together by Commander Al'erryn and sent to your team. She assured me the motive for the murders does not fit with the Moyii Tsaa. They prefer to make things personal. Like the attack on you."

Fark. And she couldn't say a damned thing.

"From what I've been told, Detective Ty'rett, the Moyii Tsaa prefer to make their attacks personal. We'll put in a request with the department to cover all bases, but I suspect we'll be told they aren't involved," Violetta replied.

It wasn't a lie, but it wasn't the entire truth, either.

"If the third body was located in the poorer section, is it possible the reason was due to the military presence at his penthouse?" Ra'keff asked. "If they remain in place there, does that mean bodies will be appearing at other places?"

"What places, aside from the arenas, does Malik frequent?" Detective Alec La Croix asked. He moved through the desks until he was near theirs. Reaching over, he grabbed a pastry. "I know he doesn't frequent his sister's bakery."

Alec La Croix was one of the newer detectives who had accepted a package deal with the military. Violetta didn't know what his job in the military had been, but had been delighted to see him. He'd been a good friend from her high school days and they'd picked up as though nothing had changed between them.

When Malik had discovered Alec was working in homicide, he'd immediately invited Alec out for drinks with them. They'd stayed out late catching up and enjoying each other's company.

"I'll have to ask him," Violetta admitted. "While going through the footage from the vidclips sent from Zane Morelli's personal cameras, I discovered an image of someone who may be the being responsible."

"There isn't a lot to go on, though," Issik added. "The being's features are completely hidden by a HAVcycle helmet with a completely reflective shield. The hair is dark, but could be either human, mixed, or of K'laisian color and style."

"Reports returned this morning, stating the being we're seeking wore gloves made of synthetic shark skin," Issik stated.

Violetta slid onto the edge of Issik's desk as he continued speaking. She hadn't checked her interface for updates yet, but acted as though she knew it already.

"According to Master Ki'monl, the gloves would not leave fingerprints of any sort." her partner continued.

"So, to summarize: a stillvid of a possible suspect with nothing to identify them. No DNA or genetics to test. The original bodies may or may not have been placed in those locations. There wasn't a lot of blood loss involved with the first two. Devries was definitely placed at the location she was discovered. They all worked for Zane Morelli. The bodies are being located where Malik Addelia, the Master of Ceremonies lives or has visited. None are native K'laisian."

"That's not a lot to go on," Ra'keff commented. He turned towards the front of the room. "Who's taking point on this, Captain?"

"Detective Cq'linns is taking point. She discovered the connection even before Morelli confirmed it. She and Ha'kksworth will be handling the cases."

Ra'keff's brows went nearly to his hairline, but he remained silent. Osing, Violetta noticed, looked like he was trying to not laugh. He held his hand out towards Ra'keff, who muttered something to him.

Looking around the room, she discovered there was a mix of amusement, displeasure, and indifference. A few looked to be exchanging currency. The captain returned to his office, leaving the detectives to talk amongst themselves.

"How soon can you get that list, Vi?" Alec asked, reaching for another pastry. He'd already finished his first. "Any idea if they did anything together?"

"I asked Malik that last night. He couldn't think of anything they all did together."

"I'll bring it by the station," Malik said in her ear. "I have a few things I need to do outside the office. Want to go to lunch together?"

"Mmm," she replied, looking at the pastries. "I'll try to catch up with him at lunch for that list, if he can't get it here before then."

"Heads up, people!" the captain called out. The talking ceased and everyone looked towards him. "Another body has been discovered on Veslore Street. Cq'linns, Ha'kksworth, take La Croix and Ty'rett to investigate."

"Yes, sir," they said together.

"Meet you there," Alec said, heading back towards his desk.

"Going to give us a lift, Commander?" Violetta asked, grabbing her trench coat from the back of her chair and pulling it on. The gift from the military had been helpful four months earlier, and she'd found herself liking how it fit her. "Or are we on our own?"

Commander Da'kaw hummed loudly. "We'll let you go in your partner's HAV this time. Just don't try to lose us and we won't have to babysit you."

"More than you already are," she teased.

Adjusting her sword and sidearm so they were within easy reach, she grabbed her interface. As the pair headed for the nearest exit, she began touching the screen and pulling up the initial report.

"Deceased is identified as Tiziano Altera." She rattled off the information from the street officers who answered the initial call as she slid into the front seat of Issik's HAV. "Malik? Did you know him, also?"

"The name's familiar. Might have met him once or twice. Think he moved here a year or two ago," Malik replied. "I'll see what I can find out from Morelli. I'll also check with some of the people I work with closely. Maybe someone has ideas on what's going on."

"See you at lunch." Violetta sighed and leaned back in the seat. "There's a link we're missing and I feel like it should be obvious."

"Everything so far is pointing towards Earth-preferred methods used against humans or those of mixed heritage," Issik stated. "There are no real clues. No vidclips. Nothing like what you had when you were framed for murder."

"Earth-preferred methods… someone who's killing from the shadows," Violetta said quietly.

"What are you thinking, Vi?"

"You listening in, Uncle Me'ngki?"

Issik began humming. "There's a code name, if I've ever heard one."

"That was his idea, not mine," Violetta muttered. "Everyone knows Dad didn't have any siblings."

"I'm here, Violetta." Mc'narrd's voice filled her ear and he sounded amused.

"Would Policy Master Zelaya be knowledgeable in methods that human assassins currently use?" Violetta asked, keeping her tone polite. "She mentioned some of her past to me earlier."

"You have the clearance," Mc'narrd replied dismissively. "I'm surprised your father didn't tell you about her first job with her native military. He's the one who helped us after our first argument."

"I never asked," Violetta admitted. "I still don't understand why, if they were such good friends, he never introduced me to her."

"That would be my fault. Until recently, you didn't have the needed clearance to even see me as a stranger," he admitted. "You were quite observant and clever, even as a child."

"Oh," Violetta said quietly. She couldn't argue his comment, even if it didn't make her feel better. "Dad must have hated that."

"More than you could imagine," Mc'narrd said softly. "I'll ask Alyssa if she'd be willing to talk to you about it. She's dealt with the IMD several times since she accepted my sword when I was the commander of the *Laedschot*."

He was referring to the military version of a marriage ceremony, where one K'laisian offered someone the mate to their preferred weapon. It was equal to being officially married in a ceremony of joining, planetside. Or even a human-style wedding.

No documents needed to be signed. Only acceptance of the weapon. Another tradition from their days as warring clans. One the military acknowledged as openly and readily as the more common method of a celebration announcing their intent, often with the exchange of rings.

As far as Violetta knew, every pure blood K'laisian who stepped foot upon a battlecruiser had two weapons: their main choice for Dueling and another, nearly identical, mate. A perfect pair, created together from the same materials at the same time. Perfectly balanced and sold as a set. Even if the being never used the matching weapon in the set, it was custom to give it to whomever they took as a spouse. Or, as K'laisians were called, a mate.

"Thank you, sir," Violetta replied. "Perhaps she will have some unique insight on what to look for during our investigation."

"We're here," Issik stated, stopping his HAV near a marked police HAV. The auburn and blue lights of the marked HAV flashed brightly. Opening the door, they met at the back of the HAV. "Was this one imported also?"

"From the report, it appears so," Violetta stated. "The body hasn't been moved yet. Shall we begin there? Work our way out, as usual?"

"Sounds good to me."

As they waited for the military escort to finish taking up their formation, La Croix spoke Violetta's name. Since the comms were connected, there was no need to yell.

When she looked towards him, he added, "About time you arrive!"

"Not everyone drives as fast as you, La Croix," Issik rejoined.

White teeth flashed as La Croix headed towards them. His voice dropped until it was only in the comm that linked all police service officers. Violetta's comm, unlike most others, also had a military frequency attached to it. Anyone in the military could chime in whenever they desired.

Which is what Mc'narrd took advantage of often with her.

"Ty'rett is getting additional scans of the scene. The body was dropped in a small alleyway between a couple buildings. Looks like it happened sometime late last night or early this morning. Took a while for someone to spot it."

"Why's that?" Violetta asked, as she walked out to meet him.

"Most people don't use the alley. It's barely wide enough for a body. Probably used by kids. Or to park 'cycles."

"I'm going to head over there, see what I can locate with my Gift," Issik said as he approached them.

Giving him a nod, she turned to La Croix as he walked off at a quick pace. "Let's see if we can find someone who used that alley last. Who found the body?"

Turning, they began following Issik at a slower pace.

"One of the neighbors. Said she heard a HAVcycle last night. Thought it was someone who habitually parked their 'cycle at the entrance. When she went out to ask, she didn't see the cycle. She did see the body."

"The being we're looking for was wearing a HAVcycle helmet," Violetta said slowly.

"I hate to tell you, but that doesn't really narrow it..." La Croix drifted off at the end.

"No, it doesn't narrow it down much at all," Violetta finished.

She looked back to La Croix, who's expression had hardened considerably. His eyes were wide and alert.

"What-" she began, just as La Croix shoved her back. As she was propelled away from La Croix, a loud, abrupt explosion happened somewhere behind and elevated from their positions. A hole appeared on the left of La Croix's chest. He grunted, convulsed, and collapsed. A large, ragged hole could be seen in his lower back, next to his right hip. His dark red blood flooded out from the ugly wound.

"*Down!*" roared Issik from somewhere.

She heard his sidearm powering up just before he began barking orders into his comm.

"Medical and Tactical protocols! Police personnel critically wounded, *hot* weapons used on the second block of Veslore Street! All available, scramble immediately!"

"Get out of there, Violetta!" Mc'narrd's voice roared equally loudly in her ear.

Instead, she knelt beside Alec La Croix, one hand above her, forming a shield. She didn't know how well it would work against the human-style weapon that had just been used. But she wasn't leaving her injured officer.

Her father's family had always had strong Gifts. Hers was the ability to form a shield of energy. She'd spent many long days learning to use her Gift. Having been taught by Vrehn Cq'linns, it had been tested to an extreme.

Her Gift had protected her against an attempt from Ziph Rc'dollph to kill her four months earlier. Now she was using it again hoping to protect herself and her fallen comrade.

Touching Alec's neck, she confirmed her fear: there was no pulse. He'd been hit in the chest. Close enough to his heart to be an instantly fatal shot.

"No pulse," she said, her voice stark.

"Get out of the open!" the admiral roared again. "That's an order, detective!"

Another roar like the one that preceded Alec's death rang out and her shield vibrated against the impact.

Well, that answers that question, she thought.

Adding more energy to the shield, she didn't take time to turn and look towards the direction of the attack. Instead, she ran in a crouch for the civilian HAVs. Criss-crossing across the short distance, she kept the shield around her head and upper back.

As she dove between the HAVs, then to the side of the larger one, she crouched low. Keeping the shield above her, she knew it wouldn't last much longer. Being only half-K'laisian, her ability to use the Gift wasn't as strong as what a full-blood native's would have been.

One downside of having a human mother. The other downside being, her mother had died in childbirth. Human women did not survive the births of mixed heritage children as easily as K'laisian women.

Another shot rang out, this time shattering the window of the HAV. That allowed Violetta the chance to turn and look up. Pulling her own sidearm, she ensured it was set to a non-lethal setting.

The words 'excessive force authorized' rang out over the comm from multiple sources. She wanted whoever had killed Alec taken alive. Dying at the hands of an officer was too good for whoever it was firing the weapon.

Following the trajectory, she moved to the side of the HAV. Looking around the HAV, she located the building number. Something moved and she noticed the shadowy form on the rooftop. Another shot rang out and she ducked back with the speed and agility few beings of mixed heritage possessed. Most beings of mixed heritage did not have a military battlecruiser commander as a father, either. One who had put their child through speed drills, honing the child's K'laisian instincts and raising them to higher-than-average levels.

Ricochet from the pavement bounced against her leg.

"Building eight-one-six, rooftop," she said in a voice that was far too calm. She glanced around the HAV again. The shadow she'd seen shifted, then vanished.

"On our way in," Commander Da'kaw said over the comm. "There's a squad moving in from the opposite side. Remain in place."

"Detective Alec La Croix has no pulse, sir," Violetta stated.

A marked military HAV pulled up near her. She darted around the side of the one she was hiding behind and jumped into the HAV.

Leaning back against the seat, she realized her face was wet. She swiped at it, only to realize it was coming from her eyes.

"Report in," Captain Os'shye demanded over the comms. "Everyone! Report in!"

"Alec La Croix is dead, shot to the chest," Violetta said over the comms. "Violetta Cq'linns: alive and well."

There was a hush over the comms before the other officers reported in. They were followed by the military personnel.

Violetta used the sleeve of her trench coat to wipe her eyes. A hand appeared over the front of the seat, offering a handkerchief. She accepted it and used it to wipe her eyes and face before tucking it into a pocket. There was no reason they'd want it back.

"You knew him?" the driver asked softly.

"We were friends," Violetta acknowledged. "Is the scene secure?"

"Repeat that, please, detective?" Captain Os'shye and Mc'narrd's voice spoke at the same time.

"How long before the scene's secure?" she repeated.

"We're on the roof now," Commander Da'kaw reported. "Not seeing anything to reveal someone was up here."

"Look for casings, consistent with Earther firearms from the past," Violetta replied. "I want to know what Alec saw before he was shot. I refuse to allow his death to go without being investigated. Was this a setup? Or an opportunity? Or someone else taking advantage of the string of murders?"

"You sound like your father," Mc'narrd commented. She could hear the frown in his voice.

"Good. That means I'm actually thinking clearly," she retorted. "How long until the scene is secure? Or I'm getting out of the HAV now." Locks clicked and she narrowed her gaze on the driver. "There's no partition between us. I will come over the seat."

"You wouldn't…" Mc'narrd trailed off, then he sighed. "Yes, yes, you would. So would have either of your parents. Though I suspect Kali would have just broken the window."

"How long?" Violetta repeated, her voice growing colder.

"Ten minutes to ensure the shooter isn't in the building, another ten to ensure the immediate area is secure," Da'kaw reported.

"Issik, you're out there?"

"What do you need, Vi?" was her partner's reply. "We're not getting anything from the military boys, other than you're secure in the HAV."

"I'll be out once the scene is secure. One way or another," she replied bitterly. "Go to the rooftop. Use your Gift. There should be a casing or something around there. You're familiar with Earther antique firearms and what they use. If we're lucky, we might get a print off it."

"On it," Issik replied. "Start at the top and work my way down?"

"I'd use the advantage of the height to search the exterior. All the way to the ground. If there's nothing close, come down and search around the house." She paused, scooted to the side door, and looked out. Police service and military were everywhere. No one had been allowed out of the buildings. "Ty'rett?"

"Here."

"Find out who owns the HAV I was hiding behind. Have the HAV taken in. There should be an Earther-style bullet somewhere inside that thing. Locate the one outside on the ground. I doubt that one will be helpful, but we can try to scan it for a print."

"How do you know so much about the weapon used?" he demanded.

"My mother was part of a merc unit before she married my father," Violetta retorted, her voice hard and cold. "The Serpent's Fangs like to visit me. I like to learn.

They've taught me a lot about Earther weapons. Even let me use a few of theirs."

"I thought they used our weapons," someone said. She didn't recognize the voice.

"They do, but that doesn't mean they don't have access to everything else. They enjoyed the fact I wanted to know everything they had to teach me about Mom's planet. Including the weaponry."

"Remind me not to piss you off," the same being replied.

"I'd just Challenge you," Violetta replied, though there was little warmth in her voice.

"Do I need to contact Malik?" Mc'narrd asked cautiously. "Your suit is reporting you as being angry, but otherwise fine."

"Let me out and I'll be happier," Violetta retorted.

"Do it," Mc'narrd grumbled. "Go with her. Whoever was trying to kill her would have been located before now. If they're still in the vicinity, they aren't going to reveal themselves by attempting it again."

The doors clicked, then opened. Violetta hopped out of the HAV. She was halfway to where Alec had died before the driver was able to catch up.

"Thought you were of mixed heritage," he muttered. Violetta glanced at him, a brow raised. "You're faster than most, even those in our military."

"So was Mom. And she was human," Violetta replied evenly.

"Ka'deshed if you aren't right," Mc'narrd said, drawing the words out. "Vrehn taught you well how to concentrate on the situation at hand. To not give into your feelings."

"Lessons learned. Lessons practiced," Violetta muttered. "I had a stark reminder four months ago. Fell apart twice in all this time. Not planning on doing it again." She paused near the blood-soaked pavement. Alec's body had already been removed. A fact she was thankful for. "Thank you, sir."

"Welcome," Mc'narrd replied, not even asking why.

Looking around, she turned towards the roof. "Issik, move towards the edge until I raise my hand." Her partner moved towards the corner of the roof until she barely noticed him. "You have your stun baton?" He removed it and held it up. "Hold it with the edge towards me, then slowly start backing up."

If he had questions, he didn't say anything. Instead, he did as requested.

"Stop!" she exclaimed. "I can just see the end of your stun baton. If it was the weapon he saw, the shooter would've had to be there or closer to the edge."

"Would the baton be larger or smaller than the weapon?" Issik asked.

"Ka'deshed if I know," Violetta answered. "We need a starting point. That'll work just as good as anything."

"I stand by my previous observation," Mc'narrd stated. "You would've been a force to be reckoned with in the military." He paused before adding, "Which is to mean I'm thankful you didn't enter the military even more, now. Your instincts are as good as your parents', but you're also too much *like* your parents."

"Funny," she retorted, though her lips curved up slightly. "There's no way they knew I'd be coming to investigate the body."

"What are you thinking, detective?" the captain's voice said over the comm.

"Maybe the reason we didn't see the suspect leaving the earlier crime scenes is because they waited a day or longer?" She paused before asking, "Do we know if there was, or is, a HAVcycle around here? Or was there something else used that mimics the sound? We need to check that alleyway for evidence of a HAVcycle, as well as the cameras."

"Probably an hour, maybe longer. So far, I'm not seeing anything on the roof. I checked the edge… what's that?" She remained silent as Issik gave directions to someone on the ground. "Spotted something. Not sure what it is."

"Found a casing," a voice exclaimed. "Scanning it now. Will bag and tag without touching it."

"I'll keep searching, but I think whoever was up here grabbed the others," Issik stated.

"Alyssa has said she'll talk to you," Mc'narrd said suddenly over the comm. "Finish up the scene, detective. There's nothing more you can do. Before you argue, you've done plenty, Violetta. At least for now."

Looking down at the blood-stained pavement, Violetta allowed herself a moment of sorrow.

"For now," she allowed. "Meet back at the station?"

"See you there," Issik replied.

Turning, she strode towards the military HAV, her mind going over the events. Whoever had shot at her had just pissed off the police service by killing one of their own.

"Should I expect to see Zh'oros when we arrive at the base?" Violetta asked resigned to her fate.

"Briefly. It won't be another six hours, I promise," Mc'narrd replied.

"Just three," she joked as she climbed into the HAV. "And I was hoping to have lunch with Malik."

"I think Alyssa is planning on taking you both out to lunch," the admiral replied. He paused. "Ah, maybe don't mention the 'uncle' thing to her."

Violetta finally found herself smiling, then chuckling. "Thank you, sir. I needed that."

"Welcome. See you at the base."

Leaning back against the seat, Violetta watched outside the window, her mind going over the recent events.

What was she missing?

Chapter Twelve

The evaluation with Zh'oros was the fastest Violetta had gone through yet. Almost suspicious, she left the medical wing to find Mc'narrd waiting for her in his office. His mate, Alyssa Zelaya, was perched on the desk in front of his console, just a foot from him.

When the door opened, she could tell they were speaking K'laisian. When she stepped into the room, her comm went completely silent.

Blinking in startlement, Violetta stared at the couple.

"Malik will be here shortly," Alyssa said cheerfully. "Surprised at the comm silence?"

"Yes," Violetta replied honestly, moving further into the room and out of the doorway.

The other woman gave her husband a smug smile. "He hates it when I do it. So do our children. But I like privacy. Once I discovered I could order complete and utter comm silence, I took advantage of it."

"Frequently," Mc'narrd grumbled. There was no missing the fact his eyes were filled with warmth and unmistakable love for his wife. "Whenever our children are home, she turns off the comms except for emergency overrides. They act like spoiled babies who just had their interfaces taken away from them."

"Says the biggest 'baby' of them all," Alyssa retorted. Her blue-gray eyes twinkled with laughter. Even as the admiral scowled.

As the door slid open, Violetta turned to see Malik stepping through the threshold. His eyes swept over the admiral and Alyssa before settling on her.

"I heard about Alec."

There was no mistaking the sadness as he held his hand out to her. She stepped into his arms and he pulled her close. His arms tightened possessively around her. Violetta could feel the slight tremble in his arms and body. Alec had been as much Malik's friend as he had been hers.

"Aren't they just adorable?" Alyssa's quipped. "As unique and determined to pave a new path as you and her father."

Violetta turned her head until she could at least see the policy master.

"Stands to reason, though," Alyssa continued, hopping off the desk. "I was the first human to be a mate to a K'laisian native. Among other things. Vrehn broke rules and traditions even before he met Kali. Both continued to do so after they wed. Did you know your mother was the first human armorer for the K'laisian military?"

Violetta shook her head. "It never came up."

"And now you and Malik will be the first mixed heritage couple to be seen in the very public eyes," Alyssa concluded. "Oh, there have been others. But they've kept their relationships rather quiet. Most take careers on battlecruisers. Returning to the planet and settling in a completely different district from where they grew up."

"So, there *have* been other offspring from mixed heritage couples," Violetta said.

She wondered if Malik was going to release her from his arms before or after he was ordered.

Both Mc'narrd and Alyssa laughed.

"Oh, yes! Those born are more human or more K'laisian. The males, if they are K'laisian, even have a Gift. It's rather inevitable. Most couples do not make it public, due to societal pressures and stupid prejudices." Alyssa's lips twisted with disgust. "I do miss that about the battlecruisers. There's nothing like that allowed onboard the 'cruisers. It was a much more pleasant life."

"Less concerning due to fewer Challenges, also," Mc'narrd commented, refusing to look at his mate.

"They all deserved it," she retorted. Her eyes flashed with irritation. "And I lost very, very few Duels."

"Most were terrified when you Challenged them," Mc'narrd teased. "They had to Duel the policy master of my battlecruiser. And it was known *we* Dueled."

"It didn't hurt," Alyssa admitted. Turning to Violetta and Malik, she grinned. "So, shall we go to lunch? I know this lovely little cafe. We can go over everything you've discovered, then I can try to help answer any questions you have."

"That would be wonderful," Violetta said. "Of course, he'll have to let go, in order for me to go anywhere."

That brought about a round of laughter from the admiral and Alyssa. Malik gave a final squeeze before dropping his arms.

"Sorry," he muttered.

"Don't be," Violetta replied, twining her fingers with his. "I'd be doing the same if the situations were flipped."

"That's one thing you'd do," Mc'narrd muttered. "Go have fun. A HAV will drive you." His eyes shifted to Alyssa. "Try to stay out of mischief this time."

The innocence on the policy master's face did not match the laughter in her eyes. "We'll see."

"Now I understand completely, sir," Malik said.

Understanding passed between the men, even as Violetta exchanged shrugs with Alyssa.

***

The restaurant Alyssa chose was near the center of the business districts. It was about equal distance to the emergency services, which included the police station, and the military base. Across the street from the building which contained the eatery was the government center.

Violetta suspected it was a favorite simply due to the centralized location of the business.

Even before the trio entered the building housing the eatery, beings approached Malik or Alyssa. She found it amusing, considering what had only recently happened. Malik kept his arm wrapped snugly around her waist, not moving it as he spoke to those who approached.

Finally, they managed to enter the restaurant.

"And you thought I would be receiving all the attention," Violetta teased him. As Alyssa spoke to a hostess, Violetta slid both arms around his waist. Her laughing bronze eyes met his. "I've yet to see it."

Malik leaned down until their noses touched. "Give it time."

Giggling, she tipped her head back slightly. "Time will tell."

"You two are so adorable," Alyssa commented. "It must drive him crazy when you two are together."

"You have no idea," Mc'narrd muttered over the comms.

"If you will follow me, please?" a pleasant human woman said.

Violetta felt as though the woman were ignoring her and trying to mentally undress Malik. A fact he knew, going by how tightly his arm tightened around her waist. She couldn't blame him. She wouldn't enjoy that sort of attention, either.

The three of them gave a nod to the hostess. Snug against Malik's side, they followed behind Alyssa. Once they were shown to a table along the left side of the room, the woman left.

"I think she completely ignored the fact you had a companion," Alyssa teased.

"She was certainly undressing him with her eyes," Violetta agreed. Her eyes twinkled. "She could have simply asked me whatever it was she was wanting to know."

Malik's eyes glared at Violetta, who batted her lashes at him.

There was a snort, then laughter from the comms.

"That was mean," Mc'narrd commented.

"She's not wrong," Alyssa said, her blue-gray eyes filled with laughter. "Call it revenge or you can cry Challenge, Malik."

Sighing, Malik slumped slightly in his chair. "Fine. I admit I earned that comment."

"We can always Duel later," Violetta cooed, her fingers trailing along his cheek.

"I feel as though I am now the chaperone," Alyssa commented. "Do I need to separate you two?"

"No, Auntie," Violetta replied sweetly, bowing her head slightly. "We promise to behave."

Alyssa's eyes narrowed on Violetta, then shifted to Malik, who wore a far-too-innocent expression. "I believe I may need to have a discussion with my husband later today."

"Oh, hox," Mc'narrd muttered. "I should have known you'd find some way of hinting at that."

"Shall we place our orders?" Malik asked cheerfully, gesturing to the interfaces at the table.

"If only because it may keep you both out of trouble," Alyssa stated dryly. Though the smile and amusement were still on her face.

The conversation quickly shifted to what was offered and what to order. It took less time than Violetta expected. Because she was working, she chose a drekka berry lemonade. Malik had chosen a cider. Since they both wore the biosuits, alcoholic beverages did not affect them nearly as fast as they would otherwise. Malik and she had quickly discovered they had a high tolerance for alcohol at a far-too-young age. The biosuits only raised their tolerance levels to a new height.

So far, they had yet to reach a dangerous level with the suits. A fact Mc'narrd had bemoaned, despite not being able to argue their logic for needing to research it. Biosuits for pure blood natives prevented inebriation. As long as they were worn long enough to cleanse the wearer's blood before the suit was removed. Only in extreme cases did it not work.

Everything had its limits, even the biosuits.

"Oh, greetings, Master Addelia!" a voice exclaimed near them.

Malik straightened in the chair, even as he turned towards the being approaching them. It was a young K'laisian native with silver hair and pale skin wearing a dark blue business suit.

"Well met and greetings," Malik said pleasantly.

As the man approached, Violetta leaned towards Alyssa. "Is this what you and Io'siph contend with frequently?"

Alyssa chuckled. "Unfortunately, yes. It was easier when our children were younger, because few beings want to interrupt a family's time together. Even now, the children deter most beings."

"They're that… formidable?" Violetta teased.

"That protective of their family time," Alyssa said with a laugh. "When Zerik and Lyza are around? I think they have a contest to see how many they can scare off with just an expression."

Violetta watched as Malik said a few words into an interface before handing it back. A pleasant expression never leaving his face.

"I wouldn't know where they would get that from," Violetta replied, a smirk on her face.

Winking at Alyssa, she shifted just enough so she could trail a finger along the curving shell of Malik's ear. Featherlight, Violetta knew it would be just light enough to cause a shiver.

The other woman kept her expression on her face the same. Although her eyes did crinkle a bit more than they had been.

Malik leaned into Violetta's touch. Tilting his head slightly towards her. The other male noticed Malik's reaction. Irritation flashed through his silver eyes until they settled on Violetta. A smirk flashed across his face.

"Lady… Cq'linns?" he said pleasantly. Violetta bowed her head, even as she moved her hand away from Malik. "Well met and greetings."

There was a definite purr to his words. It was all she could do to not laugh. The K'laisian interrupting their gathering was charming. Handsome, even. But Violetta felt nothing other than amusement towards him.

Malik, however, did not miss the sudden interest in her. His eyes narrowed slightly at the man. To keep Malik from saying anything, she leaned towards Malik.

"Greetings and well met," she replied evenly. "Is there something I can assist you with?"

Even as she spoke, her eyes kept shifting to Malik. Not hiding who held her interest.

"Ah, no, lady. I hope you enjoy your meal," the stranger said.

Violetta watched from the corner of her eyes as he gave her a final appreciative look, before bowing and leaving.

"That was so, so naughty," Alyssa finally said, no longer hiding her laughter.

"It worked," she said smugly.

"Never thought you would do something so… overt," Malik said thoughtfully.

"I never thought you'd be jealous," she rejoined. Her eyes shifted to their right. "Oh, look! Our food! I hope…"

Alyssa and Malik followed her gaze, even as a pair of servers approached their table. The plates of food were placed before them, then the pair departed once again. Beverages were settled beside each of them.

Inhaling deeply, Violetta gave a soft sound of pleasure. "I did not realize how hungry I was."

"Amazing isn't it?" Alyssa asked, picking up a fork. "My mate often teases me about it."

Malik and Violetta nodded, having already begun spearing the steamed vegetables they'd ordered. They'd both chosen a type of noodle and protein dish to go with the veggies.

At a nearby table, a group of four beings had been eating their own meal. Sometime between when Alyssa, Malik, and Violetta had sat down and when they had gotten their food, the foursome had gotten sporadically louder, quieter, and prone to giggles.

Violetta glanced over at the other table as she took her first bite. There were two women of mixed heritage, what looked to be a male human, and a female of full K'laisian ancestry. The two mixed women were giggling while looking in the direction of Violetta or Malik. The male was shaking his head while doing a poor job of appearing to be concentrating on his meal.

As for the K'laisian woman, she had her eyes locked in their direction while she spoke in a voice too quiet to hear. Violetta theorized that that particular being was staring more at Malik than her.

She looked at Malik while her fork speared more food. He was chewing slowly, but looking at her. His eyes shifted to the table she'd been looking at, then back at Violetta. He gave a dismissive shrug, swallowed, before smiling at her.

"Should I apologize? If this is annoying or overwhelming to you, I fear the fault lies with me. I did not set aside any time to prepare you for public, um, 'admiration' while out amongst our fellow citizens."

"I'm confident the 'admiration' you speak of is focused keenly on you and you alone," Violetta replied, but she had no malice in her heart or words.

"Perhaps, but give that time," Malik said in a sage tone. "There will be attention of your own to deal with. I am certain of it."

One of the girls at the nearby table gave a loud screech of either surprise or amusement. Malik gave a small sigh. He continued to eat, but began to look at his plate. Violetta decided to do the same, minus the sigh.

Their meal continued for precious minutes in that way. The food was excellent, their beverages on par with what they ate. But Violetta was sure that she'd only managed a few bites before they were interrupted. There was the distinct sound of a chair moving along the floor in haste.

More telling was Alyssa's whispered statement.

"And here we go."

Alyssa's body also shifted in her chair. She was taking up a defensive position to launch from her seat, realized Violetta.

Violetta looked up, her eyes instinctively glancing first at the nearby table. The K'laisian woman, who could barely be in her adulthood, was coming in their direction. She also looked to be the youngest of the foursome. Given the shorter lifespan of humans and human heritage, however, apparent age could be misleading.

In the moments it took the woman to walk over and stop less than a cubit from their table, Violetta realized her own body was tensing up as if a Duel was coming. That almost made her laugh aloud.

"Master Malik Addelia, youngest being to ever become Master of Ceremonies. One of only three to be not full native." The young woman practically purred the words. She did not seem to be inebriated in any measurable way. But her body language and how her eyes were locked at the side of Malik's head were not markers of someone thinking clearly.

To his credit, Malik finished the bite he had before giving the woman a neutral look and asking, "My apologies if I don't recall, but do I know you?"

"Not yet," she cooed. "But you'll be glad once you do."

Violetta realized that somehow her dinner knife had gotten into one hand without her knowing. Also, that she was squeezing its handle very tightly.

"Indeed? Do you have some grand business proposal to bring to my attention? I get so many people coming to me with such." Malik didn't have a hint of curiosity in his voice or demeanor. He kept a level gaze with the woman, but no intensity showed.

The woman hummed while her gaze went to the floor and back to his eyes.

Meanwhile, Violetta was silently commanding her stubborn hand to lessen its grip on the sharp knife. She had her sword at her side, after all.

"I have a proposal but it's not business," the woman confessed. "My friends over there are becoming mated soon. I'd love to discuss how I could arrange a private box for them to celebrate the occasion. Perhaps I could sit down and we could find some manner of barter that would be mutually desirable?"

"That sounds like business to me. The private boxes are overseen by our financial and social coordinators," Malik immediately replied.

Using the hand that was not still stubbornly gripping the knife, Violetta reached across Malik and plucked up his glass of hard cider. She took a long drink from it, watching the woman until she finally looked back at Violetta.

"All other avenues and means of exchange are currently taken," Violetta said dryly while she replaced Malik's glass on the table.

The younger woman stared at her, blinking. Her mouth became a thin, taught line.

"Before this becomes even more embarrassing for you, and blackmail material for your friends," offered Alyssa. "Let me theorize. Since you've shown an interest in our MoC, you looked at the two of us and let yourself believe we were relatives of his. That way, your hopes for a carnal exchange and preferential treatment would remain intact. At least, in your mind. Is that close to your dilemma?"

The woman, who now seemed even younger, gave a single nod.

Alyssa gave a slight nod. "This is not something even close to new for my life experience. So let's see if we can retain a sliver of hope for your dignity. Can you manage to give us a laugh that does not sound terribly forced?"

The woman gave a short, loud hum. Alyssa nodded her approval.

"Wonderful," she said to the woman. "Now if that convinced your friends, then you have this story to go with it. You came over, and gave your proposal. What none of you expected is that Malik has been courting this esteemed member of our police service. The one holding the dinner cutlery and trying not to Challenge you. Once this was brought to your attention, you gave a laugh and wished them both a lovely life together and prosperity. We smiled and thanked you. Also, I would avoid mentioning this moment when you contact the coordinators at the arena."

Alyssa gave a wide smile and nodded. Malik did the same. Violetta gave her best attempt.

The woman nodded, put a smile on her face and turned away. She managed not to hurry back to her own table.

Malik's gaze shifted to the knife Violetta had finally managed to release.

"I am sorry-" he began.

Violetta leaned over and brushed her lips across his. Against his ear, she murmured, "Mine."

When she leaned back, she found heat in his eyes, even as he wore a smirk on his face.

"So, definitely not going to object when I talk to your grandparents," he teased.

She shook her head slowly.

"That is certainly one way to deal with the circumstances you've currently endured," Mc'narrd said dryly. "Zh'oros, I might add, has been questioning the health of you both."

"Oh, just tell her it will all hit when we're both home together later tonight," Violetta quipped, sliding her hand into Malik's. They squeezed each other's fingers. "And she did clear my return to duty."

"Get back to work," Mc'narrd grumbled. "Do you need a separate HAV, Malik? Or are you going with the ladies to the station?"

Malik smiled at Violetta. "It may be best if I don't go with them."

"Wonderful," Alyssa said cheerfully. "Let's finish our meal first. With luck, there won't be any more interruptions."

Chapter Thirteen

Thankfully, no one else approached their table. Their conversation shifted to memories of Alec. Alyssa ordered a round of Earth whiskey and they all toasted their fallen friend's memory. It was, Violetta though, a pleasant way to end the lunch. Especially since Alyssa was returning to the police station with Violetta. The policy master wanted to personally share her knowledge.

Even the teasing from Alyssa about their passionate kiss before departing for their separate jobs didn't bother Violetta.

In fact, it made the trip with the woman even more enjoyable. By the time they were entering the police station, the teasing had shifted to Violetta's dilemma regarding her father's apartment. As they traversed the corridors of the station, they discussed the benefits of living within the city compared to the military housing.

"I suspect Malik wouldn't care if you kept your father's apartment as long as you spent the nights with him," Alyssa teased, nudging Violetta's shoulder with her own. "Though, I'd personally choose his penthouse. My husband was able to acquire a house with a small area we cordoned off when we had children. Being able to send them outside to Duel out their problems was rather helpful."

"How often did that happen?" Violetta asked.

"Almost hourly some days," Alyssa replied dryly. "They began with soft, foam-style weapons. They just beat each other with the weapons until they exhausted each other.

Even now, they'll grab the padded weapons and chase each other through the nature preserve."

"That must have been exhausting," Violetta commented.

"For them, not me!" Alyssa laughed. "I always sent guards out to chase after them!"

Violetta laughed merrily. She was still chuckling as they entered the 'pit'.

"About time you got back," Ty'rett snapped the moment he saw Violetta. "One of our officers is dead because you had to go out to the scene!"

"I'm sorry, but do we need to replay the recording where the captain ordered me to go?" Violetta snapped back.

"Tell him to walk it off," Issik said over the comms. "He's taking the whole thing personally. He originally transferred back to the police service because he didn't believe the military was keeping the streets safe. It's why he refuses promotions. Wants to stay where he 'can be of the most service to his city'. To the civilians."

Violetta suspected Issik was speaking solely to her because Ty'rett was glaring at her while trying to loom over her. It was possible to speak only to one being without others listening even on the police service.

Especially when Violetta knew how to program it to do so and she had shown Issik.

"You could have refused!" he retorted angrily. "Not like your military pals would dare argue with you! Not when you've got someone in your pocket! Probably one of your dad's old pals! What are you doing? Calling them up? Asking for favors?"

"Tell him to walk it off, Vi," Issik repeated. There was definite concern to her partner's voice.

"And now you're here with the world's most renowned and respected Policy Master!" he exclaimed, gesturing to

Alyssa. "You went from working hard to solve unexplained deaths to working against your own colleagues! And now you're working with your old suitor! A mix-breed who works for a criminal! We all know it, even if Morelli hides everything to prevent himself from being caught! Are you keeping his involvement hidden while you schmooze your way up the social ladder?"

"That's the best you can do?" Violetta said calmly, her eyes meeting his with ease. "Take your mewling ass and walk it off, out the door. Perhaps take a dip in Crom's Drop Lake. That'll certainly help cool your heels. I hear Harbormaster Fr'osst is very efficient at plucking people out of the deep end."

Alyssa didn't bother hiding her snicker.

"Mewling," she said, giggling. "That was your mother's favorite word."

"I Challenge you," Ty'rett snarled.

"Accepted." Violetta met his gaze evenly. Unlike the unofficial Duel with Malik, she didn't feel the least bit angry. "Meet me in the gym. I'll get the captain."

"Oh, fark," Issik muttered. "Do I need to send for the healers?"

"Well, everyone is supposed to be examined after a Duel," Violetta mused thoughtfully. "Though, unless the rules for inter-department Challenges have changed, we'll be using sparring weapons. I suppose he could demand actual weapons. If he did, I wouldn't object." Violetta paused, a smile curving her lips. "Care to join me in informing the captain, Lady Zelaya?"

"Oh, I wouldn't miss this for the world."

***

The gym for the police service was not nearly as large as the one at the military base. Nor did it need to be, since a smaller number of beings used the gym. Exercise equipment surrounded the center square of mats. The mats, in turn, were used for sparring and Duels.

The setup allowed those who were on duty the opportunity to view any spars or Duels with relative ease.

Alyssa walked in silence beside Violetta. The two women, in turn, followed Captain Os'shye. Ty'rett was already at the mats, fury on his face.

"He might as well yield," Alyssa muttered. "I'm going to enjoy watching you kick his 'mewling ass'."

Mc'narrd chuckled, but otherwise remained silent.

Captain Os'shye moved until he stood in the center of the mats. Violetta followed until she stood beside him, facing Ty'rett.

"A Challenge has been issued between Lieutenant Detective Aleos Ty'rett and Lieutenant Detective Violetta Cq'linns. Both of the 42nd Police Service of K'lais under the service of Chief of Police Endn Ta'natha. Detective Ty'rett has declared this an official Duel. Do you accept, Detective Cq'linns?"

"I accept," Violetta stated loudly and clearly. "As Challenged, I request the use of sparring weapons, to minimize the possibility of undue death. Per the rules of the police service, set forth by Military High Command."

"Do you accept her terms, Detective Ty'rett?"

"Agreed," Ty'rett replied.

Violetta gave a nod and quickly picked out a sword from the cabinet. It wasn't as good a quality as those at the base, but they were properly balanced. She'd have to ask where she could acquire one like those at the base so she could keep one on hand at the station.

Quickly, she removed the articles that might be damaged or unneeded, including her actual sword. As she held it, an idea sprang to mind. She smiled briefly, before putting the plan to the side. Shoving all but the practice sword into a locker, she pressed her hand against the interface. The lock clicked and she returned to the mats, weapon in hand.

Ty'rett was standing at the center awaiting her, tossing a sparring sword between his hands. As if that didn't make him appear arrogant and anxious enough to get started, he was also bouncing on the balls of his feet.

She strode up and stood opposite Ty'rett without hesitation.

The captain stood directly in the center of the pair, a sparring sword in his hand.

"Interfaces are recording, sir," Ra'keff said from behind the captain.

He and Osing were standing on each side of the captain against the wall.

Captain Os'shye held the sparring blade between Violetta and Ty'rett at shoulder height.

Sweeping it downward, he called out, "Begin!"

Ty'rett flipped the sword to his left hand, then brought it back to attack or defend.

Violetta flicked her wrist at the level of her hip.

The sparring blade smacked Ty'rett on his left cheek and then his right. The flat of the blade made a rough sound. It scraped against his skin both times in rapid succession.

When he blinked to orient himself, she was standing two wide paces away, holding her sword up in what humans called an En Garde position.

"Not an impressive display of your observational skills or instincts," she loudly declared.

The color of Ty'rett's face darkened harshly. He swung his sword across the air in front of him, hard enough to produce a slight "whoosh" sound.

In response, Violetta began singing the song used to introduce Malik as Master of Ceremonies before Duels. Anyone who had watched recent vidstreams from the arenas, or had been to the arenas, was familiar with the tune. She dropped the tip of her weapon to the mat and scraped a line between her and Ty'rett.

He took the bait and lunged at her, tip darting towards her midsection with respectable speed. She danced to his left and smacked the corresponding shin with her blade. He grunted, attempting to redirect his momentum. He swung wide at her with his sword, and found nothing.

She kept right on singing.

It gave Ty'rett a means to discern her position in relation to his, so he pivoted and faced her. Violetta held her sword before her in both hands. Ty'rett nodded once before coming at her again, holding his sword in the same manner.

The blades crashed against each other. Violetta pressed her body in, forcing Ty'rett to use the leg she'd struck as his lead appendage. Her intent was to make sure that if he tried to use footwork of any kind to gain advantage, he'd have to rely on the wounded leg for balance.

Ty'rett played intelligently, opting to instead use his stronger upper body mass and strength to push her back. She hopped back easily, arcing her blade to keep him from moving his sword toward her as she did. The "theme song" reached another round of the chorus, as she had sung non-stop the entire time.

Following the beat of the song, Violetta jumped in the air once, twice, and then spun in loping circles as she bounced. Ty'rett might have thought it was an attempt to mimic the dancers sometimes used on vidstreams to make more of a spectacle of Malik coming to the arena, as he began humming in laughter.

In truth, it was inspired by them, but she knew what the dancers' moves were supposed to represent. Malik had explained it to her, since he hated the spectacle. He had insisted on the moves representing ancient fighting styles of the K'laisian natives.

Violetta had made it a point to learn them since.

On the third hopping circle, her sword smacked against Ty'rett's weapon as her body began to lift in the air. It was a high strike. He reflexively raised his sword to defend his face, neck and chest from a secondary blow. This left his lower body completely undefended as she brought the sword down and up as she came around to land.

The sword struck his crotch with all the force and momentum she'd created. The result was more impressive than Violetta had hoped for.

He promptly clinched, then dropped to his knees. There was a squawking sound, then he vomited all over himself and his weapon. In that order.

"Winner by inability to continue Dueling is Violetta Cq'linns," the captain announced.

No one moved. Not even the captain.

"Anyone else care to issue a Challenge while I'm in a pleasant mood?" Violetta demanded.

No one spoke. Or even shifted.

"Are you certain? We've got the time to waste, after all!"

More silence filled the air.

Good, she thought, turning towards her opponent.

"You want to talk about injustice? Unfairness?" Violetta snarled, staring down at him. "Let's talk about the prejudice you're throwing at *me*. At those who've died. Including Alec who was a friend I cared about."

"Pity I'm not there to witness this in person." Mc'narrd's amused voice filled her comm.

Alyssa's voice came over the comm. "Mute comms, code Manticore Lost. Include Violetta Cq'linns."

The comm suddenly went silent. Violetta vowed to thank her later.

"I'm as much a 'mixed-breed' as those who died because of some sick individual. While we stand here issuing Challenges and Dueling, those people didn't get the opportunity! They died without the benefit and honor of a Duel. You're hating me because I don't spend every farking minute at the station? I spent the entire night going over those vidclips. I didn't sleep until I'd ensured I had nothing more to add to a report."

She pointed the sparring weapon at him. Ty'rett flinched, but remained where he was positioned.

"You and assholes like you are why I avoided socializing! I didn't want to be Matched with someone who considered themselves 'superior'. I've been judged since childhood simply because my mother was human. A far better being worthy of a K'laisian than what I'm seeing now."

There was a skittering of humming and snickering. Violetta noticed Alyssa was standing with her arms crossed, a smirk on her face.

"I spent my life taking down bullies, as well as prejudiced and bigoted assholes. I expected better from anyone who joined the police service. It wasn't Issik who discovered the connection, you idiot." She shook her head. "I've earned every farking thing in my life. My dad didn't give it to me. He made me work for it all, wanted me to succeed and survive. And that's why I didn't just roll over and give up when I was framed for the chief's murder months ago!"

She took a breath. Her face twisted in disgust. No one had moved and the stillness was unnerving.

"You aren't worth a Duel to the death." She tossed the sparring sword down beside Ty'rett, who hadn't moved from the mat. "But if you ever question my loyalty to my job, this district, or K'lais in general? I'll see you in the arena and it won't be with sparring swords."

Without another word, she crossed to her locker, retrieved her items, and stormed out.

The crowd parted before her.

"Well, done, Violetta. Well, done," Alyssa said. "All comms off mute."

"I just made a few more enemies," Violetta groaned. "Is Zh'oros certain I'm fit to be on duty? Because that was incredibly stupid."

"No, Violetta. You may have more enemies there, but you've solidified your position on what you believe," Mc'narrd replied.

"Let's go get a drink after you're cleared," Alyssa suggested, tucking Violetta's arm into the crook of her elbow.

"Another one?" she asked.

"You've earned it. Hox, I'd advise keeping a bottle in your desk, if it were up to me," Alyssa reassured her. The policy master glanced over her shoulder briefly. "To be honest, I want to go back and Challenge him, myself."

Mc'narrd groaned. "Stars and seas save me from short-tempered women."

Exchanging smiles, the two women departed the gym.

Commander Da'kaw fell into step beside them. The rest of the unit fell into formation around them.

"At least you don't have to worry about a brawl this time," Violetta murmured.

"Only because they'd stop the fun," Alyssa retorted.

"Not helping, Alyssa. Not helping." Defeat colored Mc'narrd's words.

"Didn't know I was supposed to, my love," was the policy master's reply.

Laughter filled the comms and Violetta finally felt her body relax.

Chapter Fourteen

When Violetta returned to the station with Alyssa, Ty'rett was studiously avoiding her.

Ra'keff and Osing flashed her smiles. Those who had been transferred from the military were giving her nods and friendly greetings. Several called out to Alyssa, having met her while in the service.

"Gather around boys and girls," Alyssa called out. She paused at Violetta's desk and inhaled the fragrance of the flowers. "I do love a man who appreciates a good courtship."

"I heard that," Mc'narrd commented. "The flowers sent weekly aren't enough? Or are you hinting at wanting more to be sent?"

"I'm not answering that," Alyssa replied, not caring that everyone else except Violetta was only hearing half the conversation. "You'll have to figure it out yourself."

She gave Violetta a wink.

Violetta chuckled. "Do you think I need to introduce you?"

"Not likely," Alyssa said with a grin. She turned to face the room. "I've been requested to come and shed some light on what human assassins are like, the methods they use, and what to look for when investigating these murders."

Silence descended over the room.

"I knew Violetta's parents. I would certainly have accepted an invitation to lunch without a second thought because of that relationship. But my friendship with Vrehn and Kali is not why I am here today." Her eyes swept the room. "I'm here today because you need my assistance and I've been cleared to give it."

"You mean, you had to get the proper security clearance to talk to us?" Ra'keff asked, leaning against his desk so he could face Alyssa.

"My knowledge of the IMD's assassins are rather… personal. It has been kept classified for decades." She paused before explaining, "IMD, for those who didn't pay attention in their classes, stands for Earth's Interstellar Military Division. Does anyone have questions about them? Or can I move on?"

Violetta had never dealt with them, but she knew about them because her father *had* dealt with them. As had her mother and the Serpent's Fangs. Both before and after her mother moved to K'lais.

Earth's military and the IMD were covered in history, governmental, and societal classes. Among others. The police academy also had courses on the IMD, though Violetta knew they weren't as extensive as what the military provided to those in the command program.

"Very good," Alyssa stated when no one spoke. "What I can tell you is the assassins prefer shark skin gloves, synthetic or otherwise, due to the fact they do not leave fingerprints. Inside the gloves or outside them." She shifted the vases around so she could prop a hip on the edge of Violetta's desk. "From my experience with Earth's assassins, and I doubt the techniques have altered much over the decades, they rely on a variety of methods. Wigs and prosthetics and makeup to alter appearances. Masks, helmets, and reflective glasses to hide their features."

"Are you thinking it may be an assassin from Earth, Vi?" Osing asked.

"No, I'm questioning if it's a human," Violetta replied. "How many people would know those methods, Lady Zelaya?"

"More than the assassins," Alyssa stated. "They're common techniques used on Earth. What sets an assassin apart is their use of both high tech and low tech to complete their contracts. They have what are called 'handlers' who assist in getting them in and out."

"You don't have to continue," Mc'narrd said over the comms. "It's been decades, but I know you."

"Your suspect, if it's someone from Earth, or who is familiar with how killers on Earth work, will have scouted his or her target prior to their death. Assassins spend weeks, sometimes months, watching their target. This being has taken the time to plan the murders." Her gaze shifted to Violetta, and she didn't like the apology shining in their depths. "You were not planned, Violetta."

"How do you know?" Issik asked.

"For one, she had the chance to escape. Alec La Croix was not the intended victim. My guess? Whoever is doing the killing, saw her, and decided her death would hit Malik Addelia harder than the rest. She was 'too tempting' to pass up."

"That fits with what we've found," Issik stated. "How familiar are you with human weapons?"

"What do you have?" she countered. He pulled out the evidence bag from a pocket and handed it to her. "You found this at the scene?"

"Violetta advised searching for that," Issik confirmed. "We have a bullet from the HAV, also."

"Could be military or civilian. A lot of ammo is used for both. After humans initiated trade with K'lais, Earth weapons were quickly upgraded to energy weapons. They're more efficient with a longer range."

"So, it's from a weapon over fifty years old?" Ra'keff asked.

"Around there, at least," Alyssa confirmed. "Brings back a few memories."

She handed the bag back to Issik before turning back to the room. "I suspect he may begin fixating on you, Violetta. The profile reminds me of a few people I knew in my past. When their target slipped out of their fingers, they became fixated on them. They would grow more and more fanatic about having to succeed. Be very careful."

"Or, we could use me for bait," Violetta offered.

The resounding orchestra of objections filled her ears: from the comms and the beings in the room.

She held her hands up before her. "Okay, okay! Bad idea!"

Alyssa chuckled. "Go further back on the vidclips and camera footage. Look for someone reappearing frequently. Don't try using facial recognition. Program for height and general frame. Weight can be altered. You can add a few inches to a frame, but if it doesn't match the arm length of physiology, it's obvious. The way a being walks can be altered. But you can't gain an extra foot without it being obvious. This person will blend in, or be trying to appear similar to everyone else in the area."

"Someone who hides their face from the cameras," Violetta mused. "Someone who is alert and watchful and knows where they are, regardless of the location."

"We can cross reference general height and frames. See if people of like sizes appear at all the locations of the bodies," Issik suggested.

"Start with the most recent," Ra'keff suggested. His eyes widened. "You have the stillcapture of that one being. If we use it, and find someone similar in the other locations…"

"We'll have a starting point," Violetta concluded. She turned to Alyssa. "And it *is* a starting place. It may not give us a name, but it's something. With luck, and a lot of work, it might allow us to put together a profile of this being."

"Delighted to be of service." Alyssa gave a slight bow. She pushed away from the desk. "If I can be of any more assistance, please contact me."

"Thank *you*, Lady Zelaya," Violetta replied. "Be well."

"You be careful," Alyssa intoned. "Whoever is doing this is unstable and ill. They aren't going to care who gets in their way. Especially now."

Bowing once more to Violetta, Alyssa headed for the main door. Her body was relaxed, but Violetta understood Mc'narrd's earlier comment. Reliving the past was always painful, and Alyssa hadn't had to do it for decades.

As everyone began discussing how best to divide up the new workload, Alyssa's words continued to echo in Violetta's thoughts.

What had caused her to become the target? Why was this being fixated on Malik?

What the hox were they missing?

Chapter Fifteen

"You aren't too exhausted to go to dinner tonight, are you?" Malik asked, leaning in the doorway to the master bedroom.

She'd been unusually quiet in the HAV on the way to his penthouse. As an effort to cheer her up, he'd suggested they go out for dinner. Somewhere elegant and fancy. Where she could dress up and wear the necklace she'd been ignoring since he bought it.

Staring at her reflection, she wondered how Malik had convinced her to try the outfit on. Let alone agreeing to purchasing it and wearing it now.

The dark sapphire blue underdress was low-cut, criss-crossing over her chest with narrow straps holding it in place. The skirt tapered to an inverted triangle in the front and back, leaving her legs from mid-thigh down bare. The tip of the triangle barely touched her knees. The actual dress, if you could call it that, was just as deeply cut in the bodice and the same shade of dark sapphire blue. The right side wrapped across her chest to button along her waist.

That was all that kept the gown from being overly scandalous to humans. K'laisians had no shame about their bodies or how much skin was shown while wearing anything. The sleeves were snug, showing her lithe figure. Tall, narrow heels gave her an extra two inches and accentuated her calves and trim legs.

She'd never been so glad to have such a trim, fit figure. The dress made her feel unnaturally unclothed.

Her eyes drifted to Malik and the formal clothes he wore.

A long fitted tunic fell to his knees. A wide leather belt embossed with ancient geometric designs wrapped around his waist. A long, flowing, sleeveless overcoat fell around him, hiding his amazing physique which was accentuated by the snug pants and tunic. Black knee-high dress boots completed the outfit.

His dark hair was braided away from his face before falling down his back in a smooth sheet. Her dark auburn hair was free of constraint and fell over her shoulders in almost unruly waves. She felt incredibly self-conscious about it, but he'd requested she leave it loose. The heat in his eyes was the only encouragement she had needed.

Watching in the mirror as he crossed to where she stood, he leaned over and opened a drawer, removing the jewelry box. From it, he removed the necklace. Unclasping it, he slid it around her neck. The gems glittered in the light as it slid against her skin, until it rested just above the valley of her breasts.

"Let's go before I change my mind," he murmured in her ear.

Smiling, she gave a nod. Together, they left the penthouse.

***

Commander Da'kaw grinned brilliantly as he opened the HAV's door, allowing the pair to climb in before joining them in the back.

No words were spoken as Violetta and Malik were driven to the restaurant.

When Violetta stepped from the HAV, she stared at the name glowing against the blue-gray metal.

Ossani's.

Malik didn't allow her time to scuttle back into the HAV. He tucked her arm into the crook of his elbow and continued towards the front door. He didn't even have the grace to wait for Da'kaw. She doubted he cared if the commander followed or not.

A K'laisian wearing a uniform of a black dress jacket, white shirt, and black formal pants opened the door for them. Malik gave him a nod as he escorted them inside the restaurant. A lovely waitress met them in the foyer. A woman of mixed heritage with brilliant bronze eyes, and dark brown hair, she wore a white shirt with a black skirt, dark leggings, and black shoes.

"Master Addelia, a delight to see you. Your party has already arrived. If you will follow me?"

"Malik?" Violetta asked. "What 'party' are we meeting?"

"You'll see soon enough," he promised.

Eyeing him warily as they followed the waitress, she couldn't help but notice everything in the restaurant was of human design with only mild K'laisian influence. Lights at a low setting highlighted the dark woods of the tables and chairs. Bright red cushions covered the seats, she suspected were conforming to ensure comfort for those sitting in them. Crystals carved to appear like candles flickered on the tables, giving them a romantic feel.

The main room was filled with tables and booths. And along the back wall were more booths. On the corner was a curved booth with a round table. Two beings Violetta recognized sat at the table.

"My grandparents?" she whispered in shock. "You… you planned a dinner here with my grandparents?"

"With you in that gown," Malik replied with a smug smile. "Yes." He paused before glancing up. "Your 'uncle' is directly above us."

"I'm going to die now," Violetta stated, her face burning.

Humming sounded in her ear.

"Correction, I'm going to remove the comm and then I'm going to hide in the ladies' room."

"He'd drag you out," Alyssa muttered. "I tried that the first time. *My* husband came into the lady's wastechamber and dragged me out."

Violetta couldn't hide her amusement that she'd used the human euphemism for 'restroom' while Alyssa used the K'laisian term.

"Oh, goodie," Violetta said. "It's going to be a family affair."

"Your grandparents have comms, too," Mc'narrd stated. "You're very lovely tonight."

"Thank you, sir," she murmured as they neared the booth.

Her grandparents stood from the booth. Her grandmother's gold eyes were shrewd as they swept over her. Violetta tucked a strand of hair behind her ear nervously.

"Here I expected to be informed you two had already wed," her grandmother teased, drawing Violetta into a hug. "Not even a ring of promise."

"The necklace is lovely, though," her grandfather, Asden Cq'linns teased, tugging her away from her grandmother. He and Violetta embraced. "Are you still concerned about what people will think?"

"No, Grandpa," Violetta said, smiling at him. "He wanted to talk to you both first."

They both raised their brows, their eyes shifting to Malik.

"Indeed," Laraeda Cq'linns stated.

"Uh oh, someone's in trouble," Alyssa said in a sing-song tone.

"He said he wanted to speak to us before speaking to you," Asden repeated. A smile curved his lips. "A traditional sentiment, but have you spoken to her first?"

"If she doesn't know I'm going to wed her even without your blessing, she hasn't been paying attention," Malik replied evenly. He dropped his arm and wrapped it around Violetta's waist, pulling her closer. "She's not getting rid of me this time. Not even if she tried."

"Good," Laraeda stated. Her eyes drifted up to where Mc'narrd sat above them. "Tend to your own business, you old ghost. We'll tend to ours."

"I'll remember that," Mc'narrd muttered, even as Alyssa snickered. "Keep watch, don't interfere, Commander Da'kaw. Initiate Code Uncle Me'ngki. All cameras off, no recording until further notice. Emergency override for outside contact only."

"Well, if you're going to be generous," Asden muttered. He winked at Malik and Violetta before gesturing to the booth. "We were informed when he intercepted the Fangs."

"Came as a surprise to us," Laraeda added. "But we were thankful when he assured us you were well and watched."

"Did he mention how much he's been watching?" Malik asked as he settled on the bench beside Violetta.

"You put me on the inside," she grumbled.

"The men tend to do that," Laraeda stated as she patted Violetta's hand. "It's to protect everyone else from us."

"Are you trying to make me spew my drink across the table?" Mc'narrd asked.

"That would be an entertaining change," Laraeda retorted.

"I believe I'm starting to understand Violetta more, now."

"Where do you think Vrehn learned it?" Asden commented. "As for how much?"

Her grandparents looked at each other and shared wide smiles.

"The last time the old ghost saw Violetta, she was three." Laraeda wrapped Violetta's hand in hers, even as Violetta stared in shock at her grandmother. "We knew him even before he was promoted. He and your father were so very close. When they each found mates? They became even closer. Brothers in every form but blood. When our world was told of his death, we all mourned."

"So, when he told me to call him 'uncle', it was because he was like a brother to Dad?" Violetta asked.

"Yes," Mc'narrd said simply.

"He couldn't break security protocols for anyone. Not even the child who should have been his niece," Asden explained. "Not when her father died. Not until something of vital importance required someone of a high rank to step in for the safety of our world."

"The Fangs told you what they did, didn't they?" Violetta guessed.

Her grandparents nodded.

"Needless to say, they enjoyed recounting everything that happened. Including seeing you two together," Laraeda replied, the smile still on her face. "They aren't aware of everything, but they deduced enough to know to watch the DA through the old chief's office. But when your uncle contacted us? We knew it was something major. Even if the Fangs didn't have all the information."

"And yet he is still involved," Malik stated thoughtfully. "Because of a familial reason? Or because of something else?"

"Good luck getting that answer from him." Asden's silver eyes met Malik's and held them. "No one holds a secret better than that man. If he's intent on being in Violetta's life? You won't be getting rid of him."

Violetta and Malik exchanged knowing looks. They hadn't yet found anything on her father's console. Though other things frequently happened every time they went to her apartment, they had taken time to look.

"So, enough about your eavesdropping uncle," Laraeda declared, squeezing Violetta's fingers. Her voice brightened as she leaned towards her granddaughter. "Have you thought about what sort of celebration you wish to have? Or would you prefer a wedding, such as what your parents had? Or a combination of both?"

"Gram'ma!" Violetta looked pleadingly at Malik who chuckled. "I've never thought about my own marriage!"

"There is a lie if I've ever heard one," Asden drawled. He leaned back against the booth's cushions. "I seem to remember a little girl, no more than seven, wearing a pretty white dress and spinning around holding a teddy bear."

"Oh, stars," Violetta groaned. She pulled her hand away from her grandmother before hiding behind both hands. "Please do not continue."

"That teddy bear had a name. I'm sure I'll remember it soon," Asden continued. "You had a line of toys, all pretending to be guests. Once you learned 'Raeda kept your mother's gown, you begged to know if you could wear it when you got married."

"I cannot believe you're retelling that story," Violetta bemoaned. "I was seven!"

"And besotted with a fellow student," her grandmother rejoined. "I must admit, it was interesting to learn it was the same student you'd punched in the face just earlier that week."

Laughter filled her ear even as Malik pulled her hands away from her burning, darkening face.

Leaning over, he kissed her cheek, then her lips.

"Are you still going to object when we go shopping for rings?" he asked, delight filling his eyes. "Will you wear it when I slide it on your finger?"

"I believe this is when you give in as gracefully as possible," Asden suggested. "He's never going to give up. And we all know you love him."

"We were actually considering contacting his sisters and discussing how best to Match the two of you." Laraeda's smile softened as the pair looked at her in surprise. "We were going to give you another year or two. But neither of you are growing younger, and she was becoming more and more reclusive. It was concerning. The fact you resolved your differences and are together? I don't think I could say I'm more pleased."

"Remember how Vrehn and Kali 'resolved' their differences?" Mc'narrd asked. Laraeda and Asden glanced at each other before making affirmative sounds. "Same method. Except they prefer swords."

Violetta's grandparents began humming loudly.

"You and Alyssa did the same," Asden said as he hummed. "Still do, I suspect."

"It's a lot less than it used to be," Alyssa admitted. "We've discovered talking works almost as often as Dueling."

"Imagine that," Laraeda commented. "The children are finally learning."

"Had to happen eventually," Alyssa quipped even as Mc'narrd grumbled under his breath.

"But, you didn't answer my question, young lady," Laraeda said, turning her attention back to Violetta. "Even if you don't desire a large celebration, I'm afraid it will be expected. You have many military friends, as well as those at the police service."

"There's also the fact, you will be the mate to the Master of Ceremonies for the arenas in your district," Asden added.

A K'laisian waitress with silver hair braided away from her face approached slowly, menus in her hands. Malik gave a subtle gesture and she continued forward.

"Greetings, ladies and lords," she said cheerfully as she deftly handed the menus to them. "May I take your orders for beverages?"

"No, you cannot get drunk," Mc'narrd said before Violetta could say anything. "You have work tomorrow, and I suspect Malik has plans for later tonight."

"Fine," she murmured under her breath. "Do you have drekka berry lemonade?"

"We do," the waitress exclaimed cheerfully. "Also, it pairs well with almost everything."

"That would be lovely," Violetta said, keeping the smile on her face.

"That's fine for some nights, but not tonight," Laraeda said in a commanding voice Violetta recognized.

"Oh, no," she whispered. "Oh, no. You wouldn't…"

"I am," Laraeda stated, looking directly at her granddaughter. "We are celebrating the intentions of Malik Addelia, the Master of Ceremonies of this district, to Lady Violetta Cq'linns, daughter of the late Vrehn Cq'linns. They have been Promised, and the Match has been approved by her grandfather and I, as well as his family."

The words were as ancient as any Violetta knew. It meant Malik had just requested to wed her. The immediate family acknowledged the pledge of an eventual joining of the families. And everyone agreed.

A formal engagement would be expected, followed by a celebration of joining or the more human-style wedding.

"Congratulations to you both!" the waitress exclaimed.

Delight warred with uncertainty on the woman's features. Malik and Violetta were obviously mixed heritage beings, but her grandparents were natives. And the announcement was pure tradition.

"Thank you," Malik said warmly.

"As such, we will have two bottles of your oldest, best, sa'apip wine," Laraeda stated. Well, demanded would have been a more appropriate word. "We will order our meal shortly."

The waitress bowed low to the table before straightening and returning the way she came.

"You'll need to go shopping soon, Malik," Mc'narrd teased. "Before your lady dies from a fear of being seen in the public."

"That won't be a problem," Malik replied smoothly. He caressed Violetta's cheek. "You did warn me."

"I did." Violetta stared at her grandparents who were wearing equally smug expressions. "Did you have to do that?"

"We could have done it five years ago," Asden stated, his gaze not wavering. "We had the right by tradition then. We could easily skip over everything and declare you betrothed now. Start the ceremony preparations and plan it all."

"You what?" Violetta just blinked at them, unable to convince her tongue to say anything else.

"When Malik spent the night in your father's apartment after the funeral," Laraeda explained. "By tradition, we could have declared you both betrothed. But we aren't beholden to tradition as strongly as others. Your parents were allowed the right to decide for themselves. Ignoring him for five years *was* causing us concern, though."

"You wanted us to get back together," Malik said suddenly.

"Of course," Laraeda said, baffled. "Vrehn was considering asking you if you desired to wed her shortly before he died. He came to us to ask for advice. He wasn't certain of a way to ask that wouldn't sound as though he were trying to force it upon you."

"Or terrify you," Asden added with a laugh. "I told Vrehn if Violetta hadn't scared you off, and he hadn't succeeded yet, then he was going to be stuck with you as Violetta's mate. Either then or sometime in the future."

"So, what sort of celebration are you going to have?" Laraeda repeated.

"Give in gracefully," Alyssa suggested. "They are correct. You'll have a lot of people wishing to be a part of the celebration, even if you have a small ceremony for the official part."

"Is it possible to have one with both our heritages?" Violetta asked, looking to Malik for support. "If we can't combine both human and K'laisian, I don't want to have anything large or public."

"Obviously it's possible," Laraeda replied. "You will need to decide what traditions you desire and then meld them all together."

"Will you help me, Gram'ma?"

"My beloved child, my darling galaxy's heart… I would be honored and delighted to help you."

"I haven't heard that endearment since you were three," Mc'narrd said quietly. "Galaxy's heart. I'd forgotten he called you that."

"I wish he could be here for it," Violetta said softly. She swallowed hard. "He and Mom, both."

"We'll find a way to have their memories involved," her grandmother reassured her. "Will you take the position of uncle, 'Zarry?"

"I'd be honored," the admiral replied.

"Good. That means Alyssa will be taking the position of honored aunt," Asden added.

"Syra can handle the cake and desserts," Violetta added. She scooted closer to Malik. "I can't think of anyone else to handle that part."

"What of his other siblings?" her grandfather asked.

"We have time to ask them," Malik replied, wrapping an arm around Violetta and holding her closer. "My parents will wish to be there, also."

"The Fangs, also," her grandmother added. "They won't care what direction you take for the ceremony. They'll just be delighted to be there."

"Then let us decide upon what we wish to have for our meal, and we'll continue the discussion," Malik suggested.

"Fine, but if I don't go to the gym soon, I'm going to become very cranky," Violetta joked. "I'll need an entire new wardrobe."

"I'm free tomorrow. Would you like to spar at the base's gym? Provided your uncle doesn't mind?" Malik suggested.

"I'll oversee the match," Mc'narrd replied. "You both need someone who can step in if tempers flare."

"Such faith you have in us," Violetta said dryly. She glanced at Malik. "Shall we meet at lunch? We can spar and then go out to eat. Provided nothing comes up, that is."

"Sounds good to me," Malik replied as he opened the menu. Violetta leaned towards it instead of looking at hers. "Shall I help you decide what to order?"

At her shock at the prices, she nodded. "I am never going to become accustomed to your extravagance."

Malik kissed her temple. "That's fine. You don't have to in order for me to spoil you."

There was chuckling from Mc'narrd and Alyssa which accompanied the satisfied expressions on her grandparents' faces.

Chapter Sixteen

"There appear to be extras today," Violetta commented as she and Malik climbed into the military HAV the following morning. "Is there a celebration you haven't told me about?"

"Both you and Malik will be having extra guards," Mc'narrd said through the comms. "I know you have duties as the Master of Ceremonies today, Malik. But it's required."

"Was there another death?" Violetta asked, reaching for her service-issued interface.

Loud humming filled the HAV and laughter filled the comm. She looked at Malik in confusion, who shrugged.

"No, nothing quite as bad as that, though you may believe so," Mc'narrd replied, now humming instead of laughing in a human fashion. "Your grandmother's declaration has become known. Several news outlets are absolutely delighted that the daughter of the decorated late Admiral Vrehn Cq'linns has been officially Promised to the city's Master of Ceremonies."

"Must be a slow news day," Violetta muttered, pulling out the interface, anyway.

Being Promised was just shy of being betrothed. But not by much. The purists would consider them one and the same. Those who were not, would be eagerly awaiting the style of ring she would be gifted. Followed by news of the ceremony.

Malik tucked it back into its sleeve. He pulled his own from a pocket and turned it on, holding it so she could see it, also. News vidclips flipped across the screen. Shots of her beside him at the arenas, all smiles and laughs appeared beside old stills of them at her father's funeral.

"Your grandmother is not the least bit remorseful," Mc'narrd added. "Nor is your grandfather. I explained to them the current events. 'Raeda threatened to Challenge me if harm befell Vrehn's daughter."

"She would, too," Violetta grumbled. "Not sure how well she'd do in the Duel, but she'd definitely issue the Challenge. Rank never mattered to Gramma."

"Laraeda is as skilled as Malik," Mc'narrd replied, admiration in his voice. "I would prefer to not Duel her. She may have picked up a few new tricks over the years."

"Delightful," Violetta said with a sigh. "What a wonderful way to start the day."

"It will only be worse once we make the formal betrothal announcement." Malik pulled her closer and kissed her temple. "Not going to run, are you?"

"No," she said with a sigh. "I'll manage. We would've done this years ago, had Dad lived."

"A fact your grandparents pointed out," Mc'narrd admitted. "They were not pleased to learn someone was targeting beings who are human and of mixed heritage. Said it reminded them of the pure blood fanatic who killed your father. They've contacted the Fangs, again."

"There are worse people to have her back," Malik stated, his voice cooling. "They protected her once. I'm certain they'll do it again."

"We'd prefer they not become involved, but I cannot argue their success rate." He paused. "We will discuss this later. You have a package awaiting you on your desk, Violetta. From your 'uncle'. As well as what you requested from your apartment."

Malik looked at her quizzically. "When did you ask him to do that?"

"Actually, I asked Alyssa last night at the restaurant. When we went to the ladies room together."

"That's what the feedback was for?" She nodded and he laughed. "Your grandmother suspected you two were talking and wanted complete privacy. Your 'uncle' was not pleased."

"There are better methods, but they were safe enough," Mc'narrd allowed. "Have a pleasant day, Violetta. We'll see you in the gym at lunch."

"I'm looking forward to it, sir."

Giving Malik a quick kiss, as was becoming a habit between them, Violetta headed into the station with her guard detail.

"It's going to be awfully boring after this," Commander Da'kaw joked as they entered the station.

She gave him a quizzical look as she stepped inside, only to hear her name being called out, followed by congratulations. Traversing the station took considerably longer as she answered questions and laughed at jokes thrown her way.

"And I don't even have a ring yet," Violetta said under her breath, a smile fixed on her face.

"Welcome to being what humans call a 'celebrity'." There was sympathy in Da'kaw's voice. "Malik's just better at wearing an outward appearance. You've never had to learn anything other than how to talk to people who are grieving or frightened. Or those who want the help you're providing."

"I almost wish the detail would keep everyone away," Violetta muttered under her breath as she moved past the largest throng of well-wishers. "Would make getting to my division easier."

"We could, but that would just alienate you," Da'kaw admitted. He patted her shoulder in sympathy. "Just wait until you're in his private box tonight."

"But I'll be with him, and I'll endure anything to be with him," Violetta said with a bright smile. "Amazing how one person can change a being's perspective."

"The right person, you mean," Mc'narrd and Da'kaw said together.

Violetta laughed, shaking her head as she entered the 'pit'. When she noticed her desk, she frowned. The flowers had been shifted and two long boxes sat on her desk.

"Call it an early betrothal gift from your beloved uncle," Mc'narrd said smoothly over the comm.

She hoped it was just to her. Da'kaw hadn't reacted, but that didn't mean anything. Those who earned the rank of commander learned how to not react to anything. Part and parcel of the job, as humans said.

"I feel like a child at winter solstice," she joked as Issik joined her.

"The only note is signed 'uncle'," Issik said. At her raised brow, he hummed. "You'll find no one more curious and willing to investigate anything than a homicide detective."

"I cannot argue that," she admitted. Removing the note, she tucked it into a pocket. The only word on it was 'uncle' written by a strong hand, with a swirl beneath it. It could have been a stylized 'm'. As she began removing the packaging, she asked, "Anything from COD?"

Issik's skittered humming at the abbreviation for criminal organization division rarely failed to bring a smile, chuckle, or even a laugh. COD, they'd quickly learned was a fish from Earth. After the phrase 'something smells fishy' had been explained, most in homicide agreed it fit the division far too well. As such, it always brought amusement to most of homicide's detectives when it was used.

"I hear you've been promised to Addelia," Ra'keff said from near her.

She looked up to find him, Osing and several others around her desk. "By my grandparents, yeah. They did."

"Laraeda Cq'linns is your grandmother?" Osing asked, his eyes widening. She nodded and shrugged her shoulders. "Congratulations. Better Malik than me."

"Not a fan of my grandparents, Ad'miryz?" Violetta asked, turning her attention back to figuring out how to take the lid off the box.

"I wouldn't want to get on her bad side by angering her only grandchild," Osing rejoined easily. "The lady was an admiral before she turned to politics. Admiral Mc'narrd, peace be with his soul, started on her battlecruiser. My father claims Mc'narrd rose through the ranks just to get his own ship so he didn't have to continue on hers."

"She wasn't an easy commander." Mc'narrd's voice sounded dismissive. "But she and Asden were strong leaders. It's no question why Vrehn was willing to disobey orders if he thought it would better serve K'lais. He got it from both his parents."

"So, you'd be afraid of them and not me?" She glanced at him from the corner of her eyes and saw him wince. "Not the smartest choice."

"I suspect Malik's not afraid of you or your grandmother." Osing's humming grew louder. "Not sure there's anything Addelia would fear."

"Losing her," Ra'keff said easily. Startled, she looked up at him. He gave a K'laisian shrug, tipping his head from one side to the other in quick succession. "He'd be a fool to not fear that. Congratulations to you both, Violetta."

"Um, thank you," she replied, trying to keep the shock from her voice. Her eyes swept the room. "Think there are many here who aren't pleased?"

"Don't know," Osing said dismissively. "Rumors have it there's going to be stronger evals to weed out those with prejudices. Bigotry, racism, racial superiority, and the such. Those who shifted over from the military aren't used to having so many beings who are prejudiced towards the people they're supposed to be serving."

"What's your take on that?" Violetta asked, finally getting the lid off.

"We've been talking," Ra'keff replied, tipping his head towards Osing. "After Ty'rett's behavior yesterday, we're thinking it's a good idea. That mentality is going to cloud how you view someone's replies to questions. You'll dismiss a suspect simply because of your own beliefs that they wouldn't do it for one reason or another."

"We're part of the military. If the main branch doesn't allow it, why does the police service?" Osing added. "Why aren't our service officers receiving the same treatment as those in the military when it's discovered?"

"Someone with a hatred towards humans and those of mixed heritage has allowed the sickness to rot them instead of seeking treatment. Now, they're beyond medical treatment," Issik added, finally joining the conversation. "It'd be interesting to see how many in our department feel the same way you two do."

"Any who objects should be the first on the medical roster," Ra'keff rejoined.

"That would've been you not too long ago," Violetta pointed out.

"It would have gotten me in, but I would've eventually passed." At her raised brow, his face darkened. "Jealousy isn't the same, and even natives experience it. Might've required some assistance from a healer, but I'm not prejudiced towards those I serve. Just sorry I wasn't the one you chose."

Violetta turned her eyes to the gifts Mc'narrd had sent, refusing to look at him.

"Fair," she allowed.

"Who sent the toys?" Osing asked, peering into the box. "We've all been wanting to know what was in it. Though I don't think anyone bet 'weapons'."

"Such narrow-minded beings," Da'kaw teased, moving closer to the group. "Female K'laisians have always loved being gifted weapons and sweets." His eyes narrowed upon the three men. All natives. "You should return to your history classes. Women have always been fierce warriors, willing to fight beside the men. Many times defending their mate when he became injured during ancient days."

"Humans, also," Violetta said, picking up the wide-handled knife.

The sheath was wider than most, easily the width of her palm. The handle had a pleasant texture meant to make gripping it easy.

"Retractable ballistics knife?" she asked no one in particular.

Da'kaw nodded. "A favored item of the military. Has a good range of three meters max. The closer you are to it? The more damage sustained by it."

Setting it back down in the box, she examined the next 'toy' Mc'narrd had sent her. She knew exactly what the fifteen centimeters of cylindrical metal was. Turning so she wouldn't hit anyone, and making certain no one was close, she snapped her wrist down.

The metal parts slid out in one fast movement, clicking into place between one second and the next. Easily seventy centimeters in length, she admired the black metal of the collapsible stun baton.

Though the police service had stun batons, theirs were not collapsible. Her fingers found a button in easy reach of her thumb. Touching it, the baton closed without a sound. There was a second button, which was arched. She knew it activated the energy charge within the baton's handle. It was the same style as used on the department's non-collapsible batons.

"Collapsible stun baton," Da'kaw said for the benefit of the others there.

"And a pair of very fashionable gloves," Osing added, nodding to the black pair in the bottom of the box.

"It helps you grip everything easier," Mc'narrd explained.

"I'll have to thank my 'uncle' the next time I see him," Violetta said with a grin. "It's always lovely to receive such delightful gifts from the military."

"Nothing like a long-lost uncle," Osing joked. "Is he adopting others?"

That garnered humming from everyone gathered around her desk, as well as Mc'narrd.

"Maybe if we had a name, we could ask," Issik rejoined. His gaze shifted to Violetta. "Because it wouldn't possibly have to do with that attack on you at the preserve."

"Yeah, if the Moyii Tsaa are after you, these are going to be helpful. Along with the sword you're wearing." Ra'keff grinned boyishly. "So, what's in the other box?"

"Swords," Violetta replied with a smirk. "Wanna see?"

More humming was her reply.

"Right," Ra'keff said, shaking his head. "Want to know what was learned about that metal bit Issik found?"

"We've also got some profiles that might match that stillclip you took, also," Osing added.

"Let's invade the meeting room again," Violetta suggested. "Did Syra send more treats?"

"We moved those baskets *to* the meeting room," Ra'keff answered. "She sent four today. They arrived with a new jakka replicator. It's in the same meeting room as the pastries. What'd you do? Complain to Addelia about our jakka?"

"If my men are going to be there, they aren't drinking the swill your police service serves," Mc'narrd retorted. "You're welcome for the gifts."

"Not me," Violetta replied. "Shall we?"

There was a great deal of nodding and the group headed to the meeting room. It might not be as comfortable as Malik's penthouse, but she couldn't complain about the company.

***

"You're going to be late," Mc'narrd's voice interrupted the discussion in the meeting room.

The room had slowly been invaded by more and more homicide detectives. Violetta hadn't realized it until Da'kaw had given up on having his own people in the room. They may have originally been drawn in by the pastries and jakka replicator. But the chairs had filled and the interfaces began being used because of the investigation.

Ty'rett had even apologized for his behavior before settling into a chair and helping himself to a pastry. She suspected it was purely for appearances sake, but she still accepted the apology and allowed him to join the discussion.

A fact that hadn't been missed by anyone in the room.

The detectives of homicide had a profile of what their suspect looked like in general. Someone had been seen at the previous locations. All within six standard days of the bodies being discovered. They still had no clues as to the being's identification or how to identify him or her. Even the gender was unknown.

Malik had given Violetta a list of places he frequented, but had also informed her he couldn't give her every place Morelli used. For obvious reasons. So if a body showed up at any of those, it would have to be explained when it happened.

The list was not short, either.

"As delicious as those treats are, might I suggest we all break for lunch?" Violetta suggested. Startlement and blinking eyes were her reply. "It's nearing midday."

"Got plans, Lady?" Valerie Carllio, one of her human colleagues, teased.

They'd all taken time to congratulate her on the official courtship. Of being promised to Malik.

"Actually, yes," Violetta admitted. "I'm meeting up with Malik for lunch."

"Planning on proposing to him?" Valeria's brilliant blue eyes danced with laughter.

"Not today," Violetta retorted with a laugh. "Shall we rejoin here after lunch?"

There were nods from all around the table, even as everyone began standing. Those who were already standing and leaning against the walls shifted or quickly left.

Violetta paused her screen and headed for her desk. With Da'kaw's advice she'd attached the weaponry to her belt earlier. The gloves had been tucked into a pocket. Tucking the second box under her arm, she headed for the exit.

Issik fell into step beside her. "Someone mentioned you were going to the base. A rematch with Malik. Mind if I watch?"

"Not at all." Violetta gave him a sidelong look, even as she smiled. "Who told you?"

Silence and a smirk was her only reply.

"I'll only say it wasn't your uncle," he finally said. As they neared the exit, he gave her a nod. "See you there."

Chuckling, she made her way to the military HAV and climbed in. Opening the box, she smiled as she stared at what it contained.

"Malik will be there, sir?" she asked.

"As I promised." There was a pause. "You're certain, Violetta? Once you do this, you cannot undo it. There will be no going back."

Drawing a deep breath, she let it out slowly. Her body sang with apprehension and nervousness. From the pocket she removed the gloves and slid them on her hands. Like the biosuits, the nanites quickly began removing the moisture forming on her palms. They would work until she reached the base. Better than wiping her hands on her clothing constantly.

"I'm certain."

"Nervous?"

"Very!" she exclaimed with a laugh. "Excited. Nervous. Uncertain."

"Why uncertain?" Mc'narrd asked in a soothing tone. It reminded her of when he'd told her she was safe and to sleep. Was that only four months ago? It felt like an eternity. "Are you worried about Malik's response?"

"I'm uncertain if this is the right choice," she admitted, holding the box and its contents tightly. "What if this is a mistake for both of us?"

"He would Challenge you if he heard you say that," Mc'narrd stated. "No one can answer that question, except you. But you already know the answer." He paused, before adding, "You both could always find someone else. It wouldn't be difficult for either of you."

"I'd rather die than be with anyone else. And I'll do anything, go through anything, to remain by his side."

"Still nervous?"

Violetta blinked. Her nervousness had vanished, but the excitement was still there.

"No. How did you do that?" she asked, baffled. "What did you just do?"

"I talked sense into you using the method your father used with me," Mc'narrd replied as he hummed. "It worked then with me. And it worked now with you. You're almost here. Prepare yourself."

***

For once in Violetta's entire life, she did not stop to stare at the sea glass or design of the base's entrance. Instead, she immediately headed for the gym. The box was left in the HAV, but what it had contained was at her side.

As she neared the main doors, her steps slowed as she recognized the human leaning against the wall, watching the corridor.

"Stella?" Violetta exclaimed, her steps quickening as she neared the woman.

The woman, five foot nothing with red hair and brilliant green eyes, was unmistakable. Not simply because she wore a standard flight suit with her merc unit's symbol on the shoulders. Violetta would recognize the hooded snake with an upper jaw showing sharp fangs and the curling body forming the lower jaw anywhere.

"It is I," Stella replied cheerfully, shoving away from the wall.

The two women embraced.

"Your grandmother told us the courtship is official and all, but Mc'narrd told us about the sparring match you've planned with Malik. Invited us to watch, since he knew your grandparents had contacted us again." Her grin widened as she noticed the weapons at Violetta's waist. "About time you learn to stay in trouble. Was wondering if you'd forgotten how to be Kali's girl."

Laughing, Violetta shook her head. "Just didn't have the opportunity before now. Gotta catch up on missed time."

"Not reassuring," Mc'narrd grumbled over the comm. Violetta thought he was teasing. "Figured you'd want them here for the match."

"Thank you, sir," she replied, tapping her ear for Stella's benefit. "Shall we?"

"Wouldn't miss this for anything," Stella said cheerfully.

The door slid open and the pair entered the room. There were as many, if not more beings this time. As Violetta made her way to the mat where Malik and Mc'narrd stood, she was stunned at how many beings could squeeze into the gym.

Nearing the front, she spotted the rest of the Fangs, all standing in a group near the edge of the mats. When she neared them, Victoria Delacruz stepped forward. Solidly built with honey blonde hair that was starting to silver, classically beautiful features, and steel gray eyes, Violetta thought she was a beautiful woman.

A formidable foe for anyone and the commander of the merc unit her mother had once belonged to.

"Good to see you alive and well," Victoria said, pulling her into a hug, which Violetta returned with enthusiasm. "Now go kick his ass."

Laughing, Violetta removed the extra items from her belt and body. "Will you watch my things?"

"I'll do it," Nathaniel McLeod, the tallest of the group said.

Nearly six feet tall, broad shouldered and muscled, he kept his light brown hair shorn close to his scalp. His dark brown eyes landed on the sword on her waist and he smirked.

Nathaniel moved away from Raymond Schwartz, the last member of the group. Raymond shifted to stand beside Stella, who stopped behind Victoria.

"You can give me a hug later." Nathaniel's blue eyes twinkled as he teased her. "You'll probably need it after the match."

Violetta handed him almost everything, giving him a very human wink, which had them all laughing. Turning, she stepped onto the mat. The moment she stood near Mc'narrd, silence fell over the gym. As she looked at Malik, she noticed Zh'oros standing to the side and behind Mc'narrd. Alyssa stood beside the sovereign healer.

Violetta tilted her head slightly in obvious confusion, but the woman merely smiled.

"I thought we were just sparring," Violetta said in a low voice.

"I sold tickets this time," Mc'narrd teased, laughter in his voice.

The comm in Violetta's ear went completely silent. She tipped her head at him curiously. His eyes shifted to Alyssa, who bowed from the waist, her eyes dancing with pure mischief.

"At least we won't be interrupted." Malik chuckled. "Shall we get our weapons?"

Not trusting what Malik had in mind, Violetta gave a slow nod. Turning, she headed for the cabinet on her side. She caught Stella's eyes and gestured for her to come over. The woman did as requested and Violetta found a sparring sword that felt right in her hands. She handed the sparring blade to Stella, who held it for her.

Violetta removed the sword, still in its sheath from her waist and gave Stella a wink.

Turning, she held the weapon from her waist behind her back and returned to the mats. Malik had not yet returned to the mat.

"You're sure you want to do this?" Mc'narrd asked, his voice too low for most to hear.

Violetta jerked around to face him. She stared at him in confusion. They'd already had the discussion. Unless he was referring to the sparring match?

"Certain," Malik said.

When Violetta turned, she found the man she loved kneeling upon the floor. One knee was bent, the other touched the mat. In front of him he held an open jewelry box at waist height. The ring she'd admired only a couple days earlier glittered inside the cushioned box.

She almost dropped the sword she was holding. It was sheer stubbornness that prevented it. Her jaw, though, was another thing entirely. It fell open until she snapped it shut.

"Will you be my mate, Violetta Cq'linns? My wife?" Malik asked, his eyes on hers. "You are the only one for me, now and always."

Violetta slid the sword from behind her back, flipping the sheath with expert precision until it rested in the palms of her hands. She held it out to Malik, the handle slightly ahead of the blade.

"I will if you will," she said softly. "Forever and always."

The silence was deafening.

Malik's eyes were as wide as saucers. He looked from the sheath to her, then back again.

"You're certain?" he asked, standing in one fluid motion. His eyes met hers again and he spoke barely above a whisper. "You know what it means if I accept the sword."

"I would hope so," Violetta replied, not lowering her voice. She held his gaze, despite the sudden nervousness she felt. In a voice that carried easily within the gym, she spoke again. "Will you accept my sword, Malik Addelia? Will you be my mate? Forever and always." Almost under her breath, she added, "Or do I have to Challenge you first?"

Mc'narrd coughed lightly. From the corner of her eyes, she noticed his lips twitching as he tried to not laugh.

Shaking his head, Malik removed the ring from the box. As he accepted the sword, he slid the ring onto the finger of the hand that had held the hilt.

"I will if you will," he parroted.

"I do," Violetta said, a wide grin on her face.

Turning his eyes to the sword, his brows rose. She knew he recognized it.

Looking back at her, he asked, "Still going to Challenge me?"

"Not today. Today I thought we were going to spar?"

"Are you two going to kiss or what?" Raymond shouted. "You're both half human! Act it!"

Raucous laughter filled the room, followed by loud cheers as Malik shrugged and pulled Violetta to him before kissing her. She melted against him. Someone took the sword and he dipped her backwards in a very humanesque manner.

When he returned her to a standing position and released her, those watching were still laughing and congratulations were still being yelled to them.

Violetta, grinning and feeling giddy, turned to Mc'narrd. "Will you still supervise the match?"

"I doubt it'll be needed, but yes, I will," Mc'narrd replied, a decidedly smug expression on his face.

"You knew he was going to do that," Violetta said suddenly. "Just as you knew what I was planning."

"The smug expression does give it away, Uncle," Malik commented. At the sour expression, Malik laughed. "You did say I could call you that when I wed her. And having accepted her sword, we are officially wed."

"Very true. And yes, I knew what you both were planning. I didn't want to spoil it for either of you, so I made certain the Fangs and your grandparents were here."

Violetta's eyes widened. "My grandparents?" Mc'narrd nodded, still smug. "You told them what we'd planned?"

"Oh, no. I told them what Malik requested I tell them. Your secret, I kept from everyone. As requested... Lady Addelia."

The use of Malik's surname caught her off guard. She knew it was custom of both K'laisians and humans to take the male's surname. It had originally been clan names, and the custom continued when K'laisians began using surnames instead of clan names.

"Ah, can we not tell everyone we're married?" Violetta asked, glancing at Malik.

"We'll announce there will be a celebration of joining at a future time for family, friends, and colleagues." Malik reassured her, kissing the tip of her ear. "Once people see the sword, those familiar with the military custom will guess, anyway. And yes, I do plan on wearing the sword. Even if I may prefer to use mine, I will not ignore the custom."

"Get your sparring weapons, children," Mc'narrd teased. "Your uncle cannot spend all day in the gym."

"Yes, sir," they said together.

Turning, they retrieved their blades from their respective co-conspirators. Stella for Violetta and, it turned out, Raymond for Malik.

It may have not been the solemn occasion Violetta had expected, but she preferred the laughter that had occurred. The mischief and jesting.

They'd never been solemn before, so why do it now?

Turning to Malik, they touched blades at shoulder height, then flipped them downward, touching them again. Each wore grins and determined expressions.

"Kick his ass, Vi!" Stella shouted.

"Give no quarter, Malik!" Nathaniel retorted.

And so began a new and different match. With shouts and good-natured ribbing from all in the gym. It reminded her of the arena Duels, except a lot more fun.

Malik playfully tapped the tip of his sparring sword against hers. He smiled as they circled each other. She wondered if he was waiting for a crescendo in the noise from the crowd around them to properly start their spar.

Not having a care or talent for working an audience, Violetta made her first move. Mostly because she didn't have the patience to wait any longer.

She came in with a hard swing to Malik's midsection, which he deflected easily. Exactly as she'd anticipated. It gave her the opening to make a quick jab at his hip or upper thigh. The intent was to start hobbling him as she had in their last battle.

Except he sidestepped her jab and slapped her blade away. Violetta had to step back to recover. Lest he'd have had an open field against her whole left side. He took the lack of attack to shift his feet, and pivoted the opposite side of his body to face her.

He came at her with a quick series of jabs, alternating which hand held the sword. She had to choose between trying to keep track of which hand held the weapon or concentrate on deflecting each blow. For obvious reasons, she went with the latter. At the moment Malik spun on one heel, she presumed the weapon was in his right hand, which he was leading the full body spin with.

It wasn't.

His empty right hand darted toward her stomach. She reflexively angled her sword to deflect the weapon that wasn't there. When the sword came at her from his left hand, Violetta barely blocked the strike heading towards her own hip. Additionally she had to stumble back to avoid losing her balance. People around them shouted in surprise and anticipation, cheering the fight onward.

On a snap decision to not let Malik continue to lead the fight, Violetta charged forward, arm back to thrust a strike at his torso. Malik came at her, then spun away as her thrust came.

She cut air. Extending her body to harness the momentum, she then easily stepped out of the range of Malik's wide swing. As she came around to face him, she saw he was grinning broadly.

Fark me swinging, he's sizing me up and enjoying it, she thought.

Violetta wondered how well he'd studied his own dancers. She began the same maneuver that had caught Ty'rett off-guard, beginning the spinning hops that would culminate in whirling the sword to sensitive or fatal targets.

She lost sight of Malik in the middle of the second hop. She heard humming from all around her just as Malik came back into view. He'd been dancing around her vulnerable back, and now popped between her arms. He locked her arms with his own, and the center of their bodies smacked against each other. Malik teasingly rubbed the tip of his nose against hers.

She responded by smashing her forehead against the bridge of his nose. A roar of approval erupted from several voices.

He used his chest and arms to push her away. She attempted a strike with her sword, and when that failed, a kick with her right foot. That also failed, and he nearly grabbed her at the ankle. She moved away, but she realized an opportunity to kick him would be much harder in this match. He wasn't letting her use the same strategies she'd relied upon.

For long, exhausting moments after that, the battle continued with neither of the pair gaining clear advantage. She would deflect or dodge his attacks, he did the same to hers.

Violetta felt her training and experience being eclipsed by Malik's, even as it was keeping him at bay. The styles he used kept changing, forcing her to improvise maneuvers or simply push her body hard to avoid being hit. Near misses aimed at her were getting closer and closer. All the while she didn't see any progress on her attacks.

Malik abruptly hopped back, turned to his left side. He made one exaggerated step, then a second, while twirling the sparring sword easily in his right hand. Violetta recognized the pattern as a "signature move" he'd used before finishing opponents in Duels, before and after gaining his title as Master of Ceremonies.

No one had managed a counter to the half turns and odd-angled thrusts that came next.

The screams and cheers were too loud in her ears now, while her brain scrambled for when she'd watched him do this move in vidclips and in person, trying to devise a counter.

He came at her. The first feint and half turn, and she pushed her sword ahead of her to stop the first thrust from striking home.

He would start changing his approach now as a result of how she'd blocked him, Violetta knew. She tried to push her body up against his, lessening the room he had to move around her.

She felt him slide past and begin to start another half turn, this time to her left. She tried to push into him again rather than dodge. His free arm wrapped around her. They spun and then she was moving away from him. Blind to what he might do next.

Glancing over her right shoulder, she saw the tip of his sword coming at her shoulder blade. Desperate, Violetta clumsily jumped away, then hopped at him, her sword held out ahead of her. Malik's blade caught hers as it was descending towards his stomach.

His blade was pushing her blade up and out of her intended trajectory. She knew she would land badly, and would have little chance to recover before he could make his next move.

She came to an abrupt halt.

Malik was two feet away, the familiar smile on his face. His sword was pushed up against the pommel of her own weapon. She couldn't push it another inch. But he wasn't moving either. Just smiling at her, eyes shining in amusement.

She then suddenly realized the room was silent. Confusion crept in.

His eyes moved down between them, then back to her eyes. He did it a second time, adding a slight nod of his chin in the same direction. Her eyes followed it the second time.

The tip of her blade was pressing against the material over his chest. Right at the top of his heart. He'd stopped her, but in deflecting the intended blow, had not stopped it from reaching him.

When her eyes traveled back up to meet his, Malik smiled even bigger and stepped back. He dropped his sword to the floor, and held his arms out to either side.

"Well done, my love. The match is yours! I congratulate you!" he said with genuine happiness and amusement.

It was then that the room exploded in cheers and laughter from everyone else.

"Next time, I'll know how to defeat you," he added in a soft voice, a twinkle in his bronze eyes. "Remember that if you want to Challenge me again."

Violetta laughed and bowed low to him, which he returned.

Her life with him just became even more interesting. There was no doubt in her mind there would be a next time. It was inevitable in their lives.

But she'd make him work for every win, just as he would do the same to her.

Chapter Seventeen

The rest of the day was a blur to Violetta. She'd received hugs and congratulations from the Fangs as well as her grandparents. The Fangs had been hired by her grandparents, though they also promised to be part of the celebration of joining that would occur at a later time. There would be a lot of planning involved and the Fangs offered to help however they could with it. After their current contract ended, of course.

She and Malik had been examined by Zh'oros in the same medical room. Violetta had collected her items from Nathaniel and Malik had hung her sword from his waist. She wore her own, as well as the ring he'd given her.

Afterwards, she'd returned to the station. Malik had returned to the arena. His duties as the Master of Ceremonies were scheduled to run late into the evening and part of the night. Violetta had promised to meet him at the arena later.

No more bodies had been discovered, which concerned everyone in the department. Had the being gone into hiding? Were they planning their next attack? Or had they killed their intended victim, using the others to hide the true target?

The day had been spent going between the meeting room and her desk with visits to COD. Though the criminal organization division had confirmed her initial suspicions, they still wanted to discuss what was going on.

With an ill individual targeting the same group as the Moyii Tsaa, the criminal organization division was concerned someone was copying the cartel's methods. Since Violetta had taken point on the investigation, she was the one talking to everyone. All the while trying to investigate as thoroughly as she typically did.

The latter wasn't going as smoothly as she preferred. She suspected there'd be more late nights in her future. Or perhaps it was due to the lack of clues.

The HAV trip to the penthouse was quiet. The trip up the stairs was equally uneventful. Commander Da'kaw left her inside the penthouse before departing the building. After giving the command for the penthouse to lock down, Violetta frowned. It was strangely quiet without Malik. She typically played soothing sounds at her apartment, but it didn't seem as appealing.

"Play my preferred listening music," Violetta said, turning towards the expansive entertainment center in Malik's living room.

"Acknowledged. Playing now," the feminine voice of the interface said.

Classical music began playing over the plethora of speakers fitted throughout the penthouse, startling Violetta. She hadn't realized Malik had set it up that way.

Heading up the stairs, she swayed with the music. Her father had sent her to dance lessons, so she was trained in formal dances. But she also enjoyed dancing in a more 'freestyle' way. K'laisians were musically inclined. Her mother had been musically inclined. Violetta inherited the ability to dance from both parents.

Her father had instilled a love for it in his daughter. A way to connect with her deceased mother and both heritages.

As Violetta was trying to decide what to wear, the doorbell chimed. Grabbing a robe, she pulled it on over her biosuit. Since she was going to the arena, there had been no reason to remove it. Unlike her night out to the restaurant.

"It's a deliveryman with flowers," Commander Da'kaw stated over the comm. "Proper clearance. We recognize the company and being."

Wrapping the robe around her, Violetta checked to ensure the biosuit wasn't visible. Since it was experimental from the military, she preferred keeping it as secret as possible. No need to let anyone know she had an extra layer of protection to go through to get to her.

The chime sounded again and she called out, "Coming!"

Grumbling under her breath, she quickly descended the stairs and headed for the door. Touching the interface, the door slid open. The delivery man took a step back, holding the large glass vase out towards her. The vase was filled with what she recognized as native turquoise-colored flowers and white roses. She accepted the vase carefully, not wanting to slosh the water in the bulky container.

"Enjoy the flowers, Lady," the man said, bowing his head slightly. "Have a good evening! I've already been paid and tipped." He turned and headed for the lift, looking at a handheld interface as he departed.

Shrugging, she turned as the door slid shut and locked.

Walking to one of the tables, she inhaled the fragrance as she placed the vase carefully on the top.

She took a moment to admire the beautiful turquoise shade of the blossoms. The petals were similar to the open roses, complete with sharp points at the ends of the fat petals. The blue-green petals centered around hundreds of stamens of a slightly darker shade that curled up, reminding her of a small bush in the center of the three layers of petals.

Brushing her fingers over the leaves, she marveled at the velvety texture of the deep purple leaves and stems. The petals of the blooms were as smooth as silk.

Her fingers began to tingle and she rubbed them together, puzzled by the sensation. Examining the flowers closer, she couldn't find anything to cause the prickling feeling. Shrugging it away, she returned to admiring the lovely arrangement.

"They're beautiful. I've seen these before, but I've never had the chance to smell them," Violetta commented. She leaned down and took a deep breath, inhaling the sweet fragrance. "They're so sweet! A little tangy, too. As though someone combined citrus with Earth's hyacinths."

Patting the flowers, she smiled at the soft velvety texture of the blossoms. The palm of her hand began itching. When she turned it over, there were red blotches covering her entire hand.

"Weird. I'll have to thank Malik for the flowers. Wonder if I'm allergic to touching them?"

Laughing, she shook her head. She'd grown so accustomed to having someone on the comms, she was now starting to talk to an empty room!

Taking out one of the roses, she twirled it in her fingers as she headed back towards the stairs, and the upper level. She managed three steps before noticing a halo around everything. Blinking rapidly, she rubbed her eyes with the back of her hands. The heady scent of the unique flowers drifted to her and she frowned. Taking another step, she felt her body tilting to the side. She stumbled forward until she fell against the railing to the staircase. Her stomach churned even as her head spun.

The entire room was spinning and it was not pleasant.

"Mc'narrd? Commander Da'kaw?" Violetta heard herself slurring the words even as she sank to the floor. "An'one?"

"Get Zh'oros on the comms." Mc'narrd's voice was muffled in her comm. "Violetta, listen to me. Stay focused on what I'm saying. What do the flowers look like, Violetta?"

Her body felt thick and heavy as she grasped the railing to the stairs. Clunky, as though the gravity had been turned up to ten times what she was accustomed to it being. She wanted to answer him, but she was having trouble staying upright. The idea of sitting was terrifying for a reason she couldn't understand. She just knew it was bad.

"Turquoise." That was right. "Native. Seen them. Never near them. Sweet. Tangy. With white roses."

She forced herself to focus, which was becoming more and more difficult as her body fought against her. The floor was becoming more and more appealing. Shaking her head, the room spun even more. Her vision was shifting from having a halo around everything to red.

"Get her out now." Zh'oros's voice was loud in Violetta's ears. "Violetta, you need to open the doors. Remove the lockdown."

"Lockdown. Off." Her tongue felt thick in her mouth, but she somehow managed it. Swallowing, she squeezed her hand around the stem of the white rose. The thorns pricked her skin. The pain gave her the needed distraction to say, "Override. Lockdown off."

"Get Malik on the comms. Ask how to vent the air," Zh'oros demanded. There was more, but it faded out before Violetta was able to focus again. "Sweet, tangy smelling turquoise flowers with white roses, 'Zarry. From a florist."

"Kyitis flowers," Mc'narrd said softly. "Farking kyitis flowers."

Somewhere Violetta heard a loud *whoosh* followed by cold air. Her body collapsed even as her vision blacked out. She felt her head hit something hard.

"We're extracting her now," Commander Da'kaw said. His voice sounded strangely muffled to Violetta, but her eyes refused to see anything but a dark red.

"The biosuit is working overtime. It's barely able to keep her alive," Zh'oros said, her voice barely a whisper to Violetta. "Get her here yesterday, Commander. We'll have a room prepped and ready."

"Get Malik. Escort him out of that arena. *Shut it down* if you have to," Mc'narrd ordered. Someone said something, Violetta's hearing had faded out again. As had her vision. "No. His mate is in critical condition. This takes precedence over anything else."

"One would think she's your daughter," Commander Da'kaw's muffled voice said over the comms.

At some point someone had picked her up and was carrying her. She could feel the arms around her. The body was oddly warm. Or she was too cold.

There was a shift and she felt something being fitted on her face. Suddenly, breathing was easier. She didn't know when it had become difficult. The air going into her lungs was cool and crisp. She felt as though she couldn't get enough of it.

"I take care of my people, Commander. This is the third attack on her life. If she were my daughter? I'd be tearing this city apart looking for the one who sent those flowers," Mc'narrd rejoined. His voice dropped considerably in temperature. "Whoever did it better be thankful I'm *not* her father and I'm not part of the investigation."

"Meet me in medical," Zh'oros ordered. "She won't be leaving anytime soon."

***

Violetta had no idea how long she was unconscious. What she did know when she awoke was her head throbbed, the lights felt too bright behind her closed lids, and her body ached from head to toe. The lights quickly dimmed to a low glow, allowing her to open her eyes. Her chest ached. It was even worse than when she'd had broken and bruised ribs.

The air in the room felt incredibly cool and clean. Though the temperature was comfortable, she still shivered under the blanket. When her body began shaking, the blanket and conforming bed began warming until it became a comfortable temperature for her.

This wasn't the first time Violetta had ever been in a medical unit or a diagnostics bed. The lights of the room, she knew, were part of the honeycomb-designed ceiling. They shifted in brightness to meet the needs of the occupant. The beds were always conforming, the hardness adjustable by the healers as needed manually. The blankets were connected to the beds and warmed or cooled to fit the needs of the occupant.

"Vi?"

Violetta turned her head to find Malik sitting near her on a chair. He slid his hand into hers.

She turned her head to face him. Even that took effort.

"Hey," she whispered. Her throat felt as though it had been shredded.

"I thought I'd lost you." The pain in his voice made her heart ache.

"Not yet," she whispered. She squeezed his fingers. A smile curved her dry lips. "Mine."

A ghost of a smile formed on his face. It wasn't very comforting. She was expecting a smile. Not worry and concern. Seeing him in only the biosuit was also unsettling.

The sound of a door opening had her looking to see who had entered. Both Zh'oros and Mc'narrd were approaching her bed. For the first time, Mc'narrd was not wearing casual clothing. He was wearing only his military special ops biosuit. Except instead of the black and purple camouflage, his was black and a silver only a shade or two above the black.

Zh'oros' gaze was on the diagnostics that Violetta knew were above her bed. They typically floated in the air above diagnostic beds in the higher end facilities, military medical wings, and battlecruisers.

"Good to see you awake," she said when she turned her eyes to Violetta.

The dim lighting, Violetta knew, wasn't a problem for K'laisians. The natives of their planet could see as easily in the dark as they could in the daylight. She had better than normal sight in the darkness, but it had never been as good as her father's night vision.

"Malik, offer her some water. Use a straw." Zh'oros' gold eyes shifted to Violetta. At Malik's quizzical expression, she raised a brow at Violetta. "Normally we would advise using ice cubes. But there is a note in her medical records stating she will eat them. Not allow them to melt slowly."

Violetta had the decency to look chagrined. Instead of meeting the healer's eyes, she looked at the bed and tried to play with the wrinkles on the blanket. But her fingers were stiff and ached. The ring Malik had given her twinkled in the light. They'd left it on her finger.

She hadn't realized how much that piece of jewelry meant to her until she saw it.

There was movement at her side as Malik did as requested. When he returned, she suddenly realized the bed had inclined on its own. It must have been gradually rising since she'd gained consciousness because she hadn't felt it shift.

She could breathe a little easier, though. Taking tiny sips from the straw took more energy than she'd expected. When she had exhausted herself with maybe half a dozen, she leaned into the bed. Malik scooted the chair closer to the bed, placing the cup on the floor near him. She noticed he still wore her sword, even if he didn't wear anything else with the biosuit.

"Why the biosuits?" she managed to ask.

"Exhausted?" Zh'oros asked. Violetta nodded once. "I'm surprised you're awake, to be honest."

"As for the biosuits, you're in a clean room. Clothing, aside from bladed weaponry, isn't allowed. The biosuits remove all bacteria and foreign particles as they develop. And though you're in a room to heal, the weaponry would never be refused," Mc'narrd explained, moving until he stood on the opposite side of her bed as Malik. She turned her head to look up at him. "You have pure oxygen being poured in here. A better alternative than the mask you were wearing in the first ten hours."

His eyes shifted briefly to the diagnostics above her bed. Her father had been able to read them, too.

"I feel run over," she managed to say.

"Save your energy, Violetta," Zh'oros said gently. "The blossoms you enjoyed smelling? They're called kyitis flowers. A pleasant flower loved by many K'laisian natives. And deadly to those of mixed heritage. They can be toxic to a human after prolonged exposure."

"And you were breathing in their particulates for several moments, in addition to taking very deep breaths of them," Mc'narrd said solemnly. "If you hadn't been wearing the biosuit, we'd be planning your funeral celebration."

Violetta felt all warmth depart her face as she sank against the bed. The bed and blanket began warming up again. She wondered if either would be able to warm her.

"That was poorly done, Admiral," Zh'oros said dryly. "Do I need to ask you to leave the room and not bring mental anguish to my patient?"

The bed's weight shifted and she felt a warm hand sliding around hers. She looked over to find Malik sitting on the bed, holding her hand.

"Except he isn't wrong," Malik allowed. She could see anger in the depths of his bronze eyes, despite the concern showing on his face. "The toxins inhaled from the flowers burned your lungs, attacked your heart, your vision, your nervous system… and that's just for starters."

"Commander Da'kaw fitted you with an oxygen mask immediately once he extracted you from Malik's penthouse. The reason you're feeling so 'run over' is due to the fact we had to inject you with nanites." Zh'oros met Mc'narrd's glare without blinking. "You are the one causing Violetta distress. Do not make me order you to leave."

"Malik hasn't left your side. He also refused to remove the sword." Mc'narrd raised a brow at the healer who gave a curt nod. "Once Malik discovered you had been attacked, he left the arena and came here. Complaining, I might add, about the slowness of his driver."

"It was rather amusing watching him ignore everyone and everything as though he were a healer and not a civilian," Zh'oros added in genuine amusement. "Already aware of the procedure required for a critical unit room such as this one, he quickly stripped down, not caring who was around."

"I informed Morelli on the way out of the arena, since he is technically my boss," Malik interjected. "He sends his wishes for a fast and full recovery. Has instructed me to take as much time off as required to care for you and protect you, as needed."

"The Fangs, I might add, are livid," Mc'narrd continued, gently squeezing Violetta's shoulder. When she looked up startled, he offered a small smile. "They're aware of the danger the flowers present to someone of mixed heritage, as well as humans. I suspect they're prepared to search for this being themselves. With extreme prejudice."

"Oh, no," she whispered, knowing the mercs wouldn't care if they killed the being behind the murders. They *might* even Challenge the person.

"The penthouse will be cleaned and decontaminated while you are here," Mc'narrd concluded.

"The nanites have to be given time to work," Zh'oros explained when Violetta looked at the healer. "Because you were so close to death, we felt it best to inject you with the nanites. They require time to adapt and learn how best to heal you. Despite being programmed for your specific genetics and DNA."

"Since I know how much you enjoy the topic," Malik teased gently. "The ones you were injected with are now communicating with those in your biosuit. Which means your biosuit's nanites will be better equipped to heal you, but it takes time."

"It also means we have to keep you here, in case of any adverse effects from the nanites," Zh'oros stated, her gold eyes on the diagnostics above the bed again. "As with the nanites in the biosuit, they are experimental. We do not have the technology to have nanites work for any being of any race or genetic makeup yet."

The words were spoken innocently. The healer hadn't even been looking at the admiral, yet Mc'narrd's jaw tightened slightly. He glanced sharply at the healer who met his gaze and held it. Something passed between the two, but Violetta had no clue what it was or if she was even seeing it. For all she knew, she was imagining things due to her exhaustion and foggy-headedness.

"We may never have that technology," Mc'narrd said dismissively. "If we can develop the nanites to where they are able to learn faster and adapt to the individuals, that may have to be enough. As it is, they're learning and working well with our current experimental biosuits."

"One never knows what the future will hold," Zh'oros said simply.

It sounded like an old argument between them, but Violetta had no clue how it involved her.

"Was it our suspect? Or Moyii Tsaa?" Violetta finally asked. Her throat still ached, but it wasn't as bad.

Malik leaned down, grabbed the cup, then offered it to her again. She gave him a grateful smile as she drank more of the cool liquid.

"We have reason to believe it was the person responsible for the other murders," Mc'narrd allowed. "If you behave and stop talking, I'll allow you an interface later."

Violetta made an annoyed expression. Leaning back, Malik placed the cup on the chair's seat.

Exhaustion was a bitch, she decided.

"Will you also be investigating, sir?" she asked in a whisper. Talking any louder hurt her throat.

"No, Violetta," Mc'narrd reassured her. When she looked up at him, he chuckled. "I will admit I am fond of you, and I'm afraid you're stuck with having me in your life. But that does not change the fact this is on you and your department to solve."

She gave a nod, understanding. They had helped only because of the clone weapon four months earlier. Even then, they'd only helped with identifying prints. Everything else had been up to her.

There were so many questions she wanted to ask, but talking at the moment was difficult.

"Does everyone know we're wed?" she asked, looking at Malik.

He just smiled, lifted the hand with the ring, and kissed her knuckles.

"You are being mean to the poor girl," Zh'oros chided. She turned to Violetta. "Malik only said an emergency had arisen involving the health of his betrothed. Then left the arena. So far, news outlets are saying you're engaged." With a brilliant smile, the healer bowed slightly to Violetta. "Congratulations, again, Lady Addelia."

"And you complained about me," Mc'narrd grumbled.

Violetta giggled as she leaned her head back and closed her eyes.

Softly spoken words were the last thing she heard as sleep claimed her.

Chapter Eighteen

For the next day, Violetta spent more time sleeping than awake. Every time she awoke, Malik was sitting beside her. She knew he slept. She also suspected the chair shifted into a small bed just large enough for him to sleep on. Yet, every time her eyes opened, he was sitting in the chair watching her.

He claimed he slept. He even appeared to be rested. No one would say he hadn't slept.

But she never witnessed it.

The second day in the room, she was more than ready to leave. She felt rested. Or, to be exact, rested enough.

Mc'narrd and Zh'oros had even allowed her the use of an interface.

When her comm chirped, she looked up in surprise. Blinking, she said, "Cq'linns."

"Shouldn't that be 'Addelia' now?" Issik teased through the comm.

She frowned, despite the fact she knew he wouldn't be able to see it.

"Not unless everyone was at the gym." Malik cleared his throat, tapping his ear. She explained, "Issik's saying I should be using your name. Thought we were waiting until the public ceremony?"

"Give me a moment," Mc'narrd said in the comm. "There. Now Malik can hear any of your conversations, but not the entire department." He snorted. "Not that he couldn't, considering his clearance level."

Malik chuckled. "Thank you… Uncle."

"You're going to make me regret saying that, aren't you?"

"I don't know what you're talking about, sir."

"What's the news, Issik?" Violetta asked, changing the topic. "I'm still here until later today. Or is it tomorrow morning? Evening? Hox if I know."

"This evening," Malik replied. "Sovereign Healer Zh'oros informed me of the tentative release time while I was preparing for entrance to the room. It depends on how well you react to treatment."

"You're going to want your service interface," Issik replied, his tone grim. "There was another death. It's someone you know, Malik."

"Who?" Malik asked quietly.

"Kazda Vescovi," Issik replied softly. "We both knew her."

"When?"

"Who was Kazda Vescovi?" Violetta asked, watching as Malik closed his eyes and leaned back in the chair.

"She and Malik dated for over a year after he left the service," Issik replied in a neutral tone. "They were… close."

"We were intimate." Malik's eyes opened and Violetta could see the unshed tears shining in them. "It wasn't love, Vi. It wasn't even close to what *we* had before or even now. But it was close enough for me to think it might work. Not knowing…"

"Thinking I didn't want you? Or love you anymore?" Violetta asked, hating the coldness that swept through her. The jealousy that was rising over someone she'd never met. Or even known existed until now. A soft chime sounded and she glowered at the air above her. "Stupid 'suit. Stupid bed."

Her chest ached from her lungs trying to figure out if they wanted to work normally or have her cry.

Stupid body.

"I cannot hate you for finding someone who made you happy. You obviously didn't remain together. And you chose me. But if you try dating or courting anyone now?" Her eyes flared with fury. And she didn't care how her chest was rebelling against it. "I'll Challenge them in a heartbeat. And then I'll Challenge you. You both may need a medbed afterwards, too."

Malik smiled, his eyes softening even as a few tears fell from his eyes. "I love you."

She crossed her arms over her chest, knowing the anger was stupid, but she still felt it.

"You said I was the only one for you."

"Oh, stars and seas save us from foolishness," Zh'oros' voice growled from the doorway. "If you believe him sleeping with another woman means anything like that? You should never have offered him the sword. Just because you remained celibate doesn't mean he had to, child. And now you're getting yourself worked up for no good reason."

"I'm fine," Violetta retorted. "Just irritated."

"Not according to what I'm seeing here," Zh'oros retorted. "You're jealous over his past when he's doing nothing but stay in this room and watch over you. I should have him admitted for exhaustion." Her eyes snapped to Malik. "And I will put you in a separate room, also."

He held his hands up in supplication. "The intimacy was briefer than the time I courted her." His bronze eyes met Violetta's angry glower. "There was no chemistry between us, Violetta. Only lust and mutual loneliness. She met someone else who made her happy, but we remained friends. I wished her well when she chose to wed him two years ago. A native of pure blood."

"She was mixed, like us?" Violetta asked quietly, her arms loosening before dropping to her lap. Malik nodded. "Fark."

"And you are staying until tomorrow morning at the earliest," Zh'oros stated, her eyes still on the diagnostics above the bed.

When Violetta remained silent, Zh'oros crossed to the bed, shot Malik a dark glower, then held her hand over Violetta's chest. Violetta could feel the familiar tingle of the healer's Gift being used and remained silent.

"Breathe deeply," Zh'oros instructed. Violetta did as bid, ignoring the ache from the process. "You're as bad as every commander I've ever had to treat."

Violetta blinked and stared at the healer in confusion. She glanced at Malik, only to find him trying to not laugh. She scowled at him which made him cough a few times before clearing his throat.

Mc'narrd remained oddly silent.

"Stubborn and refusing to admit when you're injured."

"I need to leave today, though. The murder-"

"Will remain uninvestigated *by you* until I release you," Zh'oros interjected, her gold eyes narrowing. "You aren't leaving until I allow it, Lady Addelia, daughter of Vrehn Cq'linns."

Violetta raised a brow, but remained silent.

"Uh oh," Mc'narrd murmured. "Take some advice from me, Violetta. And I'm saying this for the sake of your mental health and mine: don't argue with Keris Zh'oros. Believe me, you *will* regret it."

"Perhaps you aren't aware of how these rooms differ from those in the private, civilian sector." Zh'oros' tone was almost thoughtful. Almost pleasant. And there was absolutely no amusement in her eyes. "You're aware all healers are trained by our military on the bases."

Violetta gave a nod, choosing to remain silent. She had the impression it was safer to not speak.

"Good girl," Mc'narrd said quietly. "You may come out of this unscathed, after all."

"These rooms are identical to the ones used on battlecruisers. Complete with being able to be altered into prison cells as the needs arise. It's easier to train a healer planetside, then send them to a mock battlecruiser or one in constant dock in our atmosphere. It also allows the engineers and every other being who interacts with them ease of access."

Zh'oros gave Violetta a very cool smile that did not meet her eyes. Her gold eyes showed irritation bordering on anger.

Violetta felt her face cool as the blood rushed from it. The healer's eyes flicked upwards briefly. The smile dropped into a frown as she turned back to Violetta.

"There is no way to escape these rooms when they are used as a prison cell. No one even requires entrance during those times. Meals can be passed into the room through the door. I would prefer not having to take such extreme measures, lady," Zh'oros said, patting Violetta's left shoulder. "I understand your desire to leave, but if you are unable to breathe, you will be of no use to anyone. If you have to return to the medical wing here, you'll be of even less use to your department. And I'll never get either of *them* out of my hair."

Malik cleared his throat, earning him another glower from Zh'oros. Mc'narrd was still strangely silent.

"The admiral and Malik?" Violetta asked in confusion. Zh'oros gave a single nod. "They've been that bad? But I've barely seen the admiral."

"That's because he's been in *my* office," Zh'oros grumbled. "Why do you think he's being so quiet now?"

"Could I have my service interface, then?" Violetta asked. "If I promise to stay in bed?"

"I'll have a large-screen military interface brought to you, if you promise to stay here, stay calm, and remember Malik chose you twice-over. Well, perhaps more than that by now." Zh'oros paused before sighing. "I'm breaking protocol, but who hasn't with you two? At least once?" She shook her head. "Every evaluation Malik's had, he's shown he's only ever loved you. That his loyalty to you will always be above everything and everyone else. Think about that and try to behave."

"Oh," was all Violetta could say, her eyes on Malik. "Can he at least sit beside me on the bed?"

"As long as that's all you two do," Zh'oros retorted, eyeing them warily. "Or I will have him removed."

"Promise," Violetta said, her eyes not leaving Malik.

"Good. If you behave, it may just give your lungs time to finish healing properly from being scorched by those flowers." Her gold eyes softened slightly at Violetta's stunned expression. "The nanites are working, but chemical burns are always difficult to treat. Regardless of the race. I'll ensure you receive the interface. Soon."

Turning, she strode from the room, pausing only briefly to check the diagnostics a final time.

"Sorry for being jealous," Violetta said.

"I'm sorry I caused you grief," Malik replied, standing and moving beside the bed. "Forever and always?"

"Forever and always," Violetta repeated.

She held her arms out and Malik embraced her tightly. She could feel him shiver from repressed emotions. She tightened her arms around him, pulling him closer to her. He settled on the edge of the bed and held her tightly. His body shook gently as he mourned a friend. A former lover. His hair curtained his face, but she could feel the tears from his eyes.

And she loved him even more as he held her tightly.

Smiling slightly, she kissed the tip of his ear. He groaned softly, even as she felt his arms tighten. She wasn't the only one whose ears were sensitive to touch. Nor was he the only one willing to bring a smile. To ease the pain of heartache.

Malik gave another tight squeeze before gently pushing her back against the bed.

"My biosuit is also being monitored," he warned, though the heat in his eyes belied the caution in his tone. "Let's not test Zh'oros."

The smile she gave him finally earned a chuckle from him.

Then, her brain caught up with what Issik had said about who had just been found murdered.

"I hate being injured, medicated, and dealing with stupid emotions like jealousy and anger. I can't think straight when that's happening."

"Welcome to being mated to someone you love."

Violetta hadn't noticed Mc'narrd enter the room.

Malik apparently had, because his face was turned towards the door. Her mate shifted on the bed beside her. Positioning himself so he was close to her, he could still get up easily.

Forever protecting her. Always beside her.

The admiral smiled at her and held up a large interface easily the length of his forearm. The width was half the length. She'd seen something similar in the shops that sold interfaces, except those had been mini consoles that required an entire setup and physical attachment to a subnet. Not a hand-held interface with a wireless connection to the subnets.

Especially the police service subnet.

"You are a blessing, sir," Violetta said warmly. She held her hands out for the interface and wiggled her fingers. "The best uncle a girl could ask for."

"You say that now," Mc'narrd teased with a raised brow. He crossed to the bed and handed her the tablet. "Just wait until you meet your cousins."

Malik burst out laughing. Even as Violetta's jaw dropped.

"Goes double for you, Addelia."

That just made him laugh even harder.

"Something got your attention," Issik interjected. "What was it, Vi?"

"She was Malik's girlfriend. The relationship ended…" Violetta looked towards the ceiling calculating the time. "Two years or so ago?" Glancing at Malik he gave a short, quick nod. "Not that long when you consider how long K'laisians and those of mixed heritage live. And she was of mixed heritage, also."

Understanding flashed through Malik's eyes.

"You believe she was killed because this person didn't kill you? Or because they're now trying to remove those especially close to Malik?" Issik asked. "Either is certainly possible. No official word has been released about your health. And Malik hasn't been seen since leaving the arena in a rush."

"Anything different found with this body, Issik?" Violetta asked, knowing her pulse was elevated. She touched the interface and discovered it was already linked with the police service. "The cause of death? The location?"

"The body was located near your apartment."

"How did they manage that?" Malik asked, stunned. "There's military personnel everywhere there."

"She was shoved out of a HAV that sped off the moment the body hit the ground," Issik explained. "It was at the outer edge of the block. But there's only one reason someone would leave one of Malik's ex-girlfriends near your apartment."

"Talk about brazen," Violetta muttered.

"And sloppy," Issik added. "We found a fiber. It's human hair. We're running it through every diagnostic program and scan imaginable."

"Good. Keep me in the loop on that. What about the flowers? Do we know anything about it?" Violetta asked, bringing up the reports that had been sent to her. The screen was large enough she could have multiple reports up at the same time. "Where was it purchased? How did someone manage to deliver a flower known to be toxic to someone of mixed heritage to Malik's penthouse?"

"It isn't as though my heritage isn't renowned," Malik admitted. "Part of the reason I'm popular, as the humans say, is *due* to my mixed heritage. It's one of the reasons Morelli put me front and center as Master of Ceremonies. I could easily represent both humans and K'laisians, as well as any other race."

"I still missed out on seeing you at the main arena," Violetta grumbled. "I should Challenge whoever is doing this for that intrusion, alone."

Mc'narrd chuckled even as Issik's humming filled the comm.

"The flower arrangement was bought and paid for in currency at the store," Mc'narrd stated. "They were then dropped off at a local delivery service. It's how Da'kaw recognized the delivery person. The commander, I might add, was unaware of what the flowers were, otherwise he would have intervened. That particular delivery man is frequently used to deliver on base as well as the government center. The florist was told the arrangement was for a native K'laisian. The delivery person needed medical assistance when he found out what happened. They were simply paid to deliver it to Malik's penthouse."

"Not everyone is aware of how toxic the plant is for those of mixed heritage," Issik added. "Though, I suspect that will change once it becomes known to the public what happened."

"How do they not know already?" Violetta asked. "Is the captain staying silent on everything?"

"*We* are staying silent on everything," Mc'narrd interjected. "Until you are released from here, the military won't answer any questions as to what happened or by whom. Nor will there be an official statement until after you're released. It's standard procedure." He paused a moment before adding, "Or unless a statement is made by your mate or immediate family members."

Violetta tipped her head to the side. "Then how did you know I was well enough to talk, Issik?"

"I was notified that your comm was available. So I called."

That made sense. It wasn't as though beings in the medical wing of the base weren't allowed visitors. And her comm wouldn't have been kept turned off forever.

Violetta chuckled. "I suppose one way of making certain people are aware I'm alive and well is by going with Malik to the arena. Seems everyone in the city pays attention to that."

"Close enough. I don't think there's a lot of hermits left," Issik replied dryly. "Try to not annoy the healers more than you already have. We'd like you out sometime soon."

"Acknowledged," Violetta replied. She paused in the scrolling. "Do me a favor, Issik?"

"Anything you need, I'll do it if I can," he promised.

"Aww, he's so sweet," Mc'narrd teased. "Surprised he didn't try for your hand."

She glowered at him. Mc'narrd just grinned.

"Check in with Criminal Organization. Ask if they recognize anything we've got on the profile. Find out if the Moyii Tsaa cartel or any other group uses those flowers, that shop, has a presence of any sort in that area. See if anyone who even associates with the Moyii Tsaa fits the outline we've got."

"I'm certain Ty'rett will be delighted you're 'seeing reason'. He's still muttering under his breath thinking it's the cartel," Issik replied.

"I don't believe it's them, simply because they'd never do anything as dishonorable as using flowers. It would be too easy for the flowers to be intercepted." Violetta shook her head. "Doesn't mean it isn't someone trying to pin the blame on them. Maybe if we give the appearance we're doing exactly that, we can convince whoever is behind this to make another mistake."

"When did you become so devious?" Issik asked. "You're changing, Violence. Just not sure if it's for the better."

"I think she's only going to improve," Malik said, finally speaking up. "You weren't around her father. He'd give you a headache with all the scenarios he'd come up with for a single situation."

"I hope you're right, Addelia. Issik out."

"Do I get to keep this?" Violetta joked as she propped her legs up and settled the interface against her thighs. "It's so fast and big!"

"I'll make you a deal," Mc'narrd said slowly. She looked up at him, her head tilted to the side. She didn't hide the curiosity she felt. "You behave. You don't anger any healer or medic that comes into this room. *And* you decide where you plan on living. Malik's penthouse or your father's apartment. Give me that decision, and I'll give you the interface to keep." Mc'narrd's gaze shifted to Malik. "You know what comes with having that interface at your penthouse. We've discussed it. Now you both have to decide if it's worth it."

"If she desires to have it at the penthouse, I have an office set aside for it. I'm certain your team investigated it when you decontaminated and cleaned the penthouse." Malik raised his brows at the admiral. "Did it meet with your personal approval, *uncle*?"

"Wait… you already have an office ready for Dad's console? Just like that? But… that would mean…"

"I was going to eventually contact you," Malik admitted, with a shrug. "After Kazda, I realized there would never be anyone else and I didn't want to live a life alone. Figured I'd find a way to contact you that didn't seem like I was stalking you." He glowered at the admiral. "I didn't see a point in telling you everything. And I never expected our relationship to be encouraged so much or for it to go so fast."

"He is rather interfering, isn't he?" Violetta teased. "Could you imagine what Dad would've been like?"

"I'm still debating if he would've told us to Duel it out until we were exhausted or just declared us mates before the entire world," Malik admitted.

"With Vrehn, it's impossible to say," Mc'narrd agreed.

"Not really," Violetta argued. When the men looked at her in surprise, she grinned. "He would've done both. The true question is which he would have done first."

J.F. Posthumus

Chapter Nineteen

The following morning, Zh'oros and Mc'narrd arrived in her room together. Violetta remained silent as the healer examined her.

"I would prefer releasing you on the recommendation of no strenuous activity for a few more days." Her gold eyes shifted to Malik before turning back to her. "But I know how impossible that would be to enforce once you're outside this room."

Violetta remained silent. She even kept her expression neutral.

"Define 'strenuous'," Malik joked. At Zh'oros' dark glower, he chuckled. "She wasn't going to say it."

"Because *she* wants to leave," Mc'narrd remarked. "Careful, Addelia. Zh'oros might decide to keep *you* here."

"I'd have to turn the room into a prison cell," Zh'oros muttered darkly. She shook her head. "And change the commands to unlock the room. He had gone that far in the training."

There was a decidedly smug expression on his face.

"So, I'm being released?" Violetta asked, keeping the hopefulness she felt from her voice. She turned to Mc'narrd, who was chuckling. "I can return to work?"

"Don't know why you're looking at me," Mc'narrd retorted. "I'm not the healer."

"Yes, you can return to work," Zh'oros stated, glancing up at the diagnostics above the bed briefly. "Stay away from kyitis flowers and you should be fine."

"Thank you!" she all but squealed. Looking at Malik, she asked, "You did bring me clothes, right?"

"She does seem a bit eager to leave," Mc'narrd commented. "Have you made a decision about your father's console?"

A smile flashed across Violetta's face. "We're going to request it be moved to his penthouse. With your permission, I think it would be better to have it where I'll be living. After the official announcement and joining celebration, I'll be moving in permanently."

"I'll begin the preparations," Mc'narrd said with a nod. "It'll take some time to have it done properly. Which is why I wanted to know now. With you not at the apartment, we've had to leave a guard detail there constantly. This will make everyone's lives easier."

"Be safe, be well, Violetta," Zh'oros said, a smile on her face. "Try not to need my services as often, hmm?"

"May I ask you and the admiral a question?" Violetta asked.

Zh'oros glanced at Mc'narrd, something passed between them, but they both nodded.

"The police service is an extension of the military." The pair nodded, though they remained silent. Violetta continued after a moment. "Yet, the military does not allow prejudices such as racial superiority, racism, bigotry, xenophobia, and the list goes on and on. Those who are discovered to have such are given dishonorable discharges, if they're career military, and extensive treatment. If it's discovered when they enter their one year of required service, they're treated prior to serving their year."

"Or during that first year," Malik interjected. "It depends on the extensiveness and the illness the being is suffering from."

"All accurate," Zh'oros allowed, tipping her head to the side in curiosity. "If you ever wish to continue your training, Malik, come find me. It can be arranged."

Malik merely bowed, a smile on his face.

"Yet, you can find all of that in the police service," Violetta stated in a flat tone. Zh'oros' eyes narrowed upon Violetta. "It isn't always hidden. Why is it allowed there, but not within the military?"

"It should not be found with any who serve," Zh'oros stated in a bland tone. "May they be in the police service or the military itself. The healers for the police service have been decidedly negligent."

"Just as we were with the corruption," Mc'narrd mused. His gaze shifted to Zh'oros. "It seems perhaps the military should be taking a more thorough interest in all aspects of the police services."

"If it's occurring in one district, it could easily be occurring in others," Zh'oros added, as though she were completing his thoughts. "I'll contact my staff. We will begin interviews and evaluations of the healers in charge of the police service. From there, we will begin reevaluating the officers of each division."

"I'll inform my investigators of what is occurring. Have your staff confer with Xi'nyr in putting together a second unit to send in to investigate the police service. Ensure they have a list of questions to help your teams."

Zh'oros gave a nod. "I'll begin now. She gave a bow to Malik and Violetta. "Do you have any other questions, Violetta?"

When Violetta shook her head, the healer smiled slightly before turning and departing the room.

Mc'narrd turned to Violetta. "You realize this may cause another round of dislike towards you. Many of your colleagues will believe you're turning against them."

"Or using my father's name to get the military to step in because I'm being bullied?" Violetta asked in disgust.

"I suspect the questions will quickly turn to what influence you've created with the military," Malik said slowly. When Violetta looked at him in confusion, he shrugged. "You're being given gifts from the military. Their protection. You're known to be friends with them. Your father has been dead for five years, Vi. No one is aware of Mc'narrd's connection to you. You weren't even aware until your grandparents told you. People just know you've created friends in some unexpected places. The question is: how did you do it?"

"Most won't consider the fact is that you don't judge people on anything other than their personality and merit," Mc'narrd added. "They'll think it's because of their position in life. Your father's relationship with them. Or something nefarious."

"I can't change that," Violetta stated. She swung her feet off the bed. "But I *can* Challenge anyone who questions my honor, integrity, or loyalty."

"Perhaps we should start leaving healers on staff at the police service," Mc'narrd mused. "I'll discuss it with Zh'oros."

"If you wish," Violetta said, eyeing the admiral from the corner of her eyes. "Would either of you like to tell me where my clothes are? Because I am not going to the station in a bedrobe."

Chapter Twenty

alik had chosen a lightweight, loose tunic and matching pants for her. The shoes were her usual black military-style boots. After dressing and reattaching her assortment of weapons and tools, Malik and Mc'narrd escorted her to the main entrance. The admiral bid them a farewell and turned towards the stairs as they headed for the main entrance and the awaiting HAV.

"How are you feeling?" Malik asked, wrapping an arm around her in the HAV and pulling her close. "Truly?"

"So far, I'm well," she replied honestly. "As much as I enjoy teasing Zh'oros, I honestly don't think I'd be up for walking across the city just now."

"If you're Challenged, call me. Declare me your Champion," Malik said. She shifted to look at him. "Promise me, Vi. Just think of it as a grown-up version from when we were kids."

"If I'm Challenged today, I'll have you be my Champion," she said slowly. "As long as you promise to turn them into a bloody pile of excrement."

"Now you know what to give her for a wedding gift," Mc'narrd teased.

"And here I was thinking of more jewelry," Malik said with a heavy sigh. When she swatted him on the chest, he grabbed her hand and kissed her pulse point. "I could do both, though."

Violetta melted against him. "You two are so mean."

"But you love *me*," Malik stated smugly. "Sorry, sir. You're on your own."

"Nah, I have my own mate," Mc'narrd countered. "She's plenty."

"I'll tell her you said that," Violetta said with a smile. "We're planning to have lunch sometime soon."

There was a definite groan from the admiral.

Smiling smugly, she changed the topic to what she and Malik were planning on doing that day. When she arrived at the police station, she had the day's reports up and running across the larger tablet.

The entire path to her department was so ingrained into her, she didn't look up until someone called out her name. Looking up, she found many officers approaching her. Blinking, she found herself volleying questions about what happened.

"Get me out of here," she whispered when she glanced down at the interface.

"Sorry, folks, but we need to get her to work," Da'kaw said, moving closer. At a signal Violetta couldn't see, several other soldiers moved forward. "The lady's just been released, let's give her some room."

His words cut through the pressing crowd. Slowly, people apologized, wished her well, and moved back.

"Too much?" Mc'narrd asked. "Zh'oros?"

"Elevated readings, but nothing dangerous," Zh'oros commented. "She's going to need space for a while. If it gets worse, or doesn't lessen within a reasonable amount of time, come see me, Violetta."

"Thank you," Violetta breathed once they'd reached a mostly-empty hallway. "Never have liked crowds like that. Dad didn't like them, either. Said they made him jumpy."

"Different reasons, but no, Vrehn was not a fan of crowds," Mc'narrd agreed. "Get to work. I'll see what I can do about running interference at the department. If you need me, just ask for your uncle. Mc'narrd out."

By the time Violetta entered her division, she was eager to talk to her fellow detectives about what she'd missed. With luck, someone had some new information.

Heading straight for her desk, she found Issik already there and waiting for her.

"Meeting room?" he asked. At her nod, he grinned. "Good to see you back in one piece."

"I was always in one piece," she retorted. "Just a bit unconscious and feeling like someone ran me over with a HAV."

"I'm surprised you're back at all, much less so soon," Ra'keff commented as he approached the desk. "You could have taken a few days off."

"Nah. I've got to figure out who to thank for those flowers," Violetta joked. "They didn't leave me a card. Can't send them a thank you without a name, ya know."

"Maybe you can send them a fruit basket for the solstice," Ra'keff countered. "I can give you suggestions on what to include."

There was laughter from all around them.

"Osing should be here shortly. He went out to grab some decent drinks for all of us. Thought you'd appreciate something fresh and not from a hospital."

"Shall we, then?" Violetta asked, gesturing towards the meeting room they'd been using. The two men nodded and the trio headed for the room. "Issik mentioned a fiber was found. Any news on it?"

Ra'keff touched the interface and the door slid open. She stepped through and settled into one of the chairs. Issik followed Ra'keff into the room. Da'kaw held the door open briefly with a foot.

"You okay with these comedians, lady?" Da'kaw asked, humming lightly.

"Yeah, I don't think they'll harm me," Violetta replied with a laugh. "Thanks, Commander."

"No problem. Makes it easier if we don't have to worry about your colleagues," Da'kaw replied. Moving his foot, the door slid shut. He took a visible position near the door, but gave them privacy.

"So, the fiber is actually human hair from a wig," Ra'keff began.

He paused, looking up. Violetta turned to see Osing approaching. Da'kaw said something to him and the detective grinned and replied. After a moment, the door opened and Osing sauntered in with four cups in a carrying tray.

"I asked your guardian if he wanted to be a taste tester for you," Osing commented, removing the drinks. "Said you're on your own. Sorry, detective. I tried."

Violetta laughed and accepted the cup he offered. There wasn't much she wouldn't drink, and most of the detectives knew her jakka preferences, anyway.

"Thanks, Osing," she said, taking a sniff of the drink. "What is it?"

"Humans call it 'hot chocolate'," he replied. "My sister loves it. It's melted chocolate in warmed milk or water. She likes it in milk. Says it makes it sweeter and richer. That one has caramel and whipped topping on it." He shrugged. "Thought you might like it, too. Since I know you enjoy sweets."

"I'm guessing that's why it has her name on it," Violetta said thoughtfully.

"Didn't want to chance someone realizing it was for you," he admitted. "Not sure who this murderer is, or where they might work."

"Appreciated." She took a sip and gave a happy sound. "Delicious! Tell your sister thank you for introducing me to this." Taking another sip, she savored the sweet beverage. "Ra'keff was just talking about the fiber that was located."

"Did he get to the part about it being from a wig made from human hair?" Osing asked.

Violetta nodded as Osing settled into a chair on the other side of her. Issik had the chair closest to the door. Her back was to the window, but she didn't mind. With a squadron of soldiers sent to protect her, she wasn't concerned about her safety at the station. Her position allowed her to view the wall easily without a glare.

Ra'keff pulled up an interface and began tapping the screen. Violetta remained silent as a map of one the neighborhoods came into view. Small yellow dots were bright against the pale blue gridwork of the city.

"The yellow is where the wigs can be purchased. They're only used by entertainers at the theaters." He touched the screen again. Bright orange dots appeared. "The orange dots show where all the theaters were located."

"Where was the florist?" Violetta asked.

A brilliant red dot appeared in a neighborhood, followed by a red triangle.

"The triangle represents the delivery service that took the flowers to the penthouse," Ra'keff stated, his eyes fixed on her. "You're aware someone paid for the flowers at the florist, had them sent to the delivery service, who was paid to take them to Malik's residence?"

Violetta nodded. "Did you compare customers to the profile?"

"We got a couple hits, but the one we think did it made certain their face wasn't seen by the cameras," Issik stated. A few taps later and the stillclips appeared on the wall across from them. "Same with the delivery service. The profile fits, but it shows a different being in clothes, appearance, and weight. Shoulders were hunched in an attempt to alter their height."

"Alyssa knew what she was saying, though. When taken into account the length of the arms and the body's posture, it ended up being the same height and frame of who we're looking for." Ra'keff shook his head. "I know I don't have the security clearance, but I'd love to know the lady's history."

"I probably don't even have the security clearance," Violetta said dismissively.

"Actually, you do," Mc'narrd's voice said on the comm. "But I know why you said that."

There was scoffing from the men in the room. She tipped her head to the side quizzically.

"You're so cute," Osing teased. "Would not want to ever call a bluff from you."

"I don't bluff," Violetta countered. Then she ruined it by winking at him as a human would. She continued as though there was no change in the topic. "So, we have the location of the wig, the florist, and the delivery service. All within the same neighborhood."

"Pull up where each of the deceased lived," Issik suggested, studying the map. "Do we know if any of them lived in that area? Either now or in the past?"

Leaning forward, Violetta began going back over the reports. Ra'keff began pulling up the current residences while Issik and Osing discussed how best to locate all previously known addresses of those who had died so far.

The door to the office slid open, startling everyone in the room.

"You wed him?" Ty'rett's voice roared in the room as he stood in the doorway.

Violetta rubbed her ear with the comm as she winced. She noticed the three native males were rubbing theirs, also.

"Say it a little louder, please. I don't think the Master of the Dead heard you."

"Or those in the marketplace across the river," Osing added, shaking his head slightly. "Did you have to yell?"

"What's your problem, Ty'rett?" Ra'keff demanded, pausing the interface.

"She wed him!" he yelled. "She wed the Master of Ceremonies! Deny it! I dare you!"

"Why do you say that?" she asked in a surprising neutral tone.

Oddly enough, she didn't even feel threatened by him. Da'kaw moved forward and she gave a slight shake of her head. Leaning back in the chair, she swiveled it to face him, her ankles crossed in a deceptively casual manner.

She gave a military gesture to hold back, covering it by folding her hands together. The commander noticed and took a small step back.

"He's wearing the mate to your sword," Ty'rett snarled. He gestured towards the one at her waist. "The sheaths are identical. So are the hilts. I spent a decade in the military before transferring to the police service. I know the ceremonies used."

"So?" Osing snapped. "Who cares? She's already wearing his ring. There was a traditional announcement declaring they're promised to wed. If they wanted a private ceremony, let 'em have it. Not like Malik gets a lot of privacy, anyway."

"You jealous, old man?" Valerie yelled from across the room. "Of her landing Malik? Or because Malik got the girl?" She held up her comm in her hand. "This is how you do it, you old fool! Take the damn thing out first!"

Ty'rett's head snapped around. Valerie was leaning against a desk, a grin on her face. With deliberate movements, she tucked the comm back into her ear.

"It isn't proper," he shouted back to her. "They're both of mixed blood!"

"And?" someone else answered. Violetta couldn't tell who. "We're supposed to be worried about unexplained deaths. Not who's bedding who."

"The Master of Ceremonies just spent the past several days on the military base after his betrothed was poisoned. If he didn't love her, he wouldn't have stayed with her," the voice of Detective Carlos Santiago added. He came into Violetta's view, standing beside Valerie. "We all saw the vidclip."

"What's on it?" Violetta asked from the room. "Some of us have been working."

That garnered a round of laughter.

"Master Malik Addelia was approached by a reporter and questioned about the health of his betrothed. He informed the reporter that someone mistakenly sent kyitis flowers to Violetta in honor of their betrothal. Said he didn't believe any harm was truly meant, and she'd spent the past days being treated, but was completely healed."

"He was absolutely darling about it," Valerie chimed in. "A total hunk as he added that he hoped this would bring about a greater knowledge towards the flowers and the harm they can cause those of mixed heritage."

"Oh, it gets better!" Tiayl Sterling added, walking up with several other detectives. "The Chief of Police came on, saying anyone who tries gifting those flowers to anyone of mixed heritage will immediately be investigated for attempted murder. Advised the one receiving them to seek medical aid immediately, contact authorities, and to issue a Challenge."

"Gotta wonder if you didn't send them, Ty'rett," Ra'keff drawled, leaning back in the chair.

"Better yet, bring over COD," Osing added, his eyes narrowing on their fellow native. "He's sounding an awful lot like someone who would fit the profile of a Moyii Tsaa member."

"None of you care about your heritage?" Ty'rett demanded loudly.

Someone must have turned down the volume on his comm, because it wasn't hurting her ears anymore. From what she noticed of the others, no one else was showing signs of pain, either.

"He's going to want to shut up," Mc'narrd said suddenly. "But, please, let him continue. It'll be immensely amusing."

"None of you care about tradition? Propriety?" Ty'rett continued, oblivious to what was occurring around him.

"I thought exchanging weapons was the most ancient tradition our people had?" Osing asked, looking at Ra'keff then Issik.

The two men shrugged, except they lifted their shoulders and dropped them in imitation of a human's method of shrugging.

"I dare you say that to my grandmother," Violetta muttered. "She's the one who made the initial announcement."

Mc'narrd's laughter distracted her from whatever else Ty'rett was screeching.

"And here I thought it was going to be a pleasant day." Malik's voice carried clearly above Ty'rett's continued complaining.

Silence fell around the room, both within the meeting room and in the pit. Even Ty'rett shut up upon recognizing Malik's voice.

"I was requested to bring some information that might aid the investigation to the police service. And what do I find? A petty bully whining because two people are happy."

"Oh, fark," Mc'narrd groaned over the comms. "And I thought Violetta was bad."

"I'm surprised you haven't Challenged him, my beloved," Malik continued, stepping into a clear view of the meeting room and its occupants. He spoke in the same voice he would to discuss the weather. "I suppose you didn't regale any of them about how we met."

Violetta's eyes drifted appreciatively over Malik, enjoying how the clothes he wore fit him. She'd told him several times she loved seeing him in the formal Master of Ceremonies robes. She couldn't stop the smile that sprang to her face. Or the heat that flashed through her eyes.

"It's really rather boring," she replied dismissively.

"For you, perhaps. I'm the one you punched," he retorted, not taking his eyes off Ty'rett. "Yes, I know. Rather silly to become besotted by the girl who punched you. One you were trying to stand up for. Turns out, we both hated bullies. She insisted she could fight her own battles. I insisted that I wanted to have her back."

"It worked out splendidly," Violetta added, standing in one fluid movement. "We would often Challenge the bully on the same day, or that same week. If we felt generous, sometimes there would even be a day between the Challenges."

"You did Challenge him just a few days ago," Ra'keff offered, a grin flashing across his face. "She won that Duel faster than most I've ever witnessed in the arenas."

"Yet." Malik drew the word out. "I would have no problems Challenging this worthless excuse of a K'laisian. Then allowing the healers the chance to heal his mind while healing his body."

"To answer your question about if I wed him?" Violetta continued, raising her voice just enough so everyone could hear. Her eyes gleamed as she spoke. "Yes, I did. And anyone who has a problem can be Challenged. And those Challenges will be taken to the arena where I can humiliate you in front of everyone watching."

"Then they can Duel me," Malik added, his voice cold and equally loud.

There were loud cheers, whistles, and congratulations. Both within the room and over the comms. Violetta didn't even feel guilty. It was too late to take it back and she didn't care.

Ty'rett's eyes turned from Malik to Violetta, then back to her. Seemingly ignoring all the positive reactions from his colleagues.

"Say anything, Ty'rett, and the words *will* be spoken," Violetta warned. "I will not tolerate any more hatred towards me or my mate."

Ty'rett's jaw clenched. He balled his hands into fists. The other three men in the room stood as one group.

"Take your hatred and leave," Ra'keff ordered, taking a step closer to Ty'rett. "Violetta isn't the only one disgusted by your behavior. All you have to do is look around and see that. Your petty little group of haters can take your grievances elsewhere. We've got a string of murders to solve and you're preventing it."

"There's no less than-" Osing, always the smartass, paused to gesture as he counted beings, "-at least five beings willing to Challenge you right here. Right now." He leaned to the side and looked into the pit. "And probably several more out there, also."

Ty'rett glowered at all of them before turning and stalking away, completely avoiding Malik as he moved into the pit. He didn't reach the center of the room before Violetta noticed a commotion at the main doors. She took a step closer to the window and her eyes widened at the sight.

Three healers had stepped into the room.

"Stars and seas," she whispered. "Already?"

"Zh'oros was listening in," Mc'narrd confided. "It didn't take long for her to send people over."

"Aleos Ty'rett," the Master Healer called loudly.

"I'd rather he be treated without physical injuries to go with the psychological illness," Zh'oros said dryly over the comms.

"Yes?" he replied, uncertainly.

"Please come with us for a psychological evaluation," the healer requested politely.

Ty'rett turned towards Violetta. He managed one step before Malik and Da'kaw moved in front of the door.

Malik's hand was already on the handle of his sword, prepared to pull it.

"Ease down, Malik," Da'kaw said quietly.

Malik glanced sharply at the commander, but he did drop his hand from the sword. Then spoiled it by clenching it into a fist. Violetta chuckled softly.

The detective in question glared at Malik and Da'kaw before stalking across the floor to the healers. The Master Healer gave a nod, turned, and departed the room. Ty'rett followed behind her. The other two healers fell into step behind the detective.

"Guess the military isn't taking anything lightly anymore," Valerie said with a low whistle. "Wondered when the healers would get involved."

"Right? They're already going through everything else," Tiayl commented. She laughed. "Maybe we can finally get some work done without the grouchy men?"

Carlos elbowed the woman in the side. She pretended to yelp loudly and rubbed her side.

"Hey, Commander, will you protect me, too?" she asked, bobbing her brows suggestively.

Commander Da'kaw hummed loudly. "Sorry, lady, but I suspect my mate would object. Perhaps Lieutenant Te'soh would be willing to help you."

One of the guards on their side of the wall stepped forward and bowed slightly. He was a pure blood native with dark hair, tanned skin, and gold eyes.

"It would be a delight, commander," he stated, a playful smile curving his lips.

"A pleasure to meet you, lieutenant," Tiayl replied, bowing to the soldier. "May I share my personal information with you?"

The noise in the pit returned to its usual volume, preventing Violetta from hearing the reply, though she could see the smiles on the pair easily.

"And that is what we call Matching," Commander Da'kaw joked.

"I thought it was called 'protecting your rear'," Malik countered, causing the commander to hum loudly. Winking at the commander, Malik stepped into the room, allowing the door to slide shut behind him. "Such a shame we didn't get to Challenge him."

"I'm sure we'll have other opportunities," Violetta quipped. "So what information do you bring us?"

"It has been brought to my attention the location of where antique weapons are being sold. Such as the one used in the attack against you," Malik explained. Ra'keff moved down a chair, offering the one he'd been using to Malik, who accepted it with a slight bow. "May I?"

"You know how to use them," Violetta commented. "By all means."

Malik kept his features neutral as he touched the interface. Within seconds, brilliant green dots appeared on the screen.

"Each of those dots is where antiques are sold out of the backs of HAVs," Malik stated. "None are sold by Zane Morelli or any of his employees. They're by those who work against him."

"Why does he have that information?" Ra'keff asked, his eyes on the screen against the wall.

"He likes to know where his opponents are so he can avoid them and any trouble they bring," Malik replied. "An old Earth saying is 'know your enemy'."

"Keep your friends close, your enemies closer," Violetta said quietly. When the natives in the room looked at her, she shrugged. "Dad said it several times to me and Malik while growing up. He claimed it meant you should always know your enemies as well, if not better than your friends. Or something like that."

"If you know what your enemies are doing, you can plan a better attack against them," Osing mused. "Logical. If not oddly worded."

"Zoom out a little," Violetta asked, staring at the screen.

Before any of the others could do it, Malik had it zoomed out to show the area of the green dots.

"Show off," she muttered. Humming filled the room and her comm. Malik remained silent, though he did smile. "You even knew where I wanted it."

"If anyone here questioned the connection you two have, this just answered it," Ra'keff teased. "What are you seeing that we aren't, Violetta?"

"I think we've got the neighborhood," she said.

Touching the larger interface Mc'narrd gave her, she outlined a section of the city, then zoomed in. Within the section was the florist, delivery service, a shop that sold wigs, a theater, and several dots. One was a body, the others were residences, either recent or past, of the deceased.

There were two green dots. Each one on the very edge of the neighborhood. Zoomed out, they appeared to be on the outside of the neighborhood.

"How did…" Ra'keff shook his head. "I was wrong. I admit it. I should not have questioned you taking the lead, Vi. I'm sorry. If I ever need suggestions, I'm coming to you."

"Always happy to be of service," Violetta replied. "We have the neighborhood. But we still need a name. Or something that will help us to get one."

There was a knock on the door before it slid open. The captain stepped in, his eyes sweeping over the group.

"Take a break, Cq'linns," the captain ordered. "I don't need a healer grumbling in my ear about overworking my officers."

"I'm well, captain," Violetta began.

"You may be well. You may even have been released back to work," he stated. "But take a break. Go with your betrothed… husband… mate… whatever you want to call him. Don't know how you didn't get light duty, but I'm not taking the chance of you relapsing."

"It wasn't Zh'oros or me," Mc'narrd said quickly. "Commander Os'shye is doing this all on his own. And he's not wrong. You should have been released on restricted duty."

"You can come with me to the arena," Malik suggested. "We'll have lunch together in my office."

"Fine," she said with a sigh. "But if anything turns up…"

"One of us will find you and tell you in person," Issik reassured her. He glanced at the other two men who both nodded in agreement. "We'll go back over everything. Send units out to question the antique dealers. Maybe someone will be helpful."

"You'd need to stay out of that, anyway, Lady," Ra'keff added apologetically. "Sorry, but it's not safe for you. The next time, this person may succeed."

"Outvoted and outmaneuvered," Violetta announced. "Checkmate for you all."

That caused them all to laugh good naturedly. There wasn't a K'laisian around who didn't enjoy the human game of chess.

Malik chuckled as he stood, then pulled Violetta up with him.

"I'm certain you'll be back here tomorrow, ready to dive into it once again," he teased.

She shrugged, but didn't say anything. Instead, chose to allow him to lead her from the room, then the office.

They weren't wrong. They'd hit another block in the investigation. Maybe someone would get a lead with the antique dealers. She doubted it, but hope was eternal.

"Hey, Vi," Osing called as she and Malik stood in the door's threshold.

She and Malik turned towards him.

"Congratulations," he said, a broad grin on his face.

He stood and approached them, crossing his arms at the wrists as he neared them. Violetta crossed her own, grasping his hands in hers.

Within moments, those within the room and the pit were surrounding them. Laughter and joking filled the room. Even as more teasing and congratulations filled the comms.

Eventually, she and Malik were able to extract themselves. But she couldn't complain. It was a better way to end the day, in her opinion. Even if she didn't feel as though she needed the break.

Chapter Twenty One

Unlike the last time Violetta entered the arena, the HAV stopped at the back of the building. A large dock stretched half the back of the arena. Beings of various races unloaded foods and items from the HAVs on hoverlifts. Stairs led up to the top of the dock on each side of the wide platform.

This side of the building was decidedly slower paced and relaxed. Malik held his hand out for her, which she took with a curious look. He kissed her knuckles and tucked it through the crook of his right elbow. She recognized it as the general way of escorting a lady. Though Malik could use either arm easily, the position would place her on the inside as they entered the building. Had they been on the opposite side, she suspected he would've had her walk on his left side.

"Everything is on schedule, sir," one of the employees on the dock said as Malik neared them.

Violetta noticed the bronze eyes that marked the man as of mixed heritage. The slight blue tint to his skin suggested at least one parent was from Centauri. His hair was as straight and black as Malik's own tresses.

"A few substitutions, but nothing unexpected," he informed Malik.

"Good to hear," Malik replied, slowing but not stopping. "When's the last delivery today?"

"In three hours," the man said. He offered Violetta a smile. "Lady. Pleased to finally meet you."

"I'd like to introduce Yino Ta'kett. He's in charge of the provisions for the arena. Among other duties," Malik explained. "Sadly, we can't stay and chat. Send up the lists once you're done. We'll discuss the substitutions later. If we need to change suppliers, I'd like to have it decided well before the solstice."

"Pleased to see you well, lady," Yino replied, giving them a quick bow. "Finding suppliers won't be the problem."

"It'll be negotiating the price, I know," Malik replied with a sigh. "Be well, be safe."

"Be safe, be well," Yino replied, turning towards another group of delivering beings.

Malik continued escorting her. They passed the pallets of food and supplies, all of which were being broken down into smaller sections. Those sections were being taken through various doors along the interior portion of the dock.

Violetta watched it all in pure fascination. This was a part of the arenas she didn't know about and Malik moved through it all with ease. In fact, he appeared more comfortable with the workers than he did anyone in the main area of the arena.

She continued to watch over her shoulder as he led her through a door on the far right of the dock. His chuckle had her ducking her head in embarrassment.

"Never realized there was more to the arena than the front, did you?" he asked. She shook her head. "You should see the kitchens. They're incredible. Even if the food preparers are very touchy about who enters their kitchen."

"I'm guessing they're touchier about what you try to steal from the kitchen," she retorted. He shot her a grin and wink. "Thought so."

"So, is this all part of running the arena? As the Master of Ceremonies?" she asked as he walked her down the empty corridor. "Where does this go, anyway?"

"It's used by the staff to go from the main arena to the dock," Malik explained. "The rooms we're walking past? Those are for the performers. The dancers."

"So they have privacy and can get to and from without having to go through the crowds," Violetta thought aloud. Malik nodded encouragingly. "A way for you to move without always having to go through the main area."

"Exactly. If anything happened, and an emergency arose, I could leave quickly without being hindered by the crowd."

"Did you come this way when… when I…" she trailed off, unable to bring herself to say the words.

"When you were taken to the base?" Malik asked, squeezing her hand tightly. She nodded. "No. The guards cleared the route to the main doors for me with amazing speed and precision."

"And my other question?" she pressed.

He wrinkled his nose at her. "Not all those who are Master of Ceremonies in the other districts are as concerned about the day to day business. They perform their roles, concern themselves with scheduling, and keep the Duels running smoothly." He snorted. "I'd rather spend my time with those on the docks and kitchens than those who pay for me to spend time with them in the private boxes."

"I have a question that is completely off topic," Violetta admitted. Malik gave her a nod. "Do Uncle Me'ngki's children come often?"

"Not only do they visit the arena often, Zerik and Lyza often pay to have Malik join them," Mc'narrd confirmed over the comms. "Part of why Malik isn't concerned about meeting them. Both enjoy his company."

Zerik, Violetta knew, was Mc'narrd and Alyssa's eldest child. The only one Alyssa birthed. Lyza was one of the first children they'd adopted. A beautiful mixed heritage woman whose mother had died in childbirth. Her father had died offplanet during a battle. The two children were three years apart, but were closer than any children who were blood-related.

Both were career military with their own battlecruisers.

"Speaking of your children, sir, when will they be back planetside?" Malik asked.

"And spoil the surprise?" Mc'narrd countered. "They've been informed their favorite Master of Ceremonies is betrothed to a lovely woman of mixed heritage. Both are eager to meet this mysterious lady."

"Stars and seas," Violetta groaned. "You didn't tell them who it was? At least they can check the vidclips."

"You're presuming they will," Mc'narrd teased. At least, she hoped he was teasing. "Perhaps I suggested that it be a surprise?"

"Perhaps I'm thinking you're full of it, as my human colleagues often say," Violetta retorted.

Mc'narrd laughed. He was still laughing as Malik opened a door at what Violetta realized was the top of an upward sloping hallway.

"The docks are that far below the main floor?" Violetta asked.

"They really are," Malik confirmed.

The door opened into another hallway, except this one was wide enough four people could walk abreast. There were more people in it, too. Most wore various uniforms for the plethora of eateries. They all waved or called a greeting to Malik as they moved through the corridor.

Malik continued his trek, not pausing along the corridor. Double doors with windows revealed kitchens bustling with activity. Another door was opened to reveal a set of stairs. Her mind quickly ran over the layout of the building, the path they'd taken, and the direction they were heading.

"Sneaky," she commented as they began up the stairs.

"I should've known you'd realize where this leads," Malik grumbled. "You're a walking map."

"You can thank Dad for that," Violetta retorted. "Amazing how games end up being more than games."

"That's because it was you," Malik said with a laugh. "He probably would've just left me in the middle of the preserve and hoped I found my way out."

Violetta laughed until she was gasping for breath. They had to pause in their ascension up the stairs to allow her to breathe deep enough to not collapse.

"Oh, stars, that sucked," she gasped, a hand on her chest. "Worth it. But it definitely was not fun."

"Vi?" Malik asked worriedly, supporting her as she bent forward slightly.

She pressed a hand against her chest while the other held onto Malik. Her chest felt tight and sore, as though she'd spent hours coughing fitfully.

"Zh'oros?" Malik prompted when she remained bent forward.

"She'll be fine," Zh'oros said reassuringly. "Maybe the captain was right. Perhaps I should place you on restricted activity."

"Just how badly were my lungs injured?" Violetta asked, drawing in a deep breath. She let it out slowly. The pain eased to where she could finally stand straight again.

"You truly do not want to know," Malik said solemnly. She glanced at him sharply. "I saw the scans, Vi. And I can read the bed's diagnostics as well as the admiral and Zh'oros. It was bad. They weren't exaggerating when they said you were barely alive when you arrived at the base."

He wrapped his arms around her, pulling her tight against his chest. His lips were close to her ear. She could feel the shiver that ran through his body. His lips pressed against her head as he held her.

"I swear I thought I'd lost you," he whispered.

She held him just as tightly, knowing he needed her as much as she needed him. Perhaps she was as much his rock, as he was hers. Though there were guards escorting them, they were completely ignored by her and Malik at the moment.

"Sorry about that," she murmured quietly. "Love you."

"Love you, too." His voice was barely above a whisper. Slowly, he released her and she could see the love shining in the depths in his bronze eyes.

"Right. So, shall we continue on up? Your office is to the left, which means food should be to the right and I'm starving," she said, trying to lighten the mood.

He gave a nod, an amused smile on his face. His arm remained firmly wrapped around her waist.

"Go left," Mc'narrd suggested. "I'll have food and beverages delivered to you."

Violetta's eyes narrowed as Malik opened the door. "They don't deliver here."

"They do if you know the right people," Mc'narrd informed her.

His tone was far too casual.

"Planning on joining us, sir?" she asked in a neutral tone.

That got a laugh. "No, Lady Addelia. I will not be joining anyone at the arena today."

That caused Malik to narrow his eyes, also. They exchanged wary expressions, even as Malik led her to his office. The two guards employed by the arena stood in their usual place. Military guards had joined them. The unit that had escorted them through the corridors fanned out around the doorway.

Malik touched the interface, unlocking his office door. Three soldiers entered before him, searched the room, then vanished out the opposite side. When they returned, Violetta was perched on the edge of his desk. Malik was leaning against it, giving her an amused look as she swung her legs like a child.

The soldiers paused, shook their heads, and left chuckling and humming in amusement.

"I do hope whoever is bringing the food doesn't take long," Violetta commented. "I didn't even get to snack on your sister's pastries."

"Don't tell her that," Malik advised. "She'll give me nothing but grief."

"Wouldn't dream of it." Violetta tipped her head to the side. "You know, I keep thinking we've missed something with the murders."

Malik chuckled. "There are other things to think about, my love."

"Oh, like where we should have the ceremony of joining?" Violetta's eyes and tone were all innocence despite the question. When he winced, she chuckled. "Maybe we should have it in the arena. Have a large holographic arch over the interior, and festival explosions against the shield."

At his narrowed eyes and frown she laughed. The darker his expression grew, the harder she laughed until she was leaning against him, trying to catch her breath. Tears of pain and amusement poured from her eyes.

"I'm sorry," she managed to gasp. "I'm sorry. Too funny to not suggest."

As Malik stepped in front of her, she draped herself against him, even as he wrapped his arms around her.

"Oh, my. Are we interrupting something?" a very feminine voice said from the doorway. The voice was strong, but had a softness to it that was vaguely familiar to Violetta.

Violetta could see two forms through her tears. Pushing back, she found Malik wiping her eyes gently with a handkerchief that had appeared from somewhere.

"Are you well, lady?" Zerik Mc'narrd asked as he moved out of the doorway.

He could have been a younger clone of It'zarry Mc'narrd.

They had the same features, though Zerik had his mother's shaped eyes. Long silver hair was pulled back into a loose ponytail. He even had his father's dulcet voice. White skin was perhaps two shades darker than his father's but the smile came from his mother. The laughter and friendliness came from both parents. Brilliant bronze eyes were his own, the only indication of his mixed heritage.

"Obviously, not," Lyza replied, her bronze eyes filled with concern.

Lyza was the polar opposite of her adopted brother. Her hair was a beautiful black sheet of straight hair. Her skin was two shades darker than tan. Yet both were lithe, moved with a light step, and held themselves as the commanders they were, despite wearing casual clothing of tunics and loose pants.

"Hold these," Zerik replied, shoving a pair of food containers at his sister, who had little choice but to accept them. He crossed the room, until he stood near Violetta and Malik.

"If they didn't have the clearance, you wouldn't have told us to come today." He tapped his ear to explain his part of the conversation. "This is going to hurt like hox."

It was the only warning Violetta received before he placed his hand on her back. She gasped as a searing pain tore through her. It felt as though he were pouring liquid fire into her lungs. She dropped her head against Malik's shoulder, squeezing her eyes shut. Not that it prevented the tears from escaping. The wood bit into her palms as her grip tightened on the desk's edge.

She felt a second hand rest above her breasts and the pain grew. She gritted her teeth together, clenching her jaw until she wanted to scream. It seemed to last forever. Though she knew it couldn't have been more than a few minutes before the pain slowly faded to nothing. When the hands moved away, she discovered there was no ache or anything in her chest anymore.

Not even the heaviness she hadn't realized had been there until it was gone.

"How..." she trailed off staring at Zerik.

"Remember my mom was the first human to ever be injected with nanites?" he asked. She nodded. "When she was injected, the nanites used removed the genetic impurities that prevented me from having a Gift."

"Other humans have had nanites injected, without that result," Malik commented.

Zerik shrugged. "Those were also programmed for humans. The first ones? They were still trying to figure out a human from a K'laisian. She was the ultimate test subject.

No other human has ever lived as long as she has and retained their youth, either. Even with nanites."

"It's why his Gift feels like you're going to die when he uses it." Lyza gave Violetta a sympathetic expression, even as she placed the containers on a nearby table. "Though, he could have introduced himself before doing it."

"He wasn't supposed to do that at all," Mc'narrd grumbled on the comm. "Stubborn, disobedient child. I could court martial him for that."

"Aren't you the one who said her security clearance would allow it? Same with Malik?" Lyza countered. "Besides, you wouldn't do that to your son. Mom would have your hide."

Violetta snickered. She couldn't help it. "I could absolutely see Alyssa Challenging him over that." Turning to Zerik, who was now busily removing the food from the carrying containers. "Thank you, sir."

"Oh, stars, don't call me that," he pleaded, looking over his shoulder at her. "Not while I'm nowhere near the base, my father, or a battlecruiser."

"May your children be less insolent than mine," Mc'narrd declared. "Do I need to come there, Zerik?"

"You told me she was my cousin," Zerik said without hesitation. "Do you think I'd let my cousin continue to suffer when she has 'above a one-star admiral's' security clearance?"

"Might as well give up, Dad," Lyza suggested, as she offered a container to Violetta. "Now you know why we're commanders on battlecruisers."

Violetta laughed. "He does like to join in on the conversations, doesn't he?"

"To say the least," Zerik grumbled. He even sounded like his father. "Pleasure to meet you, Lady Violetta. It's an honor to meet the woman who is Malik's mate."

"Dad was absolutely thrilled when you chose to offer Malik your sword, Violetta," Lyza added, offering one of the food carrying containers to Malik. "When he suggested we come to the arena instead of the base, it confused the hox out of us. Until he mentioned Malik was wed. We'd only heard he was betrothed in the vidclips."

"Then he and Zh'oros were talking about your injury," Zerik continued, handing Violetta another container. "If they didn't want me using my Gift to help you, they shouldn't have mentioned it so I'd hear it."

"Especially since we suddenly had a cousin we'd never met before." The grin on Lyza's face was pure mischief. "A cousin with the same clearance as someone training to be a master healer."

"Above a one-starred admiral," Violetta repeated, eyeing Malik.

He gave a shrug. "I *had* finished my third year. The fourth year would've been more intense. And I did say I was training to be a healer who could treat admirals."

"It's seven years before they go into space," Lyza interjected with a human-style shrug. "But they're always given their security clearances at the beginning of the training. To clear them for the training, as well as to ensure they're cleared for anything they may see during training. It's a pretty intense program."

"Congratulations on the marriage," Zerik cheerfully said as he handed Violetta eating utensils. He smiled brilliantly. "And welcome to the family."

"To a bigger family," Lyza corrected, raising her beverage cup. "Congratulations to you both!"

Malik lifted his, even as Violetta and Zerik raised their cups.

They all took pulls from their cups. Malik and Violetta tapped theirs together before setting them on the desk. An old habit from their childhood. A toast to each other of a good time to come.

"We paid to have you join us. For as long as you're being Master of Ceremonies today." She nodded towards Violetta. "Doubt anyone will bother your wife with us around. We'll keep an eye on her if you need to leave her in our box for anything."

"Thank you," Malik said, giving Zerik a bow. "So, how have you two been?"

"Glad to be home. We enjoy our lives out among the stars, but we also like being home and visiting our parents," Zerik replied.

"Despite Dad's teasing, I know he likes having us home, too," Lyza said. "I know Mom prefers when we're all home and she can boss us around."

"You do know she's probably listening," Mc'narrd warned. "Keep it up and your comms will be off the moment you step foot inside the house."

Lyza's eyes widened. "I take it back. Mom is the best mother on K'lais and always does what's best for her children."

"Just buy her a large basket of chocolates from her favorite shop," Zerik advised. He tipped his cup towards his sister. "It might keep you safe."

There was a round of laughter and the conversation changed to more normal topics. By the time the pair departed for their own private box, the food had been decimated and the beverage cups were empty.

"Shall we?" Malik asked, offering his arm to Violetta.

She nodded and accepted it with a smile. "I like them."

"I've always enjoyed their company," Malik admitted as he escorted her through the hallway to his box. "When they aren't on official duty, they're relaxed and love to laugh. I'm always thankful when they visit the arena."

"How often are they on official duty at the arena?" Violetta asked, honestly curious.

"There have been a few times. On those occasions, they're as militant as their father." He paused before stepping into the box with her. "Are you ready?"

"No, but I'm going to do it anyway," she replied honestly, the smile still on her face. "This is definitely one way to tell everyone I'm alive and well."

Mc'narrd's laughter was drowned out by Malik laughing, followed by the roar of the crowd. The music began and the box moved away from the platform. When the public noticed her brilliant smile and the glittering ring on her finger, the noise level rose to an entirely new level.

Her eyes swept the private boxes until she found the admiral's children. The pair was watching her and Malik with brilliant smiles. Reaching over, Malik wrapped an arm around her waist, pulling her closer.

Raising her hand, she settled it against his chest, almost possessively. Malik chuckled. The deep blue gem surrounded by the clear stones glittered and sparkled against his dark clothes. She looked up at him and he kissed her lips.

"Welcome to what it means to be my mate," he whispered.

Violetta shifted her hand so the ring sparkled even more. "I think my newfound family might be a bit more terrifying."

"Indeed," Mc'narrd said over the comms. "Zerik and Lyza are only two of many who will be protective of you. Welcome to *my* family, *nephew*. Now treat my niece right."

"She won't want for anything," Malik promised as he raised his hands towards the crowd.

The interfaces brightened and Violetta knew it was time for him to begin his speech.

Except the crowd had yet to quieten to where he could talk.

Glancing down at the interface, she saw Zerik and Lyza laughing.

"I think the public approves," Lyza said in her ear. "At least those who don't care about you both being of mixed heritage. Or aren't aware of your heritage."

"Dad added us to the channel," Zerik explained. "You might be there a little longer than expected."

"You think?" she asked under her breath, the smile plastered to her face.

The pair burst out laughing again.

"Wave to the crowd, my love," Malik murmured, his left hand dropping to her waist.

"So nice to be amusing," she muttered as she waved.

Tilting her head back, she smiled at her mate. Impulsively, she kissed him on the neck. When he turned towards her, she brushed her lips across his. Heat flared in his eyes even as the roar of the crowd rose to an impressive new level.

"Forever and always," she whispered, a pleased look on her face as she leaned against him. "Welcome to being *my* mate."

A pair of lips touched the tip of her ear and she shivered.

"Always and forever," Malik murmured, his breath hot against her skin.

When she looked up at him, there was barely any room between them.

"I don't think anyone will ever question who's heart captured yours, Malik," Zerik said with a laugh.

"Don't you know? She keeps it on the tip of her sword," Malik joked, a twinkle in his eyes.

As the siblings burst out laughing, Malik turned back to the crowd. Raising both his arms, the crowd calmed enough for him to begin the opening words as Master of Ceremonies. Violetta remained beside him, a smile on her face.

She felt no shame. No guilt. Only love for her mate. From the glances he sent her, she knew he felt the same. And he wasn't expecting her to not show her love or affection for him. Nor did she expect him to do the same.

They would work past their jealousy. Their fears and the painful parts of their past. And in the end have a relationship that all beings desired.

Chapter Twenty Two

"Meet me in my office when you arrive." Captain Os'shye's voice filled Violetta's comm as she was eating breakfast the following morning. "Don't take long to get here, either."

"Yes, sir," Violetta replied as she pushed her almost empty plate away from her. Grabbing her cup of jakka, she drained the mug. "I love the fact these biosuits remove the need to use a bathroom."

"It is handy," Malik commented. "Think it has to do with the case?"

"I wonder if you'll be left on the channel after this is over?" Violetta wondered aloud.

"Unless either of you object," Mc'narrd's voice interjected. "I'd rather you both be able to contact each other. When it's needed."

"And now I know where to go if the comm goes silent," Malik said dryly. "He did that every time you were attacked."

"Professional-"

"Bullshit," Malik cut in, his voice sharp. Violetta snorted. She'd heard her father use that human word often and knew exactly what it meant. "You know exactly what my psych evaluations show, *Uncle*. So unless you need another to show I can handle an emergency, including one involving Violetta, you can leave the comms on."

"I'll consider it," Mc'narrd allowed. "Get to work. Both of you. Mc'narrd out."

"Have you noticed he does that when he thinks he's losing an argument?" Violetta asked as Malik placed their dishes in the cleaner.

"Or doesn't want to continue the argument," Malik added. "Yes. According to Zerik and Lyza it's a frequent thing of his. The only one who doesn't get away with it-"

"Is Alyssa," Violetta finished for him before laughing. "That's only because if he overrides her, she'll just Challenge him."

"They did enjoy informing us of that, didn't they?" Malik said with a chuckle.

Violetta nodded, still laughing as they exited the penthouse.

Less than ten minutes later, she was sitting in Major Os'shye's office. Issik sat beside her. Neither spoke as they waited for their captain to finish with his interface. When he turned to face them, his face was grim.

Issik and she glanced at each other from the corner of their eyes before looking back at the captain.

"There are a few things I wish to bring to your attention before I come to the reason for this meeting," Os'shye stated. When the pair remained silent he gave a slight nod. "First up is the healers for the department are being replaced. According to the military, they're being evaluated early."

"That's standard, even if it's early," Issik commented with a typical K'laisian shrug. "Everyone knows even healers have to be evaluated."

"Which brings me to my second point," Os'shye continued. His gaze turned to Violetta. "Every being in the department will be going through an extensive evaluation. Except you, Lady… Addelia."

She smiled at the captain. "I've gone through several already, sir. I've spent no less than twelve hours in evaluations during this case. The only time I didn't end up with one was after I was poisoned." She paused and frowned. "Odd."

"Indeed," the captain replied. "Nothing after that?"

"There were a few questions, but nothing that was three hours or more."

"Malik was there with you, though," Issik said thoughtfully. "I'll bet they had him doing the evaluation for them. So you were more at ease with answering the questions."

"Your partner's skills are being wasted at the department," Mc'narrd commented through the comm. "That's exactly what we did. And I'll be ka'deshed if Zh'oros wasn't impressed with Malik's proficiency at asking the questions during your conversations. Your answers never changed once. He handled every part of it with skill and talent. He would've made one amazing healer."

"If he did, then I want him for all my evaluations," Violetta countered. The smile didn't fade. "And I plan on using Cq'linns until our official joining ceremony, sir."

"I'll tell Zh'oros you said that," Mc'narrd teased.

"Zh'oros is listening," the healer said over the comm. "And it will be considered. Zh'oros out."

"Despite admitting to the entire department you wed him?" Captain Os'shye countered, oblivious of the conversations within the comms. Violetta shrugged. "I'll pass the word. We'll respect your request and try to ensure your privacy."

"Thank you, sir. If it becomes public knowledge prior to the ceremony, I'll reconsider."

"The third and the most important reason for this meeting is: your presence has been requested on P'yka." Os'shye kept his eyes on Violetta. "Issik has been several times over his career, but reports show you have not been before."

"Correct, sir," Violetta replied uneasily. "My presence? Specifically?"

"The being who approached the guards saying he has information about a case specifically said he would only speak to you, Cq'linns." Os'shye paused, before adding, "He referred to you as 'Lady Addelia, daughter of Vrehn Cq'linns.' So it's known you're wed."

"Who is the informant, sir?" Violetta asked, caution in her voice.

"Vylus Hy'neipi," Os'shye replied. "So far, we're unaware of how he learned of what has happened or what he knows."

"He's a known Moyii Tsaa member," Mc'narrd added. There was no amusement in his voice. "We're reviewing the recordings to locate who contacted him."

"He wouldn't have been approached directly," Violetta said at the same time as Issik. They looked at each other and grinned.

"Pairing you two together was one of the best things your previous captain ever did," Os'shye stated. "You're a good team." He glanced at his interface. "Get to the military base. Your shuttle up has been prepared. Brief her on the way up, Ha'kksworth. You're both dismissed."

"Yes, sir," they said together, standing at the same time as their captain.

"And, Cq'linns?" Violetta tipped her head to the side in question. The captain bowed to her, a slight smile on his face. "Congratulations."

"Thank you, sir."

When he didn't say anything more, she departed the office with Issik close behind her.

"Since we're going to the base, shall we just get a ride with Commander Da'kaw?" Violetta asked as Issik fell into step beside her.

"As long as he doesn't mind," Issik replied. "Would certainly make entering a lot faster for us."

"We'll deliver you to the flight field," Da'kaw commented from behind them. "You won't even have to go through the usual security checks."

"Is it your first time offplanet?" Issik asked Violetta as they headed for the military HAV.

"No. Dad would take me up to his battlecruiser when it was in orbit," Violetta said, a sad smile on her face. "I'd beg to go up every time he came home."

"It's a nebulous area when it comes to taking children to the battlecruisers," Mc'narrd commented. "But I believe every commander does it. Simply to show their children what they do and what to expect if they chose to become career military."

"My parents weren't career military," Da'kaw added as they climbed into the HAV. "But my aunt took me up to the one she served on. Met her commander and decided then I wanted to have my own battlecruiser." He hummed a little. "Decided after I found my mate I'd rather spend time planetside with my children than away on missions. Put a transfer in and traded a battlecruiser for a life with a pair of constantly warring children."

"Bet you don't regret it, either," Violetta teased.

"Only when they won't give us a moment's peace," Da'kaw admitted with a laugh. "Have to admit, you've reminded me of those days on that battlecruiser. Never knew what we'd encounter out in the vast bleakness of space. Never know what to expect with you here on our planet."

That brought a round of laughter from everyone in the HAV. Even Mc'narrd was laughing in her comm.

"Tell me about P'yka. I'm aware it's where our sole penitentiary is located and it's our moon. I know the basics that everyone is taught at the academy, but not everyone goes to it."

"First and foremost, it's run by the military," Issik began. "I'm surprised you didn't research it like you do everything else."

"I'm five years into the police service," Violetta countered. "I didn't even expect to reach lieutenant for several more years. Typically it's lieutenants and those with higher ranks who go up if someone needs to be questioned." She glanced sharply at Issik. "Though you have been up frequently."

Issik shrugged. "I have experience from when I was in the military."

Violetta frowned, but didn't push it.

"Figured you'd have time to research it?" Da'kaw asked when she remained silent. She gave a nod. "That's fair. Why worry about something if you don't need to? Allows you to keep the data fresh when it's something you'll encounter."

"Exactly," Violetta agreed.

"Tell me what you do know," Issik suggested.

"P'yka has its own atmosphere. It was terraformed when the need for a prison system was decided upon. Those who are sent there have committed grievous crimes. They aren't enough to require death, but they are enough to need the criminals away from the general population. On the moon, they can't escape as easily."

"They won't escape at all," Da'kaw corrected. His tone and expression was grim. "The shuttles used can be shut down completely from a distance. If another shuttle manages to land, then leave, it can be destroyed by any number of the battlecruisers in orbit. Including those recycled to be used as scientific vessels or communication hubs."

"Do I have the clearance to know that? Or do you now have to kill me?" Issik joked.

"We'll just leave you behind on the moon," Da'kaw rejoined. He winked at Issik, who hummed. "No, that knowledge is accessible by those who know where to look."

"The entire moon had to have an ecosystem created so that plants could be grown." Issik paused, his eyes shifting to outside the window. "That was incredibly efficient."

Violetta followed his gaze out the window and discovered the HAV was on the flight field used to shuttle beings to and from the military vessels orbiting their world. The general public and merchants used the larger flight field on the opposite side of Preserve Highway. One had to take Dra'as Avenue several kilometers out of the main city to reach it. The location lessened the traffic flow into and out of the city.

It also reduced the noise caused by the frequent departures and arrivals. The intent was to lessen harm to the local flora and fauna. The citizens also appreciated the lower impact on air and ground travel caused by the traffic.

"I know those sent to the prison continue to serve by being tasked in the care and upkeep of the farms. Those farms provide the needed food for the prisoners and military personnel. It keeps everyone from being reliant on K'lais and possible imports from other planets for survival," Violetta commented as they climbed out of the HAV.

She paused in talking to appreciate the flight field. Her eyes swept across the rows of shuttles and few merc ships parked on the field. It took less than two minutes to locate the Serpent's Fangs' ship.

A smile flashed across her face at the fact her mother's merc unit was using a place at the military base. She knew they were hired often to help patrol the nature preserves during the prime season poachers tried hunting the planet's fauna. Mc'narrd liked them, which she was thankful for, because she loved the mercenaries.

The shapes and sizes of the sleek K'laisian ships varied greatly. All were sleek with smooth lines and rounded corners. Some were meant for only one or two beings. Others could hold over two dozen beings with room left for supplies.

Violetta remembered vividly bouncing along beside her father, her eyes dancing over the ships as he led her to one of the two-being ships. Vrehn had loved piloting ships and Violetta had adored having her father's sole attention as he took her up into the vastness of space.

Her heart squeezed and her chest felt tight for a brief moment.

"It's been a long time since I've been on this field," she said to no one in particular.

Commander Da'kaw gave her a curious look, but didn't respond to the comment.

"Which one is for us, commander?" Issik asked, giving Violetta a thoughtful look.

"Old memories," she explained, her eyes drifting across the field again. "You taking us up, commander?"

"I'll be joining you, but someone else will be piloting," he answered. "Ah, there she is now."

Walking towards them in a commander's biosuit was Lyza Mc'narrd. Her dark hair was pulled back into a tight braid that wrapped around her head. Though her movement was as fluid as any K'laisian, her steps were a smidge heavier than a native. There was no missing the sharp bronze eyes or the salutes snapped from those on the field as Commander Lyza Mc'narrd approached them.

"Commander Mc'narrd," Da'kaw said, snapping his own salute to the woman. He took a step ahead of Violetta and Issik. "May I present Detective Issik Ha'kksworth and Detective Violetta Cq'linns. Both of the 42nd District Police Service."

"Lady Addelia and I met yesterday," Lyza said easily, a smile tugging at her lips. Her bronze eyes shifted to Issik. "Well met and greetings, detective."

"Well met, Commander Mc'narrd," Issik replied, bowing to her.

"I'll be your pilot to P'yka today." She flashed a brilliant smile at the trio. "If you have any questions, get them out before we arrive. Follow me, please."

"She gets that directness from her mother," Mc'narrd stated in Violetta's comm. "You'll have a smooth ride with her."

Da'kaw, Issik, and Violetta followed behind the woman. She strode towards a medium-sized shuttle. The smooth curves and polished metals shone in the sunlight. Easily twice the size of a military tactical HAV, it would easily sit a dozen beings. It was off to the side of several other shuttles of similar size.

Windows crossed over the top of the shuttle, allowing a complete view of everything outside of the shuttle. Two seats were in the front of the shuttle, while there were three rows for passengers behind them.

Weaponry blended into the sides, front, and rear. Many beings might have missed them, but Violetta's eyes latched onto every weapon visible from her angle of the shuttle. The engines were just as smoothly incorporated into the ship's overall design. A beautiful, deadly work of art and amazing craftsmanship.

As Lyza approached the shuttle, the doors slid open. Stepping to the side, she gestured towards the seats.

"Am I going to have a co-pilot or do I get to take off without him?" Lyza asked, her eyes sweeping the field. There was a pause, and a smirk took complete form on her face. It reminded Violetta of Admiral Mc'narrd, her father. "Tell him to hurry up, or I'm going up without him."

"She would, too," Mc'narrd muttered in Violetta's ear. "And she knows she's supposed to have a copilot."

"Sorry for taking so long, Commander," a male form said from behind them. Violetta turned to find a native jogging up to them. "Took longer than expected in debriefing."

"I'll have to speak to someone about that," Lyza replied evenly. "Or they could have sent someone else knowing what we were required for today."

"You're just mad because I didn't send Zerik," the elder Mc'narrd retorted. "Your debriefing begins when you return, Commander."

"Allow me to introduce my first officer, Oenik La'kasy," Lyza said, ignoring her father's comment. "He'll be my copilot."

First Officer La'kasy bowed to them, then snapped a salute to Lyza. When she gave a nod, he hurried around the shuttle. He gave them a human-style wink before sliding into the copilot's seat. Violetta chuckled as Lyza shot him a disgruntled look.

"They'll never think I'm militant now," she grumbled as she settled into the pilot's seat.

Her copilot hummed as the doors slid shut before the locks clicked into place. He settled back in the seat, checking the interfaces. Lyza's hands flew over the controls with the confidence and ease of someone who was familiar with piloting a shuttle. The steady thrum of the engines filled the air around them. A soft, constant sound that brought a smile to Violetta's face.

"Flight control, this is Commander Lyza Mc'narrd," Lyza said aloud. "Systems check clear. Space clearance requested."

"Commander Mc'narrd, this is flight control," a feminine voice said over the comms. "You're cleared for space. Flight path acknowledged, passengers cleared for travel to P'yka."

"Acknowledge, flight control," Lyza replied. Her hands settled on the controls and Violetta could feel the shuttle lifting from the ground. "Commander Mc'narrd out."

Violetta watched with the same fascination she'd felt all those years ago as the shuttle followed a gradually inclining path into the sky. The surface of their planet grew more and more distant. Soon, she could see the city far below as the shuttle entered the sky.

As they reached their atmosphere, she watched in delight as they quickly passed through, then into the vastness of space.

"When's the last time you came up, Violetta?" Lyza asked, pausing the shuttle just above orbit.

"Oh, stars." Violetta practically breathed the words. "I was in high school. Dad took me to his last command ship just before his retirement. Said it would be the last time he could take me up with ease. Wanted me to experience it one last time." She swallowed hard, her eyes on the battlecruisers that orbited their planet. "I never knew it would be the last time I'd ever experience it with him."

There were always at least half a dozen battlecruisers in active orbit around their planet. K'lais' first line of planetary defense. There could be up to a dozen, easily, at any given time. Sometimes more, depending on how many returned for routine maintenance at a single time. Currently, she counted a dozen in visible orbit, including Lyza's and Zerik's battlecruisers.

Along with the imposing battlecruisers, there were several scientific and communications spacecraft. All recycled and repurposed older battlecruisers no longer used by the military to go out into the depths of space. Merchant and supply ships docked and departed alongside travel vessels filled with visitors, dignitaries, and residents.

Violetta watched it all in fascination and a little heartache.

"Is this difficult for you?" Lyza glanced over her shoulder at her. "If so, we can just go straight to the moon."

"No, I love it," Violetta replied honestly. "I suppose it's because I didn't go into the military? This is a rare treat for me. Rarer still to have the honor of you as our pilot."

Lyza laughed delightedly. It was as musical and sweet as hearing her adopted father laugh. "We have to wait for permission to land. Glad to hear you're enjoying the view. It's one of the best parts of being a commander."

"Dad would never forgive me if I didn't allow myself to enjoy it. Even briefly," Violetta admitted. "Since I've never been to P'yka, someone should tell me what to expect."

"We'll be setting down on the military's flight pad," First Officer La'kasy stated as he scrolled through an interface.

Violetta noticed it was written in K'laisian instead of Standard. "Because it's a prison, you'll be given an escort to the interrogation room."

"Due to the being who has requested your presence, I'll be waiting for you outside the room," Lyza commented, maneuvering the shuttle among the ships with an ease Violetta admired. "First Officer La'kasy will take my position within the room."

"There will also be guards from the prison," Issik added. "Every other instance I've had to visit the moon, I only received an escort from the military personnel at the penitentiary."

"How many times have you met a not-so-former Moyii Tsaa member?" La'kasy asked.

"A few," Issik replied, his voice neutral.

"How many times have you had someone of mixed heritage joining you?" Lyza asked, piloting the shuttle beside a battlecruiser. It allowed Violetta a very close view of just how majestic and beautiful the vessels truly were. "Wave!"

She waved a hand as they passed by some of the windows. Following her lead, the rest of them did the same. Including La'kasy.

"You are just mean," Mc'narrd stated over the comms. "How many are left on your ship?"

"You're aware of how many are always left on a battlecruiser when in dock," Lyza replied.

It almost sounded like a question, so Violetta answered as though it had been posed to her. "Half the crew. Including members of the command staff. Those who aren't on the first party to the surface are allowed to leave once the first group of beings return to their duties aboard. The only time a small number is left, is when the battlecruiser requires to be docked for anything other than routine maintenance and upgrades."

"Very good," Lyza praised. "I wouldn't expect less from my 'cousin'."

"You're going to have to explain that one day," La'kasy said. "We've been granted clearance on P'yka."

"When you get the clearance," Lyza teased.

La'kasy hummed loudly. "I'm certain you'll be using that to your advantage. Especially since the lady is wed to the Master of Ceremonies."

"We're family," Lyza stated with far more indignancy than was needed. Violetta giggled. "We pay for Malik's time at our box. *We* get to enjoy his and Vi's time before and after the Duels *without* having to pay extra."

"Which is a very enjoyable time," Violetta said with great warmth. "Does everyone know we're wed? We… okay, *I* was hoping to keep it quiet until after the public ceremony of joining."

"Only if they're familiar with why he's wearing a sword now. He rarely wore one before unless he was someone's Champion," Lyza admitted, smoothly piloting the shuttle. She touched an interface, with a finger even as she turned their vessel. "My father wed my mother using the same tradition. Though she wasn't completely aware of the significance until afterwards. Which should tell you how cunning my father was. He loved Mom and didn't want to consider her being sent planetside. Wedding her ensured she'd be able to remain on his battlecruiser. Even before she took the position of Policy Master."

"Still is cunning," Zerik's voice muttered over the comms. "Someone had to say it, and no one there can do so." There was a pause. "Love you, Dad."

"Aren't you supposed to be in debriefing?" Mc'narrd asked, drawing the words out.

"Still am, but I'm with Zh'oros." There was a definite smugness to the words. "Now you know what it's like."

"You still have to answer to me, son," Mc'narrd rejoined.

"Zerik out," was the quick reply.

"Just how many people would that be?" Violetta asked. "Or is it something only career military would recognize?"

"Mostly those who went offplanet, which isn't as many as you may think," Lyza answered. "That percentage of our people isn't nearly as high as many believe. And even then, it's a tradition used mainly among native K'laisians. Humans prefer weddings or the ceremonies of joining. When you're on a battlecruiser, wedding someone is not typically on your agenda of things to do. It does happen, but not a tenth as frequently as Duels."

"Returning to the previous topic," Issik cut in. "Normally, we would go through a process of ensuring neither of us has anything that would be used against us by those in the prison. We'd be cleared for entry, go through 'processing', then be escorted to an interrogation room."

"You'll be able to skip some steps this time," La'kasy stated. He'd returned to scrolling through the interface. "Pad Saja Three Dash Nine. Code Rusek Nuwa."

"Huh," Lyza said, tapping the interface herself. "Moyii Tsaa member Vylus Hy'neipi. Sent to P'yka for… that's impressive."

"Sent for a vicious attack and judicious use of a cleaver to not kill a being but leave them in a lot of pain and misery for a very long time," La'kasy stated in a neutral tone. "Never intended to kill the being, just inflict considerable harm onto them. Apparently for not paying a certain amount to prevent the attack from occurring."

"A 'protection racket', as the humans phrased it in the report," Lyza commented. "Our own people did the same during the ancient days."

"Explains the added security requirement," La'kasy mused. "Add in the fact she's of mixed heritage? It's probably to prevent another attack from them."

"Maybe I can actually find out what I've done to garner their interest," Violetta stated, her eyes fixed on their approach to the moon. "Aside from being of mixed heritage. And being wed to someone of mixed heritage."

"Or… just breathing?" Issik teased.

"That, too," Violetta said dryly.

Lyza began the descent to the moon and there was zero question as to her skill. She obviously knew the flight path. She followed it without turning her head to either side. Violetta couldn't tell if Lyza glanced at the display, but she suspected the woman didn't need to. In fact, Lyza's hands barely shifted as she guided the shuttle.

Minimal effort for maximum effect.

Violetta's own father had done the same.

"How often have you done this?" Violetta asked in pure curiosity.

Lyza laughed. "I began even before I earned my 'cruiser. I've always loved piloting, well, anything."

"Did your father teach you?" It must have startled Lyza, because the commander's head shifted to the side towards her. "Sorry, you remind me of how my father piloted when he took me up to his 'cruiser. I figured he and your father would've been similar in their techniques at piloting."

"Oh, yes, he did." Lyza didn't look over her shoulder at Violetta, but she did give a rather human shrug of her shoulder. "Dad spoke of Vrehn often. Said he was the best pilot and commander he knew. Dad taught all of us kids how to pilot. Sometimes even letting us pilot up to his battlecruiser."

"You realize we'll have to leave them on the moon now," La'kasy joked.

"Nah, that was too long ago and Dad's too revered for anyone to believe he'd do something like that," Lyza replied with a laugh. "No one would believe it. For all anyone knows, I'm just exaggerating what he allowed me to do."

Mc'narrd's laughter filled the comm. Violetta couldn't help but chuckled also.

"She loves acting as though I'm dead," Mc'narrd admitted. "But she's right. I did allow them to pilot the shuttle up to my battlecruiser. Lyza has always had an incredible talent for being a pilot. I wanted to encourage it from the moment we adopted her."

The shuttle descended through the clouds, giving Violetta her first look at K'lais' sole penitentiary. The main building was easily as large as their city. The smooth curves of the building swept upwards towards the clouds before curving inward. There were no sharp edges anywhere. The colors were darker than what she'd seen on the planet. Dark blues, deep purples, and blacks comprised the metals used to form the buildings, guard towers, and everything else within sight.

Fields of crops were beside long rows of fruit-bearing trees. Large, long greenhouses could be seen in rows near the main building. Beings moved among the trees, between the buildings, and outside in general.

The inmates wore pale cream and white tunics and loose breeches. Their hair was cut short regardless of race. The guards carried large energy weapons in their hands. Their emerald biosuits glittered in the sunlight of the moon.

Lyza settled the shuttle down on a pad. There was one other shuttle there, but no one was near the empty craft. Several military soldiers moved away from the side of the building as Lyza shut down the engines. Her door slid open and she stepped out in one fluid movement.

La'kasy followed his commander's lead. When Da'kaw remained in the shuttle, Violetta chose to follow his lead, even as Issik climbed out.

"Commander Mc'narrd," the lead soldier said, snapping her a salute. His dark hair formed rows of braids along his scalp before being pulled back into a tight ponytail. The strands shone in the sunlight. "Everything is cleared and in place for the detectives' visit."

At the comment, Da'kaw gave a nod and stepped from the shuttle. Violetta followed him out. He gave her an approving look at her choice. Together they rounded the front of the shuttle where Violetta joined Issik.

Being the first time Violetta had set foot upon the moon, she studied everything around her. The building was a normal design, even if the materials were different. The biosuits worn by those on the moon were also typical. Even if they were a brilliant emerald green. On the left shoulder was the prison's emblem. A shieldless helm overlaying a barred circular portal, or what humans often called 'portholes'.

"Let's not keep anyone waiting, Commander At'che," Lyza stated.

The commander snapped Lyza another salute, turned on his heel, and strode towards the door. Lyza and La'kasy fell into step behind him. Issik and Violetta followed them, allowing Da'kaw to bring up the rear. As they neared the door, the rest of the soldiers fell into formation around them.

Instead of stepping into a hallway or foyer, the group entered what reminded Violetta of a recreation room. There were counters with packaged foods and beverages. Several replicators were lined up, as well as dart boards along one wall, and other methods of recreation for beings. There was also an entertainment interface hanging in the corner of the room.

At'che continued through the room and the opposite door. The formation tightened up around them as they traversed the hallway. Violetta presumed this was an area of the compound used primarily by the military personnel. It was confirmed when she noticed bunks through some of the opened doors. They were either empty or had beings lounging in them.

The general noise of conversations in various languages filtered out of the rooms. Though she knew and understood all of them, the comm translated only the snippets it picked up. Both a benefit of having the comm as a translator and annoyance. Especially when her ears were hearing things the comms missed. Or, like now, when she was able to interpret the conversations and the comms were translating them.

She could only imagine how difficult it might be for someone who wasn't fluent in multiple languages and didn't have the comms.

Once more, she was thankful for the father and grandparents she'd had growing up. For the skills they'd ensured she was taught. One day, she knew she'd have to figure out how to pass those lessons onto her and Malik's children.

That day would not be any time soon, she decided.

She wanted to enjoy a few years with Malik without children. They would have plenty of time before they discussed the whole family thing. A benefit of having a long lifespan.

Pausing before a door with a glowing red interface, Commander At'che input a series of codes. There was a click before the door slid open. The corridor it opened into shifted from a metallic gray and deep purple color to silver and white. Violetta's eyes darted around her, noticing the small openings at the top and bottom of the walls. Each one shone a brilliant blue.

She brushed her hand against Issik's fingers. He glanced at her. Her eyes darted to the objects. Issik gave a quick shake of his head. His fingers tapped hers in standard military code signaling one word: later.

She flicked his knuckles with her fingers in response. His lips twitched as he kept a smile from forming.

"They're security measures, detective," Mc'narrd said in her ear. "I'm watching the cameras in the hallway you're traveling. Very clever method you two have developed for conversing. Many beings would have tried Matching you two. Probably a good thing no one did. I suspect Addelia would've Challenged you for your hand."

"Isn't that rather primitive, sir?"

Violetta recognized the overly polite tone of Malik's voice.

"Are you saying you wouldn't have, for her?" Mc'narrd asked, curiosity filling every word.

"No, I would have," Malik reassured the admiral. "But I suspect someone very high up in the military would have informed Issik of the needed security clearance. And that he would never get it to have her as a mate."

"It's a possibility," Mc'narrd allowed.

"I suspect that same person would then have maneuvered us into seeing each other again," Malik continued, his voice still overly polite. "Perhaps even convincing certain family members into Matching us."

"Hox, I would've done it years ago if I'd known about you two," Zerik chirped up. "Long before I knew she was family. You should've said something, Malik! One of us could've convinced her to come to the arena. Even if we had to Challenge her!"

Violetta coughed lightly at the same time Lyza cleared her throat. The commander glanced over her shoulder at Violetta, amusement in her eyes. "You ready, lady? We're almost to the interrogation rooms."

"As ready as I'll ever be," Violetta replied, clearing all amusement from her face and body. Her eyes shifted to the camera in the corner of the hallway. Staring at it, her fingers signaled a request for silence.

Knowing Mc'narrd, she doubted he would do it. But it was worth a try.

Laughter was Mc'narrd's response even as At'che unlocked the door and entered.

"I'll wait for you here," Lyza said, moving to the side.

Issik followed At'che through the door, leaving Violetta to follow him. She gave Lyza a human wink as she stepped through the doorway and into a small foyer. On all sides were doors. Since only one was open, she went through.

The walls all along the next room ended at about a meter high. The windows began immediately after and continued to the peaked ceiling. She could see a single native sitting at a table on the other side of the window. His hands were shackled together, as were his feet. Both were attached to dark purple metal rings in the table and floor, respectively. Three full blood native guards stood equally spaced along each wall. None were in a casual pose and all wore grim expressions.

Commander At'che crossed to the door to the room and opened it. Issik and Violetta glanced at each other before continuing into the interrogation room. La'kasy followed, as did another native guard, leaving Da'kaw to bring up the rear.

Vylus Hy'neipi was a pure blood native with black hair cut to just above his shoulders. His dark tan skin was mostly blemish free. A narrow scar trailed along the side of one cheek, the skin just a shade or two lighter than the rest of his face. His features were sharp, made sharper by the shortness of his hair. The cream tunic and loose pants suited him well.

Violetta suspected he would have been considered handsome and attractive by most females. If he didn't have such a cold appearance.

His gold eyes darted over the full blood natives of the group as they entered before settling on Violetta.

Old habits never died, and Violetta had never allowed herself to be intimidated by anyone. A part of her mind believed her father would suddenly appear if she allowed it to happen, and so she never gave into the feeling.

She may be self-conscious when an entire arena of beings stared at her, but self-consciousness was not the same as intimidation. And she wasn't at an arena. She was at a prison, inside an interrogation room with a prisoner who was a member of the Moyii Tsaa. Who also happened to be shackled and surrounded by armed and armored guards.

Instead of shifting uneasily, or making any self-conscious movement, she met the gold eyes steadily remaining fixed in place. Her feet were shoulder width apart, knees bent slightly so they wouldn't lock and cause discomfort. Her hands were loose at her sides. Not threatening, but within easy range of her weapons.

The corners of Hy'neipi's lips curved upwards slightly. "So, you're Lady Violetta Addelia, daughter of the esteemed Vrehn Cq'linns. Beloved commander and one of best battle strategists our world ever had the glory of witnessing."

Violetta lifted her chin slightly before lowering it in a K'laisian nod. "I am. You are Vylus Hy'neipi, member of the Moyii Tsaa. I'm afraid I do not know your clan name."

The comment made the man snort, a smirk flashing across his features. "Well played, Lady Addelia."

She bowed slightly at the waist. "I was informed you wished to speak with me about something occurring within the 42nd District of K'lais."

The declaration was the right choice of words. Vylus Hy'neipi straightened even more in the chair and his eyes flashed with anger.

"I was instructed to speak with you in regards to restoring honor to the Moyii Tsaa," he stated. His gold eyes didn't waver from hers, even as the military personnel grew even more alert. It was as though he didn't care. "We're aware of what has been happening. Someone has brought dishonor to the cartel. We desire to rectify that, and in so doing, restore honor to our name."

"What do you know?" Issik demanded. "If you have a name, then speak it."

"You are here because she would not be allowed to come alone," Hy'neipi snapped, his gold eyes snapped to Issik. "You are not the one who controls this discussion. If she wants the name, she agrees to the terms."

"Explain, please, how dishonor has befallen the Moyii Tsaa cartel?" Violetta asked politely. "And what it has to do with me?"

"Eyes and attention have turned to the Moyii Tsaa due to the attacks upon you, Lady Addelia," Hy'neipi declared. "The being responsible is known to us. He, yes it is a male, has approached us multiple times with the desire to join the Moyii Tsaa."

Violetta remained in her casual stance. She could have adopted a standard 'at rest' position, but she refused to show any discomfort or annoyance. Her face remained neutral, her eyes remained fixed on Hy'neipi.

"Please, continue," she requested, her tone never changing. "How has this being brought dishonor upon the Moyii Tsaa when he is not a member?"

"He has attempted to kill you and has killed others using subterfuge and at a distance," Hy'neipi snarled.

His entire face shifted into one of pure disgust. The native prisoner stretched his neck until popping sounds filled the room. Violetta refused to flinch or wince at the sound. Her father had done it frequently when he was thoroughly angry. It had not occurred often, but it had happened. She always hated the sound. That had not changed in the past five years, either. Not that she was going to show such in front of Hy'neipi.

"No one, absolutely *no one*, would attack you in such a disgraceful and dishonorable fashion, Lady Addelia," Hy'neipi continued, biting off each word in absolutely fury. "We would come at you, allowing you the honor of defending yourself. Not dying by inhaling the scent of a deadly flower."

"Or being shot at from the top of a building using an antique Earther weapon?" Issik added, disgust in his voice.

"Both are dishonorable, but most especially the vase of flowers," Hy'neipi allowed, his eyes flicking briefly at Issik before returning to Violetta. "The Moyii Tsaa are actually pleased you healed from that event. And it is because of that dishonorable action that we are willing to give you the being's name."

"Honor will be restored if I, personally, request the name of this individual?" Violetta asked. "Please forgive my ignorance, but I am confused due to the fact I was attacked, not Challenged, at the nature preserve."

Hy'neipi gave a stiff nod. "Clear the Moyii Tsaa's name. Make it known this individual is not a member. Agree and I will give you the name of who you're seeking. As to the others, they disobeyed protocol and direct orders. The survivors were dealt with."

There truly was little choice, in her opinion.

"It will be done," Violetta promised, bowing at the waist. Her entire upper body remained a straight line as she did so. "Even if I must make the statement myself. I thank you for answering my questions."

"We have an accord." Hy'neipi's eyes narrowed on her. "Obviously it will be known if you do not uphold your side of this agreement."

"I have no reason to not keep my side of the agreement. Your statement confirms my suspicions. If this individual is not a member of the Moyii Tsaa, it should be known. It *will* be known when he goes to trial for the murders he has committed. As well as the attempts upon my life."

"Yinko Si'elos is the name of the K'laisian native you need to seek out," Hy'neipi said, his voice calmer. The fury still gleamed in his gold eyes, but it wasn't twisting his face anymore. "Locate Si'elos and you will have your murderer."

"Your assistance, and through you the assistance of the Moyii Tsaa, has brought honor back to them," Violetta stated, knowing it's what they sought more than anything else.

"Do you believe this is an absolute truce, Lady Addelia?" Hy'neipi suddenly asked, a cruel smile curling his lips. "This is only temporary. But when we do come after you, rest assured, you will be allowed the honor of defending yourself."

Every native with a weapon stiffened at the declaration.

The corners of Violetta's lips curved upwards slightly. "Will you permit a question?"

Hy'neipi tipped his head to the side, but he lifted his chin in a nod.

"What have I done to warrant their attention? They attacked before I wed Malik. He had not even gifted me the ring yet. I am not aware of insulting a member of the Moyii Tsaa."

"Liar," Mc'narrd's voice said in her comm. "Though I only know differently because I heard you do it over your comm four months ago. Admittedly, there is no way anyone would know otherwise, since all those members are dead."

Hy'neipi scoffed. "That's a well spoken lie, Lady Addelia."

"Please, explain that. Perhaps my memory of a conversation is considerably different and I am unaware of the insult I spoke."

"We were informed you insulted Asharii at the business where your mate purchased the ring. I'm certain the military is aware it is one of our legit businesses the Moyii Tsaa owns," Hy'neipi retorted. "Insults, you're aware, are taken seriously by the Moyii Tsaa."

"Indeed? Perhaps we should allow the camera footage of that event to speak for itself," Violetta suggested.

Her hand was removing the interface and her fingers flew over the screen before anyone could object. Even Hy'neipi appeared impressed with her quickness. Within only a few heartbeats, she had the vidclip of the event up and paused. It wasn't difficult, considering she knew exactly what day it was, as well as the time. Having access to it only helped in the quickness of her retrieval.

Stepping forward, she slid the interface across the table to him. He jerked in startlement as the interface stopped at his hands.

"How is a Halfer capable of being as fast as a native?" he demanded, tapping the screen to play to vidclip.

"My father was Vrehn Cq'linns. My mother Kali MacLeod, a human mercenary who could trace her family name back for centuries to an ancient warring clan on Earth," Violetta replied with pride in her voice. "Simply because I am not a pure blood native, does not mean I am not skilled."

Hy'neipi replayed the vidclip several times before finally sliding the interface back to her.

"You said very little in the business. At that interaction, you were nervous, eager to leave. Malik demanded nothing more than the respect any customer should be given." He studied Violetta, seeming to search her for unease or any negative emotion. "Yet you show nothing remotely similar here. Even as you wear the mate to bures'o Addelia's sword, as well as the ring he gifted you."

"I'm not comfortable shopping for such," Violetta explained in a neutral tone. "I'm more comfortable with those I swore to protect when I graduated from the police service's academy."

"That will certainly change," Hy'neipi muttered. His eyes watched as Violetta turned off the interface and slid it into its sheath. All without removing her eyes from him. "I'll make it known neither you nor your mate insulted Asharii or anyone at the business."

"I appreciate your assistance and for watching the vidclip." Violetta bowed once more at the waist.

Hy'neipi returned the gesture as well as he could, considering he was sitting in the chair. Violetta turned and left the room. The door ahead of her slid open and she continued through it without waiting for the other men. A power play to show she was equal to those around her. Not a being wishing to be protected.

She waited until she was through the second door to draw in a deep breath and let it out slowly.

"And that is why I am thankful I did not enter the military," she admitted. "Having to continue that charade for long periods of time? I don't know how Dad, or really any of you, manage it."

"You learn," Lyza said, giving her an understanding expression. "We aren't encountering new races nearly as often as you may think. Or even encountering races who wish to battle us at every meeting."

Violetta leaned against the wall across from Lyza, allowing herself to relax as they waited for the others. "I can do it, but I still hate it."

The door slid open and At'che walked through with the others. He glowered at her but she just shrugged.

"Let's get you back to your shuttle," Commander At'che said, taking the lead again.

They fell into the same formation as the one they'd entered with, allowing Violetta time to consider what she'd been told.

"That explains why they wanted to speak to you," Issik said quietly as they traversed the corridors. Violetta glanced at him sharply. "The vase of flowers."

"I still don't understand that," Violetta admitted with a sigh. "Why wait until that was sent to me?"

"Because you truly did almost die from that," Lyza stated. She slowed until she was walking beside Violetta. "It's no secret how badly you were harmed. Many people questioned if you were actually dead when you came out of the penthouse."

"How…" She trailed off, then sighed. "Vidclips?"

"Guessed it the first time," Lyza teased. "You were then seen being loaded into a military HAV that took a few routes only a military HAV could take in an emergency. At the same time Malik bailed from the arena and wasn't seen for days. Not even a peep from him about what was going on."

"Until he was questioned at the arena after you were released," Issik added. "Didn't take long for someone to order the Chief of Police to make that announcement about kyitis flowers."

"It should have been done decades ago," Lyza grumbled. "Not like it's a new thing."

"Makes you wonder why now?" Violetta mused aloud. "Because it happened to someone in the public's eye? Or because it happened to someone in the police service, and ultimately, the military?"

"You are technically career police service and a being of interest to the military," Lyza stated. At Violetta's confusion, the older woman laughed. "Five years on the force with no interest in ending the career. You're rising in the ranks. You have exposed not a small amount of corruption in said police service. That's just what I've heard. I'm certain there is more."

"You do seem to bring all sorts of… problems… we'll call them 'problems' to the military's attention," Issik added. "You've never been one to allow an injustice to go unanswered, if you could prevent it."

Violetta shrugged. She couldn't deny it.

Lyza gently added, "What you discovered four months ago would cause you to be a being of interest to the military. Once someone garners the military's attention? They aren't going to stop watching you. Especially when you continue to find information considered important to the military."

"You brought something harmful to K'lais security to the military's attention," Mc'narrd interjected. "Lyza is aware it would take something of a high security concern to involve me. Despite all appearances to the contrary, my main duties are with special operations, covert operations, that require the highest security and secrecy."

"You believe someone further up in the military demanded that declaration," Violetta commented. She met Lyza's eyes. "Wonder who it could've been?"

Lyza shrugged. "Mom is one of the highest ranking Masters of Policies. Maybe she said something to someone. I think she's met every three-star admiral and healer in our district."

"She did indeed." Mc'narrd grumbled. "She demanded to know why it took me so long."

Why did it? Violetta signed the words using military symbols, using the hand nearest to Lyza.

Her fingers moved just enough to form the words. If Da'kaw noticed, he remained silent.

"Cute," Mc'narrd stated coolly. "You are still under my command, Violetta. Regardless of how many ranks may be between us, you're still *under me*. Allow me to remind you that the entire police service is under the military. My military ranking is even above most of the beings at the base. It was an oversight. It's been corrected. Don't push, *lieutenant*."

"*I* am not under your command." Malik's cool voice said over the comms. Her eternal rock in the storm. "Even had I remained in the military, I would have been outside your command as Master Healer. And so *I* will ask: What else have you overlooked? Who else has to die, or come dangerously close, for a similar reason before you or anyone else decides to become involved?"

Violetta glanced sharply at Lyza who shrugged slightly. They'd traversed the building and the last room was in front of them. Everyone remained silent as At'che led them outside to the shuttle. The silence continued even as they all entered the shuttle.

"Be safe, be well, Commander Mc'narrd," Commander At'che stated, snapping a salute to the woman.

She returned the salute. "Be well, be safe, Commander At'che. Our thanks, again."

At'che smiled, bowed, and patted the shuttle's side before striding back to the side of the building.

"Did you forget I could hear the conversations, sir?" Malik continued in that same cool tone.

Lyza turned her complete attention to the shuttle, her hands steady as they moved across the controls. First Officer La'kasy began checking the interfaces.

"Flight path cleared, Commander Mc'narrd," a voice said from one of the interfaces. "You may leave at your leisure."

"Acknowledged," Lyza replied as she piloted the shuttle into the air.

Following a similar path back up into orbit, she slowed the vessel's speed once they hit the vast openness of space. There was still silence between Mc'narrd and Malik.

"How about a trip around the planet?" Lyza suggested cheerfully.

"Trying to avoid the return, daughter?" Mc'narrd's voice was deceptively neutral.

"Yes," Violetta said. "That… would be appreciated."

Issik gave her a curious look. She tapped his hand, using their signal for discussing it later. Her eyes slanted to his ear before looking in the general direction of their planet. Understanding flashed through his eyes.

"I suspect they're hoping it will give you time to calm down," Malik replied over the comms. "It's a valid question. One I hope you think long and hard about, *sir*. Addelia out."

Even as La'kasy tapped the interface, Lyza piloted the shuttle forward, heading for a leisurely tour of the planet and the orbiting ships.

"Enjoy the view," Lyza commented. "Trips to P'yka are rare. So unless you plan on a trip offplanet, this will be the last time you come up for a good while. Care to take some vidclips for them, La'kasy?"

"Setting it up now, commander," he replied. "Better hope you don't get reprimanded for this."

"I'm considering it," Mc'narrd snapped. There was a pause, then a heavy sigh. "But I'd have to contend with your mother if I did that."

"I believe I'll be safe this time," Lyza commented, keeping her voice neutral.

Without another word, Lyza maneuvered the shuttle onto a course that would circle the planet, allowing them to pass by the moon a second time. The course was easy to view on the interface, and Violetta recognized it as one similar to what her father would take.

Violetta turned her attention to the exterior, determined to remember everything. Issik, she noticed, was doing the same. A thoughtful expression on his face.

The view was a much better option, in her opinion, than wondering what sort of reception she'd receive from the admiral once they landed.

Unlike Lyza, she did not have Alyssa to protect *her* from a reprimand.

Chapter Twenty Three

The tour around the planet took less time than Violetta expected. Perhaps it was because she hadn't done it for over five years. Or, perhaps Lyza hadn't taken quite as long as her father. The trips with her father, Violetta had to admit, included a lot of questions from her and explanations from her father. Lessons and quality time with her beloved father rolled all into one.

"Meet me in my office," Mc'narrd ordered over the comm.

"I'll walk with you," Lyza offered. To Issik, she explained, "My commanding officer is wishing to debrief her about the visit. Standard military procedure. You will also need to be debriefed, Detective Ha'kksworth."

"Fark. I suppose he would," Mc'narrd grumble. "Fine. I'll take Violetta and set Ha'kksworth up with Admiral By'kett. Da'kaw, escort Issik. Lyza…" he trailed off with a sigh. "Don't make me regret this."

"I'll escort you to Admiral By'kett," Da'kaw offered. "His office is on the third level, detective."

Issik gave him a narrow-eyed look, but remained silent. The last time Violetta and Issik had spoken to By'kett had been on a ground-level office that had actually been Mc'narrd's office.

"No, sir," she replied in a demure voice. There was considerable grumbling from the admiral that Violetta couldn't make out. Lyza smirked and gestured for Violetta to follow her. "Would you like the vidclips and stillclips on a chip, Vi?"

Holcrom data cards, or poker chips as the humans referred to them, were what everyone used to store data.

Because they reminded humans of round or multi-sided poker chips, the name had caught on. Most beings referred to the data cards as 'chips'. The chips varied in storage size, design, and color. A being could place a password on the cards just as easily as they could a console or interface. The ones used by the military could be protected by DNA sequences, passwords, or a combination of the two. Some types of chips could only be read by military devices.

Violetta still had a few of those types amongst her father's possessions.

"I would enjoy that, thank you," Violetta replied, grateful for the change of topic.

"I'll put them on a chip for you while you're being debriefed," Lyza offered.

"Thank you," Violetta repeated.

"Happy to do it, cousin," Lyza replied cheerfully.

There was a slight emphasis on 'cousin', which elicited more grumbling over the comm. She shot Violetta a very human wink. Their conversation shifted to more casual topics as they traversed the corridors to Mc'narrd's office.

"Good luck," Lyza said softly, stopping in front of Mc'narrd's door.

"Thanks," Violetta replied. She touched her hand to the interface. The door slid open, allowing Violetta to enter.

Mc'narrd was standing next to his desk. He was looking at something on his interface display. He smiled without looking towards her and said, "Violetta, come in."

From the interface, the voice of Zh'oros said, "Thank you for joining us. Would you prefer to sit?"

Violetta opened her mouth to answer, then closed it. Her eyes remained on Mc'narrd, uncertain of what the admiral would prefer from her. "Sir?"

Offering a single shrug, Mc'narrd replied, "Whatever you'd like to do. I will be standing for the moment."

"She did it again," cut in Zh'oros.

A second display projected from the desk. It was nearly the same as the projection closer to Mc'narrd. A full body display from a medical scan, along with measurements of bodily activity such as pulse, respiration, and such. An image of a brain was being projected between the body and the statistics. The brain had a large area marked in light blue, with a series of small dots pulsing.

Violetta looked at this display, and tried to look at the other. The readings were mirror opposite, so she could not immediately recognize the numbers. When she did, it was evident the numbers were not the same as the display in her eye line.

Mc'narrd sighed. As he did, the readings changed on the display facing him. The brain display changed colors, as did portions of the body display.

"Don't say it. I can see I'm doing it as well," grumbled Mc'narrd.

"You're making progress already," observed the voice of Zh'oros.

"I'm very confused," admitted Violetta.

As the words left her mouth, she noticed the brain display facing her had changed. What looked like green lightning was dancing along one portion of the brain. The heart rate and pulse had also increased.

"Is this a medical scan of me? One in current time?" Violetta asked.

"Yes," said Zh'oros. "With less than 2 milliseconds of lag. I'm projecting the readings from your respective biosuits so you can see how your bodies are reacting."

"Our Sovereign Healer has identified a series of psychological responses that she considers worth bringing to our mutual attention," said Mc'narrd. His voice was tired and amused in equal portions.

The green lightning subsided on Violetta's display, to be replaced by a pink glow in a different section. A spike in thermal temperature and circulation on the body display, specifically from the neck up.

She didn't need a mediscan to know she was blushing.

"So, in the first minute, we have witnessed several phases in physiology and brain function," Zh'oros announced in a sweet, maddening tone. "Do we need further data to confirm my theories, Mc'narrd?"

"Not to me, but you will explain them to the detective. I'm getting a headache just trying to recall all the medical words you launched at me before she arrived."

A low hum came from Zh'oros. "Violetta, this is not a dangerous concern or condition I am bringing to both your attention and the admiral. But I have repeatedly witnessed your response to Admiral Mc'narrd being subjectively consistent with that of a child wanting to please a parental being. Would you agree that this is a likely behavior?"

Violetta had to push her brain to find denial and data to back it up. Finally, she groaned and admitted, "Yes, it is. I do find myself thinking of my father while interacting with the admiral."

"You owe me a private box and drinks, It'zarry. She is far quicker to grasp this situation than you have been." Zh'oros sounded just a teensy bit pleased with herself.

"Conversely, I often respond to your well-being with the same level of concern as a parent does for their child," Mc'narrd added.

He seemed slightly deflated, as though some measure of resolve had been surrendered.

Violetta found herself looking at his display, desperately trying to discern changes in the readings. Then, she stopped herself. Nor would she let herself look at her own readings. Now that she was aware of their function and the circumstances, the displays seemed unsettling.

"And Violetta is already attempting to improve on this," said Zh'oros cheerfully. "The concern is not that you both are developing a close rapport, Violetta. It's that doing so without refrain will one day lead to one or both of you making decisions using your emotional connection as the driving factor, rather than information and rational problem-solving. Even before we began dealing with other races, K'laisians recognized the inherent, often fatal mistakes that came with such styles of decision making."

Violetta nodded in at least partial understanding. Then wondered if the Sovereign Healer could even see her nod.

She said, "I understand."

"Now that you are both consciously aware of this, I am confident that all parties will work towards a positive resolution. This will be a part of your respective evaluations from this point forward. Thank you for your attention."

Zh'oros shut down the displays, and her voice was not heard for a few seconds. Mc'narrd finally sat behind his desk.

"I hate when she does things like that," he confided.

"That is completely understandable," Violetta agreed, crossing to a chair and settling into it. "Do you have this difficulty with your children, sir?"

Mc'narrd gave her an honest, if not tired smile that met his eyes. "All the time. It often takes a conscious effort to treat them the same as every other commander and soldier under my command. They're brilliant beings, and they test the limits of the laws and protocols they're trained to follow. But, just as I did, they often have to deviate from the rules to achieve the goal best for the circumstances. I, in turn, have to ignore the fact they are my children and consider their actions as if they were any other commander."

Violetta nodded, a thoughtful expression on her face. "Until we met, I will admit, none of my supervisors reminded me of Dad." At Mc'narrd's chuckle, she couldn't help but smile and duck her head in a very human fashion. "I know. Dad was a very impressive and imposing being. Few could ever stand close to him. But you do, sir. I will endeavor to remember, at least while I'm on duty, you are my commanding officer. Even if we do have a friendship."

"More of a familial relationship, but friendship as well. I mean no offense, but you may well discover it is a deeper struggle for you, since you are part human," Mc'narrd rejoined. "My spouse has often displayed more significant issues in putting some emotions 'to the side', as she refers to it."

"I… okay, we should be honest, at least to each other. I was afraid to admit how much you have come to mean to me," Violetta stated frankly. Mc'narrd's face softened. "I value the familial relationship and I believe it's something I covet." She gave a very human shrug. "If I fall into that 'trap', please let me know? And remember it's most likely subconscious on my part?"

"Indeed," he replied while smiling. "As it will likely be on my part as well."

"Agreed," Violetta said, with definite warmth in her voice.

"Now, tell me about what happened at P'yka," Mc'narrd stated, touching the interface. "We'll start there with the debriefing."

Chapter Twenty Four

By the time Violetta was able to meet Issik in the main entrance, only two hours had passed. Having the discussion with Mc'narrd and Zh'oros solidified some questions and raised others. But, at least now she didn't question the depth of meaning behind Mc'narrd's request to call him her uncle.

Somehow, within the past four months, she'd managed to wed her childhood sweetheart and gain a considerably larger family. Ah, well. After five years of being a reclusive hermit, was it truly so surprising?

"How long did your debriefing take?" Violetta asked Issik as they headed for the HAV.

"Not nearly as long as yours," he teased. "I've already spoken to Ra'keff and Osing. They've had the data analysts working on gathering information on Yinko Si'elos. The profile should be complete by the time we arrive at the station."

"It's a short trip to the station," Violetta commented.

"It'll be awaiting us," Issik reassured her.

Violetta pulled out her interface and input the name. Issik moved closer so he could see the screen. Together they began discussing the information Violetta could pull up. It wasn't a lot, but it was better than remaining silent.

By the time they arrived at the station, they were eager to leave the HAV. Instead of choosing the main door, they jogged to a side door. Violetta input the code to enter. The door slid open and they entered into an empty hallway. Their steps quickened as they headed for their department.

"Any news from COD?" Violetta asked in the comm.

There was a moment of silence before Ra'keff's voice filled her ear. "They're supposedly sending someone over. They're a bit… cranky at the moment."

"What's going on?" Issik asked, glancing sharply at Violetta, who shrugged her shoulders. "Never heard you use that term before, Hy'szolis."

"Seems the healers have decided to do evals of their people. Several have been pulled from active duty to be treated for psychological illnesses," Ra'keff replied in a cool tone. "The same policies for the military are being implemented for the police service."

"Ka'desh," Issik breathed.

"They're down several people already," he added. "How far out are you two?"

"Walking in now," Violetta replied, opening the door to their division. Her eyes landed on her desk, only to find more flowers on it. "More?"

"Not all from Addelia, either," Osing called. "Valerie was wondering if she could have a vase or two for her desk."

Violetta spotted the woman at the other side of the room. "Hey, Val," she said in the comm. When the woman looked her way, she waved. "Osing said you've been admiring the flowers. Want a vase or two? I think my desk may turn into a garden if they stay there."

Valerie's laughter filled the comm. "Thanks, Osing, for ratting me out! You sure, Vi?"

"Absolutely. If you want some, Tiayl, help yourself," Violetta added. "Though, Val might take 'em all, if you aren't careful."

"Hah! You wish!" Valerie retorted.

There was considerable laughter and humming as Violetta paused by her desk to check the cards that had been sent with the new flowers. There were several new ones from Malik. As well as a vase from her grandparents, several from military personnel she recognized, and a large arrangement from Zerik and Lyza.

"Just leave the ones from Zerik and Lyza," Violetta requested. "I'll have to thank them later."

"We'll just take the ones from Malik," Valerie replied with another laugh.

"Yeah, you can have the others," Tiayl joked. "His orders are always fancy."

"Thanks, ladies." She didn't bother hiding the grin. It was nice having such a good camaraderie with her colleagues. Different and definitely more enjoyable. "Are we taking over the meeting room again?"

"We should just put our names on the door," Osing joked. "Move our desks in there, too."

"Think the captain would sign off on it?" Violetta asked, heading to the room with Issik.

"The captain can hear you comedians," Os'shye interjected.

None of them appeared the least big chagrined, Violetta noted with amusement as she settled into one of the chairs.

"So, is that a yes, sir?" Ra'keff asked in an innocent tone.

"Keep dreaming, Detective Hy'szolis," Os'shye retorted.

"Every day, sir. Every day," Ra'keff rejoined, sorrow in his voice. "But so far, none of them have come true!"

"I should have stayed with the military," Os'shye grumbled. "Os'shye out."

Ra'keff had a decidedly pleased expression on his face.

"Let's not wait for whoever COD is sending over." He gave a snort. "They may not even send anyone."

There was a quick round of agreement from all of them.

"We've pulled up the medical files we have on one Yinko Si'elos," Ra'keff began, his hands tapping away on the interface before him. "His place of employment is a theater on Bl'icherat Avenue. He's an opera singer there, not an actor."

Osing touched his interface. A hologram of Si'elos appeared in the center of the table and began turning in a complete circle.

"His physical appearance fits the profile with only a little variance. According to the current healers, it's within an acceptable amount to fit the profile we have on our suspect," Osing stated. He paused the hologram so it faced them. "I'll admit, I was not expecting a native K'laisian."

"Does he have any connections with Malik?" Violetta asked, studying the face. "Is the name Yinko Si'elos familiar to you, Malik?"

The three other natives remained silent, accepting the fact she could contact him with their comms. They didn't even appear surprised.

"Yinko Si'elos?" Malik repeated, as though tasting the name. "No. It's an unusual name, even for a native. Sorry, beloved."

"We're not locating a direct connection, either," Mc'narrd stated over the comms. "We did check, due to the direct attack upon you."

"He's not familiar with the name," Violetta informed her colleagues, with a shake of her head. "So, still no connection that we're aware of."

"Or motive," Issik added. "He does live in the right neighborhood for the florist, delivery service, antique dealers, and some of our victims."

"And the name was given to us from a known member of the Moyii Tsaa," Violetta added. She paused before turning to Ra'keff and Osing. "You're both familiar with why we went up to P'yka, yes?"

The pair nodded.

"We've been briefed by Issik. Captain? Do we have enough for a warrant to search and seize evidence?" Ra'keff asked, all humor from his voice. "The sooner we can search Si'elos' residence, the sooner we'll know if we were told the truth."

"I'll contact a judge," Captain Os'shye stated. "You may have to plead your case, Detective Cq'linns."

"Tell him to contact Judge Io'siph Ta'ba," Mc'narrd instructed. "I'll sign it without making you plead your case. We need this being brought in before he kills again."

Violetta didn't even blink. "What about Judge Io'siph Ta'ba? Would he be willing to sign the warrant?"

"I'll check to see if he's available, but he's a good choice," Captain Os'shye replied. "He would definitely want us to move forward before this being kills again."

With only a few touches of her interface, Violetta shifted the hologram to the end of the table. A replica of the street in and around Si'elos' residence began forming in front of them on the table.

"You're confident we'll get that signed," Ra'keff commented, his gold eyes on her.

"No, I'm confident we'll get a judge to sign it one way or another," Violetta corrected him. "We need to plan out our approach so when we do get it, we can move in immediately. Especially if Issik and I have to plead our case."

"Sorry, 'Keff, but I may request Vi take the lead on more cases," Osing stated as they stood to lean over the display.

"None taken," Ra'keff replied. She glanced up, startled. His eyes locked with hers. "I'm going to do the same."

"Let's finish this case before you two start planning out my future for me, hmm?" Violetta asked, a smile on her lips. She touched the screen of her interface. Blank-faced copies meant to resemble street officers appeared in a line along one side of the table. "Now, how do we want to do this?"

There was a round of skittered humming as the men began discussing the best method of approach. Mc'narrd even added a few suggestions she hadn't considered, which she spoke to the group.

By the time the admiral had signed the warrant, under his alias of Judge Ta'ba, Captain Os'shye had joined them in the meeting room. They finished plotting out the best plan to secure the residence and street around it as the signed warrant appeared on their interfaces.

"If he isn't there, we'll have to move to the theater," Violetta commented. "Thankfully there are fewer entrances and exits he can take there."

"We'll be able to secure it with more ease, certainly," Osing concluded.

"This is being sent to the street officers and your fellow detectives," Os'shye declared. "Go get this *t'iach* and bring him in. Alive, if at all possible."

The four of them exchanged grim expressions as they all stood.

"He'll have to commit suicide in order for him to come in any other way but alive," Violetta vowed.

The men glanced at each other then smiled at her. It was lovely to know they were concerned about her temperament.

"Dismissed," Os'shye ordered.

The four of them departed the room.

"We'll take an unmarked HAV, detective," Da'kaw stated. "You three take your own."

There was a round of nods and agreement. The walk out of the building was deceptively silent. All of them had their own thoughts. Violetta wasn't going to intrude on the men. Not when she had her own to contend with, ones that required the privacy of a military HAV.

The moment she was in it, she spoke. "Was that a bit of preferential treatment, sir?"

She checked her tone to ensure it wasn't familial and gave a nod. It was just as professional as what she typically used with the captain.

"No, detective," Mc'narrd said with a smile in his voice. "The military gifts you've received were preferential. Allowed due to the attack from the Moyii Tsaa, but still considered preferential. I've signed a great many warrants for the police service over the years. It's required to keep my alias active. Your current case was enough to gain public attention, which means Ta'ba would have heard about it."

"You visit the arenas frequently," Violetta guessed with a grin.

"Unlike you, detective, my spouse and I do watch entertainment vidfeeds as well as newsvids," Mc'narrd replied with a laugh. "But, yes. I go often. Alyssa also enjoys going. Though, our children prefer having their own boxes when they accompany us. In fact, when the entire family is together, we will all spend a day at the arena. Pay for all the private boxes, and see who can convince Malik to spend the most time with a particular group."

"It's why I was so suspicious of him when we first met," Malik chimed in. "I'd seen him many times at the arena with bronze eyes and dressed as more Earther than

K'laisian. Despite his supposed obvious mixed heritage." There was a good deal of laughing before Malik spoke again. "Your wife and entire family could have been actors, sir. One would never know the truth from how you all act."

"Alyssa taught our children from an early age," Mc'narrd admitted with loud humming. "Her skills and talents had been honed by her military and the years spent in their cold, cruel hands."

"We're arriving, detective," Da'kaw stated. "Your colleagues are already there awaiting you."

"Time to bring an end to these murders," Violetta stated.

She removed the gloves Mc'narrd had given her from a pocket and pulled them on. If she was going in, she was wearing the best of everything possible. The gloves were so comfortable and conforming, she could barely tell she was wearing them. The moment the HAV stopped, she unlocked the door and it slid open.

Climbing out, she paused in front of her fellow detectives. "You're all ready?"

"Everyone and everything is in place," Ra'keff stated.

He turned towards the building. Violetta followed his gaze. It wasn't the elaborate elegance that held Malik's penthouse. This particular building was older, the steel having seen decades of weather. She doubted cleaners visited this building to wash the windows weekly.

In fact, moss sprouted from the window ledges, violet flowers blooming in the shade. There was a feel of age and decay that one would expect from the poor section of the city. Her gaze shifted to the other buildings. They were a mixture of older style, straighter buildings and newer architecture. The older buildings showed age and some signs of decline, such as the moss and a few cracked windows. The newer buildings shone their brilliance and newness in the daytime sun. Their windows were reflective and not a sign of moss or decay anywhere on them.

"Let's go," Violetta said, heading for the front door.

There was no interface to keep anyone out. It slid open to reveal a small foyer. Doors lined each side with stairs leading up to a landing. Looking around, she didn't see a lift anywhere. She frowned at how only those who could walk and move with ease could live in this particular apartment building.

"I haven't seen those before," Violetta admitted, gesturing towards the doors. There was a rectangular interface set inside a metal box. The doors didn't appear to slide into the wall anywhere. In fact, it appeared to have hinges.

"None of these have safety interfaces. They're all older models. You unlock the door with the interface and they swing inward," Osing commented as he studied one of the doors. "Old school door with a newish tech."

"So, not only not very accessible for anyone injured, old, or disabled, but also not the safest," she muttered.

The door appeared as though if you hit it too hard it would just break into pieces.

"Or even those with children," Da'kaw added. "Ever try to carry groceries with an infant or toddler who thinks he or she can fly?"

"I have," Issik commented. Osing and Ra'keff were nodding.

"Unfortunately, no," Violetta admitted. "Single child of a single child. Hermit for five years, remember?"

That caused skittered humming as they began up the stairs.

"Be thankful," Ra'keff commented. "Little children wiggle and squirm worse than a wet fish fresh out of the water. Just barely more difficult to drop."

"Unless you're bathing them," Osing teased. "Then they're worse than a wet fish."

"You two remember her current marital status, yes?" Issik interjected. "Keep it up and she may decide to never have children."

Ra'keff and Osing looked at each other before bursting out into loud humming. It didn't stop as they climbed the second set of stairs. The second flight angled over the stairs they'd just climbed.

"Right," they both said together.

"I'm afraid to even ask," Violetta muttered.

"One of the many reasons those of mixed heritage choose a K'laisian as a mate isn't simply due to societal pressure." Zh'oros' voice surprised Violetta. She'd expected Mc'narrd to say something or tease her. "The admiral suggested it would be best if I explained. It isn't a topic he would be comfortable talking about, even with his own children."

"One more flight," Osing said, still humming.

"Indeed," Violetta said, trying to keep the pair from knowing she was trying to respond to Zh'oros at the same time.

"K'laisians, the natives who are of pure blood, are capable of taking birth control. It's effective and complete. It does not work as well for humans," Zh'oros continued as though she'd spoken an affirmative to continue. "It does not work at all for those of mixed heritage. Of either gender."

Her steps faltered as she began up the last flight of stairs behind the men. She blinked in startlement at what Zh'oros had said.

"No one told me that," Violetta muttered as she forced one foot in front of another. "Why wasn't that in biology class?"

"Or any other class," Malik added. He sounded as stunned as Violetta felt.

"I think she just figured it out,' Issik stated dryly. "You look rather dumbfounded, Vi."

"Someone took pity on me and informed me," she retorted. "And just for that, you all can babysit for me."

The three looked at each other then back at her.

"Can we discuss that?" Osing asked. "Because if your child ends up anything like you…"

"Careful. She *will* Challenge you," Ra'keff warned, smacking his partner in the back of the head.

Humming from Zh'oros filled her comm. "It was still considered an option as you were just entering those years. But, no. There is no effective birth control for either of you. You'll have to use the ancient method of timing your body's cycles and hope it works." There was more humming. "And neither of you even asked before continuing your relationship. Somehow, I suspect that information would not have stopped either of you."

"Fark," Malik said suddenly. "That's why your grandparents said they could've declared us a wed couple. If… if you'd become… if I'd…"

"I haven't. I didn't. And, we'll discuss this later. Work now… *that* later," Violetta retorted, shaking her head. Climbing the last few steps, she peered over the edge. "Ka'desh. That's a long drop. And a longer climb."

"No, no, Lady! You are not allowed to jump today," Ra'keff teased. "Wait until after you've had a child. Then you can contemplate the sanity of it."

"You don't even have kids," Osing grumbled.

"I've got two nephews. They're plenty."

"They're twins," Osing rejoined.

"You two are pathetic," Da'kaw cut in. "Neither of you have had kids of your own. I've got four. If she can Duel the Master of Ceremonies and handle herself, she can handle a child. Whenever it may happen." He gave Violetta a nod. "For your sanity, I hope it's many years in the future."

Violetta shot him a grin as she approached the door to Si'elos' apartment. This door, at least, appeared solid. Two members of the Search and Seizure team followed behind her. She moved to the side, allowing them room to work. They attached their interfaces to the door with several devices.

She watched as the interface drew a diagram of the apartment's interior. After two minutes, it indicated no life readings within the apartment. Violetta wasn't entirely certain how the devices worked, but she knew they were accurate.

"Yinko Si'elos, this is Lieutenant Detective Violetta Cq'linns of the 42nd District Police Service," Violetta called out loudly.

She knocked on the door as was standard procedure. Even if someone wasn't home, an officer announced their presence by calling out the name of the being, who the officer was, then knocked loudly. Just in case the being arrived from an unexpected location.

Three knocks, then they could enter.

On the third knock, the door vibrated beneath her hand. There was an odd sound, almost as though something had snapped, and the door swung inward. Her sidearm was in her hand even before she realized what she'd done. Her body was in a crouch. From the corner of her eyes, she noted those within her peripheral vision were in similar positions.

"Fark this," she muttered. "Readings show it's safe and no one's home, anyway."

With one cautious step after another, she entered the room. Much to the muttered complaints of every being around her. Mc'narrd remained oddly silent as she scanned the entrance of the room. She moved to the right, even as Issik moved to the left. Keeping her back to the wall, she scanned the room, the sidearm following her eyes.

Issik darted around the door, checking behind it before moving further left. He, also, kept his back to the wall. As Violetta moved further to the side, she paused as the rest of the officers and soldiers moved into the room.

"Stay in position there, detective," Mc'narrd's voice said in her comm. "Let them sweep the rooms."

"Yes, sir," she replied, her voice no different than what she'd used earlier with her captain. A brief smirk flashed across her face at the fact.

"Good girl," was her only reply.

Making a face, she bit back a retort. Instead, she chose to focus on the room she stood in, even as the teams called out when each room was clear.

Against the far right wall were floating shelves. Each one held holograms.

Several were ones remembering a deceased being. Common gifts given out at funeral ceremonies. Violetta knew any not claimed after a celebration of life were easily reprogrammable by the Master of the Dead's employees.

The remembrance holograms each had an image of a being that rose from the center of the fifty millimeter by fifty millimeter pedestals. Near the bottom, not obscuring the majority of the image, was the name of the being. The dates of birth and death varied in style, depending on what the family chose. Most had the date of birth on the left with the date of the being's death on the right. Others were photos of what Violetta presumed were living beings.

Beneath the floating shelves were wooden shelves filled with books and what appeared to be dried flowers. Small statues and other display pieces sat at the ends of the shelves and in front of the books.

Against the opposite wall was a smaller entertainment interface. She suspected it was a half-meter to three-quarter meter screen size. The one at her father's apartment was larger, but even it paled in comparison to Malik's wall-size interface. Several conforming chairs had been placed in front of it with a long, short table between the chairs and the entertainment stand. She recognized it as what humans often called a 'coffee table'.

The main room opened into what was obviously a small kitchen. There was a small table with four chairs. A replicator, a refrigeration unit, and stove. Cabinets lined the area above the stove. A wide door was to the left of the refrigeration unit. Since no one entered it, she suspected it was used for storage of some sort.

There were no consoles anywhere she could see. Her eyes, though, kept returning to the shelves. Ignoring Mc'narrd's order, she crossed to the shelves.

"Weren't you told to stay in place?" he asked in the comm.

She didn't reply as her eyes swept over each of the remembrance holograms from the funeral ceremonies. None were names of any of the victims. Several appeared in some of the holograms beside the remembrance 'grams. Si'elos was in only two of all of the holograms that filled the shelves.

"There's something about these," she commented aloud. "I don't know what, but there's something here."

"I recognize him," Ra'keff said from over her shoulder. She glanced at him, a brow raised in question. He pointed to one of the remembrance 'grams. "He died in a Duel. Refused to yield." Ra'keff's gaze remained fixed on the hologram as he added, "Malik was the Champion for that Duel. I can still remember the disgust on Malik's face when his opponent refused to yield."

"Such is our way," Osing stated dismissively. "It's our life. And the price for being Champion in a Duel. Taking the risk that someone will refuse to yield and you'll be forced to kill."

"You two sound like you admire him," Violetta said evenly. "Malik, that is."

"He's a stronger man than me," Ra'keff said easily. "I wouldn't be able to serve as he does."

"I remember that one," Osing said, pointing to another remembrance hologram. "Malik wasn't Champion, but he was Master of Ceremonies. Some woman fought her. I should've remembered that. Xela Devries. She was a frequent Champion for Morelli."

"I was not aware of that," Violetta said quietly. "Malik?"

"She didn't typically Duel at the main arena, and I don't remember all the Duels. But I do know she would be Champion for Morelli. Depending on who declared the

Challenge," Malik replied in a neutral tone. "I… I'm sorry. I didn't even think of that as a possible connection."

"So, we have two people who knew Si'elos, killed in Duels by Champions of Morelli," Violetta said thoughtfully. "There's a lot of people here who don't have names. We need someone to analyze these images and see if they've all been Challenged and the results of the Duels, if they were. Did all these beings in the remembrance 'grams also die in Duels? If so, were they in Challenges against Morelli? Or one of our victims?"

"Tiayl and Carlos, get up here," Issik said over the comms. "You two heard what's needed. Get started."

"Yes, sir," the pair said together.

"Detective, we've found something," one of the sweep teams called from another room.

Violetta turned away from the shelves.

"That used to be my job," she muttered as she followed Issik to what appeared to be an office.

"Too late to complain," Issik retorted. "You're on a fast track up the ranks. Get used to having to delegate."

"Not much choice," she replied. "What do you have, Stevens?"

A human with an uncanny knack for finding anything unusual, held up an evidence sack.

The sacks, once sealed, would reveal if they were opened and resealed. It was a method to prevent tampering, once an item was placed into a sack for evidence. This one was large and already vacuumed shut to protect the evidence that sat at an awkward angle in the bag.

There was no mistaking it for what it was: an antique Earther gun.

Violetta took the bag and studied the weapon. "Where was it?"

"Shoved under several boards in the bottom of the closet," Robert Stevens replied.

He shoved aside some clothing to reveal the location. Violetta peered down at the raised boards. Then her eyes traveled up to the clothes he was touching.

"Have you checked those?" she asked, her eyes on a leather jacket. "Looks similar to the one in our vidstill."

"Tag on the inside shows it belongs to the theater," Stevens said thoughtfully. "Got that image on your interface?"

Issik had his interface out and the 'still up before Violetta could pull hers out. He held the image up beside the jacket. Since all of them wore gloves, as it was standard, there was no worry about contamination of the scene or any of the evidence. The difference between Violetta's and theirs was the fact her gloves were made of military-grade nanites.

"Looks like a match to me," Stevens commented as he raised his own interface and began scanning the garment. "Good catch."

"Let's check the bedroom," Violetta suggested.

Issik gave a nod and led her to Si'elos' bedroom. It was smaller than her bedroom at her father's apartment. She took a moment to acknowledge how much she'd come to enjoy the spacious room she enjoyed at Malik's penthouse.

A conforming bed was against one wall with framed posters of famous operas along the wall. There was a small nightstand near the bed. A dresser lined the wall beside the door. But it was the closet that caught Violetta's attention. As did the wig another of the sweep team was removing from it. That, too, was being dropped into an evidence sack.

"You should see what we found in the kitchen," Ra'keff said over the comms.

"Let us know if any of you locate a HAVcycle helmet," Violetta stated as Issik departed the bedroom for the kitchen.

Her comm filled with acknowledgement from every being inside the apartment. Which meant thirteen people talking all at once. She took a moment to filter through the voices and realized it was easier than she'd expected. Blinking in startlement, she gave her head a slight shake before ignoring the conversations again.

"What do you have, Ra'keff?" she asked as they neared the main room and subsequently, the kitchen.

He held up a long evidence bag. "He kept it."

"Is that… that's a muya p'ek," Violetta said in disbelief. "He used that? On one of the victims?"

Humans referred to the round cylindrical objects as 'rolling pins'. The K'laisian word translated to 'kitchen pin' because it was used for baking and cooking.

"It has evidence of blood on it," Ra'keff replied. "It matches the DNA of one of our victims."

"Check the floors, walls, furniture. Including under and behind everything. Everywhere, including the bathroom," Violetta ordered, her eyes sweeping the rooms again. "He could have easily reorganized any of these rooms to cover a stain. We need to rule out anything happening in this apartment. Especially if that p'ek was found here."

"It'll take longer, but it'll be done," Steven's voice said over the comms. "I'll call in a second team to assist."

"Acknowledged," Violetta replied. "Do we have a current location for Si'elos?"

"Officer Dr'ildaw here, ma'am," a feminine voice said over the comms. "Yinko Si'elos has not been seen leaving the theater."

"Where are you currently, Officer Dr'ildaw?" Violetta asked, gesturing to the other three detectives as she headed towards the apartment door.

"Currently watching him perform inside the theater," she replied. "I volunteered to come in out of uniform to watch from the inside."

"Is that common?" Violetta asked as she jogged down the stairs.

"Yes, ma'am," Dr'ildaw replied in a quiet tone. "Practices at this theater are open to the public, but you have to pay to see the actual performance with everyone in costumes and such. I come frequently, so my presence would be less likely to cause alarm."

"Stay there, officer," Violetta ordered in a pleasant tone. "If he leaves the stage, see if you can stay with him. Be his biggest fan, if you need to. Just stay safe. Do not, I repeat, do not attempt to apprehend yourself."

"Yes, ma'am," she replied.

It wasn't difficult to hear the strong low timber of a male's voice singing operatic notes.

Violetta ran down the last two flights of stairs. The natives kept up with ease. All of them wore grim expressions. When they reached the ground level, they separated to take their different vehicles to the theater. It was faster in the HAVs than by foot and none of them wanted to risk Yinko Si'elos evading them.

Chapter Twenty Five

The HAV was silent as it traveled the short distance to the theater. Even the comm seemed unusually quiet to Violetta. As though the entire department was keeping silent as the four detectives worked together to stop Yinko Si'elos.

Violetta felt a calmness settle around her as they stopped directly in front of the theater. The auburn and blue strobes of police HAVs surrounded the theater.

The exterior of the theater was made of a metal that resembled a dark wood grain. It curved alongside an interface flashing the names of the operas and plays being performed. The smooth curves glided up along the side, as though they were wings. The roof had several points that reminded her of the crowns worn by ancient K'laisian clan leaders and ancient Earth nobility.

"Doors are covered. Multiple beings inside," the words came over the comms from someone Violetta didn't recognize. The voice was so even and lacking inflection, she couldn't tell if it was male or female. "Yinko Si'elos is inside, currently on stage."

Violetta strode from the military HAV to where the other three detectives were converging. They'd all arrived at the same time.

"One more time before we enter." Violetta stated as they stood outside the main doors. "What's the interior like?"

"One stage, box seats above. Large seating area. There's a small food court, as the humans term it, at the front near the main entrance. Lavatories to the sides. There's a considerably large area backstage and changing rooms to each side of the stage. A basement holds props," Ra'keff recited. Violetta found it amusing he used the Standard phrasing for what K'laisians referred to as wastechambers and humans called restrooms.

"Exits?" Issik prompted, turning towards the six doors at the front.

They could see the outer doors emptied into a small foyer, then there were another six doors. The second set of doors opened into the main interior.

"Four on the left and right sides, three exits in the rear. All have military and police officers waiting at each of them. Non-lethal force in place to intercept and apprehend," a male voice said over the comms.

"Let's go," Violetta said, striding to the front doors of the theater.

"You'd never know someone was trying to kill her," Ra'keff commented. Though the words were spoken with amusement, his eyes weren't smiling. "Like, maybe, the person we're going to arrest."

"She's never allowed anything to stop her before now," Issik rejoined. "Not even an entire police service hunting her. Why should a single being who kills from a distance give her pause?"

A smirk flashed across Violetta's face briefly.

"Not wrong," she said as they entered the theater. Each of them stepped through a separate door as it slid open.

Violetta paused inside the main entrance, waiting for her escort. She took a moment to acknowledge the uniformed police service officers standing alongside military personnel just inside the main entrances. Once her military escort, the dozen uniformed police officers, and her fellow detectives had entered, she continued forward to the large doors that opened into the theater.

Rows upon rows of conforming seats filled the room. Each row dropped slightly as they neared the stage. Dark blue curtains covered the walls. The stage ahead of them was barren aside from the dozen beings who had stopped moving on it. A set of wide steps rose from the floor up onto the stage.

Violetta knew the opened semi-circle in front of the stage could hold dancers, singers, or even a full orchestra. There were two dozen beings sitting or standing in the rows watching Yinko Si'elos perform.

Pausing at the furthermost row, she signaled to the officers to go to aisles nearest the walls. Once they had taken position, she headed down the middle aisle.

Striding ahead of everyone else with Issik a step behind her, Ra'keff and Osing took a position behind them and to the side. She could hear Da'kaw grumbling under his breath on the comms, but she refused to allow anyone else to be in front. Her sword rested heavy on her hip and her gut said there would be a need for it. The gloves kept her hands cool and she appreciated the comfort afforded by the nanites.

A K'laisian native who matched the description and hologram of Yinko Si'elos watched their approach.

The only word she could think of to describe his expression was frigid. The sharp features were made even sharper in the lights of the theater. His long silver hair was braided back from his face. Silver eyes were cold with disgust as he watched her nearing the stage.

The opera singer turned his head slightly to the sides, but didn't move from his position in the center front of the stage. He wore a long black tunic belted at the waist, dark brown pants, and multiple lightweight overcoats of various pastel shades that gave the impression of multiple, voluminous robes.

An odd ensemble, in her opinion, but she also didn't know what opera he was supposed to be performing.

"Yinko Si'elos, I am Lieutenant Violetta Cq'linns, a detective with the 42nd District Police Service. I have a warrant for a search and seizure of your residence as well for your arrest," Violetta stated in a clear voice once she reached the semi-circle in front of the stage. "You are being arrested for the murders of multiple K'laisian residents, as well as the attempted murder of myself. And the suspicion of attempted murder of Master of Ceremonies Malik Addelia."

"That was added on?" Issik whispered behind her. "Who added that on?"

"Judge Ta'ba," Ra'keff replied. "It's at the bottom. After everyone else. Including Violetta's name."

"If you wish to arrest me, I cry Challenge," Yinko Si'elos declared.

"Accepted," Violetta replied without blinking.

She crossed to the stairs and started up them. She could have easily leapt onto the stage, but she had more decorum than that. Her steps were silent in the theater, despite the heavy boots she wore.

Thank you, Dad, for those lessons, she thought.

"Hox," Issik muttered.

"A Challenge has been issued and it has been accepted!" Commander Da'kaw declared loudly in the theater. "Do you wish to Duel here, now? Or schedule it for later?"

"Here and now!" Si'elos all but bellowed, his voice echoing in the nearly empty theater.

"Agreed," Violetta repeated as she paused at the top of the stairs.

She wasn't about to approach until the others were in position.

"I will oversee the Duel," Da'kaw announced in a loud, clear voice.

With equal solemnity, the commander crossed to the opposite set of stairs and ascended them. Without even conferring, the other detectives did the same. Issik went right, following Violetta's path, while the other two went left. They fanned out around the stage, even as Da'kaw stepped into the very center.

"Place the lights on automatic settings," Da'kaw demanded. "An official Duel has been placed and accepted. No theatrics!"

The lights shifted until they illuminated the entire stage. Then dimmed to a more natural setting.

"Lights are under our control," a voice said over the comms. "You're clear to begin, Commander."

"Cameras are set up," another voice said.

"As are ours," Issik added.

Violetta glanced at her partner to see that he, Ra'keff, and Osing all had their interfaces out, pointing towards them. Ra'keff stood on the right of the stage, Osing on the left. Issik was in the center, behind and to the right side of Da'kaw.

"I am Commander Toriz Da'kaw of the 42nd District's Military Service, under the command of Admiral Diash By'kett," Da'kaw stated. "A Challenge has been issued by Yinko Si'elos, opera singer of the T'kashi Theater of the 42nd District of K'lais. Si'elos has Challenged Lieutenant Violetta Cq'linns, a detective of the 42nd District Police Service."

"Call her by the proper name," Si'elos snapped. "Lady Violetta Addelia! Mate and wife to Master of Ceremonies Malik Addelia!"

Violetta didn't even blink at the declaration. She remained silent and poised.

"Do you accept the Challenge, detective?" Da'kaw asked, ignoring Si'elos' statement.

"I accept," she replied simply. Her bronze eyes never wavered from Si'elos' crazed gaze.

"Do you have any other statements, detective?" Da'kaw asked.

"Yinko Si'elos is accused and will be arrested on the suspicion of murdering multiple K'laisian citizens, as well as his attempt on my life and suspected attempt on the life of Master of Ceremonies Malik Addelia. I accept the Challenge. Afterwards, he will stand trial and face K'laisian justice."

Shrugging off the plethora of outer robes, Si'elos threw them all over the edge of the stage. Beneath them all, he wore a sword belt with a well-polished weapon. He unsheathed the blade, turning it so the light glinted off the metal.

Violetta unsheathed her own, holding it simply at her side. Unlike Malik, she didn't try to showboat. She didn't need to work a crowd, nor did she have any interest in doing so.

Duels were a way of life and she'd been taught to take them seriously. She'd never been one to toy with her adversary. Not like Malik enjoyed doing.

Go in, fight, and leave the opponent on the ground.

She preferred to humiliate her opponents, who were generally bullies. But this was different.

Humiliation had no part in this Duel.

"Do you even know how to use that?" he sneered, gesturing towards her sword with his own blade.

Rolling her eyes, she heaved a sigh. "Let's just do this."

"Very well," Da'kaw stated. Unsheathing his own blade, he held it between the pair at shoulder height. The sides of the blade faced both Violetta and Si'elos. "Begin!"

With a fluid ease, Da'kaw swung the blade down. As the blade passed between the pair, he slid back several paces, giving Violetta and Si'elos room to maneuver.

Violetta wasn't skilled at working a room, but she *was* skilled at interrogations. The time had come to see if she could integrate that skill into Dueling. As Malik had done with entertaining a crowd.

"This isn't a captive audience, and no one here cares to hear you sing," she said in a bored tone. Her sword stayed at her side. "Would you prefer to have some of your friends here to cheer you on? Keep your fragile ego from collapsing when I don't fall under your swordsmanship right away?"

She found some emotional trigger of Si'elos' in that brief provocation. His eyes blazed, and when he swung his teeth were bared. His attack was still respectfully fast and strong, as Violetta's deflection of his blade caused her own to vibrate more than anticipated.

The extra time sparring with Malik had been time well spent. Violetta saw the pattern of his attack immediately. Keeping her expression neutral, she side-stepped his follow-up swing.

"Yep, still here and standing," she observed. "Perhaps you should see if Saiya or Vesech are available to come and remind you how awesome you are. Because you're not impressing me."

"Fark me, Violence, that's cruel. Maybe we should start calling you Vicious, instead," Issik whispered in her comm.

Both beings she named had been two of the K'laisians on the remembrance holograms in Si'elos' apartment.

The smile that came to her face from her partner's comment was unintentional, but had more of the desired effect on Yinko Si'elos. He shrieked, spinning his sword with a practiced ease, building momentum to strike as he came at her again. Violetta subtly shifted her stance to brace for impact.

Sparks flew from the clashing swords as he gave three hard swings. Violetta countered them each time. She gave almost no ground, but only because she had been prepared. Their bodies were quite close when the blades clashed and held against each other on the third blow.

"Keep talking, ignorant ajla," Si'elos hissed threw his teeth. "You have no right to even speak their names."

Violetta's knee came up and connected with Si'elos' thigh. He gasped in pain even as she shoved him back.

"I dislike being called a bitch in any language," she declared. "And if you're going to call me ignorant, best prove it."

She emphasized her statement by spinning her sword with a flourish used by Malik. A popular move played frequently during public broadcasts.

"You *would* cheat and use his moves!" Si'elos roared.

Although he had to favor the injured leg, he still came at her with considerable speed. He changed tactics by thrusting his first attack, followed by an overhand swing, and then thrust again. Violetta had to shift her position and give a little ground to volley each, but she managed.

He overextended slightly on the third thrust. Violetta used the brief opening to punch him in the ear. This time he howled and stumbled back. She leapt forward, forcing him to lose ground. He had to parry against her stabs and more finessed swings.

All the while, his free hand clutched his swollen ear.

"Irrefutable Rule Number One," she said loudly. "The weapon in hand is not the only weapon one may use during the Duel!"

"Irrefutable Rule Number Twelve," he shouted back. "Fight with honor or do not fight at all!"

"How much honor did you show to Xela or Lorenzo?" she demanded.

She feigned a thrust at Si'elos' left shoulder. When he brought his sword up to parry, she pushed his own blade down until the tips of both swords stabbed into his left hip. He screamed into her face.

She gave him a hard grin.

"Not so easy to win when you face a superior opponent in a fair Duel, is it?"

He punched her in the nose. Her nose didn't break, but blood flowed down into her lips.

She smashed her head into his nose. There was a sharp crack. As he stumbled back again, wide-eyed and covered in his blood as well as hers, she blew him a bloody kiss.

"Is that the best you have? Nicholas and Kazda would have handed you your ass in a fair Duel. Perhaps even with an encumbrance against them! Shall I hold my free hand behind my back? Would that make you feel more confident?" she taunted him.

"Farking Halfer," Si'elos spat through his bloodied lips.

And there it is, Violetta realized. The missing piece of motivation she didn't have. Just a bit more provocation and they'd have the rest.

"Oh, no! You've cursed my unclean heritage! I'm going to wither away from shame!"

Her voice was overly dramatic as she placed the back of her free hand against her forehead.

Somewhere, one or more of those on comm was humming with laughter. She dropped her free hand down to her waist, then looked around innocently.

"It seems I'm not going to, after all. Got a plan D? Or are we at needing a plan E, yet?"

"I should have gone after your grandparents, next. They violated tradition first, after all. Resulting in… *you*. No telling how far back I'll have to go to find where Malik's family turned against their own kind," Si'elos countered. He was wiping blood from his face, and seemed to have regained some of his confidence.

"They'd have kicked your ass, too. You suck at Dueling almost as badly as you sing."

"Okay, Vicious, maybe you can just let him talk and lose, now?" Mc'narrd said stiffly via the comm in her ear.

"Fark you! And Malik! And especially Morelli! You've all ruined the lives of anyone I care about!" Si'elos screamed, lunging towards her.

The strike against her blade was strong enough to force her to the side. She spun as he attempted to stab at her unprotected side. Her foot came up and connected with his right knee. It was a glancing blow, but enough to make him howl again. It was also unable to support his weight.

As he struggled to stay upright, Violetta took a risk. Punching with the pommel of her sword, she swung past his weapon, connecting with the socket of his right arm at the shoulder. His sword scraped her face, giving a three inch cut along her cheekbone.

The injury was worth it, in her opinion.

His right shoulder separated from the impact, shifting unnaturally against his body. His sword fell from his now useless hand. Si'elos made a dry, retching sound in her ear.

She leapt back to avoid any possible mess caused by his heaving stomach.

He was shaking, looking with confusion at his right arm as well as his weapon. There seemed to be some confusion as to how the latter had fallen to the floor.

"Pick it up," Violetta demanded. She shifted her own sword to her left hand. "Show me your so-called honor and continue to fight."

Her father had drilled into her the need to be able to be ambidextrous when it came to Dueling. That skill hadn't been required in the past, but she'd kept the ability sharpened and honed to a precision.

A fact few knew. A skill even fewer bothered to learn.

He looked dazed as he bent over and picked up the sword with his left hand. His fingers gripped the weapon too tightly, as though unfamiliar with its weight and balance.

"Why not just go after Morelli," she asked conversationally. "Since he's just as guilty of everything as Malik and I, in your mind?"

"He makes all the money. Profiting off of the spectacle that's been made of our traditions. He's probably going to make a fortune off of you two halfers becoming joined. And too many of my fellow natives don't even see how this is damaging K'lais!"

"Is that what Nyis thought? Or Ataine?" she asked, using the names of the other two beings from his remembrance holograms.

"Lives taken! Death might have been a mercy! All from halfers who were already taking services from those of us who are actually from this planet!"

Violetta made a false stab at Si'elos. He brought the sword up awkwardly. She tapped his weapon and he nearly lost control of it. She stepped back, holding her own to her side.

"You planned on hurting Morelli by killing beings that worked for him. Was Malik supposed to be the last?" she asked, knowing what she proposed was probably wrong.

Yinko Si'elos, she suspected, would have continued his self-appointed task until he was brazen enough to attempt to go after Zane Morelli.

"Every one of them is responsible for a full-blooded K'laisian losing life or livelihood! Each of them cheated! Exploited the weakness of 'acceptance' for paths against our sacred ways."

Violetta nodded. He swung clumsily at her. She gave ground easily, barely having to exert herself to deflect the pair of attacks. But it boosted his confidence and kept him talking.

"Since they cheated, I returned the gesture! Even soiling my own blood by using methods the ka'deshed Earthers brought to our home. The police service might have found me if they had stayed pure, but they've been as thoroughly corrupted as everything else!"

He attempted an oafish overhead swing. It was slow and she could have easily moved out of the way. Instead, she brought her sword up with both hands, acting as though it was a grand effort to keep his blade from getting closer. He was smiling now.

"If an 'uncorrupted service' had discovered you, would you have surrendered peacefully?" she prompted while holding his sword at bay.

"I wouldn't have had to surrender! I wouldn't have killed your mate's associates because the police would have kept the Halfers and Earthers in their place! You wouldn't have been around to interfere! To force my hand to try and eliminate you as well, for that!"

"You avoid my question," she said, and pushed against his sword. His arm was shaking already. "Would there have been any scenario where you would have surrendered peacefully?"

"No! I would have Challenged whomever came after me! I would either have been victorious or died with honor! Since there would have been no cheating!"

That was more than enough. Everything had been recorded. As was expected and required with official Duels.

Violetta let go of the sword with her right hand, swung back, and smashed the side of her fist into Si'elos' left elbow. There was a thick popping sound as the cartilage gave way. His sword fell away for the final time. She used a backhanded swing with her left to smash his jaw with the sword's pommel. He crumpled to the floor.

Although unneeded, Violetta kicked his sword away, where one of the police service members could gather it as evidence. She glared down at Si'elos.

Da'kaw spoke up, voice ringing with authority.

"Both upper limbs rendered useless. Right lower limb questionable to sustain body weight. Blood loss approaching a critical level for cognitive function. Multiple head injuries. Si'elos is unfit to continue. The undisputed winner of this Duel is Lieutenant Detective Violetta Cq'linns of the 42nd Police Service."

"Why couldn't you just die?" Si'elos whined through his broken jaw and shattered teeth.

"Such a boring question. Yinko Si'elos, you are held accountable for the murders of K'laisian citizens. Evidence has been gathered and you are being taken into custody. Your personal belongings will be cataloged and accounts held until trial. You will be afforded the opportunity to be defended by yourself or others during said trial."

Chapter Twenty Six

When the four detectives returned to the police service station, cheers and applause erupted around them as they entered. Violetta paused inside the main doors, blinking in wide-eyed startlement. They had stopped at the base long enough for her to be evaluated, treated, and released.

All three of her colleagues refused to continue to the station without her. They had all departed together, and they insisted they would return together.

"Well done, detective," Os'shye's voice said in her comm. "Good job, all of you."

"Sir?" Violetta asked, glancing at Issik.

"The department is aware of the events that have occurred," Os'shye replied. "Vidclips from those at the theater have been uploaded to various social subnets."

"Ah," Violetta replied as the foursome traversed the hallways.

She kept a slight smile on her face, as she waved and replied to compliments and shouts from those around her.

Issik stayed on one side of her, Ra'keff on the other. Osing remained directly behind her. Da'kaw had taken point, effectively blocking her in.

"How are you doing, detective?" Da'kaw asked.

"So far, so good," Violetta replied. "Thank you. All of you."

"Good to know you don't mind protection sometimes," Ra'keff teased.

"Only with crowds," Violetta rejoined. "Besides, gotta give you men a reason to walk behind me."

"Her ass, I might add, is not scrawny," Osing deadpanned.

"Now I'm regretting it," Violetta muttered, feeling her face growing warm.

There was humming from all of them as the door to their division slid open.

"I've been saying that for months," Malik's voice interjected over the comms.

"Not helping," Violetta groaned.

"Wasn't aware I was supposed to help," Malik teased. "I saw the 'clips. I'm pleased to hear he was caught. Think you'll be able to lose the babysitters now?"

"I'm sure it'll be discussed later," Da'kaw stated.

"Let's finish wrapping this case up into a lovely, inescapable package for our new district attorney," Violetta suggested as she headed for her desk. A small package sat on her desk. It was wrapped in blue and silver paper with a silver bow on top. She eyed it warily. "Okay, so I've graduated from flowers to gifts."

"We've scanned it," Tiayl stated, sauntering up to the desk. "Nothing dangerous, but no clue what's inside it."

"Malik?" Violetta asked, picking it up and examining it.

"I've only sent flowers," Malik admitted. "Your uncle?"

"No note," Violetta stated. Turning the package over in her hands, she examined every inch of the small box. There were no clues on the exterior. It didn't even rattle. "He is being very silent."

"So, open it!" Tiayl encouraged.

There was a lot of laughter from everyone except Violetta.

"You're all certain that it's safe?" Violetta asked. "I seem to remember a delivery that I thought was safe. Ended up with me in the medical wing at the base from it, too."

"It's been scanned by the team," Tiayl repeated. "As in, a complete scan for every biometric in the data bases. Complete with potential poisons."

"Then they should know what it is," Violetta stated, carefully removing the ribbons.

"Stevens did the scans, but he refuses to say what it is," Tiayl replied dryly. "Only that it isn't dangerous."

"Stevens?" Violetta asked.

"Nope, not telling," Stevens' voice said on the comm. "I'm not spoiling the surprise from whomever sent it."

The silver string took only a few seconds to remove, the paper a few more. Even with her being careful with removing it to reveal a small silver box. There was nothing to denote where it was from.

"I should be in the meeting room putting the report together," Violetta said, uncertain if she wanted to remove the lid.

"Si'elos will be undergoing severe psychological evaluations. It'll last a few days, at least," Issik reminded her. "A few minutes to enjoy a pleasant surprise isn't going to alter that timeline."

"Logical, as always," Violetta grumbled as she removed the lid.

Within the box was an antique brooch, of a very Earther design, on a soft velvet lining. With deliberate care and gentleness, Violetta set the box on the desk before reverently lifting the antique brooch. She recognized the piece from holograms, vidclips, and stillclips of her mother.

"This…" she sat hard in her chair, her eyes staring at the antique Earth thistle brooch. Her fingers ran over the rough surface of the jewelry.

Earth diamonds set throughout the prickly leaves, stem, and round bottom of the thistle glittered in the lighting of their office against the gold metal of the brooch. The flowerhead itself was a purple gemstone Violetta knew was an amethyst from her mother's home planet.

She'd seen the image so many times throughout her life. She'd asked her father about the beautiful brooch and he'd explained what it was and why it had been dear to her mother. The thistle was the symbol for Scotland, where her mother's ancestors had originated.

"Violetta?" Issik asked, placing a gentle hand on her shoulder.

"It… it was my mother's," she said in a soft voice, still staring at the brooch in her hands. "She wore it all the time. At least, in all the images I've seen of her, she was wearing it. I thought Dad had buried Mom in it."

"Your father gave it to me not long before he died," Mc'narrd explained gently. There was sadness and warmth to his tone. "If I'd realized how deeply it would affect you, I would have given it to you personally. Anywhere but at your office."

"It's a shock to see it, that's all," she said quietly.

"Vrehn asked me to make certain you received it, in case anything happened to him. I thought he was being overly cautious at the time," Mc'narrd admitted. "He said it was an heirloom, passed down from mother to daughter upon the daughter's betrothal."

Violetta drew a breath and let it out. Taking a moment to pin it to her tunic, and ultimately the biosuit, she shook her head. "Next time, sir? Let's have this chat in person, okay?"

"I'm certain there will be more opportunities to shock you," Mc'narrd teased. "And no, it will not cause harm to the biosuit."

Pushing herself up from her chair, she shook her head slightly. "Right, so, about that wrap up."

There was a round of murmurs as she led the way to the meeting room. Once inside, she settled into a chair. Within a few minutes, everyone who had worked on the case filled the room, including those who had been part of the search and seizure.

"What do we currently have?" Violetta asked, pulling up Si'elos' image on the wall.

"The wig was an absolute match for the fiber we found," Ra'keff stated, pulling up the report. "A helmet was also found hidden in the apartment. Hairs found in the helmet match, also. There was evidence of blood, and the DNA matches with several victims."

"What about the Earth weapon?" Issik asked, pulling up the image of the weapon.

"Violetta's suggestion about the bullets and the… casing?" Osing asked. Violetta gave a nod. "The casings are a match to the Earth weapon and what was located in Si'elos' apartment."

As everyone spoke, Violetta was typing and maneuvering the files and information on the larger tablet Mc'narrd had given her. She gestured for him to continue as she compiled the report.

"Did we find a link between the holograms and the victims?" Violetta asked, turning to Tiayl and Carlos. "Or are you two still pulling that together?"

"We dragged in Valerie," Tiayl replied. "The three of us were able to use facial recognition on the unnamed beings to compile the data." She touched her interface and sent the list of names to the wall. Beside the names were lines leading to the victims, Malik, or a number of other names. "Those beings in the holograms, listed on the left, participated in Duels, and subsequently lost in those Duels, to the names on the right."

Valerie leaned over Tiayl's shoulder and tapped the screen a few times. Lines appeared going from the left to the right. All the red lines matched up with a being who had died or had been attacked. Several lines led also to Malik

"Malik has multiple lines, because we discovered he was the Master of Ceremonies for several Duels. He wasn't the Champion for all, but he presided over several," Carlos explained. "And every single being on the right either currently works for Zane Morelli, or has in the past."

"And you became his irritation when you just wouldn't die," Tiayl concluded.

"He wanted to hurt Malik pretty badly. He just didn't expect to go up against someone as stubborn as you," Ra'keff chimed in. The grin on his face softened the words.

"He obviously wasn't paying attention a few months ago," Violetta retorted. Mischief danced in her eyes as she added, "Guess I'm *not* the only hermit in the city."

That brought about a round of laughter from all the beings in the room.

"We interviewed his colleagues at the theater," Carlos added, as the laughter and humming lessened. "He was known to complain about how unfair it was that humans and 'halfers' were 'stealing the services' provided by K'laisians. He believed they were simply being given the positions in the theatrical, operatic, and musical divisions simply because they were humans or of mixed heritage. That the Duels at the arenas are rigged."

"He said all of that to his colleagues?" Violetta asked, pausing in her organizing and data compilation. Carlos, Tiayl, Valerie, and several others all nodded. "What were their responses?"

"They humored him because he could have a temper. He'd never harmed anyone, but he loved to yell and scream," Tiayl stated, disgust in her voice.

"A few natives stated he bemoaned the fact that the Moyii Tsaa wouldn't accept him. Said his ideals were too 'strict' and claimed he had no honor," Valerie added. She made a scoffing sound. "I wonder why they'd say such a thing."

"I suspect once the healers have concluded their investigations, this will all just be another report to go on a thick stack," Osing grumbled.

"Perhaps, but it's important to ensure he receives a fair trial," Violetta stated. She leaned back in the chair and stared at the images on the wall. "To give him the fairness and justice he didn't allow any of the victims. Yes, it would have been easier to kill him in the Duel. But that doesn't allow for the closure the families will receive by allowing the healers to completely and thoroughly evaluate his psychological state. No one will question the results they will give. Not like beings would if he died in a Duel."

Silence filled the room. Maybe they'd forgotten she'd dealt with something similar five years ago. Without realizing it, her fingers touched the brooch on her chest.

"They can learn, without a doubt, why he killed those beings. Having that answer will bring considerable peace to the families of the victims," she concluded, her voice softer than she'd intended.

Something she had never been given. Even now, five years later, there was still the question of why that fanatic had killed her father.

"Let's get the reports filled out, in detail, and on our desks by tomorrow morning," Issik stated, bringing attention back to their jobs. "Let's make certain Si'elos has no way of talking his way out of what he's done."

"And show the D.A. our department has only improved from four months ago," Ra'keff added.

With those words, everyone settled in front of an interface or left for their own desks. Conversations shifted to the case and where who was meeting whom for drinks later to celebrate.

"You coming, Vi?" Ra'keff asked. Violetta looked up, surprised. He grinned. "Bring your... betrothed? Mate? Whatever he is at the moment, if you want. I'm sure Malik will enjoy being possessive and witty."

"I am not possessive," Malik's voice said in her ear. "But I'd enjoy joining you and your colleagues for an evening out in celebration. I may even buy everyone a round of drinks."

"I'd enjoy it," Violetta replied, smiling. "I suspect Malik will, also."

Epilogue

Three weeks later the trial of Yinko Si'elos ended and the native was found guilty on all counts of murder and the attempted murder of Violetta. As per K'laisian laws, he was sentenced to death.

Yinko's severe racism, and racial superiority had caused a hatred for Zane Morelli. When many of his colleagues and friends died in lawful Duels, or lost their positions in various services, he'd turned a general dislike into hatred. The hatred had settled on the human who he saw as the reason for a great many injustices towards fellow K'laisians. A human who appeared to prosper while seeming to mock some of their oldest traditions.

When Malik was then seen courting another being of mixed heritage, it sent Yinko over the proverbial ledge. He began killing others in a way in which he knew he could succeed, deciding to make Malik his ultimate target. That is, until Violetta refused to die.

Yet another ill, unbalanced individual who refused to seek aid for their sick mind.

"Your mind is anywhere but here," Malik teased, wrapping his arms around Violeta's waist. He kissed her eartip, knowing exactly what it did to her. "Should I be concerned?"

"Just thinking about Si'elos and his trial. How you were the focal point of such an ill being simply for being successful. How much my life has changed in the past several months," Violetta admitted.

"The fact multiple beings, including two native K'laisians, have tried to murder you instead of seeking medical aid?" Malik added.

She nodded. "And the fact that my personal family has grown seemingly overnight. And now, we're making everything with us official. Publicly."

"Ah, investigating murders is sounding incredibly appealing, then," he joked, leading her down the small hallway to his private box. They stood at the edge, waiting for their cue to enter the box, and subsequently the field. "I did warn you there was no going back."

"I'd rather move forward." Violetta met his eyes with hers, smiling softly. "I did say you were stuck with me."

Malik laughed. He pulled her close and kissed her.

"You're going to ruin the look," she teased.

"Not even remotely possible," he rejoined.

She slid her hands over her mother's wedding gown. It had needed only minor alterations to fit. She refused to touch her hair. It had been braided and curled to an inch of its life by Victoria and Stella. Who then added gloss to her lips and extra makeup to cause her eyes to stand out. It was very light, but it was enough to make a difference. Both women had remarked that she resembled Kali on her wedding day to Vrehn.

Malik had chosen traditional K'laisian attire of a heavily embroidered and beaded tunic and matching pants. The overrobe was just as long and elegant with the same designs as the tunic.

The designs were as ancient as the clan emblem that was his mother's ancestry. He wore a ring bearing the clan's symbol on his left hand's first finger. She wore her father's clan ring on the first finger of her left hand. The thistle brooch that had been her mother's had been pinned to the left side of her wedding gown.

K'laisians believed life was represented on the left. Just as the sun rose from the left and traveled right across their planet. And so, everything of importance was placed upon the left side of the body.

Flowers had been woven through her hair, the tiny buds and vines as much a tradition of human brides as they were K'laisian. The necklace Malik had bought her twinkled against her chest. As the music began rising, they stepped into the box together.

Both ensured the train of her gown was tucked into the box before the door slid shut.

"I cannot believe you convinced me to have the ceremony here," he murmured as the box moved away from the edge.

"It's the only place large enough," she replied, as the crowd erupted into a deafening roar. She smiled and waved, even as Malik did the same. "We have most of the military and police service here. As well as most of Morelli's people. Not to mention your beloved fans."

"I may just Challenge *you*, my love," Malik muttered, a wide smile on his face.

"None of that tonight, children," Alyssa said over the comms. Though there was no mistaking the laughter in her voice.

"I would think they would have other plans for their wedding night," Zerik chimed in, cheerfully.

Violetta felt heat rush to her face, even as Malik kissed the tip of her ear, which caused the crowd to grow even louder.

"Behave," Alyssa chided as Malik's box neared theirs. "Comms and cameras go live the moment you get here. And don't believe we aren't aware of Verisa Ta'kelo."

"Ah," was Zerik's only reply.

As the box neared the northeast box, she could see Alyssa, Zerik, and Lyza standing in a row beside Admiral

It'zarry Mc'narrd, who wore traditional K'laisian formal wear despite the contacts that changed his eyes to bronze. Except where Malik wore black with silver embroidery and varying shades of dark, earth tone beads, the admiral wore shades of silver and pale blue.

The pale shades suited Mc'narrd, Violetta thought, despite the fact he had the whitest skin she'd ever seen on a K'laisian.

Alyssa wore a more traditional formal gown of dark emerald that wrapped around her trim figure, flattering her, while leaving her arms free of confinement. Both of their eldest children had chosen to wear their biosuits, only these had their command stripes and ribbons on full display. Complete with every medal each had earned. As the box approached them to dock, they shifted until they stood behind their parents in a formal stance. An interface within the Moc Box displayed another box with the rest of the children belonging to Alyssa and the admiral.

The box beside the one they stood in held Violetta's grandparents, both wearing formal K'laisian attire instead of military uniforms. Malik's entire family, aside from the young children, were in both boxes.

It'zarry Mc'narrd, in his persona of Judge Io'siph Ta'ba smiled warmly at them. There was nothing but compassion in his eyes as he nodded to them both.

"Comms and cameras are yours, Judge Ta'ba," a voice said over the comms.

Violetta didn't recognize the being, but Malik did. He gave a slight nod, a hand touching the interfaces before him with the barest shift of his body.

Alyssa stepped forward, her hands raised for all to see. A universal gesture for silence.

"Master of Ceremonies Malik Addelia and Lady Violetta Cq'linns, lieutenant detective of the 42nd Police Service's homicide division have arranged a unique surprise for all gathered here tonight! They have requested Judge Io'siph Ta'ba to preside over their ceremony of joining this night!"

Malik's private Moc Box joined with the private box that held Mc'narrd, Alyssa, and the rest of the family. Once they were secure, the doors unlocked and opened.

There was another loud roar of excitement from the crowd. She raised her hands again, the cameras zooming in on her. When a hush settled over the arena, she dropped her hands, gesturing to her husband. Mc'narrd crossed into the Moc Box where he stood before Malik and Violetta. As the crowd hushed even more, he began speaking the opening words to a traditional ceremony of joining.

Everything had been arranged to pure perfection.

There would be multiple parties and receptions over the next several weeks, as was tradition. But tonight they would enjoy the private boxes with their families while the entire arena viewed their wedding.

Exchanging smiles, Malik and Violetta turned towards the admiral.

"Forever and always," Violetta whispered softly.

"Always and forever," Malik replied in an equally soft tone.

They slid their fingers together as they bowed formally to Mc'narrd.

Whatever was to come, they would face it together.

End.

We hope that you enjoyed this title and look forward to many more to come. Please, leave us a review! Reviews matter to all of our authors.

Take a look at some of our other award-winning series at https://threeravenspublishing.com/series-universes/

Visit us at https://www.threeravenspublishing.com and sign up for our newsletter for the latest and greatest news on upcoming titles and events.

Other series and titles you might enjoy.

JOINT TASK FORCE
13
HOLDING THE LINE
BETWEEN HEAVEN AND HELL
AMAZON

B.E.N.T.
BIOLOGIC   ENHANCED   NASCENT   TALENT

STARFLIGHT

IT CAME FROM THE
TRAILER PARK

You can also keep up to date with our latest release announcements on Scifi.radio and get some of the best fandom programing on the planet.

Scifi for your Wifi

And don't forget to check out our other Sponsors and Affiliates

A southern Appalachian jewel for craft beer lovers, Buck Bald Brewing offers something for everyone.

To discover more visit us at buckbaldbrewing.com

Revolution X is a testament to the power of collaboration, blending four unique styles into a cohesive, revolutionary sound. When these four individuals unite, the result is nothing short of musical Revolution!

Would you like to learn how to write and market your own titles? The following affiliates links might be helpful.

Don't forget to check out the latest edition of Car Warriors: Autoduel Chronicle fiction series.
https://threeravenspublishing.com/car-warriors-autoduel-chronicles/

…or the latest in the *Car Wars* game series

http://www.sjgames.com/car-wars/

Or the other amazing titles from
Steve Jackson Games

http://www.sjgames.com

Comprised of active or retired servicemen and civilian volunteers, Shepherd's Men enthusiastically raises awareness and funds for the SHARE Military Initiative (SHARE) at Shepherd Center in Atlanta, GA.

This nationally renowned program focuses on assessment and treatment for American military veterans who have sustained mild to moderate Traumatic Brain Injury (TBI) and Post-Traumatic Stress Disorder (PTSD) during post-9/11 service.

Find out more at: https://www.shepherdsmen.com/